Hey Kid,
Thanks for supporting me
no matter what.
Happy Birthday. ♡

THE ONE THAT GOT AWAY

THE ONE THAT GOT AWAY

MYK RICHELLE

Library of Congress Control Number: 2020907593
ISBN: Hardcover 978-1-7960-9995-9
Softcover 978-1-7960-9994-2
eBook 978-1-7960-9993-5

This is a work of fiction. Names, characters, places and incidents either are the product of the author's imagination or are used fictitiously, and any resemblance to any actual persons, living or dead, events, or locales is entirely coincidental.

Print information available on the last page.

Rev. date: 04/25/2020

To order additional copies of this book, contact:
Xlibris
1-888-795-4274
www.Xlibris.com
Orders@Xlibris.com
812926

Acknowledgements

This novel has been in the making for the last five years. The completion of this novel could not have been possible without the care of so many people who have pushed me forward to continue writing no matter how often I thought about giving up. I'd like to thank my Mom for believing in me and pushing me forwards to write. Without her positive words and feedback, I wouldn't have persevered and finished this work. Thank you to all relatives and friends who in one way or another whether that be physically or financially have supported this work.

www.shotbydevan.com
twitter.com/shotbydevan
instagram.com/shotbydevan
facebook.com/shotbydevan

www.shotbydevan.com
twitter.com/shotbydevan
instagram.com/shotbydevan
facebook.com/shotbydevan

Light blinded her. Her hands shot to her face and covered her eyes. The brightness was nearly unbearable. She could feel just how fast her heart was racing. Every beat felt quicker and quicker. It felt what a gazelle feels when it's not sure if it's being watched. When it stands up straight, alert, flicking its ears, trying to determine whether something is stalking it. And right when it decides its safe, the lioness pounces and it knows it's only a matter of moments before its life ends in a vicious bloodbath. She knew that it could be then. Those moments alone in the bright but damp room, could very well be her last moments alive.

The squeaking of the doorknob as it turned made her breath catch in her throat. She didn't dare move her hands away from her face. She didn't want to see the nightmare that was behind them. But then she felt it. A hand was touching her leg, slowly finding its way up their length. She could feel the goosebumps on her arms as every second that went by, he made his way up her body. She didn't dare move her hands. She felt his lips brush against her ear. She was frozen with fear. His hand on her leg lifted and flew over her body and grabbed one of her wrists. He yanked one of her hands away from her face with such force that he lifted her slightly off of the bed. Her eyes were blood shot and she was lachrymose.

A charming smile spread across his gorgeous features and for a second and only a second, she had almost forgotten how wicked he truly was. And then he laughed. It was the most chilling laugh she had ever heard. He still had one of her wrists in his hand. He lifted it so the back of her hand was approaching his lips. She couldn't move. He kissed the back of her hand three times and then gave it a small squeeze, all the while staring into her eyes.

"You...are so beautiful." He whispered. His voice was cold as ice, the edge on it could cut glass.

Tears stung the backs of her eyes. She felt like she couldn't breathe. Suddenly, his other hand swung forward and grabbed her by the side of her head. He had a fistful of her dirty brown hair in his grasp. He held it so tightly it pulled against her scalp. She could feel a couple of the hairs being pulled right out. He yanked her by the hair and she let out a sharp cry. The tears barreled over the rims of her eyes and fell down her cheeks. He pulled her into a sitting position and brought her face close to his. His eyes bore deep into hers. She could feel their intensity but didn't look away. She knew he was violent and she wanted to prevent antagonizing him in any way.

He smashed his lips into hers and held her head there by the hair that was knotted in his fist. She could taste the saltiness of her tears as he forced his tongue into her mouth. And that's when she had her idea. She could feel his tongue exploring the inside of her mouth. It was rough and tasted like day old beef. She bit down hard. She could feel the blood gush into her mouth.

He pulled back fast and screamed. She spat the blood that was in her mouth at him. It splattered across his face. She brought one of her legs back and kicked him in the stomach. He fell backwards but didn't lose his grip on her hair. The fistful of hair that he had ripped from her scalp, the roots bloodied. She cried out, the tears pouring down her cheeks. She hurled herself off of the bed and ran for the door. He was laying in the fetal position on the bed, screaming and clutching his stomach.

Once she crossed the threshold, she turned and slammed the door behind her. She whirled around and ran weakly down the hall. She was dehydrated and had a hard time sucking in a breath. She rounded a corner of the hallway and noted the exceptionally clean walls and flooring. It was almost off putting; how tidy the place was. It was not what she was expecting. She stumbled through a doorway at the end of the hall and found herself in his kitchen. A door to the outside world was less than ten feet from her. She stretched out an arm and reached for the doorknob.

He grabbed her in a choke hold and tore her away from the door. She tried to scream but he tightened his grip around her neck. He dropped to the floor, slammed her small body against the kitchen linoleum. She let out an inaudible gasp as she clawed at his arm while she tried to gather an inhale. She used all of her strength to move her arm forward and then brought the point of her elbow back against his body right under his ribcage as hard as she could. His grasp around her neck broke as he started coughing hysterically. She pulled away and tried to scramble to her feet. He kicked his foot out and knocked her back down to her knees.

"Help me! Someone, please help me!" She screamed; panic filled her shaky voice.

Blood dripped from the corners of his mouth and splattered on the floor as he slowly opened it to show her his tongue. It had a deep gash along the top and the deep scarlet liquid coated the muscle. He gradually stood up, not taking his eyes off of her terrified face as she lay helpless on the kitchen floor. Her eyes were filled with awful fear. She begged and pleaded with him through the petrified look on her face.

He brought his leg back and booted her hard in the side. She screamed and curled up in a ball. He drove another hard kick to her stomach and then strode quickly across the kitchen. He had spotted a roll of fishing line that sat on his counter next to a calendar with a large red salmon on the front. He swiped up the fishing line and began to unroll it. She was laying on the kitchen floor, tears streaming down her cheeks, pain racking her body.

He dropped the roll on the floor, letting the line unravel. He ambled back across the kitchen towards her body. Her eyes fell on the line in his hand and they widened with dread. She turned to her stomach and gasped as pain shot through the tender wounds on her body. She tried to crawl away from him as he got closer and closer.

He knelt to the floor, rage seethed within him, his blood hot and coursing through his veins. With a low throaty growl, he brought the fishing line around the front of her throat and began wrapping it around her neck. She clawed at the floor, trying to pull herself out of his deadly grip. Once he had the thin, clear line around her neck twice, he started to tighten it. Immediately she could feel her air supply get cut short.

She gasped. Her mouth open, she tried to suck in breaths but found herself failing.

He grunted as he pulled the line tighter. An indent became visible on her throat as a thin row of crimson started to drip. He knew he could decapitate her if he tightened the fishing tool enough. The thought sent a shiver down his spine and thrilled him to no end. But that wouldn't work for him then. He couldn't do that to her. Not yet.

She slapped the kitchen floor twice as her eyes started to roll back in her head. Blood had started to drip from her nose. It was only a minute later and he finally relaxed. He let the line drop from his hands which resulted in her head slamming back down against the linoleum. He sat back on his palms as he stared at the limp dead weight that lay there. And then he felt the rage start to boil up inside of him. He frowned at the fresh corpse on the floor and the anger that filled him erupted.

He stood up fast and spun towards the counter. He eyed his knife block that sat next to the sink. The large chef's knife glimmered under the kitchen light. That was the one. He swiped it off of the counter and twirled back to face the girl. He used the heel of his boot to turn her to her back. Fiery hatred swam through his eyes and across his face. With a loud scream, he dropped to the ground over her body and shoved the knife deep into her stomach.

Over and over again he stabbed the knife into her torso. He never stopped screaming. Blood gushed out of the wounds spilling over her body and onto the white kitchen floor, staining it red. Finally, the absolute rage that fueled his rampage began to subside. He dropped the knife beside her mutilated body. The tears started to fall. Horrible sadness replaced the anger that had filled him.

"Look what you made me do. Look what you made me fucking do." He whispered, his voice shaking with anguish.

He glanced towards the doorway that led back to the hallway they had emerged from. A round analog clock was situated above the door. The hands read eleven thirty-two. Panic raced through him. He was running out of time. He was not about to miss *their date.* He needed to get rid of the mess he'd just created and get to the university before one twenty.

He wiped the tears from his face and coughed once. He could bleach and mop up the blood when he got home. He needed to get rid of the body before he did anything. And he knew exactly where he wanted to go. He stood back to his full height and walked steadily towards the hallway. He just needed to grab his car keys from his bedroom. He had left them in there before he went to the room where she had been staying.

He passed the room where his guest had previously resided. A small smile crept across his features. He had experienced anger and sadness over her but now he was experiencing the thrill of what he had just done. And that's what it was. A thrill. He passed by another door. It had three locks on the outside of it. He smiled at that door and let a hand fall across it as he moved. His bedroom was next. His car keys sat on the dresser that was directly beside his door. He didn't even have to enter the room in order to retrieve them.

Once he was back in the kitchen, he reached under the counter under the sink and pulled out a garbage bag. He ripped a hole in the bottom of it so he could fit it over his clothing. He didn't want to get her blood on his clothing. When he reached down to lift her, he noticed she had released her bowels. Fecal matter and urine stained the buttocks of her pants and had spilled out onto his floor. It took everything in him not to gag.

He struggled for a moment to pull her to her feet. Once he had her there, he lifted her with ease and let her body flop over his shoulder. He held his keys by the ring and let out a huff of air as he turned to walk towards the door that lead to his driveway. He reached for the knob and twisted it slowly while he tried to keep her body steady on his shoulder. The door opened silently and he shuffled his way out. He noticed that blood was steadily dripping as he hauled her body out the door. It dripped down the driveway to his vehicle. He wasn't worried about it. His closest neighbour was over fifty kilometers down the road. No one knew where his cabin was. He had complete solitude in his little corner of the woods. He never had visitors, except the ones he brought home for himself. He wasn't worried about a little bit of blood in his driveway.

An hour and a half later, he sat himself down on the metal bench and leaned back. He glanced at the matte black watch on his wrist and watched the little arms ticking away, counting down the minutes. He knew her schedule by heart and he never missed their make shift rendezvous. It was the most important part of his day. The planning, the meticulous planning. It's all that mattered and all that counted if he wanted his work to go the way he so desperately needed it to.

The watch on his wrist beeped once, twice, three times, alerting him that it was precisely one twenty. His gaze fell across campus and on the heavy maroon coloured doors at the other side of the quad which were opening at that very moment. He held his breath as she appeared through the frame.

He watched her toss her head back and laugh as she walked down the sidewalk with Bella Donaldson and Jennifer Kassidy, her two blonde friends who were so utterly insignificant and did not matter to him whatsoever.

He watched them all approach the large, decorative fountain in the middle of the Ridgeway University campus. To him, the massive stone raven that protruded from the top of the fountain was very tacky; that the fountain could have been beautiful had it not been for that fucking raven. It symbolized the mascot of the Ridgeway campus, the "Ridgeway Ravens", but couldn't they have just made the gorgeous piece of work with little raven inscriptions along the base? He shook his head. That stupid raven ruined all of the beauty in the world for him. Except for her. She was...she was something else.

He watched her hug each of her two friends and kiss their cheeks. He wished she would kiss him. He watched her wave goodbye to them. She sat down on the edge of the fountain, her many textbooks resting in her lap. He knew what they were. He knew they were her Criminal Justice and Law Enforcement books. He knew she wanted to be a lawyer.

He watched her lift her arms and slide her maroon coloured RU hoodie over her head, mussing her hair slightly. That angered him. She had beautiful hair. She placed the hoodie gingerly on the edge of the fountain, careful not to let it dip into the water which was, more than likely, very cold on that mid-March day.

She leaned her black book bag against her shins. Slowly, she tucked a stray strand of her ebony brown curls behind her ear, exposing one side of her jaw-line and neck. The way the sun hit her, outlining her, made her look like the most beautiful of all the angels that could ever walk the Earth. He licked his lips and shifted on the bench; he wanted to see her better but couldn't risk being exposed. He wanted to be able to hold her, to kiss her whenever he wanted. He wanted to feel her naked flesh pressed against his as he thrust into her. He wanted her.

He watched her open one of her textbooks. He knew her routine. He'd been watching her long enough to know exactly what she did every day and where she went. He day dreamed he could be with her. He watched her flip through her book, and every so often she would pick up her pencil and jot down a note or two in the royal blue journal that she kept close to her at all times. He knew that the journal was extremely important to her. She never took notes on single sheets of paper. She was very particular in keeping a journal for every single class that she took. It was one of the quirks that he loved so much about her.

He watched her touch the tip of her index finger to her tongue and use it to help her turn the next page. He watched her furrow her brow and lean closer to the book. She scrunched her nose and tapped her chin with her pencil. She looked up. He froze as she looked around the campus. There were enough students milling around the fountain that there was no way she could see him. She wouldn't be able to with all of the activity going on.

After only a moment, she looked back down at her book and flipped a page. She was so beautiful doing the simplest, most mundane things. He licked his lips a second time and adjusted the lump in his pants.

No matter what happened, he would get her back.

Soon.

Soon, she would be his again.

This time, he wouldn't let her go.

1

Detective PJ Richards sat at her dining room table; a cup of steaming black coffee snuggled between her hands. The morning newspaper was open to page number three.

The big, bolded headline stared up at her, she stared back down, blankly.

The headline read *'King's Strike Leave 5 Dead'*. The article highlighted a Mexican street festival that had been in Ridgeway one week ago. According to the article, the festival was attacked by a gang of white Supremacist men who labelled themselves, "The White Kings". Three Hispanic men, one woman, and one fifteen-year-old teenager were beaten so badly that all five of them tragically succumbed to their injuries that same night in hospital. "The White Kings" were all arrested at the scene of the crime and the festival had shut down early.

PJ shook her head when the words processed in her mind. She remembered that day. She was one of the detectives on scene that weekend. She remembered all of the nasty things that "The White Kings" had to say. She shut her eyes tightly and pushed the thoughts out of her mind. She certainly did not want to relive that day.

She opened her eyes again and while she stretched her mouth open in a wide yawn, she wiped her tired eyes with the back of her hand. She had forgotten to take her makeup off the night before, and what was left smeared onto her pale forehand. She sighed.

It was Saturday, and seven twenty-three in the morning.

PJ lifted the piping mug to her lips and slowly blew on the top before taking a little sip. Delicious. She reveled in the moment. She hardly got to enjoy her coffee in the mornings. Her friend and boss, Brock Carter, the Chief of Police at the Ridgeway Police Department usually called her, needing her assistance on a mundane task or for some intense case that - for some reason - she was the only one that could actually manage to do without screwing it up. Maybe that was because she had been on the force longer than almost anyone else.

She lifted the mug again, about to take another sip, but just like she expected, the little black iPhone resting on the table beside her elbow burst to life in a fit of ringing.

"Detective Richards." PJ answered without looking at the caller ID. She had a bad habit of doing that.

"I just love hearing your voice, *Detective*." The deep, manly voice responded right away. PJ began to giggle like a twelve-year-old school girl who had her first crush.

"Charmer. How are you, hon? How was the plane?"

He coughed.

"It was alright. Little bit of turbulence, nothing too crazy, surprisingly enough. You know how I am with flying." He paused.

"I miss you already."

PJ smiled to herself. How did she get so lucky?

"I miss you too, Nick. Now hurry up and get home."

Nick coughed again. PJ heard some scuffling in the background and another voice she could barely make out.

"I'll be back soon enough, girl. I love you."

"I love you too."

The phone clicked off, signaling the end of the conversation.

PJ smiled to herself again; images of Nicholas Redford filled her mind. Strikingly handsome, he had a broad chest, wide shoulders, chiseled facial features and a strong jaw-line. His wavy black hair was always perfectly quaffed, his sparkly sea blue eyes always shining, happy to be alive. He resembled a young Clark Kent. It also helped that he was the most sought-after lawyer in all of Ridgeway.

PJ looked back down at her coffee; she had almost forgotten about it. She picked it up and blew on it again, getting ready to have the delightful, hot brew flowing down her throat, warming her entire body and getting her prepared for the day.

Wishful thinking. The ringing of her cell phone interrupted her thoughts.

"Detective Richards."

"Come to the office immediately."

PJ sat up straighter. Her boss didn't intimidate her, but she could hear the urgency that laced his voice and she realized that something was seriously wrong.

"I can be there in about fifteen."

"See you then."

She didn't get a chance to say goodbye. The chief had rushed his last words and hung up on her, signaling the end of that conversation.

PJ glanced down at her mug, and shot it a sad look. It was very quickly becoming colder and colder. She shook her head, stood up, and spun on her heel. She reached above her head and opened a cupboard that sat above her counter. She pulled out a stainless-steel travel mug that was laced with black rubber trim around the bottom for non-spillage and around the middle, for grip. Shutting the cupboard, she turned back around and lifted the mug. She poured the liquid swiftly into the travel mug and placed the lid on top. She placed the mug back on the table and decided she would deal with the dirty dish at the end of the day.

She took long strides out of the kitchen and through the hallway. When she got to the stairs, she took them two at a time, like usual, making it to her bedroom in half the time she would if she took them one at a time. She bypassed the bathroom, no time for a shower today.

Once in her room, she dug through her dresser and pulled out a pair of dark blue jeans. She slid them over her long legs and had to do the wiggle dance to get them over her butt. Thirty-six years old and still doing the wiggle dance.

Next, she pulled out a flowing white tank top and pulled it over her head, mussing her brunette hair only slightly. She grabbed her favourite brown leather jacket off of the hook behind the bedroom door and yanked it on to complete her look. She stopped in the bathroom on the way back to the kitchen and grabbed her toothbrush.

She was sure that the Chief could wait for two extra minutes while she took care of her teeth. Dental hygiene was one of the most important parts to her morning routine. As was a shower, but then she'd have to make him wait for about twenty extra minutes and she knew he wouldn't appreciate that in the slightest.

She flipped off the light switch and left the bathroom quickly and ran down the flight of stairs. She jogged through the kitchen, swiping her car keys off of the counter and her cell phone off of the table. She glanced at her phone, the time said seven fifty-two. That left her eight minutes to get to the PD office. She bit her lip. If there wasn't any traffic, she should be able to make it in the nick of time.

She made it outside and double checked to make sure she locked her front door and then she quickly got into her vehicle. She thanked her lucky stars. There was very minimal traffic on the suburban road, making it incredibly easy for her to get to the main street through town. Still minimal traffic, which she was more than thankful for. She figured it was because it was Saturday. Everyone was probably at home, sleeping off their Friday night hangovers.

She pulled into the RPD building's parking lot and glanced at the time. Seven fifty-nine. She made it to the office in seven minutes. Record timing. She could congratulate herself later. She got out of her car and slammed the door shut, pressing the lock button on her key fob twice and pulling on the handle to make sure it was, in fact, locked. She ran to the front door, taking the four steps up to it, two at a time and pulled the glass doors open effortlessly.

"Good morning Detective Richards!"

Hilary, the bright, young blonde at the reception counter smiled happily. PJ thought she looked too happy to be at work at such an early time. Especially for such a young thing like her. She *should* be recuperating from partying. At least, had PJ been her age again, she would definitely be taking the day to re charge from a long night of drinking.

"Good morning Hil. How many times have I told you, please, please call me PJ."

Hilary started to blush.

"I'm quite sorry Dete—PJ! PJ." She stuttered and bit her lip. She gave PJ. a soft smile and PJ shot her a small, warm smile back and turned to walk down the hall. She ran right into a tall, lanky man.

"Oh shit. Sorry Brock."

PJ apologized automatically. Without a word, Brock ushered her into a room situated about a foot up the hallway. He firmly shut the door behind her. PJ looked around the room. She had been in there plenty of times, but the atmosphere today seemed colder. Frigid even.

She noticed two plain-clothed officers that she recognized as Daniel Martin and Philip Walters, sitting at the rectangular table in the middle of the room.

"What's going on? Brock?"

She looked around the room again, and that's when she noticed the picture board. Her feet carried her to it, before she even realized she had told them to.

"Oh my god." She whispered.

"Kelly Smith. Found early this morning." Daniel piped up.

Daniel Martin was a young cop. He'd been on the force for two years but he was good at his job. So good in fact that he went from desk duty to field to detective in that short amount of time. He had dusty brown hair and brown eyes to match. His face had freckles sprinkled across his nose. He had those boyish good looks that every woman he charmed, fell for. His partner, Philip Walters, had been on the force for even less time. He'd been working with the RPD for a year and a half. He too was excellent as his job, receiving the same promotions that Daniel had. Philip had a head full of jet-black hair and deep blue eyes.

PJ's eyes scanned the photographs. A young woman, couldn't be much older than eighteen was lying stark naked in the dirt. Multiple stab wounds were visible on her chest and stomach, a thin red line was visibly indented around her throat and dark purple bruising polka dotted her face and ribs. Her brown hair was matted and dirty with dried blood. PJ noted a chunk of hair approximately the size of a fist was missing from the side of her head. PJ spun around and bore her eyes in Daniel's.

"Give me the lowdown."

"Nineteen-year-old Kelly Smith. She was reported missing by her seventeen-year-old boyfriend last week..."

"Why is this the first time I am hearing about this! Brock!?" PJ snapped. Brock coughed into his closed fist.

"You were working on a separate case. You remember, the Bobby Jackson case?"

"Yes, I remember. But still. Why didn't you tell me about...this! Please, go on Dan."

Daniel stood up and walked over to the picture board so that he was standing right beside PJ.

"She was reported missing by her younger boyfriend last week. At first, we thought she may have just met someone her own age. But then her professors and roommate reported her MIA."

"Professors?"

"She goes...she went to RU."

"So what? She cheated and the younger boyfriend goes rage crazy and murders her? Star crossed lovers? Any signs of a fight? Any signs of sexual assault?"

PJ turned back to the board and studied the photographs again, looking for anything. Any sort of sign that could tell her what happened.

"No signs of a fight. My guess is she was being beat through the time she was kidnapped until she was found. To your second question, yes. Turned out she had an allergy to latex. Our unsub used a condom when he was assaulting her which resulted in her having a nasty allergic reaction down south."

Phil offered helpfully from the table.

"What's the M.O? This is some serious over kill. Someone was obviously pissed off at her over something."

"Official cause of death was asphyxiation. The autopsy showed signs of a struggle while she was being strangled. Beaten before and during, hence the bruising. She also has a few broken ribs and fractured wrist. Stabbed several times post mortem."

Phil continued on. Daniel sat next to him, staring at the board with deep intent. PJ shook her head again and then looked at Brock, her eyes filled with fierce anger.

"Local, nineteen-year-old girl goes missing and a week later, her body turns up used, abused and practically mutilated. Why the fuck was this not on the news? Why wasn't I informed?"

It was not rhetorical question, PJ didn't expect a response, but Brock felt the need to answer her anyway.

"Parents' wishes. Phil called Mr. and Mrs. Smith the moment she was found, but no answer. When they were notified that she was missing, they requested that it stay off the news. They really didn't want this public. You know Mr. Smith. He owns that diamond store in the middle of town. He's one of the wealthiest men in the country. Are you surprised?"

PJ sighed.

"First vic like this. Let's try and keep it that way, shall we?"

Daniel coughed once. Brock shot him a look.

"What?" PJ asked quickly.

"That's where it gets a little messy." Daniel said from the table. PJ whirled around and faced him.

"I don't like that."

Daniel nodded in agreement. PJ crossed the room and pulled out a chair from the table and slowly sat down. Her head dropped into her palms. Her finger tips rubbed her temples in a very monotonous way.

"Okay. Hit me."

"She's not the first. She's the third." Daniel stated matter-of-factly. PJ's fingers stopped their circular temple massaging movement. She very slowly raised her eyes and met Daniel's. She held up three fingers.

"Three?"

She said through gritted teeth. There was an icy cold edge to her whisper.

"There have been three identical homicides and I'm only hearing of this now?"

PJ slammed her hands down on the table, pushing herself back to standing. She shot Brock a hard look.

"Show me all three files, now!"

PJ demanded. She knew she shouldn't have spoken with such anger to the Chief, but she felt she couldn't hold back. Besides, she could have been in that position. PJ Richards, Chief of police. But no. She graciously turned that promotion down when it was offered to her two months ago, just so her longtime friend, Brock Carter, could live his dream. The two of them did have an agreement. Brock was the Chief, but PJ. was his very close second. She had just as much power as Brock, with the exception of firing. Brock didn't hesitate. He already had three large manila envelopes in his grasp. PJ snatched them and tossed them onto the table.

"You two. Help me put the photos on the board."

Daniel and Philip didn't hesitate. Each grabbed an envelope and started pinning the pictures from each file in order of each homicide. After each file was properly displayed, PJ tucked her hands in her jeans pockets and paced in front of the board.

"Talk to me. Don't fuck around right now. All three former or present RU students?"

PJ stopped and looked at the first photo. Same deal as Kelly Smith. She was lying naked in the dirt, multiple stab wounds, thin red line around her neck and bruising on her face and ribs. PJ could only bet that she had a couple broken ribs as well.

"No. Not all are RU students." Phil was the first one to speak up. PJ looked at him.

"Okay so what? They don't look under eighteen."

Phil moved closer to the board so he could point at the first victim, a young redheaded woman.

"Denae Crossman. Seventeen years old. Went to Ridgeway High. She was in her senior year. Same thing as Kelly. Younger boyfriend first reported her missing and then her friends and teachers said she stopped coming to school."

"When did she first go missing?"

"February twelfth."

"That's nearly a month ago."

"They found her body a week after she went missing."

PJ shook her head for the millionth time.

"What about her?" She pointed at the middle picture.

"Carly Bew. Eighteen. Senior at Ridgeway High."

PJ looked at the girl, Carly, in the middle picture. Long black hair. The dark purple bruising all across her torso highlighted the midnight blackness of her thick hair. She looked absolutely beautiful even in her demise.

"Did Carly and Denae know each other? Maybe dated the same young guy?"

PJ didn't need Phil or Daniel to inform her that there was a younger boyfriend who did the initial first missing report.

"According to both sets of parents, no. Neither mentioned that their daughters had known each other. As for dating the same guy, they had no idea." PJ looked from the photos to Daniel to Phil then back to the photos.

"Clearly hair colour is not the common denominator. Redhead, blonde, and black hair. The high school isn't either because Kelly went to RU..."

"Well, actually." Daniel chimed in.

"We haven't shut out RU yet. Both Denae and Carly were touring the university just days before they were abducted."

PJ narrowed her eyes.

"So, Denae. Abducted February twelfth. Found February nineteenth. Carly. Abducted February..."

"Sixteenth."

"Sixteenth. That's three days before Denae was found." PJ observed.

"That's right." Daniel said slowly.

"So abducted the sixteenth, probably found February twenty-third. Let me guess. Kelly was taken on the twentieth." PJ was starting to figure out the loop. Phil nodded solemnly.

"And you said you found Kelly this morning. That means...shit."

PJ paused, letting the new information come to rest in her brain, and also realized something troubling.

"That means if the unsub sticks to routine, he will have grabbed his next victim three days ago. Get me all our recent missing persons reports, asap!" When Phil and Daniel were both out of the room, PJ walked over to the table and slammed her fist down.

"Fuck!" She screamed. Brock walked up behind her and touched her shoulder.

"I'm very sorry I didn't include you or inform you about any of this. You were dealing with so much. I didn't want to put more on your plate." He said softly. PJ reached up and put a hand on top of his. She squeezed gently. All was forgiven. Only a few moments of silence passed before Daniel and Phil returned with a very small stack of white, standard size papers. They lay them out on the table and PJ slowly sunk back down into the seat she was previously in. In front of her, four faces were staring up. Three girls. One boy.

"Stories? Dan. Go." PJ said, trying to remain calm even though the fire of pissed off rage burned in her gut.

"The boy, Joshua Martin, no relation, went MIA yesterday after a blow-up with his parents. Sixteen years old. Detective Sarah Rogers is on his case."

Daniel said, sliding the boy's picture away from PJ's grasp. She eyed the three girls. Two of them looked around the same ages as Kelly, Carly, and Denae. The third looked mid-thirties to early forties. PJ had to make sure her case was being taken care of before she could let Phil take the picture away.

"Is her case under control?"

Phil nodded, knowing very well what PJ was thinking.

"Amy Rothwell is on hers."

Phil took the picture away from PJ and set it at the other end of the table. PJ pointed at the two younger girls.

"Stories. What happened here?"

"The one on the left, the blonde, her name is Michelle Clifford. She's eighteen, goes to Ridgeway High, she went MIA two days ago."

"Who reported her missing?" PJ asked quickly, pulling out a notepad from her jacket pocket, ready to take notes down about the two girls.

"A fourteen-year-old girl and her mother. Sasha Brown and Lisa Clifford-Brown."

Daniel replied, looking directly at PJ. She was staring down at the girl. She had a big smile on her face, her green eyes were sparkling and her blonde hair flowed down around her shoulders.

PJ bit her lip.

"Was she touring RU also?" Phil shook his head and looked at Daniel.

"As far as we've been told, she was planning on touring St. Louis campuses instead." PJ chewed on the inside of her cheek.

"That doesn't fit." She stated softly. She kept staring at Michelle Clifford. This girl was just as beautiful as the victims.

"How about her?"

PJ picked up the second report and held it above her head so Brock could see.

"Mya Swanson. Seventeen. MIA two days ago. Difference is, she was going to Ridgemont Private School. That's Ridgeway's private high school. She wasn't touring RU before she disappeared, but she was there, visiting her father who works as a professor at the university."

Daniel informed her. She dropped the paper back down to the table. This girl too, was abnormally beautiful. She had wavy chocolate brown hair and icy blue eyes. The smile on her face was wide and showed her teeth. She looked happy and without a care in the world.

"Two days ago, that still doesn't fit. Who uh, who reported her missing?"

Daniel and Phil exchanged a glance.

"You're going to love this."

Daniel tapped the photo of the missing teenage boy, Joshua Martin, with his index finger.

PJ let out an exasperated sigh and started to rub her temples again. She could absolutely go for a massage.

"I want the names and contact info of all the citizens that reported these girls missing. I want the contact info for this guy's parents. Now."

PJ snapped her fingers a couple of times. She was still fuming over the fact they hadn't clued her in or kept her informed about any of this for the past few weeks. Soon after Phil was laying a neatly typed paper with seven names on it, down in front of her.

Amber and Christopher Martin 555-5635

Lisa and Jeffery Brown 555-6626

Kyle Bellfry 555-4170

Jacob Miller 555-7733

Jordon Gardener 555-1020

PJ looked up from the list.

"Which boy reported which girl?"

"Kyle Bellfry reported Denae, Jacob Miller reported Carly and Jordon Gardener reported Kelly."

Daniel replied, helpfully. PJ made a note on the paper.

"You said they were all younger. How old are they?" PJ inquired.

"Kyle, the one who was romantically involved with Denae, is sixteen, almost seventeen."

"Almost seventeen?" PJ interrupted.

"Seventeen in a couple of weeks or something. Didn't think to clarify." Daniel replied, apologetically. PJ shook her head.

"What about Jacob and Jordon?"

"Jacob is sixteen. Jordon is seventeen."

"Oh, that's right. I remember."

PJ paused and looked at Brock, who was leaning against the wall, arms crossed, staying silent.

"So Chief."

PJ tried to lighten the mood by letting out a small chuckle.

"Do you mind if I take over as the lead on this?"

Brock shook his head, without saying a word but a small grin slid its way onto his lips. PJ. was a fire cracker all right.

"Wonderful. Let's pay the missing boy's parents a visit first."

She paused and looked at her silver Rolex watch. Nine forty-six.

"Daniel, call them. Amber and Christopher, now. Come get me after. I'll be compiling some notes."

2

Where am I? The girl, the young and pretty brunette girl sat up and rubbed her head. She blinked hard a couple of times, her vision still a little bit foggy. Blurred. She felt around the darkened walls, looking for a light switch or something to make it easier for her to see her surroundings. The walls felt slightly damp and that's when she realized just how warm it was in the room. She hadn't noticed that she was sweating.

"Ah, Mya. Finally. You're awake."

The brunette, Mya, shook her head and looked around the dark room.

"Yes. I'm awake. What. What's going on?"

Mya felt her heartbeat start to quicken. *Stay calm. Stay calm Mya.* She thought silently. Suddenly the entire room lit up. Mya had to close her eyes because it became too bright, too fast. She made a mental note that the lighting was LED. She slowly opened her eyes, letting her pupils take in the light and become accustomed to the brilliantly lit room. She was sitting on a twin sized bed that was pushed up against the wall furthest from the doorway.

The room had pale blue walls, a dirty looking brown carpet and a couple of posters plastered to the walls. They were those motivational ones someone would see on the walls in a class room. There was a dingy dresser against the wall opposite the bed. Mya looked up and focused on the man standing in the doorway. He was lowering his finger from the light switch.

"Are you hungry?" He asked with a surprisingly charming voice. Mya was taken aback. Her captor didn't sound scary. He sounded like a very normal, loving guy. She nodded slowly.

"Yes-yea. Very."

She tried to keep a strong voice, but it was much harder than she anticipated.

"I thought you might be. You've been sleeping for two days."

Mya tried hard not to react.

"Two days?"

She repeated, tasting the words on her tongue and not liking it. What had he done to her in those two missing days? The man nodded.

"I was surprised. The others woke after only a day."

That was when Mya could hear just how chilling his voice really was. The slight bone trembling edge that laced his words.

"Others?"

Mya said, her voice barely coming out of her mouth above a shaking whisper.

"You're my fourth. My fourth beauty. You're so very pretty..."

He paused and strode through the room, sitting down next to her on the bed. It took everything inside her not to flinch and scramble away. He lifted a hand and reached towards the still girl. She didn't mean to, but she flinched.

"Don't be afraid of me, pretty girl."

He brushed the back of his hand across her cheek, his fingers lingering on her jaw bone, only an inch away from her voluptuous lips.

"God, you're so pretty. Beautiful, even. But not quite perfect. No, not quite perfect."

He was speaking more to himself than to her. He paused briefly and licked his lips. He ran his index finger over Mya's bottom lip.

"You'll do. Yes. You'll do."

His voice had grown gruff and husky, want and need filling it. Mya couldn't stop herself from shaking.

"Shh. Shh." He whispered as he leaned into her. She tried to pull away, but he grabbed the back of her hair in his fist and pulled her back into him. She let out a little shriek of pain. He had pulled a little too hard on her sensitive scalp.

"You're hungry. You're hungry. I'll get you something to eat, my girl."

He pressed his lips into Mya's before standing up and leaving the room. He smiled at her before firmly shutting the door. Mya heard a tiny click and realized that he had locked the little bedroom's door from the outside, effectively keeping her put on the other side of the one exit. She let out a heavy sob that shook her entire chest and a thick pain settled behind her ribs, right in the middle of her sternum. The tears welled up in her eyes, weighing down on her rims. Two days? He'd said she was sleeping for two days. What had he given her? Where the hell was she? She wanted Josh. She loved him. She wanted him. She wanted his comforting hug, his soft kiss on her forehead.

She flung herself backwards and laid down on the bed. She didn't want the tears to fall, but she couldn't help it. They stung the corners of her eyes. Another sob escaped her chest, making her ribs feel like they were even tighter than they were and making it especially hard for her to breathe. Taylor. Was that even his name? She doubted it. She tried her hardest to remember what had all happened. He had approached her while she was at school. He had told her she was beautiful. She told him she was flattered, but taken. What else had happened? She just couldn't remember no matter how hard she tried. She grabbed her head in her hands and began to rub her temples almost as if she was trying to coax her brain into remembering the missing details.

It seemed like no time had passed when she heard the click of the damned lock on the door again. She rolled onto her stomach; she didn't want to see him. She prayed that if she looked away, he'd dissipate into thin air. Wishful thinking. She wanted to be able to open her eyes and be lying next to Josh, safe and have everything be okay.

"My girl, I brought you some eats."

Mya froze at the sound of his voice. That fucking voice. She was completely astounded by how insanely normal it sounded. The chilling edge was gone. Had she dreamed it? No. She knew she hadn't. She squeezed her eyes shut tight. She prayed to God that when she opened her eyes, she'd be curled up next to Josh's side and they'd be stuffing their faces with Dill Pickle flavoured popcorn and watching *Dexter* on Netflix.

She felt his hand on her lower back, tracing her spine and pausing in between her shoulder blades. Her breath caught in her throat.

"Hey, wake up. Eat. We don't have all damn day."

Mya did not move a muscle.

"Oh dear. Mya. Baby, if you don't eat, then we're going to have a much more serious problem. An even bigger problem than you fucking a sixteen-year-old." He paused, waiting to see if he could get a reaction from her. She sniffled and then slowly turned over. His hand was still resting on her back, so when she turned, it rolled across her shoulder and over each breast. Mya didn't say a word. She stared at him; tears still very apparent in her eyes.

"How-how do you know about Josh?"

She croaked in a mute voice. His eyes narrowed, adding a hint of danger that wasn't there before.

"Oh, Mya. I know more about you than you think. I know your full name, your birthday, where you were born, your parents' names, where you go to school, what colleges you were looking at...you get the gist."

Mya gulped. She was still lying down, staring up at him. He leaned down into her, brushing his lips against her cheek.

"C'mon my girl. Eat."

He grabbed her hand and pulled her to a sitting position. She was apprehensive. He slid the tray from his lap onto hers. A sad looking piece of burnt toast, a couple of wilted pieces of lettuce that made a pathetic green salad and a bruised apple were the contents that the tray held.

Mya very slowly took a bite of the burnt toast, choking as it slid down her dry throat. This, she could barely manage. He stared at her as she nibbled the food. The longer she took to eat the food, the longer it would take for him to do whatever he was going to do to her. She kept her eyes trained on the sustenance, and even though she didn't want to eat it, she finally realized she was starving. Her stomach began to growl ferociously.

After struggling to down the horrendous food on the tray, she finally finished the very last bite and sighed with relief. He grabbed the tray from her hands and set it on the ground, without taking his eyes off of her. He sat back up and took her hands into his. She didn't move, didn't take her eyes off of her lap.

"Mya, look at me."

She didn't reply.

"Mya."

She flinched, but didn't look.

"Mya!"

He yelled and smacked her hands. That startled her. She looked up and into his eyes with such caution. But then she noticed them. It was like it was the first time she had. She hadn't taken in exactly just how beautiful they were. The irises were dark blue that faded into a light green-blue closer to the pupil. They were so deep she thought she was going to get lost in them.

"That's better."

He slid an arm around her shoulders and put the other on her knee. He pulled her into him and pressed his lips into hers. She whimpered and squirmed, trying to get away from him. He held her more tightly and opened his mouth. He poked his tongue against her lips, prodding for an entrance. She pursed her lips tightly and tried to turn her head away from his kisses. He grabbed the back of her head with the hand that was around her shoulders and squeezed her knee, digging his fingers into the fabric and right into a pressure point.

She cried out and a couple of tears managed to escape from her eyes. He didn't care that he had hurt her. He kissed her cheeks, licking her salty tears into his mouth and then planting another kiss on her mouth. She still wasn't kissing him back.

He pulled away from her face and looked at her again. She turned her face so she didn't have to look into his beautiful, luminescent eyes.

"Mya. Why do you have to be such a bad girl?"

She gasped as he tightened his hold on the back of her head.

"I don't want to hurt you, Mya. If you don't behave, you'll have to be punished."

Mya sucked in a deep breath and gradually turned to face him. Her entire body was vibrating under his touch.

"Please, just let me go home. Please. Taylor. Please."

He froze when she used his false name. He didn't think she was going to remember it.

"Please."

She stared right into his eyes, trying to portray a 'damsel in distress' sort of feel, trying to make it so that he would release her. His hand slowly let go of the back of her head. He still had a hold on her knee, so she didn't move. She didn't notice his hand ball into a fist next to him.

"Let me go and I can help you."

She whispered. She put a hand up to his face, trying to remain calm.

That made him snap.

"I don't need help!"

He screamed and the hand on her knee lifted and grabbed her wrist. His fist connected with her ribs and she cried out in severe pain. She could feel one or two cracks inside of her. He shoved her onto her back. The tears didn't hesitate when they spilled over the rims of her eyes. They barreled down her cheeks. He hit her again.

"Shut up! Shut the fuck up!"

He opened his fist and smacked her across the face, open palm. The pain was imminent. She shut her mouth quickly and turned to look away. He grabbed her face, squeezing her cheeks between his thumb and fingers. He pressed right into the red hand print materializing on her pale cheek and made her look at him. She closed her eyes, trying to hold back the tears.

"Look at me! Bitch, look at me!"

He shook her face in his hand and screamed at her. She slowly opened her eyes, all the while shivering from fear. The tears wouldn't stop.

"You'd rather fuck a boy, than a man? You'll fuck a sixteen-year-old kid over an experienced adult man? Go ahead. Scream. Scream Mya May Swanson. Yell, cry, tear your fucking hair out. No one will hear you."

He screamed at her, shaking her face, tightening his hand around her cheeks, squeezing them together tightly.

"You don't know where we are. So, go ahead. Make a fuss. I'm still going to do what I brought you here for."

He ended his screaming rant with a whispered threat through his gritted teeth. Mya held her breath. She couldn't talk. Her voice refused to leave her throat.

He let go of her face and slid his hand down her side until it reached the zipper of her jeans. He felt her tense, stiffen, trying to make it harder for him to pull her pants off. He didn't mind putting up that fight. He liked feisty women. Not sassy, back-talking broads but he enjoyed a little bit of a fight in bed. Rough sex could get him off easier than that soft, romantic shit. After a couple minutes of slight struggling to get her pants off, he managed to pull them and the pink panties she was wearing over her slim hips and down her long legs. She stayed frigid. Unmoving, as his fingers frantically tried to pull her shirt off. She wouldn't lift her arms.

"Come on, Mya. Help me out here, baby."

She didn't answer him. He couldn't get her shirt off, without her lifting her arms. He was not about to give up. He bit his lip and tried not to get angry.

"You're going to be this way, are you? That's okay."

He grabbed the front of her low-cut tank top and with all of his strength, he managed to rip it right down the middle, exposing her blue bra. He licked his lips and lowered his head. He grabbed her breasts and squeezed, licking the sides of them. He ripped the middle of the bra so it fell off to each of the sides, leaving her breasts out in the open. Mya cried silently, sobbing and begging him to stop. She screamed in pain with his first thrust. She silently sent prayer after prayer, begging it would end. He didn't stop, she thrashed about, trying to throw him off of her, but she was famished, and he outweighed her by a hundred pounds. He grabbed her wrists in his hands, holding her down, and he had his eyes closed as he made one final thrust, exploding inside her. A short moment later, he slowly sunk down right on top of her. He kissed her naked chest, her collarbone, the curves of her neck and finally, her lips. Her face was wet with tears. He used his thumb to wipe away the streaks, then looked at her in her eyes. Mya stared back, a blankness covering her face, nestled deep in her eyes. He slowly pulled himself out of her.

"Clean up, get dressed."

He ordered her.

"I have to go somewhere, but don't you worry your pretty little head. I'll be back for you, my girl."

He planted another kiss on her lips and stood up. He was naked from the waist down. Mya turned away from him, facing the wall. She brought her knees up to her chest.

He pulled his jeans back up above his hips. He looked at her once more, then retreated from the room. He got into his car and drove down the silent street. He couldn't help but be completely pissed off at the fact that he had lost two days with her.

Two days. Two fucking days. The chloroform affected her differently than the others. She should have woken up at least a day ago. Angered thoughts jumbled his brain. He drove in silence, trying not to think of how much of a setback this was. He didn't think of anything until the university appeared in the distance. A massive smile crept onto his face. He pressed down on the gas. He had to see her. Knowing she was only a couple of minutes away; he could barely hold onto his enthusiasm.

He arrived at the university about five minutes later and found his favourite parking spot, right around the many other cars, hidden in plain sight. He climbed out of the car and slammed the door shut, pressing the lock button on his key fob more times than necessary. He walked to the trunk and slowly lifted it. Inside, there was an open suitcase filled with shirts, ties, pants, hats and jackets. He decided that what he was wearing was going to be fine enough. He just needed to add the finishing touch. He pulled out a maroon and white coloured varsity jacket, with the school's insignia on the upper left chest.

He closed the trunk softly, and turned towards the school. He walked swiftly towards the fountain. He never missed their 'date'. He looked at his cell phone. It was one fifteen. He knew that Saige D'Leo's Criminal Justice course ended at one. He knew she would wait for her two friends that he just couldn't stand, the two blonde bimbo looking young women who Saige spent her time with. The three of them would exit the university by one twenty. They'd walk together until the fountain, where her friends would continue on and Saige would sit on the side of the fountain, next to one of those gaudy ravens that he hated so much, and study for about half hour. Finally, she'd return to her dorm. She'd be alone. So deliciously alone.

He sat down on a bench that was not too far from the fountain and in the perfect position to watch her as she would study. He was dressed in his jeans, a white t-shirt and the varsity jacket he had so recently pulled from the trunk. He pulled his cell phone from his jacket pocket and leaned over it, pretending to be texting furiously. He could easily pass for a student, texting a girlfriend or he could be mistaken for waiting for a friend. It was a perfect disguise. Hidden in plain sight. The moment the time turned to one twenty, he looked up. There she was. He gulped hard as he, once again, watched her emerge from the doorway and strut her way down the sidewalk, her friends flanking her side as always. He gulped again and licked his lips. He watched her laugh; the sound was music to his ears. He couldn't wait to hear it more. She flipped her hair over her shoulder. He licked his lips again. He could feel them becoming raw. He would need to buy some chap stick.

She flipped her hair again and laughed even harder at something her friends said. God, he wanted to run his fingers through her silky looking loose curls. They approached the fountain. She stopped walking and smiled at her friends. Her smile. He crossed his legs, trying to prevent what was happening in his boxers. She hugged each of her friends and kissed both their cheeks. She smiled, waving goodbye. That's when she noticed him. He froze. He didn't think she was looking at him. She couldn't be. He'd been sitting there, watching her for months. She didn't notice him. He was just another student. Just another student. Except he wasn't.

Just sit down. Just sit down.

He thought frantically, as if trying to see if she could read his mind, which, obviously she couldn't. She didn't sit. She adjusted her book bag on her shoulder, shifted her textbooks in her arms and, to his extreme horror, began to walk in long strides towards him. He told himself to just breathe normally and everything would be okay.

"Hi there."

Oh god. Her voice.

"Hi."

He responded softly. *Hi? That's all you can say? You're a fucking moron.* He yelled at himself in his mind. Saige gestured to the seat beside him.

"Is that seat taken?"

She smiled directly at him. At *him.* He shook his head, nervously.

"May I?"

"Please."

His heartbeat quickened as Saige, his Saige, took a seat next to him. She didn't waste a second.

"Have you been following me?"

She accused. He was completely shocked. Had he been so obvious? He thought he was doing a great job at being hidden plainly. He faced her. How dare she.

"No. What makes you say that?"

He responded, even toned. She shrugged and wrapped a silky brown curl around her finger.

"I see you sitting here, every single day at the same time. I never see you around campus though."

It wasn't a question. But she phrased it like one, with the end of the word going up into a higher pitch.

"I go to class. I go home." He replied. He looked into her eyes. Her chocolate brown eyes shimmered, the sun glinting off them in such a beautiful way. Everything about her was just beautiful.

"If that's true, why do you sit here, then? Why this spot?"

He noticed she put emphasis on the word, 'this'. She was trying to get into his head.

"I write poetry."

He said, before he even thought. *Poetry? What the fuck!*

"Poetry? That's exciting! I wouldn't mind hearing one. If you wanted to share?"

She smiled at him again. He melted.

"Sure. One day. Maybe."

They sat in silence for a minute or two. Saige was the one that broke it.

"My name is Saige. Saige D'Leo."

He swallowed hard.

"Hi Saige. I'm Michael."

False name of course. No, he wouldn't tell her his real name. Not until she was his again.

"Nice meeting you, Michael."

She paused and touched his knee.

"I'll see you around?"

She said hopefully. He smiled at her and nodded. She stood up, cradling her text books against her chest. She walked about three feet and turned back to him.

"I look forward to reading that poem."

He gave her the thumbs up. *A fucking thumbs up? Kill yourself.* He'd beat himself up over that for the next week. The moment she turned to continue walking away, he bent over himself and adjusted the lump in his pants. He waited until she was out of sight, and then got up and walked towards the parking lot.

Saige. He knew that was her name, of course. Having her come up to him and introduce herself was a dream come true. He hadn't expected that. Not in the slightest. He smiled to himself the entire way to the parking lot. He was in such a state of complete amity, that he never noticed the blonde girl walking towards him, head down, buried in her books. He ran right into her, knocking her to the ground, her books falling around her on the pavement they were standing on.

"What the fuck?"

He exclaimed as he stumbled, but managed to catch himself before hitting the cement. It was another story for the blonde. She was sprawled out on the walk-way. He almost left without helping her up, but he had to act like a university student. They were kinder these days than when he was in school. He reached down; hand extended.

"I am so sorry."

He tried to sound as sincere as he possibly could. The blonde smiled up at him, obviously taking in how attractive he really was.

"Oh, it's no problem. Totally okay."

She gushed. He kept a straight face as she stood all the way up. She brushed her legs and butt off with hands that had long, false nails glued to the tips of her fingers.

"Bella."

She stated and held out her hand.

"Uh, Michael."

He replied. That's when he recognized her as one of Saige's horribly annoying blonde friends.

"Well, Michael. Since you just kind of knocked me on my ass, I think you owe me a coffee."

She was flirting. He knew that.

"Maybe, hey."

She touched his chest with her hand.

"How about, I get your number, and we'll figure something out?"

He was hesitant. Did he want this annoying bobble-headed bitch having his cell phone number What could the harm be? He decided he could use her to get closer to Saige.

"Sure. Here."

She handed him her phone, all the while giving him googly eyes. He punched in his phone number and couldn't help but notice her wallpaper picture was of her and Saige kissing each other's cheeks. He was jealous. He wanted that kind of picture on his phone. He handed it back to her but she didn't take her eyes off of him.

"I got to go..."

He started to say. Bella interceded.

"Yea, that's cool. I'll text you later, cutie."

He brushed past her and rolled his eyes.

"Alright, start again. From the beginning."

PJ smiled, reassuringly. Amber and Christopher Martin sat on a black leather sofa, clutching each other. Amber had tears running down her cheeks. Christopher sat with a blank stare.

Daniel Martin stood at the edge of the sofa, notebook in hand.

"Joshua had recently started seeing this girl. Mya Swanson. Very, very nice girl, but a year older than him. She's seventeen and Joshie is only sixteen..."

Amber paused as she choked on the last couple of words. Her hand flew up to her chest, as if she was trying to hold in the heart wrenching sobs. Christopher rubbed her arm gently and kissed her temple.

"That girl, Mya, stopped talking to Josh a couple of days ago. Just stopped out of the blue. He was really torn up about it. He came home, crying. Said Mya was gone."

"What do you mean by 'gone'?"

PJ leaned forward. Christopher exchanged a look with his wife.

"I'm not sure. He said gone. I guess we thought he meant they broke up."

PJ jotted down a quick note.

"Then?"

"We said, 'Mya is a seventeen-year-old girl. She probably found a boy her own age. You're in grade ten, baby. You've got your whole life ahead of you to be dating, especially someone whose got post-secondary to focus on.'"

Amber paused again, stifling a sob.

"He got mad. Yelled at us. Said we didn't know what the fuck we were talking about. Said Mya wouldn't leave him without being real. Said she'd break up with him first. That is what confused us. We had assumed that they had broken up." Christopher paused and looked down at his lap. He shook his head slowly.

"So, we told him to calm down, think clearly. He said don't tell him to calm the fuck down. He was going to go out and find Mya. He would save her. And then he left."

Christopher finished. A massive sob exploded from Amber, resulting in her whole body shaking violently. Christopher squeezed his arm around her gently, trying his best to settle her down. She dropped her face into her hands and cried hard. PJ was jotting down notes like there would be no tomorrow. She slowly looked up.

"Sounds like he thought Mya might have been abducted."

Christopher bit his lip.

"What is it, sir?"

PJ asked, curiosity filling her voice.

"One night, Mya was here. I heard her telling Josh she felt like she was being watched. That there was this guy at school who had been watching her, following her. Coming onto her. She said she didn't feel safe."

PJ looked over her shoulder at Daniel, who was writing furiously in his notepad.

"Did you over hear anything else?"

Daniel asked, before PJ could speak. Christopher slowly shook his head. PJ glanced at Daniel. They exchanged a look.

"Did you know your son's friends very well?"

"Joshie's friends wouldn't make him run away."

Amber exclaimed through tears.

"Did you know his friends?"

PJ repeated herself, directing the question to Christopher. He nodded.

"Mostly. I knew the ones that he played sports with. They were the same hooligans that would come trash the game room on the weekends."

"Do the names Kyle Bellfry, Jacob Miller, Jordon Gardener, or Sasha Brown ring any bells?"

Christopher thought for a moment, then looked at Amber. They both shook their heads.

"No. Not really. Sorry."

PJ made another note and smiled at Christopher, then at Amber.

"How about Denae Crossman, Carly Bew or Kelly Smith?"

Christopher shook his head again.

"Sorry Detective. I don't know those names."

PJ made one final note and stood up from the sofa.

"Would you mind if we had a quick look around?"

PJ asked, looking at both of the parents. Daniel followed her lead and stepped away from the sofa as well and looked at Amber and Christopher. Christopher shook his head. Amber was too busy sobbing.

"Go ahead. Josh's room is the first door on the left, down the hall."

PJ made her way around the sofa and gestured for Daniel to follow her.

She twisted the knob to the bedroom door, holding it open for Daniel. The room looked unkempt. She figured it was because Amber and Christopher knew better than to mess with his things. Could very well be used as evidence if the case went sour. PJ pulled a pair of plastic gloves from her pocket. She always made sure to keep a pair handy just in case. Daniel did the same. PJ motioned to one side of the room, the side furthest from the door, by the window. The bed was positioned under the window. PJ noticed there was a trunk at the end of the bed.

"You look over there; I'm going to tackle the closet."

Daniel knew better than to question the Detective's orders. He crossed the room swiftly and with a gloved hand, lifted the trunk's lid, which was surprisingly heavy. He didn't see anything suspicious at first glance. The trunk was filled to the brim with a couple of hockey pucks, a basketball, a soccer ball, a few different sports jerseys, and a porn magazine. Daniel laughed out loud and shook his head. PJ looked over.

"What is it?"

Daniel reached into the trunk, chuckling. He held up the magazine and PJ stifled a giggle.

"Hustlers."

PJ couldn't stop the guffaw that escaped her lips.

"He is a sixteen-year-old kid. I'm not surprised he has a nudie mag. I *am* surprised he only has one."

Daniel chuckled again.

"Think again."

PJ said as she pulled something from the back of the closet. Daniel squinted his eyes as she held it up.

"We've got a box of Hustlers and Playboy."

"That's it? I had those, Juggs, and Asian Babes. They were definitely well used."

PJ shot Daniel a disgusted look but a small sly smirk crept its way onto her face.

"Fuck off Daniel. That's fucking disgusting!"

She teased. Daniel shrugged, a cheeky smile on his lips.

"Welcome to a lonely man's world, P."

"You have a wife!"

PJ exclaimed. She turned back to the closet and set the box back down. She started digging in a storage shelf.

"Yea. I do. And Lorrayne is pretty terrific. I'm talking about my teenage years."

He dropped the magazine back into the trunk and closed it.

"Okay, okay enough! I so don't need to hear about your lonely life as a teenager and your disgusting, over eager masturbation habits."

PJ chuckled. They searched in silence for a couple of minutes.

"What's this?"

She said softly. Daniel didn't hear her. She could still hear him scrounging around somewhere behind her. She carefully unfolded the piece of paper. It was a handwritten note.

She needs a man. Not a boy. Say goodbye.

"Daniel, take a look at this."

PJ spoke up quickly. She heard rustling behind her and Daniel peered over her shoulder.

"Whoa."

He said. PJ nodded her head. "Did you find anything?"

Daniel shook his head.

"Let's take this to the lab. Get them to run finger print scans. Look for any form of DNA. See who the fuck sent this to Josh."

PJ and Daniel left Josh's room, shutting the door behind them. They left it the way they went in, for the most part. When they got back to the family room, Christopher stood up.

"Did you find anything of use?"

PJ and Daniel exchanged a glance.

"We found a note. May or may not be from the person who we're starting to suspect has abducted Mya."

Christopher and Amber looked at each other. Tears flooded Amber's eyes for the millionth time.

"We're going to take it with us. Run some tests."

Christopher was not about to stop them. PJ extended her hand to Christopher.

"Thank you for your time Mr. and Mrs. Martin. I understand this can't be easy for you. We'll be in touch."

She shook hands with both of Josh Martin's parents and walked swiftly down the stairs and out the door. They hadn't even made it ten feet out the door before PJ heard her name.

"Detective Richards?"

PJ looked over her shoulder and saw Christopher walking towards her.

"What can I do for you Mr. Martin?"

Christopher looked around uncomfortably.

"You guys think that Josh thought Mya got kidnapped...that's really true? Did that poor girl get kidnapped?"

PJ decided to tell him the truth. She was planning on hosting a press conference on Monday. Slowly, she nodded.

"That's our theory now, yes."

Christopher's eyes glossed over.

"Do you think...do you think he's safe? He said he was going to look for her...oh god."

His hand raised up and covered his mouth. PJ touched his shoulder.

"As far as our evidence goes, our unsub strictly sticks with females. I'm sure your son is fine."

She paused and looked into his eyes. She could tell that he wasn't sure whether or not to believe her.

"We will find him."

Christopher finally nodded.

"Thank you, Detective."

He turned and made his way up the walk and back inside. PJ turned back to the cruiser and saw Daniel holding the door open for her. She shot him a quick smile and ducked inside.

Daniel got inside the driver's side and looked at her.

"Spill it. What do you really think happened to that kid? Thinking what I'm thinking?"

PJ bit her cheek.

"That depends on what you're thinking."

"Well I'm thinking that he found who kidnapped his girlfriend, and had gotten himself killed in the process."

"Yes. I'm thinking what you're thinking."

PJ kept her eyes on the road ahead of her. Shouldn't take them too long to get to their next destination; Sasha Brown's house. It turned out that the Brown's lived about ten blocks over from the Martin's. PJ looked at her notepad as Daniel pulled up in front of a quaint white house with blue trim around the windows and door. A white picket fence lined the yard. The lawn was cut and very tidy. Two pink plastic flamingos sat in a small garden off to the side of the house. There was a large red rose bush situated opposite the flamingos on the other side of the garden. Daniel pulled up to a stop along the curb outside of the house and put the car into park. PJ. and Daniel got out of the cruiser and walked on the skinny sidewalk that cut through the center of the too green lawn. PJ raised a fist and knocked twice.

"Hello?"

The door opened a crack and a tiny voice, that sounded like it could belong to a Who of Whoville, escaped.

"Who is it?"

They asked in a sing song voice. PJ assumed it was a small child. She held up her creds, even though something like that didn't matter to a kid.

"Detective Richards. Detective Martin. We're from the Ridgeway PD. I spoke with a Lisa Clifford-Brown a couple of hours ago on the phone."

The door opened all the way and a small girl, could only be five, maybe six, stood in the frame.

"Mommy!"

She yelled, while staring in awe at PJ and Daniel. It only took a moment for a smartly dressed woman to appear behind the kid. She extended a hand over the little girl's head.

"Hi, I'm Lisa Clifford-Brown. Detective Richards, Detective Martin, please, come inside. Faye, move out of the way." Lisa ushered Faye out of the doorway, allowing PJ and Daniel to step inside. The interior of the house was just as fascinating as the exterior. PJ felt overwhelmed by the amount of family photographs that clung to the walls and the mind-boggling number of shoes that littered the entrance way floor. The brown tiles on the floor were dirty and just one tile looked to be smeared with Vaseline or some other kind of greasy substance. PJ narrowed her eyes.

"Sorry about the mess. We've been cleaning and getting rid of stuff, including all of those."

She nodded slightly at the massive pile of footwear. PJ smiled at her and Lisa told them to follow her. They walked up the stairs and entered the family room. A brown suede sofa took up one wall and a matching love seat was positioned opposite. A large flat screen TV was hanging on the wall above a small fireplace at the front of the room. The glass coffee table that sat between the two sofas was clean and tidy. Nothing was out of place. It was a massive change from the entry way right down the stairs. PJ sat on the loveseat, Daniel stood behind it, his arms crossed over his chest, observing. Lisa sat down opposite of PJ, Faye jumping up next to her.

"Okay Mrs. Clifford-Brown, as I said on the phone, we would be by to interview your daughter, Sasha..."

"Sasha's my step-daughter."

PJ met Lisa's eyes.

"Yes, I'm sorry. Your step-daughter. Because she was the one that reported Michelle missing."

PJ paused, taking a breath.

"However, because Sasha is fourteen, she is classified as a minor, so I will need your permission to speak with her."

PJ could now see the tears that were welling up in Lisa's eyes.

"Michelle. Michelle is my daughter."

PJ looked up at Daniel. He shrugged; a confused look plastered to his face. PJ looked back to Lisa. She was standing now, grabbing something off of the fireplace mantel. She turned and walked across the room to PJ and presented the small black iron picture frame to her. PJ took it gingerly and looked at the photograph that it contained. It was of Lisa and whom she presumed to be Michelle sitting in front of a tree. Lisa's arms were wrapped around Michelle and they were both laughing. Michelle's blonde hair was all messed up from Lisa or perhaps a gust of wind.

"She's a beautiful girl."

PJ stated softly. And it was true. She was a beautiful girl. She made a mental note that the unsub's MO was to go after a certain kind of pretty. Lisa nodded.

"Yes. She is...uh...let me go get Sasha for you."

She hustled down a hallway and was gone, leaving PJ, Daniel and Faye alone in the glorious family room. For a moment, no one said anything. PJ and Daniel were waiting patiently. Faye started bouncing up and down in her seat. Faye's eyes met PJ's. Her eyes matched Michelle's to a T.

"Are you going to bring 'Chelle home?"

PJ leaned forward.

"We will do our very best."

Faye slid off of the sofa and stood up.

"My sissy said she was gunna go on vacay. What's vacay?"

PJ's eyes widened.

"Vacay is vacation. Like a trip."

Faye's eyes also widened.

"What! I wanna go on vacay! Do you think she went to Disneyland? Oh man."

She was getting really excited.

"Faye, did Michelle say she was going with anybody?"

PJ questioned. She had to be careful how many questions she asked. Faye was five. That was definitely a minor.

"Hmm...she said not to tell anybody. She said 'Okay Faye.'"

She paused and started to giggle.

"That rhymes."

She giggled again.

"She said, 'Okay Faye, 'Chelle needs to go away for a bit. 'Chelle's goin' on a vacay. You can't tell anyone. Keep it hush, okay?'"

PJ looked at Daniel. Faye's smile turned upside down.

"Oh no! I just told! Pretend I didn't tell you. 'Chelle will be mad if I told you."

PJ mimed zipping her lips and throwing away the key. Lisa finally returned with a scrawny brunette girl next to her.

"Sit."

She pointed at the sofa and the girl sat down next to her. Faye squeezed herself in the seat between Lisa and the girl, whom PJ could only assume was Sasha.

"Detective Richards, Detective Martin, this is Sasha."

Sasha feebly lifted a hand and waved.

"Mrs. Clifford-Brown, would I be able to speak with Sasha privately?"

Lisa's eyes widened, but she stood up.

"Uh, yea, sure. C'mon Faye."

Faye slid off of the sofa and ran over to PJ. She cupped her hands around her mouth and PJ leaned down so Faye could whisper in her ear.

"Remember, don't tell."

PJ held her pinky out and Faye made a pinky promise, sealing the secret she had just told away for good. PJ knew that she was going to spill the beans anyway. She had to if she even had a sliver of a chance on finding the missing teenager. Lisa reached for Faye's hand, she slid it into her mother's tight grasp. PJ waited for Lisa and Faye to be gone before turning to Sasha.

"What do you want me to tell you?"

Sasha said, before PJ could ask a question. PJ tilted her head.

"The truth. What were you and Michelle doing leading up to her disappearance? Who was she hanging out with? Why does Faye think she went on a 'vacay'? Just tell me whatever you know."

Sasha looked around the family room and then down at her hands. She sniffled.

"C'mon Sasha. You can tell me."

Sasha looked back up. Her blue eyes were glossy.

"I don't know where she went. I just know that Hannah, Stephanie, Rachel and Michelle were talking about some big college party. She said that David told her about it. That she should hit it up. Smoke weed, get high, get drunk, do what teenagers should be doing. And then Stephanie got all butt hurt and asked if that meant David was breaking up with her and Michelle said no, he wasn't, but..."

She trailed off.

"But?"

PJ coaxed.

"But people were getting suspicious. They had to keep their relationship on the DL. Michelle said that, apparently, David's daughter was starting to figure out what he was doing, where he was going after his classes..."

"Sorry, Sasha. Classes? Daughter?"

PJ had to interrupt. Sasha didn't respond right away. She bit her cheek and looked around the room again. The poor girl was clearly uncomfortable sharing her step-sister's secret to the police.

"Yea...David is a professor at Ridgeway University."

PJ's jaw dropped open. She immediately closed it and looked back at Daniel; whose arms dropped to his side. A look of total astonishment glued to his face.

"How do you know all of this?"

PJ finally managed to speak. Sasha shrugged, halfheartedly.

"When Michelle has her friends over, I sort of eaves drop."

PJ had to stifle a small chuckle. She managed to compose herself. She had to remain professional and laughing at a fourteen-year-old girl was definitely not that.

"Do you know what professor?"

PJ wondered even though she had a strong feeling she already knew what the answer was. Sasha hung her head.

"No. They never said his last name. But they did say, 'it's all his slutty daughter's fault.

If it wasn't for that preppy bitch, Mya, then everything would be okay. Just because she goes to private school, she thinks she is better than me? She's..."

Sasha paused and looked directly at PJ.

"Do you want me to quote her?"

PJ thought that was an odd question coming from a kid. She shrugged and nodded.

"If you remember exactly what she said, then yes. Please. It would be most helpful."

Sasha pursed her lips and nodded back.

"Well, she said 'she's fucking a sixteen-year-old and I'm fucking her dad."

PJ's jaw dropped again. Sasha confirmed her suspicion. Mya and Michelle were connected through Mya's father. PJ could not believe all of the new information that she and Daniel had just received. She glanced back at Daniel. He was clutching the back of the sofa, white knuckled. PJ stood up.

"Thank you, Sasha. You've been extremely helpful. Extremely."

PJ shook Sasha's hand enthusiastically.

"We're done here!"

PJ said a little louder, hoping Lisa would be able to hear her so that she and Faye could return to the family room and be comfortable.

"Officer Richards?"

PJ didn't bother to correct the title. She just looked at Sasha.

"Please, find my sister."

PJ couldn't respond. This girl was so innocent.

"How'd everything go? Did you get what you were looking for?"

Lisa asked, a hint of concern filling her voice. PJ turned to her. Faye was clutching Lisa's hand. PJ gave her a reassuring smile.

"Sasha's been a great help."

Lisa shot Sasha a look and then returned her pained stare to PJ.

"Just find my baby."

PJ didn't reply. She shook Lisa's free hand and left the little house. Back at the car, PJ and Daniel met each other's eyes.

"Holy..."

"Shit."

They were both completely blow away by the new intel. Michelle knew Mya and now they were both missing.

"I say, let's go surprise our naughty prof, David Swanson."

Daniel suggested. PJ had to agree.

"I have this strong feeling that he won't be around. I have a feeling that he and Michelle ran off together."

No time to waste. It was now three seventeen and if PJ was right, David Swanson would have been on 'vacay' for two days and would be gone for an undisclosed amount of time. They tore into the RU parking lot and grabbed a free spot as close to the main entrance as possible.

PJ looked at Daniel.

"This will go so much faster if I go in alone. I'll be right back, keep the car running."

Daniel didn't care. He grabbed the seat adjustor and tilted the seat back. He closed his eyes and drummed his fingers on the steering wheel. PJ wondered how the hell he could be so relaxed. She got out of the car and tried walking calmly. She found herself jogging up the main walkway and bursting through the doors. She was in the main hallway. A couple of students were milling around. Some had textbooks open, some had their phones out. PJ shuffled through the groups. She had no idea where the hell she was going.

"Excuse me?"

She tapped a girl on the shoulder. She turned to look at PJ and PJ was filled with awe. This girl was absolutely stunning. She didn't think she had ever seen anyone as beautiful as her. Her brown hair cascaded around her shoulders in perfect wavy curls, her deep brown eyes were shimmering and her perfect white smile could have been blinding.

"Yea?"

She asked. Even her voice was beautiful. PJ was thrown off guard by it.

"Could you please tell me where the Dean's office is?"

"Oh yea, sure. If you go down this hallway and turn right at that little corridor in the middle, his office is the first door down that hallway. On the left."

She smiled at PJ.

"Thank you!"

PJ rushed down the hall and shook her head. She easily found the door that the girl had been talking about. She knocked once. Waited. No answer. She could hear a couple of voices behind the door. One was very stern. She knocked again.

"One minute please."

Someone yelled from inside.

"Detective Richards with Ridgeway PD. I need to speak with the Dean immediately."

PJ ordered. There was a shuffling behind the door. The lock clicked and it swung open. The Dean was standing, wearing a dark gray suit and blue tie. His brown, thinning hair was gelled, almost like he was trying too hard to make it look like it was fuller than it was. A young man, obviously a university student, judging by his black faded jeans, sports jersey and beautifully quaffed brown hair, was sitting at the Dean's desk. He sat with his back against the back of the chair, but his legs were apart. He was slumped over; his fingers were tapping the arms of the black chair. The Dean stretched out his hand.

"Hello Detective..."

"Detective Richards."

She interrupted. The Dean smiled.

"Hello Detective Richards, I'm Dean Williams. Dean Brody Williams. What can I do for you?"

PJ peered around Dean Williams' shoulder and looked at the student.

"May we speak in private?"

PJ requested, bringing her attention back to Dean Williams. Dean Williams gave her another smile.

"Of course. Matt,"

He paused and turned towards the student.

"Matt, please wait in the hall. We aren't finished here."

The kid, Matt, shrugged, stood up and brushed past Dean Williams and PJ.

"He's brilliant. Doesn't look it, but that young man could win the next Nobel prize if he tried."

Dean Williams admired as he shut the door behind Matt. He shook his head sadly and turned back to PJ. He gestured towards the chair that Matt was recently occupying. PJ sat down, though she really wasn't planning on staying long. Especially since Daniel was waiting in the running car, burning gas.

"Can I get you coffee, tea, water?"

Dean Williams offered politely. PJ smiled at him but shook her head softly.

"No thank you sir."

She waited for him to sit in his massive black office chair. He did and folded his hands on the desk in front of him.

"What can I do for you Detective?"

PJ shuffled the chair closer to Dean Williams' desk.

"Well, sir, I'm here because a high school student has recently gone missing and there is reason for the RPD to believe that she has potentially run off with one of your professors."

Dean Williams' eyes bulged. He didn't know how to respond. He had never been faced with this sort of issue in his fifteen years as the Dean.

"So, can you tell me if Professor David Swanson is at the university and teaching or has he gone on vacation?"

Dean Williams gulped and grabbed at his tie, loosening it.

"Professor Swanson, uh, yea...He requested a week off so he could take his wife and daughter to a hotel for a little time away."

PJ pulled out her notebook and jotted that tidbit down.

"Do you know which hotel?"

Dean Williams shook his head apologetically.

"No, I'm very sorry. I do have his cell phone number if you'd like?" He offered. PJ slid the notepad and pen across the surface of the desk. Dean Williams quickly jotted down the phone number and something else. He gave the notepad and pen back to PJ. She looked down at the pad. There were two numbers on it. The first one had David Swanson's name written underneath it. The second had Brody Williams written underneath it. PJ held in a chuckle.

"Detective, I assume you will be launching a full investigation when he returns from vacation, am I correct?"

PJ nodded at him.

"Very correct."

Dean Williams stood up.

"Consider Professor Swanson hereby on temporary suspension, until the case is adjourned and the proper consequences can be taken into consideration."

PJ stood up and tucked her notepad and pen back into her pocket. She stretched out her hand and shook Dean Williams' meaty hand in return.

"Thank you again Mr. Williams."

"Please. Brody."

"Thank you, Brody."

"If you need any more information, please don't hesitate to call me. Or if you just want some company...you've got the number."

He smiled at her. She smiled politely back but Brody Williams just wasn't her type. Speaking of her type, she suddenly missed Nick a lot.

"Thank you, sir. If I need more information, I'll be sure to call. You have my number as well, so if you hear anything, please, make sure you give me a holler."

He walked her to the office door and pulled it open. He shook her hand once more and she exited the office. Matt was still standing outside the office, and when PJ left, he went back in. PJ was amazed. When she was in college, no one would have waited if they had gotten a free pass out of the office. Halfway back to the main office, PJ pulled out her cell phone.

Three fifty. She dialed Nick's number and held the phone up to her ear. She continued walking to the outside world.

"Hi, you've got Nick Redford, sorry I missed your call, leave me a message and I'll catch you later."

PJ was discouraged to hear the voicemail answering message.

"Hi babe, it's PJ. Call me back when you can. Love you."

She hung up the phone and slid it back into her pocket just as she approached the main doorways. She pushed the doors open, suddenly feeling very weak. It had been a long day.

She accosted the cruiser and noticed that Daniel had turned the idling car almost off. He left it on auxiliary. Daniel was rocking out hard to some kind of dance-able music. PJ pulled open the door, just as 'Sweet Child O' Mine' was ending.

"Took you long enough."

Daniel said, jokingly.

"Sorry for doing my job!"

PJ exclaimed back with a gentle teasing tone. Daniel started laughing and grabbed the key that stuck out of the ignition, turning the car all the way on.

"So, what happened? Dear professor teaching or on vacay?"

PJ sighed, feeling defeated.

"What do you think?"

Daniel made a sharp left turn.

"Vacay."

PJ sighed again.

"Mr. Williams, the Dean, says David Swanson asked for a week off to take his wife and daughter to a hotel getaway. Michelle and Swanson's daughter, Mya both disappeared two days ago, so my guess is he doesn't even know she's gone."

Daniel shook his head in disgust.

"So where now? Talk to Swanson's wife? Track down whichever hotel he's at and bust 'im? What?"

PJ stomach made a fit of nasty loud growls.

"How about the McDonald's drive-thru? I'm fucking starving."

He sat in his car in the driveway, tapping the steering wheel. She had approached him. She had actually come up to him, sat beside, spoke to him, *touched* him.

He shivered.

He could still feel the heat of her hand through his jeans on his knees.

He turned the car off and got out. Then he locked the door and walked up the three steps to his front door. He pulled out his large number of keys and found the one that opened the front door, leading him into the main entrance way.

Once he was standing in the mostly empty front entrance, he turned to face the door and locked the key lock, the dead bolt and lifted the chain as the final touch. Security.

He looked around his entry way, which was just his kitchen.

Tidy. Not clean. But tidy.

He decided that his white marble floors could use a sweep and a mop but that could wait until he was finished his business.

Instead, he walked through the kitchen and into the hallway. It was dark. All of the doors to each of the rooms in the hall were shut.

Locked, of course.

Security.

He walked the full length of the hallway and put his hand on the doorknob that belonged to the room at the very end. He still had his key collection jingling away in his hand. He found the one that belonged to this room, one of his favourite rooms. He slowly unlocked the door. He didn't want his friend on the inside to know he was coming in. He shoved the many keys into his pocket. He was going to need both hands, just in case his friend decided to act up, again.

"Wake up, boy."

He said angrily as he saw the young boy curled up on his side on the bed. He stormed over and kicked the kid, hard in the back. He cried out and reached back, rubbing the pained area as best as his abilities allowed.

"Get the fuck up!"

He screamed again. The boy slowly sat up and turned to face him. His face was horribly bruised and bloody. His clothes, tattered and ripped.

"Are you going to answer me yet, or no? What do you know about me!?"

His voice was getting louder, the angrier he got.

The kid coughed, blood spattering onto the dirty carpet. He didn't reply.

"I know you saw me. I know you know I have Mya. You know what that means for you, right?"

He said, his voice had lowered, the tone was terrifying. The boy on the floor didn't look up. He coughed a second time; more blood sprinkled the dirty carpet.

"I bet you'd love to see her. Wouldn't you?"

That seemed to spark the kid's interest.

"She's-she's still alive?"

The kid barely managed to whisper, still without lifting his head. His energy was drained and he was broken. He rolled his eyes.

"Of course, you fucking moron! She's still useful to me."

The kid placed his palms flat on the floor and used all of the energy he had left and stood up on shaking legs. He was very pale, and looked as if he was going to faint at any possible moment. He thought the sight was delicious to see.

"I would love to see her."

The kid whispered again, this time his voice had come out a little louder, obviously hard for him to speak with such power. His chest hurt so much; he could hardly push enough breath out to talk louder than a whisper. He smirked and grabbed the kid's shivering shoulder.

"Does she know I'm here? Has she been asking for me?"

The kid asked as he tightened his grip on his skinny shoulder.

"No..."

He responded, and then decided to get the kid worked up. It would be so much fun.

"She's been too busy enjoying my dick to be worried about you."

The kid didn't know how to react. He thought he felt his heart stop. He knew it couldn't be true, but the words still cut into him, deeply damaging.

"I still want to see her."

He rolled his eyes again; he did not get the reaction he had wanted. He'd hoped for screaming, crying, upset sounds of betrayal. He tightened his grip on the kid's shoulder even more and pulled him out of the room. He didn't bother locking that door. No one was in there, so it didn't matter.

They reached the door at the opposite end of the hallway. He kept one hand on the kid, though he was positive that if there was the smallest chance, he'd see Mya, he'd behave.

He pulled his keys from his pocket of what seemed like the hundredth time and picked a silver key that had a couple of pink polka dots decorating it and slid it into the deadbolt and unlocked it. He heard rustling behind the door. Mya wasn't very sneaky.

"I'd back away from the door if I were you, Mya, my girl. I have someone that wants to see you and you wouldn't want to do anything to get him killed, now would you?"

He said through the door. More rustling and finally the squeaking of the bed frame. He slowly pushed open the door and poked his head in.

"Hi Mya."

He smiled. The more he did that, the creepier it became, Mya observed. She was sitting with her back against the wall, her knees pulled under her chin, her arms wrapped around her shins.

"Please, don't touch me."

Her voice shook. She was traumatized from the last time he touched her. He chuckled and used his foot to kick open the door all the way and he shoved the kid inside.

He landed with a thud on his knees and caught his breath in his throat. It felt like the wind was knocked out of him.

"Mya."

He whispered as he tried to stand, unsuccessfully. Mya couldn't move. She stared in disbelief.

"Mya, babe."

The kid gasped, clutching his gut, trying to regain control of his breathing and the aching pain in his abdomen. He tried again to pull himself to his feet, but the pain in his bruised and cracked ribs was too much and he had to stay down.

That's when it hit Mya. She realized who she was looking at and the happy tears instantly welled up in her eyes.

"J-Josh?"

She stuttered.

"Yes, honey."

He whispered again, pain lacing his voice. Mya scrambled off the bed and grabbed Josh in her arms. He gasped and sucked in a deep breath. Mya gingerly touched the bruises and lacerations on his face.

"Josh."

She whispered as she held him. Seeing him felt like a dream. Josh wrapped his arms around her waist. The two of them held each other on the floor, getting lost in the moment of them being together again, that they had forgotten where they were and who was standing at the doorway, watching their every move.

"It'll be okay My. Everything will be okay."

Josh whispered into her ear, his lips brushing against her lobes.

A loud, obnoxious laugh came from the doorway.

"Everything will be okay, My. Everything will be okay."

He mocked Josh's comforting words.

The couple glanced up and saw him standing there, leaning against the door frame, arms crossed, a stupid, sly grin plastered to his chapping lips.

Mya tightened her grasp on Josh like she thought if she wasn't touching him, he'd just disappear.

"Enjoy your time together. I'm leaving again, but I'll be back soon."

He didn't leave right away. Instead he strode through the room until he reached Mya and Josh. They stiffened and he grabbed Josh's arm and pulled him away from Mya easily.

A sixteen-year-old teenager was no match for a thirty-two-year-old man.

He shoved him over, and Josh winced in pain. Then he grabbed Mya's shoulders and pulled her to her feet. He grabbed her chin and kissed her hard. She whimpered and tried to pull away.

"Stop!"

Josh managed to exclaim. He pulled himself to his feet and limped towards Mya. She was trying to pull herself out of his arms, but his grasp was just too strong. He shoved Mya backwards and turned just as Josh threw a punch. He may have been weak, but he was damn sure he was going to try and protect Mya. Their captor looked down at Josh, who had fallen to his knees after throwing his one punch. He chuckled and knelt down and stared into Josh's eyes. A small smile crept into the corners of his mouth and he shook his head. He threw a fist into Josh's gut.

"No!"

Mya cried from the floor on the other side of the room. He had thrown her pretty far and she was struggling to stand. She was just as weak as Josh was. He punched Josh again. Mya was crying. Josh was lying on his side. He pulled a hunting knife out of his belt and knelt down so his face was a foot away from Josh's.

"Don't fuck with me, boy. I told you what was going to happen. I was going to be kind enough to let you have some time with her while I was gone. I was being a good person. But you just had to go and try and stop me. Now look what you're making me do."

Josh groaned. Mya was still crying. She scrambled across the carpet as quick as she could go. He grabbed one of Josh's shoulders and plunged the knife deep into his abdomen before Mya could reach her boyfriend.

Mya screamed.

She finally reached Josh who was now gasping, hands covering his gut, blood spurting through his fingers.

He stood up and met Mya's angry, tear streaked face glaring up at him.

"I'll be back soon, my girl."

She looked him right in the eyes. The beauty of them no longer had any effect on her.

"Go to hell."

She pointed her middle finger at him and pulled Josh's head into her lap.

He smiled at how silly she was being and left the room, making sure to lock every lock from the outside. The moment he was gone, Mya pulled Josh closer.

He was holding his gut and his breathing had become shallow.

"Josh, oh my god, Josh."

Mya was saying over and over. She kissed his forehead.

"What do I do? I don't know what to do."

Josh didn't answer at first.

Tears poured down Mya's cheeks, creating streaks through the dirt on her pale face.

"I don't know how to help."

She sniffled. The tears barreled down her face like a bowling ball headed for a strike.

"Everything will be okay."

Josh said slowly, between heavy breaths. He slowly looked up, into Mya's watery eyes.

"I'll be okay."

He whispered. Mya reached down and touching one of his hands, bloodying her own. Josh winced.

"I love you Josh. I love you. I'm always going to love you."

Mya whispered.

"Don't you dare say that. Don't say your goodbyes. I'm not going to die. Not here."

Josh grimaced and reached a blood-soaked hand up and touched her cheek, smearing the crimson liquid across her face. He may have only been sixteen years old, but Josh was wise beyond his years and he knew that Mya needed him now more than ever. He knew he was in danger of dying and that it was very likely he would perish in that exact spot, however, he refused to let Mya know that. He was going to be strong for her in those coming last moments of his life.

Mya's tears had stopped, but her eyes were still watery, her face still tear streaked.

Josh closed his eyes, his breathing labored. Mya's heart skipped a couple of beats.

"Josh, stay with me. Stay with me, baby."

She tried to keep her voice steady and strong. For him.

"I'm okay, my love. Just resting."

He said slowly.

"Open your eyes Josh. No resting. Look at me. Don't close your eyes."

Mya tried to coax him. His eyelids fluttered.

"Mya."

"Yes, Josh, yes I'm here."

Mya grabbed his hand and held it tight.

"Listen to me, okay?"

Josh whispered, blood leaking out of the corners of his mouth and staining his teeth a rusty crimson colour. Mya didn't reply. She squeezed his hand tighter and ran her other hand gently down the side of his face.

"You have to get out of her. You have to get out and get help."

The tears that lingered over the rims of Mya's eyes teetered dangerously close to falling.

"I can't...I can't leave you."

"You...you have to. Mya, you have to. I need help. You need to do this."

Mya's eyes lifted off of Josh's face and scanned the room. There were no windows at all. The only way out was through the door which was triple locked.

"Okay, babe. I will. How do I get out?"

Her eyes fell back down to his face. His eyes were closed now, his lips slightly parted. Blood was slowly drying to the corner of his mouth.

"Babe?"

Mya squeezed his hand and held her breath. The inevitable had happened.

"Josh. Josh no."

The tears tipped over and regained their momentum of pouring down her cheeks. One dripped off of her chin and fell onto the center of Josh's forehead. She noticed the bleeding had stopped and Josh was now lying in a puddle of scarlet.

"Oh hey! Hey! Over here!"

She called to him as he entered the little coffee shop. She stood up and hugged him as he reached the table.

"Hi Bella."

He said smoothly. The platinum blonde, ice blue eyed freshman at RU smiled as the hug ended. She looked like a complete ditz, but she was incredibly smart. She was in RU majoring in Criminal Justice and was one of Saige's closest friends. This was the same blonde he had run into right after leaving Saige. She had become really intrigued by him for some odd reason. He'd remembered to tell her his name was Michael.

He sat down at the cafe table across from her. She kept smiling at him. He sighed. She was one of the blondes that he always saw walking out of the school with Saige at one twenty.

"So, Michael. What are you studying at school? What's your major?"

Her voice was slightly high pitched, almost whiney.

"Arts."

He responded without thinking. *Fuck. Who majors in arts?* He could punch himself.

Bella giggled.

She reached across the table and touched his hand. He forced himself not to flinch or pull his hand away.

"So, what would you like to do? I'm so happy you agreed to come here. I mean, I'm not surprised after you knocked me down earlier."

Bella asked, chattering away.

He shrugged. Honestly, he just wanted to go home. He had some business to attend to. Bella batted her overly make-upped eyes. She tilted her head and flashed a smile.

"How about we go for a walk?"

He suggested. He felt claustrophobic in the tiny cafe. He felt like the walls were closing in on him, pushing the annoying bimbo even closer than she already was. He needed air.

"Okay cutie."

She smiled again. They stood, Bella grabbed her cup of coffee and slung her book bag over her shoulder. He followed her out the door. When they were outside, Bella slid her arm through his, clutching it tightly.

He glanced at her. Oh, how he wanted to torture her and bring her a miserable death. He could imagine his hunting knife sliding into her skin, the flesh ripping and tearing as it created a massive hole in her body and having her guts spill out, blood splashing everywhere as she gasped for breath and clutched onto his arm, her eyes begging for help. The imagery was appealing.

They were walking, strides matched, Bella clinging to his arm, when he saw her again.

His heart started pounding, he felt sweaty and clammy. He prayed they wouldn't see each other, which was wishful thinking because he also knew that the two of them were friends. They could detect one another in a burning building if they were both there.

"Oh look! Hi! Hey Saige!"

Bella's shrill voice squealed over the crowd. He squinted. Her voice hurt his ears. He held his breath as Saige turned around to look at who called her. That smile that he loved so much appeared on his lips. She waved at the both of them.

"Oh, let's go say hi!"

Bella exclaimed. He looked down at her as she dragged him towards Saige. Towards his angel.

"Hi Saige!"

Bella squealed. She let go of his arm and hugged Saige tightly. After the embrace ended, Saige surprised him. She stepped into his arms and hugged him to her body.

"Hi Michael."

She greeted warmly. He felt his heart quicken. He hugged her back, not wanting to let go, ever. She was his.

His.

She stepped out of their hug and he felt his erection coming back. He quickly thought of unappealing thoughts to stop the obvious movement in his crotch. Now was not the time to get a stiffy. Saige looked from him to Bella and then back to him.

"You two know each other?"

She questioned, a hint of jealously lining her voice. He could definitely hear it. He started to shake his head but Bella's annoyingly high-pitched pig-squeal pierced his ears.

"Kind of. I ran into him in the parking lot of the uni earlier...well actually, he ran into me and completely knocked me on my ass. He asked me to get coffee. He's so sweet."

She gushed, smiling at him. His eyes met Saige's. Her's were smiling, a hint of laugher lingered through the depths of them.

"I doubt that is how it went."

Saige joked.

"Okay, so maybe I asked him, but what's the big difference."

Saige looked around, as if she was trying to spot someone in the small crowd. Bella had regained a grip on his arm. Both of his hands were in his jean's pockets, trying to limit contact between himself and Bella.

"Oh, hey, Sai, maybe you and Matt could join Michael and I for dinner one night?"

Bella exclaimed. His eyes went wide. He looked down at Bella.

"Wait, what?"

Saige giggled.

"Maybe."

"Hold on!"

He cried out. Bella shook his arm.

"What?"

He didn't answer right away. Either he could go along with it and be a partially functioning piece of society, or he could melt back into the shadows from which he came. The latter would have been his preferred choice. The other question being, who the hell is Matt?

He looked down at Bella, then, he found himself gazing back up and looking at Saige. They were both staring at him, thinking he'd gone insane. He could feel himself drifting away in the depths of her beautiful brown eyes.

"Nothing. Never mind."

He said, before he realized he'd made up his mind. Functioning piece of society it is.

Saige smiled at him and then turned her attention back to Bella.

"Yeah, I'll talk to Matt later on tonight and get back to you."

There's that name again. Who the fuck is Matt?

"Oh, you'll talk to him alright. You'll talk to him with your pu..."

"Okay, stop. Don't be gross. Don't be that girl."

Saige interceded before Bella's statement could get too vulgar. He was personally disgusted. Bella was not a lady. What lady spoke that way in public, let alone at all? His gaze fell back on Saige, and before he realized it, he'd gone full pokey.

He had to get out of their before it became too apparent and one of them noticed. He brushed Bella's arm off of his.

"Well ladies. It's been a pleasure. Until next time."

He bowed and quickly tried to readjust before standing up again.

"You're leaving!?"

Bella exclaimed. He was standing again, his erection tucked up into the waistband of his boxers.

"I must go. You know how to contact me."

He smiled at Bella.

He wanted to kill her.

He hated her.

She stood on her tip toes and kissed his cheek.

"Okay, well I'll call you."

He wanted to drag his hunting knife across her throat.

"Okay."

He turned to Saige.

She was so beautiful.

"Nice to see you again, Michael."

He nodded.

"You too, Saige."

He wanted to hug her and kiss her and love her unconditionally. She stepped forward and hugged him. He hugged her tightly, never wanting to let go. But he did. She couldn't be his. At least not yet. He had to perfect himself. Make sure he was ready for when the time actually came. He could not let her slip away from him again. Not like the first time, that was too painful of a memory. He had to replace it with a new one. Getting her back and keeping her would be perfect.

He started to walk away.

"Oh, Michael!"

It was Saige's voice calling him back. He didn't hesitate to turn and look at her.

"Yes?"

"I'm still looking forward to hearing that poem."

Bella looked at her, eyes wide.

"Poem?"

"He didn't tell you? He writes poetry."

Saige smiled.

"No! Oh Michael! You write poetry. That's so romantic!"

It took everything inside of him not to charge at her and choke the lights right out of her empty head.

"You'll hear it soon, Saige. See you both later."

He continued walking swiftly down the sidewalk. He had to get out of there before Bella could demand he write her some romantic ass piece of shit poem.

He climbed back into his car, which was parked right outside of the little cafe he and Bella were previously sitting in. He climbed in and started the engine, but didn't drive away right away. He slammed his hands down on the wheel.

"Fucking Bella. Fucking stupid dumb Bella. Stupid fucking bitch. Fucking little fuck. God damn it!"

He could feel his cheeks getting hot. That girl was ruining everything for him. Now he had to be so much more careful of everything that he did. He had to be more careful with his plans, especially the ones involving Saige.

They watched him get in his car. He was kind of...different. In a charming way.

"So, what do you think?"

Bella asked excitedly. Saige shrugged one shoulder.

"He seems like a nice guy. Don't know a whole lot about him though."

Bella giggled.

"Have you met him before? You know about his poetry?"

Saige bit her lip.

"Yea I met him earlier today. I guess right before he met you. I feel like I've definitely seen him somewhere. Not sure where though...Do you have that feeling?"

Bella shrugged and scrunched up her cheeks.

"Yes. I've seen him in my dreams."

Saige half smirked and shook her head, holding in a chuckle.

"You're a nut."

Bella didn't even care.

"He's just so fucking good-looking. The things I would do just to put his di—"

"Seriously? Bella, shut up. That's disgusting."

Saige interrupted before she could finish her statement. She loved Bella but she had a really filthy mouth.

"Anyway, I'll catch you later. Matt's waiting for me."

She said quickly. Bella hugged her.

"Let me know about that double date!"

Saige pulled out of Bella's arms and looked at her, smiling widely.

"Sure will. See you later, girl."

She gave Bella one last squeeze and then hustled off towards the parking lot a few feet away from where they were standing.

She reached the sleek, black Chevy Cobalt SS and paused as she approached the driver's side door. She slowly reached for the door handle, trying to peer into the tinted back window. She'd locked the doors, but there was such a thing as lock-picks and people that knew how to use them were certainly not scarce. She didn't see anything suspicious staring out at her, so she climbed into the driver's seat. Matt was nice enough to let her use his car; but that's exactly what it was. His car. His rules. He wanted her back at his place within the hour.

She put the car in gear and realized her mind was stuffed full of questions about Michael, so that is exactly what she thought about as she made her way back to Matt's apartment.

Where had she seen Michael before?

Could it be just from school? Probably. But she couldn't help that feeling she had; that one that embedded itself deep in her gut, insisting that she knew him from somewhere.

She shook her and laughed at herself.

"You're being stupid, Saige. You just met the guy. He's Bella's eye candy of the week. He's very nice. And he's going to show you poetry soon. Yea. He's nice."

She scolded herself. Didn't matter how many times she said that, she just couldn't shake that nagging feeling.

It took a while, but she finally pulled up to Matt's building. She admired him for getting an apartment for himself. His family travelled around a lot, they were marine biologists and animal rights activists. She admired Matt because unlike the many other students that attend the school, he lived in an apartment. They all, including herself, lived in dormitories or at home with their parents, if they had originally lived in Ridgeway.

She had asked him why he chose to get an apartment right away. His response being,

"Well, Sai. I could live in a dorm, like everyone else, and have that space for four years while I'm in school. Or I can get an apartment and have this place to fall back on when schools over. Most of the kids in the dorms will end up moving back in with their parents, post-grad. Considering mine are wherever the hell they are now; I don't have that cushion when school is out."

he brought his car into his designated parking space and slowly turned it off. She climbed out, making sure to lock the doors twice, like Matt had requested. She ran her hand along the top of the car.

"Well Cassandra, we made it back, safe."

Saige said, utilizing the car's 'name' that Matt had blessed it with. The sleek car was Matt's most prized possession.

She walked up to the front doors of the building and inserted one of the many keys that Matt had told her was for the building. He had tons and tons of keys and had given her copies of most of them.

Matt lived on the second floor of the building, so after she'd entered the main doors, she walked up the short flight of stairs and went for the apartment door right on the corner. She put in yet another key and easily pushed open the apartment door.

She was surprised to see the apartment was so dark. After the darkness registered in her brain, fear took over.

"Matt, I'm back."

She said loudly. She put her keys back into her purse and flipped the light switches closest to her to the on position. The small unit's kitchen was the first room she walked into after opening the apartment door.

"Matt?"

She called again. No response. She looked around the kitchen, listening intently for any sort of sound or movement through the apartment. Nothing.

"Matt are you here?"

She yelled. Her heartbeat slowly quickened. She didn't like being alone, which was why she hardly stayed at her dorm anymore. Her roommate had graduated and she still hadn't gotten a new one. She was just about to give up. She turned to walk back to the door to leave the apartment when she heard a groaning creak coming from somewhere in the apartment.

"Matt?"

She called again, voice shaking. She knew Matt's knife block was on the counter behind her. She spun and reached for one of his stainless-steel steak knives.

Someone screamed and grabbed Saige around her waist right before her palm could close around a handle.

She let out a blood curdling scream and instantly began to cry.

"Sai? Sai, shh. It's okay. It's me. Matt. Shh."

Saige turned in his arms and found herself staring up into Matt's eyes. She put both hands on his chest and shoved him away from her, hard.

"I'm sorry, Sai. I'm sorry. It was supposed to be a joke."

Matt said softly, taking a small step towards her. She had one hand up, signaling for him to stay back. Her other one was against her face, frantically wiping away tears.

Her mind flashed back to when she was eight years old.

Her eyes fluttered open slowly. She blinked a couple of times, trying to help her eyes adjust to the dimly lit room. She tried to stand up and immediately fell back down. A chain rattled against metal. She looked down and to her extreme horror, she found that she was handcuffed to a heater. Sweat was beading on her forehead. Her clothes were tattered and her wrists were bleeding from the handcuffs rubbing the skin raw. She was in a house all alone. She looked around the dank room. It was a bathroom. She could tell that much. The tile was rough on her scarred and bleeding knees. The light bulb overhead flickered, casting terrible shadows onto the walls, making them dance in the light.

"Mommy!"

She whispered, not able to muster anything louder. Her throat was dry. She felt like she hadn't eaten in days.

"Phoebe!"

She cried again, knowing very well Phoebe wouldn't be coming to rescue her. The memory was coming back.

She heard a creak coming from just outside the bathroom. She started to panic. She kicked the heater, her tennis shoes protecting her feet from getting burned. She knew he was just outside. She knew he could hear her, panicking. Her heart started to race even quicker than it had been. The sweat on her forehead dripped down, rolling down the bridge of her nose and tickling her upper lip.

She looked up and seen a shadow appear in the doorway.

She shook her head quickly, bringing herself back to the present.

"Sai. I'm really sorry. Please, talk to me."

Matt was still saying. He had finally reached her again and he very slowly pulled her into a hug. She wrapped her arms around him and hugged him tightly back. Her tears soaked into the front of his shirt; her sobs muffled because she pressed her face into his chest.

Matt rubbed her back and kissed her head.

A couple of long minutes later, Saige slowly lifted her head and looked into Matt's eyes.

"Not funny."

She whispered through one last little sob. Matt kept her in his arms, safe and protected from harm.

Saige had met Matt when she was ten years old. His family had owned the Ridgeway Aquatic Animal Rescue Center, which is where she had met him. She was looking at the penguins and laughing at them. He had walked up to her, and handed her an ice cream cone. Together they watched the penguins and then the dolphins and finally the beluga enclosure where they got completely soaked when one of the whales came to the surface and hit the water hard. Over the last ten years, she and Matt had formed a very tight bond. He'd been her first kiss when she was twelve. He'd asked her to junior prom when she was fifteen and then again for senior prom when she was seventeen. He was there for her when her mother had passed away two years prior.

Yes, they'd known each other for quite some time and she had told him almost everything...everything except for that one missing year of her life, just after her eighth birthday.

She wanted to tell him. Oh god did she want to tell him. She just couldn't seem to find the right words or the right time. Besides, how was one supposed to say, 'By the way, I got kidnapped when I was eight and he kept me for a year and did so many awful things to me before I managed to escape.'

Suddenly, she realized just how much she was shaking. She took a couple of deep breaths and pulled herself out of Matt's arms.

"I'm really, really sorry Sai."

He said again.

"Please, just don't ever do that again."

She whispered.

"I won't. I promise."

Saige had stopped crying and used the back of her hand to wipe away the last few salty tears. To distract herself from the memories that haunted her, she shot Matt a quick grin.

"So, guess what."

Matt shrugged and looked into her eyes, curiosity filling his.

"Bella's got a new piece of arm candy."

Matt scoffed.

"What poor soul has that leech hooked into now?"

Saige stifled a laugh. She smacked Matt's arm playfully.

"Hey. Be nice."

"I'll be nice when she comes back with negative STD test results."

Saige hadn't meant too, but she burst into a fit of giggles. She loved her friend but Matt had a point. That girl got around faster than a flu in flu season.

"So, I guess that's a no for a double date then?"

Matt looked at her, bewildered.

"Are you kidding? It's a yes. I have to warn the poor dude."

It was Saige's turn to roll her eyes.

"Please, be civil. She seems really happy."

Saige knew very well that Bella and Matt used to be exclusive. It was not something that Matt was proud of. Especially considering that he had taken her back twice after catching her cheating on him.

Saige also knew that after one of Bella's straying moments, and Matt had been kind enough to take her back, she had ended up giving him Chlamydia. He'd gone to the doctor and gotten the medication to get rid of it, but he had despised Bella ever since.

"Saige!"

Saige looked up at him.

"Yea? What?"

She replied quickly, looking confused.

"I said, when is the date? Jesus girl, get your head out of the clouds."

Saige bit her lip and pulled her cell phone from her pocket.

"I didn't even expect you to say yes. I'll have to ask her."

She composed a quick text, the way young people do, and put her phone on the counter behind her. Matt brushed some of her hair behind her ear. Her eyes twinkled up at him.

"I love you, Sai."

He murmured against her lips as he leaned in to kiss her. He pressed his lips against hers and she kissed him right back, with just as much, if not more, passion.

She reached up and grabbed a fistful of his shirt to pull him closer. His hands ran down her sides and over her hips. They reached around and grabbed her butt, squeezing gently. She let out a small moan, and leaned in closer to him and then her cell phone erupted in a fit of singing and jingles from 'Bootylicious' by Destiny's Child. She jumped at the sound and Matt chuckled.

Saige held up a finger. She reached behind her and grabbed her phone. Her eyes scanned the small text.

"Well, I guess we have a date tomorrow. Bella's got it all set up."

Matt coughed.

"I don't know, Sai. Tomorrow? I think I'm getting sick; I can't go."

Saige shot him a look.

"Really? You just said you wanted to go! To warn the poor guy. So now you're too sick? Fine, well then that means no sex either."

"I'm kidding! Babe, I'm kidding!"

Matt begged her, grabbing her arm. She held in her laughter.

"I am kidding!"

He cried. That did it, she started laughing.

"Yea, yea okay. But seriously, dinner, tomorrow night. Be nice okay?"

Matt kissed her cheek.

"Yes, I'll be nice. Now what do you want for dinner, tonight? Pizza?"

5

The sound of the front door unlocking echoed through the empty house.

The door swung open and PJ dragged herself inside, shutting the door firmly behind her. She tossed her car keys on the counter and put her cell phone more gently next to them. She had a large McDonalds cup in her other hand. She lifted it to her mouth and took one last long sip, slurping the very last remnants of the Diet Coke from the bottom of the cup. She shook it for good measure and tossed it into the garbage can with a swish.

She pulled a chair out from the table and sat down with a heavy sigh.

"What a day. What a long fucking day."

She started rubbing her temples again, eyes closed. It was well past nine pm by now. She should be getting ready for bed. Tomorrow would be Sunday. She should be sleeping in until noon, having a late lunch with her mom and brother like they did every Sunday. Then she'd come home and usually Nick would come over and they'd cuddle and watch movies the rest of the day. This Sunday, however, Nick was out of town and PJ had one bitch of a case to work on.

No 'Sunday Funday' for PJ.

She sighed. The case filled her mind.

When she learned that Joshua Martin was connected, she immediately took over from Detective Rogers, with a little persuasion from Brock, as Sarah did not want to give it up. PJ couldn't seem to wrap her mind around the case.

There were too many connectors, too many missing persons and not one unsub, with the exception of Professor David Swanson.

PJ didn't think he was their guy. She wasn't quite sure what it was, she just didn't get *that feeling.* That could change. She knew that. She hadn't seen him. She hadn't talked to him. That *feeling* could absolutely be there after they finally had him in custody and got to speak with him.

Although, she was one hundred percent sure that he had definitely disappeared with Michelle Clifford, but that girl was eighteen, over sixteen, therefore not illegal. She qualified as a consenting adult.

PJ bit her lips.

"Okay, yea. So, Swanson's forty-seven and Michelle's eighteen. Consenting, yeah."

She spoke her thoughts out loud. No one was around to hear her.

"But Swanson's gone with Michelle, his own daughter is also missing. He probably is unaware. He could be killing Michelle or whoever is with Mya could be our guy, I just don't know who that is yet."

PJ ran her fingers through her hair.

"For fuck sakes."

She crossed her arms and lay her face down in the crevice. She had no idea. Tomorrow she'd have to either hunt down Swanson and Michelle, contact the three boys that reported the three girls post mortem and see what they know, or hunt down any other potential witnesses or anyone with any information at all. She knew she'd end up doing all of it.

PJ slammed her hands onto the table.

"God dammit!"

She exclaimed. She wished this could be easy. She wouldn't be a Detective if it were easy. She sighed and stood up.

"Looks like I'm going to bed early tonight."

She said out loud, even though she was the only one in her house. She got the living daylights scared out of her next. Her phone began to ring. She looked over her shoulder at it like it was some foreign object.

This late at night, it might as well have been. She quickly retraced her steps to the counter and grabbed the phone before the ringing could stop. She had a habit of not checking the call display. She didn't change that now.

"Hello?"

"Hi sweetie."

PJ could feel her chest loosen.

"Nick."

She smiled to herself.

"Sorry for calling so late."

He apologized.

"Don't be sorry. I miss you. It's been a crazy day."

PJ sighed. She wished she could hug and kiss her handsome man.

"I know what you mean. Judge can't seem to hear enough debating. Jury can't make up their damn minds. Ugh."

Nick's smooth sounding voice, sounded even smoother and manlier over the phone. PJ missed him even more.

"When do you think you'll be back?"

PJ asked slowly.

"I really don't know. I was thinking sometime mid-week, but the way this trial is going, I might not be back until Christmas."

It was a joke, but PJ could barely muster a hearty laugh. She just managed a soft chuckle.

"Just get home, please."

Nick let out a guttural laugh.

"I'm doing my best, my girl. Get some sleep. I'll call in the morning. I love you."

"I love you too, good looking."

They made kissing noises to each other through the phone and hung up. PJ smiled down at the cell phone in her hand. She placed it gently on the counter, as if it were a piece of Nick Redford and she didn't want to break that little piece.

Her hips suddenly felt very heavy. Her holster weighed down on her. She was too tired for this. She unclipped the holster and put it on top of the counter, the Glock twenty-two, sitting in it, safety on.

PJ smiled at her gun. That was her favourite toy that came with being in the RPD.

She loved her gun.

She turned her tired body and managed to drag herself down the hallway to the stairs. Getting up the stairs was a little trickier. Her feet just didn't want to lift. She forced them to carry her up the flight of stairs to her bedroom.

She almost made the decision to bypass changing into her pajamas, but decided that sleeping in jeans would be way too uncomfortable.

She shimmied out of her jeans and pulled her white tank over her head. She faced her full-length mirror, standing there in her lacy black bra and matching boy-cut panties. She admired herself.

She liked to think she wasn't bad looking. She had silky brown hair and blue eyes. Slim waist and long legs. She wished she could have been blessed with perhaps a C cup breast size and fuller behind, but she had to work with what she had.

Her eyes skimmed over the thin, jagged, mean looking pink scar that ran down her leg, starting just under her hip, extending all the way down to mid shin.

Now that, she could do without.

She remembered that day like it was yesterday.

She was seventeen again. She had taken a police academy course in high school and was goofing around with one of her police academy friends. They'd just watched some cop movie. In the movie, the cop partners would drive at each other and they'd jump on the hood of the vehicle and roll off.

She and her friend thought it had looked like fun, so they grabbed the keys to her friend's Dodge Ram and started the engine. She drove at her friend, Brandon Wilkinson first. She went five miles an hour, very slow, just to get him used to the jump first. He'd managed to do it like a pro. Made the movies look like amateurs.

Then it was PJ's turn.

Brandon thought it would be funny if he went slightly faster than she had. She jumped, but went airborne too late. The top of the fender caught one of her legs, snapping it in two. She tumbled over the hood, screaming bloody murder.

Brandon slammed on the breaks, sending her flying off the hood, landing ten feet from the parked truck. Blood was gushing from the massive gash in her leg.

"Call nine one one!"

Brandon had been screaming.

PJ blinked and she was no longer bleeding to death in the middle of that old, dusty dirt road. She was back, staring at her reflection and the huge scar that marked where her life had come too close to ending.

A shiver rippled through her and she grabbed her cheetah print fuzzy pajamas and slid them on, covering the evidence of any stupid behavior in her teens.

She slowly sunk down into her king-sized bed, pulling the quilts up to her chin.

She reached over to the night stand and pressed play on the iPod docking station. She had a set playlist that she listened to every night that helped her fall asleep just like every other night, she was knocked out before the end of 'Whiskey Lullaby' by Brad Paisley.

"What do you mean, you don't believe me?"

Tears were running down her dirty face. PJ stared at her.

"You're being silly, Mellie."

PJ turned her head away from the girl. She grabbed PJ's arm.

"Penny. Please. Mom doesn't believe me. I don't feel safe. I need someone to believe me."

PJ looked up, but not at her.

"Let go of me, Melissa. Do you think maybe mom doesn't believe you, because you constantly tell stories? It's like the boy who cried wolf."

Melissa, the girl standing there, grasping PJ's arm, tears stinging her eyes, shook her head.

"Penny. Please. He is out there. Not right now, but he is. He's been coming to school and talking to me and talking to my friends. He's creeping us out. I caught him following me the other day. Penny. Penny."

PJ let out an exasperated sigh. She turned to Melissa. She grabbed Melissa's wrist and pried her hand off of her arm.

"Stop telling stories. 'He' doesn't even have a name. If he was talking to you at school, don't you think you'd have asked for his name? Tried to find out who he was?"

She turned back to her book.

"I told you before. He said his name was Sam. Samuel Thomas. Penny, please believe me. He was following me!"

"Yea I'm sure he was."

"Penny!"

"Get out of here, Melissa. I'm busy, studying. I do have an exam this week. I have to pass or I won't even have a chance at RU."

"Penny..."

"Get. Out."

PJ snapped. Melissa hung her head.

"Fine."

She headed for the door, but stopped just as she reached it.

"What if I died, hmm?"

PJ looked up; eyes narrowed.

"What if?"

Melissa slowly nodded.

"Yea. What if I died. Today. Tonight. Tomorrow. I don't know. But what if I'm actually telling the truth and Sam kidnaps me and kills me? How would you and mom feel?"

PJ rolled her eyes.

"Well you're not going to die because Sam doesn't exist. So, I'm sure we'll feel just fine because you're still standing here."

Melissa's tears started again.

"I hate you."

PJ shot up in bed, breathing hard, sweat pouring down her face. She rubbed her eyes and looked around the room. Her eyes landed on the clock. Six thirty. She wiped blindly at the sweat dripping into her eyes.

It couldn't be the same person.

It couldn't be.

She knew very well it was. Melissa's body had been found the same the other girls had been.

PJ didn't want to believe it. Didn't even want to think it. But she owed that to her sister. She had to find this guy. She owed Melissa that much.

She rubbed her eyes again and yawned. She didn't have time to mess around. She threw back the covers and swung her legs over the side of the bed. She scratched her head, stood, and yanked the pajamas off without hesitation.

Sunday.

Six thirty-four.

March twenty eighth.

Another day, another dollar.

"Actually, another day, another missed chance to find our missing girls."

PJ said out loud. She was standing in front of her full-length mirror again. Her eyes scanned her body once more, running over the scar. That seriously pissed her off. Bikini season sucked.

She opened her dresser drawers and found a pair of black jeans she hadn't worn in a while. She stared at them, debating her options.

Eventually, she decided against them. Hell, it was Sunday. Lazy work day. Kind of.

She shoved the jeans to the back of the drawer and edged the drawer closed with a little bit of elbow grease. She pulled open the drawer beneath and reveled in the multitude of black leggings. She grabbed a pair of fleece lined ones and smiled at her choice.

She shimmied them over her hips and walked to the large closet on the other side of the room.

She pulled it open and walked right inside. She ran her fingers along the hangers and stopped at a cream coloured, oversized knit sweater.

Sunday.

She left the bedroom, dragging herself towards the stairs. She trudged down them.

The sound that left her frozen on the second last step was the front door clicking. She felt paralyzed. She heard the door slowly creak open. Out of habit, she swung her arm back to her hip, where, to her horror, her holster was not attached. And that's when she remembered she had taken it off in the kitchen the night before.

Some prowler had just broken into her home and had her twenty-two in the same room.

She held her breath on the staircase.

The house was old, even the smallest movement made the old foundation creak and groan.

After what seemed like an eternity, the house was still quiet.

PJ knew someone was in her kitchen, doing god knows what, and she didn't have any way to defend herself if he had decided to snoop and stumbled upon her.

After another eternity, she decided she couldn't just stand there and wait for whatever horrible thing to happen. She very slowly stepped down the last two stairs, surprisingly not making any extra creaks.

She stepped into the hall and the overwhelming scent of fresh coffee drifted through her nostrils. She hadn't been downstairs at all this morning so she hadn't set the timer yet. She hadn't set it the night before either, she had completely forgotten.

Whoever broke in was making coffee and then going to kill her.

Her mind was going wild.

She had to keep going. She had to make it to her gun and defend herself or die trying.

She took the last few steps to the kitchen doorway and peered around the corner. She saw a stocky build sitting at her kitchen table, back to the door. She could see the corner of the newspaper just past his shoulder.

She instantly recognized his thick, black hair and the way he heaved his shoulders when he exhaled.

"Nick?"

She said quietly, stepping fully into the kitchen. The man sitting in the chair swiveled around and smiled hugely at her.

"Hey, P."

She dropped her arms to her sides, jaw dropped.

"What the hell!"

She screamed. She ran across the kitchen and flung herself into his arms, wrapping her legs around his waist, her arms around his neck. She planted kisses all over his face.

"Why are you here!"

She exclaimed. Nick was hugging her back, kissing her cheeks.

"I wanted to surprise you."

He smiled.

"I was kidding on the phone last night. I was on my way back as we spoke. Guess what."

She couldn't believe it. Her Nick was back finally.

‘What?”

She was genuinely curious.

“I won.”

PJ’s face lit up.

“No way! Congratulations babe! That’s amazing!”

Nick kissed her nose and lowered her back down to her own feet.

“I was thinking we could celebrate tonight. Let’s get away. Hotel. Fancy dinner. Wine. Roses.”

PJ backed out of his arms.

“That sounds fantastic, but I can’t. I have to work. Big, messy, shit storm of a case.”

Nick pouted.

“PJ...”

He was cut off by PJ’s cell phone. Her eyes widened and she rushed to the other side of the table and grabbed her phone off of the counter.

“Good morning. Detective Richards.”

“PJ. Can you get here soon? Something’s happened.”

PJ recognized the urgency in Brock’s voice.

“Yes. Be there in fifteen.”

She hung up and glanced over her shoulder at Nick.

“I’m sorry. I have to go. Make yourself at home. I’ll try not to be too late.”

She grabbed her holster off of the counter and strapped it around her waist, adjusting it so that her twenty-two was in the perfect position for her to grab it if she needed to.

Nick was pouting at her. She tried not to look at him. His face could make her feel so guilty. She grabbed her keys off of the counter from where she’d thrown them, shoved her phone in her pocket and ran out the door.

As she drove down the quiet, suburban street, she was trying to decide what could have possibly happened. It was too early for a body. They still had a few days. They still had time!

She was so thankful that the Ridgeway PD office was only ten minutes away from her place. It sure made getting to Brock a whole lot easier.

She pulled into the RPD parking lot. For a Sunday, there were quite a few vehicles in the lot, she observed.

She saw Brock's little Miata, Daniel's Honda civic, Phil's Toyota Camry, and three other vehicles she couldn't identify.

She climbed out of her car and locked the door.

It was completely routine. Getting out of the car. Walking across the lot. Taking two stairs at a time to get to the main doors. Saying good morning to whichever preppy, blonde receptionist was in that day.

It was beginning to drive PJ crazy.

"Talk to me, Brock."

He handed her a coffee, which she was surprised to see was steaming and actually piping hot. She silently praised the lords.

Brock put his hand on her back and directed her into the same conference room as the day before.

PJ glanced around the room. Daniel and Phil were sitting at the table, mimicking the day before.

Oh. Shit.

She recognized the uniforms.

Feds.

She turned her attention to Brock. They shared the same thought; she could tell by the look that both sets of their eyes shared.

The feds. The fucking feds. Dealing with the feds was like dealing with a nightmare straight from the deepest parts of hell.

PJ turned from Brock and extended a hand out to the group of the FBI Agents.

"Good morning. I'm Detective PJ Richards. I'm the lead on this case."

"Good morning. I'm the SAC, which you know, means I'm in charge now. I'm Agent Brinker, these are Agents Hamm, Maynard, and Darbyshire."

The fed that spoke first, also stepped up to her, and shook her hand firmly.

PJ narrowed her eyes and forced her hand out of Brinker's tight grip.

"So, Detective Richards, you know this means you cannot get in the way of our investigation."

PJ laughed. She hadn't meant to, it slipped out.

Brock shot her a horrified look, whereas Agent Brinker raised a brow and stared her down. PJ turned her back on him and looked at Brock.

"On the phone you said something happened...is everything okay? What went down?"

Before Brock could reply, PJ heard the Special Agent in Charge; Agent Brinker, pipe up.

"Young man. Stabbed multiple times in his chest and abdomen."

Brinker turned and grabbed a large envelope from one of his Agents and tossed it on the table. It slid off to the side.

Daniel stood, grabbed the envelope and opened it gingerly, careful not to tear the contents.

He met PJ's eyes.

"We know who his latest vic is now. And it's not Michelle."

He quietly said.

PJ reached out and grabbed the papers from him. She almost dropped them.

The sixteen-year-old kid, Joshua Martin was lying face down in the dirt in the first shot. He was wearing boxers and nothing else.

In the second shot, the forensics team and coroner had turned him over where she could see several deep gashes, where she could see at the time had been bleeding profusely.

PJ looked up.

"Daniel..."

She started, but Agent Brinker cut in.

"I want you to tell us everything you know about this case. We'll get the BAU to analyze a profile."

PJ stared at him. She did not want to lose control of this case. She couldn't. She owed it to her sister.

She wished she could tell Brock or Daniel about that night, so long ago.

"Detective."

Brinker snapped. PJ zoned back in and looked at him.

"Or you could let me handle this."

Agent Brinker's eyes widened.

"Because you're doing such a fine job at it right?"

Sarcasm laced his words heavily. PJ slammed her files on the table and the entire room went completely silent.

"Look, I understand you're the feds and I understand you apparently have 'seniority', but this hasn't even gotten out of Ridgeway! Why are you involved? This is my case! I'm the lead on it. Stay out of my way. Please."

PJ swore she could hear a pin drop.

"I'm not putting you in charge. But I'm willing to work together. I really need to know everything possible so the BAU can determine a profile."

PJ sighed at Brinker's words. She looked down at the teenager in the pictures. She felt herself well up but she blinked hard, fighting back the tears. She swallowed, trying to choke down the lump in her throat.

"I need someone to inform his parents."

She looked up.

"Daniel, you were with me when we spoke to them yesterday. Please. Take Agent Maynard with you."

PJ glanced at Brinker, trying to show him she was going to be civil and include his men. Daniel smiled at her and nodded slowly. He got up. He didn't need to be told twice. He gestured to Agent Maynard and the two briskly left the room.

PJ looked at Phil.

"Can you help me set up the board again please."

Phil nodded solemnly and pushed himself away from the table. PJ nodded at the table, suggesting non-verbally that all of the Agents take a seat. They did as Phil and PJ worked together to put the vic board back together.

Luckily, it didn't take too long. Most of it was still up from yesterday. PJ could sense the horrifying amount of tension that hung in the air.

She dug in the drawer of a small desk that was pushed behind the board and found a laser pointer. Those things could be found in almost every desk at the PD office. She trudged to the back of the room and flashed the laser pointer on the board. She briefly described how each homicide involved several stab wounds, strangulation and sexual assault. She explained about the connections to RU and how each girl that went missing was abducted around two to three days before the previous girl was murdered and found. Each girl usually missing for about a week.

Agent Brinker tapped his fingers along the surface of the table.

"If that's true, we've got today, possibly tomorrow to find him before he takes his next girl."

PJ nodded.

"Yes sir. Now, here's one more thing. Two missing girls. We know one of them is at a hotel with a professor from RU. Second is the professor's teenage daughter. Still unknown whereabouts."

"Do you know which hotel? Professor a suspect?"

"We have officers working on finding which hotel. Narrowed it down to the Marriot and the Prospera. Professor's name is David Swanson and he is the only name we have gotten on our suspect list, currently trying to compile a list of possibilities; however, we haven't figured out a motive for him to harm his own daughter."

Brinker looked to the side and caught Agent Hamm's eye.

"Go now. There's no time to fuck around. You and Darbyshire. Check Prospera first. You are to apprehend Swanson at first sight. Get that girl in custody as well."

Agents Hamm and Darbyshire didn't waste time getting to their feet and getting out the door.

Brock, PJ, Phil and Brinker were the only four left in the room. Brinker got to his feet.

"Detective Richards. I'm going to bring this info to Janet, she's a specialist on our BAU team. She should have a profile back to us by afternoon."

PJ nodded. Brinker was charming in an incredibly egotistic, arrogant way. PJ turned away. For some reason, his eye contact was making her uncomfortable. As arrogant as he was, he was incredibly good – looking, with his wavy, ashy, blonde hair, bright blue eyes and olive complexion, he looked like he could have been a surfer god in a past life. She had to get out of there. She looked at Brock.

"I'm going to interview Swanson's wife. See what she knows."

He had his ear pressed to the bedroom door. Her screaming was pleasing to the ear. He pulled the keys from his pocket and unlocked the door.

He slipped soundlessly inside and shut it behind him.

She didn't see him at first. She was crying so loudly he was almost surprised that no one could hear her, until he remembered that they were at his cabin.

He stood inside the doorway, arms crossed, sly grin plastered on his face.

"Are you done with this incessant noise?"

Mya looked up from her tear-soaked sleeves.

"You-you killed him! You fucking killed him! Why him!"

She screamed, tears pouring down her cheeks. She struggled to stand. She felt weak.

Drained.

She wished she could die too.

He laughed at her pain.

Her heartbreak.

She pulled herself to shaking knees and almost fell right back over. She looked at him, anger and hurt filling her eyes.

She staggered towards him.

She didn't have enough energy left. He hadn't fed her the last day.

He was pissed at her for 'cheating' on him with Josh. The smile left his face. An image of Saige filled his mind. He pictured her in the arms of another man. He felt red hot anger boiling inside of him.

He imagined her, Saige, his beautiful perfect angel with another man's erection in her mouth.

"No! Get out of my head!"

He screamed, just as a sobbing Mya reached him. She grabbed his arm.

The sudden contact brought him back to the room. He saw Mya clutching his arm, but instead of seeing Mya's face, he still saw Saige's. He brought his other hand across Mya's face, smacking her with a backhand, knocking her already weakened body to the ground.

He looked down and still saw Saige. He saw her gorgeous brown eyes staring up at him, tears pouring down her cheeks like waterfalls.

He knelt down over her and grabbed her jacket by the collar.

She coughed and whispered,

"Please. Please kill me."

But what he heard was a beg from Saige.

"Please, please fuck me."

He dipped down and plunged his tongue into her mouth. His hands ravaged her body. She squirmed and cried and pounded her fists against his arms and back.

He stopped kissing her and looked down at her. She gulped hard, tears glistening in her eyes. Saige's image shuddered and dissolved. He found himself staring back into Mya's eyes. He was instantly repulsed.

Mya was beautiful but compared to his Saige, she was a dog.

He lifted his hands from her waist and felt them closing around Mya's throat.

"You're not her. You're not her."

He growled.

Mya gasped and clawed at him. Her face changed from white to pink to purple. Her eyes rolled back in her head.

He realized what he was doing and quickly pulled his hands away.

"It's not time. Not yet."

Mya coughed. She breathed deeply and stared at him with more fear in her eyes than she had ever had before.

He still leaned over her, she lay frozen, paralyzed in place.

His eyes filled with tears. He couldn't keep looking at her. Not the way she was. Just as one tear trickled out of the corner of his eye, his closed fist connected with Mya's delicate jaw.

He hit her again and again as he sobbed.

She screamed and tried to pull herself out from under him.

He put one of his knees on her chest and connected his fist with her ribs. He heard a loud crack and Mya let out one last ear-piercing scream. She shuddered once and went quiet.

He got off of her.

He knew she wasn't dead. She couldn't be. Not yet.

He wiped the stray tears from his eyes and slowly backed out of the room.

He first noticed the blood soaked on his hands when he was locking the door again. His blood. Also, hers. Ninety percent of it was hers. He reveled in the sight.

He slowly backed away from the door. He was getting messy. Not as organized as he had once been. Saige was weighing heavily on his mind more and more each day.

He was seeing her everywhere. He couldn't get her out of his head. He was going to need to move fast. He needed to get her back.

The vibrating of his cell phone made him jump. The damn thing was a major annoyance. He looked down and pressed the little white envelope icon at the bottom of the screen.

He remembered he'd given his cell phone number to that fucking Bella. He had to keep up the appearance he was into her. Especially if he wanted to keep seeing Saige.

He wanted to throw his phone, smash it into tiny pieces.

"Hi Michael. Saige and Matt will join us for dinner tonight. Blah blah blah shut the fuck up."

He read angrily.

He stormed down the hallway into his living room. He stared at the cell phone in his hand. How should he reply? How did teenagers' text?

He hummed and hawed over it for several minutes. He needed to make sure it was convincing. Finally, he decided to 'k' her.

Like he really cared.

Whatever.

He tossed the phone onto the couch. It bounced off the cushion and landed with a thud on the ground. He really didn't care.

He grabbed handfuls of his hair and screamed. Everything seemed like it was falling apart. Saige was not supposed to notice him. Not until their time to be together came. She wasn't supposed to want to hang out with him. He wasn't supposed to kill that kid. He wasn't supposed to be so disorganized.

He needed Saige.

He needed her to fill the void in his heart that she had left when she ran away from him so many years ago.

He was damn lucky her hypno-therapist had done such an excellent job at making her forget.

He was damn lucky he had done such an excellent job at disappearing the night she did.

Yes.

He was damn lucky.

He threw himself down, face first on the living room floor. He needed a nap. It wasn't even eight am and he needed a nap.

And right there in the middle of the carpet was going to be the perfect spot.

He woke up that morning, feeling amazing. He knew that it was coming up. He was almost ready to get her. His precious girl. The only girl he knew that he would ever want. They would be happy together.

He pulled himself from his bed, folding the blankets back under the pillows, smoothing it all over. He pulled each corner tight. He liked a perfectly made bed.

He walked happily down the hallway towards the kitchen, but once he reached it, he veered off. There was a small corridor between the kitchen and a doorway heading to the backyard. Off of the corridor there was a little closet. He opened the closet door and knelt down. He dug his fingers into the corner of the carpet and pulled back hard. He peeled the carpet away from the floor and out of the closet, flopping it over on itself in the hallway.

Under the carpet in the closet, there was a small door in the floor. He lifted it slowly and then flicked a light switch on the inside of the closet. The space in the floor lit up a ladder, which he slowly lowered himself onto.

He clung to each rung of the ladder, one by one, lowering himself into the dank hidden basement. When he got to the bottom, he was surrounded by a few different shelves. They all held supplies, like water bottles, nonperishable food items, batteries, and a few flashlights. To the untrained eye, it looked exactly like a bomb shelter. Which is what his excuse would be if anyone that wasn't supposed to be down here, somehow stumbled upon it.

He grabbed one of the flashlights and walked silently to the far side of the room between two shelves stocked with hardware items. Two large bags of lye were sitting side by side on the floor against the wall. He put the cord of the flashlight in his mouth and reached for the bags of lye. He grunted as he pulled them to the side. They were very heavy. Underneath where they sat, was a little door, big enough for the entry to a possible crawl space.

He pulled his keys out of his pocket and unlocked the door to the crawl space and then got on his hands and knees. He pushed the door open and ducked his head as he edged himself into the small space.

Once he was inside, what looked to be tiny on the outside, was much bigger on the inside. He'd built this little room by himself. No one knew about it. He looked around the inside. He could stand, just barely brushing his head against the ceiling. But he could stand. That was a big deal to him.

He walked around the tiny room. There was a thin foam mattress lying in one corner of the room with a bunch of dirty blankets piled up on top of it. He was stressing out just looking at the mess. The walls were plastered with pictures of her. His Saigey. Pictures of her playing in her front yard, just down the street. Her running through the sprinkler in her little bikini. Her eating ice cream. His favourite was a picture she had wanted to take of the two of them.

He knew he'd gained her trust. He stopped by her yard everyday she was outside. She'd come to know who he was. Or who he had told her he was. She had come to trust him and come to really appreciate when he stopped by to play Barbies and Transformers with her. He knew that was her favourite part of the day.

He stood there now, staring at the picture in the center of all the other ones. Saige had pressed her soft cheek against his. They both had a hold on the camera and were making funny faces.

He lifted his hand and ran a finger down the photographed cheek.

He started to get emotional.

"Enough, Red."

He said to himself, wiping away a tear that seemed to make an appearance on his cheek. He hated to cry. He hated it. He didn't want to be in the room anymore. The only reason he came down here was when he wanted to see his pictures. He slept in here when he wanted to be closer to her. Soon enough, maybe even today, he'd have her, finally.

Speaking of her, he looked at his watch. It was close to the time where her parents would be leaving and Phoebe, that annoying babysitter would show up. But that also meant that Saige would be outside. He wanted to see her.

He scrambled backwards, falling back to his hands and knees so he could get out of the crawl space quickly. He locked the door behind him and dusted himself off. With another grunt, he pulled each bag of lye back in front of the small door, hiding it perfectly.

He retraced his steps out of the shelves and back towards the ladder, stopping momentarily at the first shelf where he'd gotten the flashlight he was holding from. He turned it off and opened the battery compartment. He'd forgotten to take them out last time he used it. He pried them from their compartments and put them next to the flashlight, where the many boxes of batteries were piled up.

Finally, he pulled himself rung by rung back up the ladder and into the closet. He slowly closed the door in the floor, didn't want to seem too eager to get outside. Take it easy. She'd be out there. He knew she would.

He folded the carpet back down over the door and pounded it into the corners with his fist, making it look like it hadn't been disturbed before. He slid the closet door closed and wandered back down the hallway. Saige filled his mind. Saige Laeyke D'Leo. His baby. Forever.

When he reached the kitchen, which also acted as an entry way to his house, he looked out the window solemnly. From his kitchen, he could pretty much see the entire street. He was located in the center, which sometimes he didn't like. Sometimes it seemed too in the open, but then again, he was also hidden in plain sight, just as he liked.

Looking out the kitchen window, he studied the quiet, suburban street. Nothing was happening on the road at all. That seemed normal enough, he figured. He slowly turned his eyes to Saige's house.

Perfect timing.

He saw the door open and an excited Saige leapt down the three stairs from her door to the sidewalk. She landed on her feet but instantly dropped to her knees and crawled to the grass, clawing at the air, acting like some kind of animal. He chuckled. She was adorable.

Then he saw Phoebe. She left the house behind Saige, leaving the door open. He felt his heart drop. He knew she was going to be there, but he wished she wasn't. She was a cute girl but not who he wanted. He watched Phoebe sit down in the lawn chair that was on the grass, beside a tree. She peeled off her shirt, revealing a bikini top. She was wearing shorts. She leaned back in the chair and closed her eyes.

He looked back to Saige. She had a pink backpack with her, no doubt containing her multitude of Transformers and Barbies. He couldn't watch anymore. He wanted to get over there. Although, today's would be different.

He left the window and walked over to his front door. He slowly exited his house, this time, not locking his door.

He walked casually across the street and a house down.

"Hi Saige."

He greeted. Saige looked up and made his heart swell when her eyes lit up.

"Sammy!"

She exclaimed. Usually, he hated being called 'Sammy' but coming from Saige, he just couldn't help but love it.

"How's my favourite girl?"

He asked, loving that he was able to say that out loud.

"Oh, hi Sam!"

He pursed his lips and turned to look at Phoebe. He plastered a false smile across his lips.

"Hello, Phoebe."

Phoebe had pulled herself to her feet and walked over to him. He looked down at her. She had a skinny build. He noted that she had a naval ring. She trailed her finger down his chest and smiled up at him. He knew he was good looking. He knew she knew he was.

"How are you, Sam?"

She asked, her voice sounded sultry. He had to do everything not to roll his eyes at her. He had to stop himself from looking down at Saige, who, no doubt wasn't even paying attention to them.

"I'm fine."

He responded slowly. She bit her lip and leaned in a little closer, hooking her fingers into the pocket of his jeans.

"So, I was thinking, maybe one day when I'm not babysitting Sai, we could hangout."

"Or we could hangout right now."

He found himself saying. That was not part of the plan.

"Oh?"

She asked, curious as to what he meant. He had to think quickly. He looked down at Saige.

"Hey, Sai, how would you and Phoebe like to go get ice cream?"

That got Saige's attention. Her head snapped up and a massive smile spread across her face.

"Yes! Yes! Phoebe! Please?"

Saige exclaimed. She jumped to her feet and grabbed one of Phoebe's hands and one of his. His heart almost stopped. She was holding his hand. She was actually holding his hand.

Phoebe looked from Saige to him and then back to Saige. She gradually smiled and met his eyes.

"Yes. Okay. We can go. Sure."

He smiled back at her but in his mind, he was smiling at Saige.

"Let's run across the street and grab my car, hey?"

Saige was jumping up and down, tightly holding onto his and Phoebe's hand. The three of them walked across the road and a house up to get to his quaint three-story house.

"My car keys are inside."

He said slowly as he opened the front door.

"Please, come inside. I'll only be one minute."

Saige's excitement was overwhelming. Phoebe's adoring gaze was annoying.

"Ice cream, ice cream, ice cream!"

Saige was chanting monotonously. They entered his house and he shut the door behind them, flipping the dead bolt and locking it.

"Your home is so cute."

Phoebe said to him, touching his arm as he approached her and Saige again. Saige climbed up onto one of the kitchen chairs.

"Hurry up, Sammy! Ice cream!"

Saige exclaimed. Her voice was melting his heart. He was so in love with that little girl. He turned towards the sink.

"Just. Give me a quick second."

He said, pausing slightly. Phoebe stared at his back.

"Is everything okay, Sam?"

She asked, softly. She took a step towards him. He turned around and stared her in the eyes. His hand balled into a fist and swung it towards Phoebe. She didn't have time to react as his knuckles collided with the side of her face, cracking into her cheek. She hit the floor with a thud. Her hand flew up to her face, grabbing her cheek, tears rolling over her rims.

"Sam!"

She exclaimed. He dropped to his knees and grabbed her by the hair. His reddened knuckles hit her face again, and then he hit her in the stomach. She doubled over.

He was so focused; he didn't hear Saige's horrified screaming.

Phoebe was laying on her side now, he had let go of her, she was unmoving. He stood to his feet and crossed the kitchen to the spot where he kept his wooden knife block. He pulled out a large silver steak knife; and then he felt the little hands grabbing his arm.

He looked down and saw Saige's hands wrapped around his elbow.

"Sammy, Sammy stop!"

She was crying hard, tears pouring down her cheeks. He wasn't focused on her. The only thing on his mind was disposing of Phoebe. He shoved Saige away from him, she stumbled backwards and fell to her knees.

"Sammy!"

She cried, her chest heaving the word. He ignored her. He leaned towards Phoebe. He grabbed a fistful of her hair and lifted her head up. Her eyes were closed. She was breathing but she was unconscious. He lifted the knife in his other hand and with a quick, all in one movement, sliced the knife across her throat.

The result was imminent. Blood gushed instantly. She sputtered once as the blood sprayed out of the wound, sprinkling him with the scarlet splash.

7

Saige shot up in bed, beads of sweat dripping down her face. She breathed deeply, trying to center herself. She knew Matt was already out of bed. She checked the clock on the night stand next to the bed.

Seven fifty-seven am.

With a shaky hand, she grabbed her cell phone off of the stand and dialed a number straight from her memory. She held the phone next to her ear, hand still trembling. With her other hand, she wiped the sweat from her forehead, instantly glistening her hand with the moisture. It felt like forever until the phone was answered.

"Saige. Hello sweetheart. How are you?"

"Cara. I need to see you. Please."

Cara, the woman on the phone recognized the urgency in Saige's terrified filled voice.

"I'm full until three. Come in then, okay?"

She responded quickly, trying to let Saige know that she was concerned for the young girl.

"Thank you."

Saige replied quietly and hung up. She'd had the dream again. She hadn't had the dream in a year. She thought it was done. She was so confused. The dream was always so vivid. She could swear it was just a dream, but it felt way too real. She could remember specifics. She could remember them better than anyone was supposed to remember stuff from dreams.

Slowly, she pushed off the comforter, revealing her long legs and slim torso in an oversized tee shirt and short shorts. She shivered at the temperature change outside the down filled comforter. She flung her legs over the side of the bed and shuffled her feet along the thin carpet in search of her bunny slippers. Those were one thing she couldn't let go of. Her bunny slippers were her favourite things in the world. When the slippers were on her feet, she stood up to her full height of five four and stretched her arms over her head. She yawned and let her hands fall to her face. She wiped her whole face with them, trying to get the last of the sweat. She felt disgusting. She really wanted a shower. Maybe she would see if Matt would join her.

She trudged down the hallway and saw Matt standing at the counter. She could smell the eggs and hear the bacon sizzling.

"Smells good in here."

She said as she stepped up behind him and wrapped her arms through his and around his waist. She pressed herself against his back, hugging him tightly. She planted a kiss on his bare back, right on the black ink of his native American wolf tattoo.

"Hasn't anyone ever told you that you shouldn't cook bacon without a shirt on?"

She teased. She ran her fingers over his chest, tickling him slightly. He flinched but didn't move out of the way. With a black plastic spatula in hand, he flipped some of the bacon strips in the frying pan. Then he spun around and grabbed her face in his hands, brushing his lips against hers.

"Yes. But I'm a pro bacon cooker."

Saige rolled her eyes with a smirk on her face.

"Whoa. Okay babe. No bacon for you."

He spun in her arms again and faced the stove, picking the spatula back up.

"No! No! Sorry babe. Matt! Matt, baby, please."

Saige pleaded. She clung to his arm and waist. She heard Matt chuckle and then a tiny popping sound. Matt jerked in her arms.

"Holy shit! Ouch! Ow!"

He shoved her gently away from him and stepped away from the frying pan, tossing the spatula onto the counter. Grease was popping from the frying pan onto the counter.

"What happened?"

Saige asked, a smirk on her face. She knew very well what had happened. Matt pulled a white tank top off of a chair in the kitchen. He slid it over his arms and down his chest, covering his abs and tribal tattoos. He shot her a look.

"I told you."

Saige teased. Matt pretended to be hurt. He pouted, adorably in Saige's opinion. She crossed the kitchen and stepped back into his arms. She wrapped hers around his waist again.

"I'm only kidding honey. C'mon, let's eat and then cuddle."

Saige smiled up at him. She turned and skipped back to the oven.

"Hey, you have to come here and finish making this stuff. I really need a shower."

She said as she picked up the spatula and flipped a piece of bacon. She glanced over her shoulder and saw Matt staring at her.

"Damn. Your ass looks great in those shorts."

Matt admired. She looked over her shoulder. He had his arms crossed in front of his chest, a crooked smile on his face as he checked out her rear end. She bit her lip and wiggled her butt.

"You think?"

Matt bit his lip as well.

"Oh, fuck yea."

He took two long strides and then jogged the rest of the way to her and grabbed her butt in his hands. He started kissing her collarbone and neck. He brought one hand around her and grabbed one of her breasts in his palm. She closed her eyes and leaned back into him.

"Turn off the stove."

She whispered, huskily.

"We'll eat later."

She turned in his arms. He reached over her and turned the dials that controlled the elements to 'off'. She grabbed his face in her hands and kissed him hard. His hands were on her butt again, ravaging her body. He lifted her up. She wrapped her legs around his waist. He carried her like that back to the bedroom, kissing her, tongues dancing together.

He tossed her onto the bed and scrambled on top of her. His hands frantically ran up and down her body, hooking onto the bottom of her night shirt and sliding it up and over her head. She had her arms around his shoulders, digging her nails into his skin, raking them down his back.

"No wait. I need to have a shower!"

She exclaimed. Matt ignored her. She pushed at his chest, trying to get him to move off of her. He grabbed her wrists and pinned her down. He moved one hand down her body, feeling every inch of her womanly stature. He had both of his hands on her breasts, kissing down her neck, collarbone, and down her chest.

She had her head back, eyes closed, mouth slightly agape as Matt kissed her whole body. She sat up, pushing him off of her. She stared into his eyes. They were filed with desire and lust, but more importantly, love.

"Let me take care of you. After I have a shower!"

She whispered. She put one hand on his chest and pushed him back. She slowly slid out from underneath him and rolled off of the bed. He turned onto his side as he watched her strut out of the bedroom. The moment she was out of site, he did just what any man in his position would do.

He followed her.

He saw her standing in the bathroom, hands on either side of the sink. She was staring at herself in the mirror. He paused in the hallway. In all the years since he'd known Saige, she had never looked so unguarded. She put her hands on her hips and turned from side to side. She ran a hand through her silky brown hair. It fell around her shoulders in those curls that Matt loved so much. He took the last couple of steps, crossing the threshold into the bathroom. Saige jumped at the sound of the floor creaking. She turned and looked at him.

He didn't say a word as he approached her. He slid his arms around her waist and planted a small peck onto her full lips. Saige returned the symbol of affection and held her arms above her head.

Matt kissed her again as he lifted her large tee shirt up her body, sliding it delicately over her arms. Saige glanced down at her body. She felt self-conscious. Matt could tell by the way she tensed up and brought her arms back around her stomach.

"Sai..."

Matt whispered. He reached for her hands and pulled her arms gently away from her stomach.

"We've known each other since we were nine years old, Sai. I've been in love with you every single minute. You don't have to hide yourself from me."

Matt kissed both of her hands. Saige's eyes watered up. She looked back down to her body anyway. Matt followed her gaze. Both sets landed on the nasty scars that marked her stomach. Matt knelt down and kissed each scar.

"I can only hope one day, you'll tell me what these are from."

He whispered. Saige pulled Matt back to his feet.

"I just can't."

She whispered back. Matt grabbed her face in his hands and kissed her hard. She wrapped her arms around his waist and kissed him back just as passionately as he was kissing her. She knew Matt wouldn't force her to tell him about the scars. She knew he wouldn't push. He'd wait until she was ready. She pulled away from Matt and stared deeply into his eyes. Saige slid the muscle shirt up his torso, revealing nicely toned abs and pecks.

He lifted his arms to grab the top for her, helping her pull it over his head. His muscles rippled. Saige trailed a finger down his smooth chest, running it over the bumps and ridges of his defined abs. She let her finger dangle over a tribal tattoo on his waist, right next to his v-line. She didn't know what his tattoos meant, but she knew that they had very significant meaning to him. And that's all that mattered.

He helped her roll her shorts over her butt and down her long legs. She helped him with his boxers until they were both standing in the bathroom, naked both physically and emotionally.

Matt reached around Saige and pulled the lever on the tap in the shower, starting up the spray of water into the tub. He let the water run over his hand until it felt hot enough for the two of them to climb in. She hugged him close to her as they both stepped back, lifting their legs to get into the tub. The moment the spray hit Saige, she let out a soft gasp and moved closer to Matt. It was a moment of such intense, unguarded intimacy. The water ran over both of them as they held each other. Matt's dark hair clung to his forehead and neck. His muscular arms held Saige close to him. She stood on her tiptoes, careful not slip and fall on the wet floor of the tub.

She pressed her lips into his neck and collarbone. Planting small pecks along the ridges of his collarbone. She let herself fall back onto her feet, Matt keeping her steady. She slowly lowered herself down to her knees. The spray of the water dripping down her face, was making it a little harder for her to breathe steadily. Matt picked up the shampoo bottle and put a little bit into his hands. He started massaging it into Saige's hair. She blew water out of her mouth and grabbed Matt by his legs. He let out a soft moan as her hot mouth wrapped around his manhood. His fingers twisted in her hair and his eyes rolled back in his head. His breathing was labored. He could feel the warmth of her mouth and he could feel her nails digging into his legs. He braced himself on the wall as his whole body began to tingle.

"Saige,"

He started to say. She didn't give up.

"Saige,"

He repeated, his voice wavering. She held tight. His one hand that was left in her hair was gently trying to urge her away from him. She resisted. That was all it took, that little bit of resistance, knowing she wanted to give him the best that he had ever got, that was all it took. He cried out and shuddered. The act almost brought him to his knees. Saige slowly backed away, water dripping down her face. She gave him an infinitesimal smile. He helped her to her feet and brought her into his arms. He kissed her hard on her mouth, his juices hot and musky on her tongue.

"Now it's your turn."

He said tacitly. Saige didn't complain. He started kissing back down her body, running a tongue over each taut nipple and down the tightness of her tummy.

"I don't know! Are you serious? You're the police! You're supposed to be telling me where my husband has gone! Where my daughter is! But instead, you're telling me that my husband has run off with a high school student. That my daughter, my darling Mya has been.... has been kidnapped! This is bullshit."

Harriette Swanson exclaimed. She was waving her hands in the air and pacing back and forth. PJ was sitting in the pristine living room. She noticed the tears sparkling in Harriette's eyes. Her blonde hair had grey streaks and was piled into a frizzy bun atop her head. PJ held up her hands.

"Mrs. Swanson, if you would please take a seat..."

Harriette shot her a distraught look and continued pacing. PJ noticed her tidying items around the room as she moved.

"Mrs. Swanson, your daughter has been missing for three days now. Is there anyone that might want to harm her?"

"You're not saying someone murdered her."

PJ expeditiously shook her head.

"No. No, no, no way. That is not what I'm saying. However, it's something we haven't ruled out. I really need to know whatever info you can provide. Mrs. Swanson, if you want me to find your daughter... husband...you need to tell me whatever it is that you can."

PJ did her best to try and persuade the discomposed woman. Harriette languidly sat on the couch across from PJ and dropped her head into her hands. She started to sob.

"I really don't know where David went. He...he told me he didn't love me anymore. That he has fallen in love with another woman. He said he was going to get a lawyer to finalize a divorce between us. And then he was going to move in with his new girlfriend. You said she was a high school student..."

PJ felt really sorry for the poor woman, but she needed to push her.

"What about Mya, Mrs. Swanson?"

Harriette coughed and stifled another sob.

"She said his name was Tyson or something. She knew she was in trouble. She just knew. She told Josh. She told him she was scared. She tried to tell me...oh god."

She choked on a breath and hid her face in her hands again. PJ was bewildered.

"What exactly did she tell you?"

Harriette desperately searched for the right words.

"She said, 'Mom. I don't know who...not really...or why. But someone has been following me. I've seen him a couple of times before...I don't know. I don't feel safe."

She paused and choked on a sob.

"I didn't believe her. None of her friends ever mentioned anything when they were here. I never saw anyone lurking around outside. I thought she was looking to get some more attention. Or make Josh jealous."

She started to bawl. That was her breaking point.

"Thank you, Mrs. Swanson. If you can remember anything else, please don't hesitate to call me."

Harriette looked up, tears streaking her face, mascara running rapidly down her face, resembling the darkest of rivers. PJ stood up from the couch to leave the house through the door behind it. She reached for the doorknob. Harriette grabbed PJ's arm just above her elbow.

"Please. Find her."

PJ didn't have time to respond. Her cell phone began to ring. She looked apologetically at Harriette Swanson.

"I'm going to do the best that I can. As well as my team. But I'm sorry. You'll need to excuse me. I have to take this."

She pressed the green answer button on her jingling iPhone and pulled open the door. She stepped outside.

"Detective Richards. Talk to me."

"Richards. It's Brinker. We've got Swanson and Michelle Clifford in custody."

PJ shocked herself when she sighed with relief.

"What did you get from the missus?"

Brinker's deep, manly voice spoke with an urgency. PJ shook her head.

"Not much. Mya told her she wasn't safe. Mrs. Swanson didn't believe her. Mya went missing. That's about it."

Brinker scoffed through the phone.

"What kind of mother doesn't believe their child when she's scared?"

PJ didn't reply at that time. Her mind went back to when her baby sister was panicked. Neither she, nor their mother believed she was in any real danger. What Harriette had said inside, about not seeing anyone or hearing anything of it from her friends hit home with PJ. It was all too familiar.

"A bad one."

Was all she could muster as a reply.

"Well, get back to headquarters. Swanson's in the interrogation room."

Brinker clicked off, leaving PJ standing there in the slight wind, phone in hand.

The door clicked open as she was about to head for the car on the road.

"Detective?"

PJ turned and met Harriette Swanson's eyes.

"Can I come to the station?"

Her question was hushed. Her eyes darted around the street. PJ had a curious look across her face.

"I may know something. I may know something about my husband, but I want to be sure that I am safe. I don't trust him."

Her eyes stopped scanning the suburban roads. She focused on something down the road a little way. Her eyes widened. PJ turned again to see what Harriette had frozen, looking at. She didn't see anything of interest. A cat ran across the street.

Harriette grabbed PJ's shoulders, her fingers digging into the fabric of her sweater. The fear emanated from her eyes, bearing deeply into PJ's.

"Please."

That one word stabbed through PJ's inner core, forcing itself through her veins, coursing through her blood. The terror in that miniscule word sliced into PJ's brain. She couldn't shake the feeling that Harriette passed onto her. Especially in all of her years on the RPD, she'd never seen that kind of emotion in one person's eyes. Finally, she nodded.

"Yes. Okay. Come on."

Harriette spun around, grabbed her bag off of a hook just inside the front door and spun another one eighty, slamming the door shut behind her. PJ began walking back down the little sidewalk that cut through the lawn towards her police cruiser she used during work hours. Harriette hustled alongside her. PJ never noticed how diminutive she was. Sitting on the couch, Harriette seemed to tower over her. Now, reaching the car, PJ noticed how truly dwarfish she looked. She couldn't have been more than five feet tall.

At the vehicle, PJ reached forwards and pulled open the door, holding it open for the frazzled looking lady to duck her head and get inside the vehicle. Harriette didn't say a single word. The drive to the department was quiet. Steady and fast but quiet. Harriette stayed in the backseat, eyes down. She wouldn't look outside and she wouldn't look to the front. PJ tried to meet her eye on more than one occasion but Harriette stayed strong in her defiance.

As the precinct loomed into view, Harriette tensed up. PJ could feel the change in the atmosphere inside the vehicle. It was cold and unfeeling. PJ glanced in the rearview mirror and caught another look at the frayed woman. She was now looking out the window, eyes trained on the doors of the department as if something or someone was watching her, stripping her of her privacy.

Once PJ had parked the vehicle, she was out and reaching for the handle to the door that Harriette was sitting behind. PJ could see her fidgeting behind the glass of the window. PJ cracked open the door for her and she slinked out of the car. Her short stature seemed even more diminished next to PJ's frame. She escorted the small woman to the front doors of the station. Reporters shot them looks and jumped up. PJ threw them a deadly gaze that told them not to even try or she'd throw them in jail for harassment. The last thing the little Harriette needed was a hundred reporters shoving their microphones down her throat looking for a scoop.

Inside the RPD, Harriette looked around, her eyes wide and wild with genuine fear, like she was going to be killed. PJ wondered what it was that was putting her so on edge. They passed the reception desk and wandered down the hall towards the interview rooms. Harriette had been adamant that she had something she needed to say. PJ didn't say anything as she walked in front of Harriette down the hallway. They were approaching the room quickly.

When they reached the room, PJ opened the door and Harriette scuttled inside. She was like a spider, small and moving with speed and accuracy. She perched herself on one of the chairs and tucked her legs under the desk. PJ sat opposite her, resting her arms on the table.

"So, Harriette,"

PJ started to say.

"I think my husband might be after me."

She interrupted; her eyes were darting around the room. PJ glanced around too but didn't see anything out of the ordinary.

"What makes you think that, Mrs. Swanson?"

PJ asked, her tone of voice soothing, motherly.

"He caught me cheating."

Was her response. PJ sat back in her chair. She kept a straight face.

"With his best friend."

PJ nodded her head slowly. So, this was a Derek-Addison-Mark type of situation.

"I need protection."

Harriette continued.

"He's going to kill me."

PJ pursed her lips and put her hands on the table in front of her. She pushed herself to her feet.

"Everything will be okay, Mrs. Swanson. Sit tight."

PJ walked to the other side of the room and opened the door. She exited smoothly and didn't look behind her.

"I don't know anything! Do you think if I'd known my daughter was missing, I would have remained with Michelle?"

David Swanson was sitting at a steel table in a dimly lit room. He was wearing a black tee shirt and a pair of dark wash blue jeans. One of his wrists was handcuffed to the table leg, so he was slightly hunched over. It seemed like he was some big time criminal, instead of a man with a very young girlfriend. Brinker was standing, pacing the table. He stopped, mid stride and looked straight at David.

"But you did know she was missing, didn't you?"

David looked down, un answering. Brinker took one step towards him.

"Didn't you!"

"No!"

David finally screamed back. Brinker slammed his palms onto the table, rattling it on the cement floor. He glared at David.

'You killed your daughter or hired someone to do it for you so you could be with that little girl!"

David's eyes lit up with an intense anger.

"Are you fucking stupid? Why the fuck would I kill my daughter and leave my wife?'

Brinker leaned down even further. He could tell that David was trying not to flinch or look away. Signs of a guilty conscious. Brinker smirked and stood up straighter.

"So, she'd suffer. You don't love her anymore. You hate her for what she did to you. You hate her and wanted her to live the rest of her life completely alone."

David didn't reply. He glared back at Brinker, tears beginning to show in his eyes. The testosterone was heavy in the air.

"I would never hurt Mya."

David managed to whisper. He bowed his head, eyes meeting the silvery handcuffs that jingled against his wrist and table leg. One tear fell from each of his eyes. Brinker began to pace again. He had his hands behind his back. His face was red from yelling. He turned back towards the table with the slumped over man. He was just getting ready to scream at him again when a couple of knocks on the steel door interrupted him.

He shot one last look at David and made his way to the door. He pulled the heavy thing open.

"Ah, Detective Richards."

He stepped aside to let PJ into the room. She studied the man sitting at the table. He was not what she was expecting. From the looks of his wife, she expected him to be small, shrimpy, and maybe bald. What she saw, was a very well put together, good looking man with a full head of wavy brown hair, a little bit of morning stubble upon his face. His tee shirt fit him perfectly enough to show off his muscular arms. PJ was impressed. He was a very handsome man.

"You must be David Swanson."

PJ stated firmly. David didn't respond. PJ smiled at Brinker.

"Thank you, Agent Brinker. I'll take over."

She was so glad that the federal Agent was nice enough to work as equals. She was glad that he didn't completely take over her investigation. Brinker didn't leave, however. He leaned against the wall, right next to the two-way glass. PJ pulled the chair out from the table and gradually sat down.

"So, David...May I call you that?"

David didn't respond. He shrugged and looked back down towards the handcuffs. They were on tight enough to rub into his wrists when he moved them a certain way. He jiggled his hand, the cuffs clanging against the metal of the table.

"Would you like coffee? Tea? Water?"

She smiled at him and folded her hands across the table, interlocking her fingers. She hoped she didn't look very intimidating. He smirked.

"I know what this is. The good cop, bad cop routine won't work on me."

PJ chuckled. She sat back in the chair and folded her arms in front of her chest. She learned that if she held herself a certain way, she looked bigger than she really was. She liked looking more muscular than her normal self.

"Why not?"

"Because I did not kill my daughter. I didn't kill her."

He paused, taking deep breaths, attention turned back towards PJ and away from the handcuffs. PJ stood up from the chair and caught Brinker's eyes. They exchanged a look.

"I just spoke with Harriette."

David followed her with his eyes.

"What?"

PJ walked around the room, killing time. How anxious could she make him? Would he crack? Did they even have the right guy? The more she thought about it, she wasn't sure if her instincts were telling her the right stuff.

"What did she say?"

David did his best to stand up. His arm was slightly restricted due to the cuffs. PJ turned back to him, observing the way he was sort of slumped over, trying to stand up straight, but failing as he was restrained to the table. PJ also took in his size. He was a big guy. He had to stand at least six or seven inches above her five-foot six frame.

"What did she say!"

He exclaimed again. His voice echoed through the cement and steel room.

"I think you know."

David slammed his free fist into the table.

"Whatever she said is bullshit!"

PJ walked slowly back to the table.

"Sit."

She said sternly. He didn't sit. He frowned at her; his eyebrows knit together tightly. Brinker stepped forward a couple of steps, but not all the way to the table.

"Sit down!"

He said, voice raised. David still didn't sit.

"What did she say? What did that bitch fucking say? I didn't kill my daughter! I didn't hire anyone to kill her! She's...she's my baby girl."

He very slowly sunk into the seat and put his face into his free hand. He was sobbing slightly. PJ turned and met Brinker's eyes again. She sat back down into the seat opposite of David Swanson and intertwined her fingers a second time.

"What your wife said was that you walked in on her with another man. A close friend of yours. Ryan Beal. You walked in on your best friend giving it to your wife really good. So, you snapped. You found yourself a good-looking young girl to make her jealous, then you served her with divorce papers."

"Yea, that's true."

David whispered, looking back down. PJ leaned forward, resting on her arms.

"But not without threatening to kill her."

David's eyes widened and he shook his head.

"I wouldn't actually kill her. I was angry. You know when people get pissed off, they say stupid shit."

"Just be truthful, David. Honest. Did you kill your daughter? To get even with your wife?"

David couldn't hold back the tears anymore. A couple escaped from his eyes. He immediately began to shake his head again.

"No, I didn't. You guys need to look at someone else."

PJ shared a third look with Brinker. She could tell that he was becoming incredibly pissed off and restless with the uncooperative man. PJ used her eyes to gesture towards the door. She pushed herself back from the table and followed Brinker to the hallway, making sure to securely shut the heavy door.

"What do you think?"

PJ asked him as they got to the observation room. They both faced the two-way glass. They could see David sitting at the table. His leg was shaking underneath, he was tapping his fingers on the table top.

"I don't know. Besides a couple of tears, he doesn't seem upset enough. His daughter has been missing for three days. We're fast approaching the seventy fifth hour of her disappearance. That man should be hysterical. A friggen mess. But he barely showed any kind of emotion."

"Besides being enraged with Harriette."

"Yea. Besides that."

Brinker leaned closer, squinting his eyes, looking harder. He studied David Swanson. PJ put her hand on his shoulder.

"Michelle knew Mya. Maybe she knows. Have you or has anyone talked to her yet?"

Brinker shook his head, but didn't turn away from the mirror.

"No. You can take the lead on that. I'm going to stay here. See if I can make Swanson crack."

PJ didn't have to respond. She just patted Brinker's shoulder and left the observation room without as much as a second word. She walked down the hallway and stopped at another room closer to the main doors. She peered through the blinds into the office that belonged to Brock. She saw a pretty blonde sitting in one of the office chairs, hands clasped together tightly. She was looking down at her lap, her leg twitching nervously. She was alone. PJ guessed that her family had not been notified about her reappearance.

She looked down the hall as she heard quiet footsteps and noticed Brock on his way to where she stood. She turned back towards the window and re focused her gaze on the inside of the room. Brock stopped next to her. He put his hands behind his back and stared in with her.

"What did you get out of Swanson?"

PJ shook her head and scrunched up her nose.

"Nothing useful. He swears up and down that he's innocent."

"Do you think he is?"

PJ observed Michelle in the office and thought about that question.

"I want to say he's innocent. Brinker noticed it too. He just didn't seem torn up enough. Brock, you have a daughter. How would you feel if you found out Paxton was kidnapped?"

Brock's eyes immediately fell to the floor. PJ could hear his breathing get heavier.

"I would be absolutely devastated. I'd do anything and everything in my power to get her back."

PJ flung her hands into the air.

"Exactly. That is exactly what I am saying. Swanson just doesn't seem to care. Actually, he seemed more concerned with what his wife had to say about him."

Brock averted his eyes from PJ and looked back into his office.

"So, you want to tackle this one?"

PJ agreed.

"Sure would. This is my case."

She twisted the cold metal of the doorknob and entered the office. Michelle looked startled for just one moment but her expression went right back to being nervous and even a little angry.

"Hi Michelle. My name is PJ Rich..."

"You can't arrest him! Or me. It's not illegal. I'm eighteen. It's consensual."

Michelle interrupted PJ's greeting. PJ gave her a soft smile.

"ards. PJ Richards. I'm a Detective here at the Ridgeway Police Department."

She finished anyway. Michelle ignored it.

"You can't arrest either of us."

PJ sat down next to Michelle. She noted that she moved over slightly, almost as if she was uncomfortable sitting next to someone of authority. She flinched when PJ reached towards Brock's desk that was sitting right behind her. PJ moved slowly, to show Michelle she wasn't going to harm her. She pulled his notebook and pen off of the desk.

"You're right, Michelle. We can't arrest David for sleeping with you. We can arrest him for manslaughter."

She watched Michelle sit up straighter, her back pushed up against the brown suede chair.

"Manslaughter."

She repeated, her voice quivering.

"That's right. We can arrest you too for being his accomplice."

PJ's voice was stern.

"What-what are you talking about?"

Michelle stuttered. PJ studied her pick at the skin around her nails. It seemed like she was doing it subconsciously.

"I'm talking about David's daughter. Mya Swanson. You joined together to kill her so a, his wife would be completely alone and b, you guys could be together with him having zero attachments to his previous marriage. So, the two of you conspired it. Came up with this scheme."

Michelle instantly teared up.

"No. No it's not true. David, he wouldn't kill his own daughter. He wouldn't. Yea, he was pissed at Mrs. Swanson. Of course, he was. I don't blame him. But he wouldn't kill Mya to get back at her. Mya is his, as much as I hate to say it, his baby girl."

PJ tucked the notebook and pen into the crack of the chair cushion. She leaned forward, resting her elbows on her knees and put her chin in her hands.

"He might not. But would you? To get whatever you want? In this case, David."

Michelle shook her head furiously.

"I don't like Mya. But I wouldn't kill her. I'm not that person."

PJ sat up straight. She was having a hard time sitting in one position.

"I was going to try and get you to come clean on your own. Looks like that isn't working. We know you two did it. David admitted it."

PJ kept calm as Michelle's sad eyes widened. She tossed her head side to side, tears streaming down her face.

"He wouldn't. He's lying. He really didn't."

PJ took in the way the girl was acting. Maybe she was wrong. She wasn't so sure of her instincts anymore. The teenager was bawling.

"He really, really, really didn't."

PJ stayed very still. The way Michelle was reacting, picking her nails, biting her lip. PJ got a very strong feeling that whether or not Michelle had done it, she most certainly knew something. She stood up quickly, the room racing around her. She grabbed the box of Kleenex off of Brock's desk and tossed it into Michelle's lap. That crying girl paid them no mind at all. PJ crossed the office and exited the room. Brock, who had witnessed the whole scene, slowly looked towards PJ.

"She knows something."

He said, before PJ even got the chance.

"I'm going to give her a second to calm down. Can you retrieve Brinker from the interrogation room, please?"

The chief of police, and also one of PJ's closest friends, smiled at her and patted her shoulder. He made his way back down the hallway from which PJ had originally come. PJ focused her attention back on Michelle inside the office. Her eyes lit up, heart beat quickening. As quickly as she could, she re-entered the room. Michelle had stopped crying; she was now wiping her face with a Kleenex.

"Michelle."

PJ's voice was soft. Michelle didn't respond. She sniffled silently.

"Where will we find Mya's body, Michelle? Woodland park? Like the rest?"

Michelle's head snapped up.

"That girl doesn't deserve to die, Michelle."

"She's not dead."

The short phrase came out of Michelle's mouth, barely above a whisper. Had PJ not been paying attention; she wouldn't have heard her say it.

"She's not. At least she shouldn't be."

Michelle whimpered. Her shoulders were heaving up and down heavily. PJ could tell she was having a hard time with this.

"Michelle, I need you to tell me what happened. You won't be in trouble."

PJ couldn't promise her anything. Seeing how Michelle was not a minor, she'd be able to convict her with any possible felony and have her sent off to a women's correctional facility anywhere she pleased. She snuck a quick peek at the window, Brock had returned with an intrigued looking Agent Brinker. Michelle was no longer looking at PJ, but at the wall behind her.

PJ didn't think she was looking at the framed photographs of Brock's family or the pictures of six-year-old Paxton. She definitely didn't think she was taking an interest in Brock's prized hockey jersey, a Montreal Canadiens jersey that used to belong to his favourite player,

'Guy Lafleur'. He'd had it framed, showing the back of the jersey with a big autograph though the zero of the number ten.

PJ gestured to Brock and Brinker to come inside the room.

"Michelle, this is chief of police, Brock Carter, and this is federal Agent, uh..."

She realized she had never been told Brinker's first name.

"James. James Brinker."

He piped up, finishing the introduction for her. Michelle didn't reply.

"Michelle, will you please come with us? We need to go to a different room, something a little quieter than Brock's office."

"The interview room."

Michelle said bleakly. PJ, Brock, and Brinker didn't say anything. She sniffed once and coughed. Her face was red from crying.

"I know how it works. You'll take me to the interview room so you can put my confession on tape and then you'll throw me in jail. I know how it works. I've seen C.S.I and Criminal Minds."

She stood up and nodded towards the door.

"So, let's go."

PJ was dumbfounded. She led the way out of the room with Michelle following her and Brock and Brinker taking up the rear. Michelle stayed silent the whole way to the dreary, flat gray room. There was a one-way mirror in that room as well as a steel table, two blue plastic chairs and a video camera set up on a tri-pod. Michelle sat down in the chair farthest from the tri-pod. PJ was the only one who went into the room with her.

Brock and Brinker were watching with genuine curiosity from the observation room.

"State your name, age, and town you're in."

PJ felt like a warden. She hated administering the taping sessions.

"Michelle Gwyneth Clifford. Eighteen. Ridgeway, Ontario, Canada."

PJ made a couple of alterations to the camera, fixing the angle and the focus.

"Alright. Go ahead."

Michelle folded her hands together and looked directly at the camera lens.

"I did not kill Mya Swanson. It is true that her father, a professor at Ridgeway University, David Swanson and I are in a romantic relationship. It is also true that he is leaving his wife and he hates her. And it is true that he had absolutely nothing to do with her disappearance. I… I uh…I may have been jealous of how much he loved her. Mya, I mean. I was talking about it with a friend of mine at school one day.

"This guy came up to my friend and me and asked if she was a problem. I, jokingly, said yea, she was. He said he could take care of it. He said he had a crush on Mya. Said he would gladly keep her occupied so I could have time with her dad…I mean David."

Michelle paused to brush away a tear. She coughed a couple of times. PJ glanced over her shoulder towards the mirror. She couldn't see Brinker or Brock's reactions, but she could only assume they were having a hay day in there.

"I thought he just meant ask her out. I knew she was dating Josh, but there was this super good-looking older guy that liked her? I thought she'd go for him."

"How do you know she isn't dead?"

PJ leaned forward, being careful not to lean too far into the frame. Michelle slid her eyes from the camera to meet PJ's.

"She…she called me."

PJ stood up so fast her head started to spin.

"Please. Tell the camera exactly what happened."

She said, stuttering only slightly. She very slowly sat down. She could only imagine how Brock and Brinker were reacting behind the one-way glass to that shocking news.

"She called me. Or he did. She was crying. She was having a hard time talking. Then…then she screamed. Someone hit her. Then she said, 'Thanks Michelle. For hooking me up with Taylor. He's amazing.' I think he forced her to say that. She tried to say something else, but he hit her again and then he…he talked to me. He said 'I was coming for you, Michelle. But Mya is just so much fun.'"

She paused and more tears fell over the rims of her eyes. She turned back to PJ again.

"Can we please be done?"

"Bye Matt! I'll be back soon and then we're meeting Michael and Bella for dinner!"

Saige yelled as she pulled her set of keys from her purse.

"Bye baby!"

Matt yelled back just as she slammed the door shut. Matt was letting her borrow his car again. She just had to stop at her dorm to grab extra clothes and then get to Cara's office. The drive to her dorm was quick.

Silent.

She didn't think about anything.

Quiet. But quick.

She parked in a 'visitor' spot and made sure to lock the door. The dorms were quieter than normal. She tried not to let the deafening silence bother her, but her mind had other ideas.

It took her back twelve years. Back to that room, being cuffed to the heater or radiator.

She was bruised, dirty, bleeding and crying. She desperately wanted her mother.

"Hi Saigey."

She looked up and through the dim lighting, she could see a silhouette in the doorway.

"Saigey, you have to talk to me. Be a good girl."

The unknown male moved across the hardwood floors without making a sound.

"I want my mom."

She whispered.

"You won't see her anymore, my girl. We're happy together. We're happy."

"I'm not. Sammy, please. I want to go home."

She started crying again. Her shoulders shook which resulted in the handcuffs to rub into her wrists, making them bleed more and the flesh rawer. The male, her captor, sat down on the floor beside her. He put his hand on her knee. She stiffened, still blubbering.

"It's okay, Sai."

He insisted. He reached up and stroked her dirty face. She flinched.

"Looks like it's time for a bath."

He whispered. He leaned towards her. She pulled away, not getting very far as the handcuffs kept her movement limited. She was sweating, the heater kicking in, only inches from her.

"Don't touch me."

She wept. He kept one hand on her knee and took her cheek into his other hand.

"You need a bath or at least a shower."

He planted a hard kiss onto her cheek as he reached into his pocket. He pulled out a tiny key and slid it into the handcuffs, twisting until it popped open. She instantly started rubbing her raw wrists. She looked up at him with big, sad eyes. He pulled her closer to him, grabbing her dirty pink tee shirt by the hem.

"Saige!"

Saige jumped and realized that she was sweating profusely after her flashback. She spun around and caught whoever called her.

"Oh my god. Danni. You scared the crap out of me."

She felt her hand fly towards her chest.

"Sorry girl. Just not used to seeing you around here anymore. How are you?"

Danni, a redheaded girl who was slightly overweight walked up to Saige and gave her a hug. Saige hugged her back.

"It's okay. You're right. I'm hardly around. I've been..."

"Staying with Matt."

Danni interrupted. Saige smiled at her.

"Yea. With Matt."

"Well, I've got some papers I really have to get working on. So, I better get back to those. Maybe I'll see you later."

Danni had a very warm smile. It made Saige feel so much better.

Safe.

"Sure. See you around."

Saige replied, trying to generate the same warm smile as Danni. Danni retreated into a dorm room, leaving Saige alone again. Scarily alone.

She found her dorm room and held her breath as she slid the key into the lock. She very slowly twisted it. The door opened smoothly, revealing a pitch-black room. Saige flipped the light switch right at the door. The light flickered twice but managed to illuminate the room.

Everything looked untouched. Nothing seemed to have been disturbed. Saige exhaled and took a couple of steps into the room, shutting the door behind her and putting the chain on.

Out of habit, she looked in the closet and under the two beds. She didn't see any evil eyes peering back at her.

She drew her best calming breath, but wasn't surprised when her body shook slightly. Even after twelve years, he haunted her. She wondered if he'd ever go away.

She dug around in her dresser and realized she had a very limited amount of clothing left. Most of it was at Matt's apparently. She grabbed the last two pairs of jeans and four tee shirts that were in the drawers. She stuffed them into her oversized purse and without a second thought, shut off the light and banged the door shut.

Back in the hallway, she felt herself calm down a little bit. She was isolated in the hall but she knew that other students, her peers, were just behind closed doors. It was also two forty pm. No one would attack her in broad daylight...or would they?

She hustled out of the dormitory building as fast as her legs could carry her. She didn't waste even a millisecond unlocking Matt's precious car and jumping in behind the steering wheel, but not before first checking the backseat for any unknown or unwelcome bodies.

Cara's office was more than twenty minutes away. Saige hoped she'd be able to make it. If she got lucky, there would be minimal traffic. Saige pulled onto the main road through town and let out a very thankful yelp. There were only a few other vehicles on the road. It was Sunday, so everyone was probably at home getting ready for the long work week ahead of them.

Saige glanced at the clock on the dashboard.

Two fifty-seven.

She pressed down harder on the gas pedal. She was still about five minutes away. She glanced at the speedometer and took in that she was about twenty kilometers an hour over the speed limit. She prayed no police officers were around. She got her wish as she finally pulled into Cara's parking lot, not a cop in sight.

She scrambled out of the vehicle and into the building, running right into a blonde bombshell.

"Oh my god!"

They both exclaimed. Saige brushed herself off and looked up at the blonde.

"Oh. Cara."

She said quickly. The tall, curvaceous blonde held onto Saige's arm, just above her elbow.

"Hi Saige. Thought you forgot about me. Generally, you're at least ten minutes early."

Saige nodded apologetically.

"I know. I'm sorry. I got held up at my dorm."

Cara didn't reply. She let go of Saige's arm and smiled at her. Saige noticed that Cara's smile was not as bright, in fact her whole demeanor seemed less bubbly than usual.

She was not about to ask her. She followed Cara into her office and took her usual seat in an oversized blue eggshell chair. Cara sat in her big, leather, lazy boy recliner.

"So, you had the dream again?"

Cara asked, her voice soft.

"Mostly. It started off the same. But changed. It got worse. It turned really bad."

Saige replied, her voice beginning to shake slightly. She clenched her hands together, twitching them.

"Would you be able to tell me without being under the influence of hypnosis?"

Cara asked, leaning forward in her chair. Saige stayed silent for a couple of minutes. She was looking at the floor, at her hands, at the ceiling. Finally, she met Cara's eyes.

"I can do it. It's been a year since the last time."

She paused and breathed slowly, trying to steady her shaking self.

"We've done this before, Sai. If you need, we can do the hypno..."

"No. No thank you. I can't keep letting hypnosis fix my problems for me."

Saige interrupted. Cara sat back in her chair, crossing one leg over the other.

"Take your time."

She tried her best to send Saige a heartfelt smile. Saige closed her eyes.

"It started like it usually did. I was eight years old, playing in my front yard. The door was open and my parents were fighting. I could hear my mom screaming profanities at my dad. I tried to block them out by making my T-Rex transformer eat one of my Barbie dolls. There was this boy that lived up the street from me.

"I wasn't sure how old he was, probably late teens, early twenties at least. His name was Samuel Thomas, but he went by this nickname. 'Red.' He'd stop by my yard whenever I was outside and talk to me and he'd play with my Transformers and Barbie dolls with me. He'd keep me occupied while my parents fought. His face is kind of fuzzy. When we blocked him out, I haven't fully been able to remember what he looks like..."

Saige paused but did not open her eyes.

"Are you okay, Sai?"

Cara asked, softly. Saige held up her hand.

"Yes. I'm fine...so then, my dream changed a little bit. My parents were gone and my babysitter was sitting in the yard with me. She was tanning while I played. Red, Samuel Thomas, came to my yard again. I was always so happy to see him because he was always so nice to me. My babysitter, Phoebe was hitting on him. He asked us if we wanted to go get ice cream, his treat. We went with him back to his house to get his vehicle, which is when everything turned around. He hit

Phoebe. He hit her over and over until she wasn't moving. I was scared. I couldn't move.

"I couldn't scream. I watched him grab one of those massive kitchen knives and he slit Phoebe's throat. I don't think I've ever seen so much blood. I still couldn't scream. He dropped the knife and looked at me. He said, 'I'm so sorry you had to see that Sai. I'm so sorry baby.' And then he walked over to me and knelt down and looked me in the eyes. He said, 'I did what I had to do to make you mine. I love you, Sai. I love you.' And then he grabbed my face and kissed me...Wait...wait, oh my god.

"That wasn't a dream! That wasn't a dream. That...that happened."

Saige paused and grabbed her head in her hands. She shook her head and dug her fingers into her scalp. Cara sat up and reached towards her.

"Saige."

She said softly. Saige bit her lip and scrunched up her face. She was trying so hard not to cry.

"Saige. Saige, listen to my voice. It's me. Cara. Listen to my voice. You're okay. You're in my office. Everything is okay."

"He kept me for a year before I managed to escape. He kept me for one entire year thirty feet from my own house. Thirty fucking feet and no one even found me."

Saige stopped and opened her eyes, letting her hands drop from her head. The cuss word left a dirty taste in her mouth. Tears had built up behind her closed eyelids, and her body was trembling.

"Saige. It's okay. Breathe. It's just you and me. You're safe."

Cara said softly.

"Do you want to block out those memories? We can take them away; help you start re-living a normal life."

Saige shook her head again.

"We've tried that. Last year. And It worked, for the most part. Until now. I don't know why my dream is back. Why my flashbacks are coming back. I don't know why."

Cara stood and picked up her clipboard from the coffee table that sat between them. She sunk back into her chair.

"Have you made any new friends? Has anything in your classes as the university possibly triggered something in your brain, making you remember? Perhaps for your own safety?"

Saige chewed at a fingernail.

"The only person I've met is this guy named Michael."

"Michael. Is there anything about him?"

"He's Bella's new toy. I met him yesterday, officially. He always sits at this bench a few feet from that Raven fountain where I like to study. He writes poetry."

"Is there anything about him? That feels familiar, maybe in a not so good way?"

Cara asked, trying to dig a little deeper.

"No. He seems like a really nice guy. Quiet. Reserved. But nice."

Cara made a few notes on her clipboard.

"What's his last name? What does he look like?"

"I never thought to ask. Uh, he's tall. Stocky. Muscular. He's got dark hair. Looks very healthy and shiny. Oh, and his eyes are absolutely gorgeous. They're like this dark blue that fade into a blue-green. They are stunning."

"Does he remind you of Samuel Thomas in any way?"

Cara responded. Her hand was fluttering across the page, writing notes furiously. Saige's eyes widened.

"I already said no. You blocked him. I don't really remember at all. I'm almost positive that Sam had blonde hair and these cold blue eyes, though."

Cara made a humming noise and wrote one more note. She looked up and met Saige's eyes.

"It's up to you, where we go from here. I can take the block off. Or I can put it in again, stronger, or I can fully erase the worst memories."

Saige coughed twice.

"You know what. I think I'm okay. I don't want the full block. Maybe my mind is forcing me to remember, for my safety, like you said. I don't want to take it off either, though. If I keep some of it gone, then great. Until the wall fully comes down, I think I'll be okay."

"What about your flashbacks?"

Cara said, holding the clipboard steady on her lap.

"I don't want to be hypnotized again. Talking about it helps a lot."

Saige pulled herself to her feet, out of the comfort of the egg chair.

"I appreciate you listening to me, Cara."

Cara smiled again, softly.

"I'm not just a hypnotist. I'm also a therapist. It's what I'm here for, sweetheart."

Saige gave Cara a hug. She felt like their relationship was more than client-therapist, but friend-friend.

Saige started for the door, but when she reached it, she turned back to Cara, who was reaching for a Kleenex box on the coffee table.

"Cara."

Cara flinched and looked up.

"Yes, Sai?"

Saige pursed her lips and bit her cheek.

"You can talk to me too. Is everything okay?"

That little act of friendship seemed to shatter Cara completely. She broke down, crying.

"My brother was found this morning, stabbed to death in the forest at Woodland Park."

Saige's jaw dropped. She crossed the room and hugged Cara tightly.

"Cara! I'm so sorry!"

Saige said softly. And she was. She felt terrible. She'd never known Cara's brother, but she did know Cara and him were close.

"He didn't deserve it. Josh was a good kid."

"I'm sure he was. No one deserves to die."

"He was only sixteen."

Cara whispered. Saige didn't know what to say.

"He was looking for his girlfriend. He texted me telling me that he was positive Taylor took her. I don't know who Taylor is. I don't know anything. I miss him. My brother. Poor Josh."

Cara was crying and sobbing. Saige had no idea what to do. Then something switched in Cara. She wiped her face with her sleeve.

"I'm sorry, Sai. So unprofessional of me."

"It's okay."

"You better go now. I have another client in five."

Saige nodded.

"You'll be okay, Care."

Cara half-heartedly smiled at her.

Saige shut the door behind her as she left. She exited the building, feeling utterly devastated for Cara. She liked her a lot. She didn't deserve to lose her best friend. It hadn't seemed to matter that she and Josh were fifteen years apart. As far as Saige knew, the two told each other everything.

She slowly climbed into Matt's car. Cara's loss weighed heavily on Saige. She wasn't sure why. She shook her head and thought about what Cara had said about Samuel Thomas and Michael. She couldn't really make out Samuel's face, but she was certain that there was zero connection between them. Michael was warm and friendly. Samuel was a cold-blooded killer. Saige couldn't help but to think about how Samuel hadn't been caught after she'd escaped. He'd simply disappeared. She tried not to think about the possibilities of hair dye, coloured contacts, or facial reconstruction.

11

He stood at the door; ear pressed against it. He couldn't hear anything from the inside. He prayed she wasn't dead. She was still useful. She satisfied his needs. Upon not hearing anything, he slowly pushed open the door. He saw her laying on the ground, next to the puddle of blood he so recently lifted that kid, Josh, from. A small smile crept onto his face.

That kill was thrilling. He'd disposed of a threat. He'd disposed of someone trying to get between him and his girl. He zoned back in on Mya and saw Saige's face take over Mya's body. He suddenly felt awful. He rushed into the room and pulled Mya into his lap. She was passed out, but still breathing. He brushed her hair behind her ear.

"I'm so sorry you had to see that, Sai."

He whispered, tears filling his eyes. Mya twitched in his arms. He held her tighter, sobbing softly over her still body. Her eyelids fluttered. She opened them, finally and looked up. She saw him, holding her, crying, his eyes closed. This was the first time she'd ever seen him show emotion, other than his usual, sadistic smile. She didn't move.

"I'm sorry, Sai, I'm so sorry baby. I wish I didn't have to but she stood between us. I love you, Sai. I love you."

He was muttering. Mya didn't dare move. She'd never seen him so unguarded.

"I'll take care of you. I'll take care of us. We only need each other, Sai."

Mya regulated her breathing, trying to control her heartbeat so she didn't give herself away.

Who is Sai?

She wondered to herself. She closed her eyes again, trying her best to focus on her memories as far back as she could possibly remember. Was she connected in any way to this 'Sai' person? Is that why he'd taken her? She couldn't figure out if she knew her. 'Sai' didn't ring any bells. Didn't even come close to ringing any bells. She slowly opened her eyes again and gasped, flinching in his arms. He was staring down at her with wide, wild eyes. As soon as their eyes connected, his gorgeous limpid pools of blue turned dark, so dark they almost blended into his pupils.

"You're not my Sai."

Mya froze. He shoved her off of his lap and scrambled backwards.

"You're not her."

He whispered. His hands flew up to his face, covering it. Mya swore he was sobbing. She slowly shook her head, even though she knew he couldn't see her.

"No, I'm not. But...but if you let me go, I'll...I'll help you find her."

She whispered, unsure if her bait would catch the fish. He slowly raised his head. Mya's breath caught in her throat as she noticed his eyes were back to normal. She thought it was strange that they could turn so dark so quickly. Tears sparkled on his cheeks.

"You'd do that for me?"

She nodded quickly, maybe a little too quickly.

"Let me go and I'll help you find whomever you'd like."

He started to smile. Mya noticed it wasn't his typical sick, twisted smile. Instead it was a warm, heartfelt one that spread like sunshine across his face. Mya slowly stood up.

"So, let's go."

She gave him a soft smile and turned her back on him. She started walking to the door. He pushed himself off the ground and clenched his fists. He stared at the back of her head as she walked towards the door. He started breathing heavier, his face going red.

"You liar!"

The two words exploded from his chest. Mya inhaled a sharp puff of air and lurched for the door. She started twisting the knob. When she found out it was locked, she started banging with her fists, screaming.

He sprinted across the room and grabbed her by the shoulders, pulling her away from the door, throwing her like a rag doll over his shoulder and onto the floor.

"You're a filthy little liar!"

He screamed, while standing over her as she lay on her back, tears brimming her eyes. She held her hands up as some sort of shield to protect herself in case he swung.

"Taylor...Taylor, it's okay."

"My name's not Taylor!"

He screamed, cutting her off. He bent down and grabbed her throat in his hand. She pushed on his chest with her hands.

"No! No stop!"

She cried, the tears trickling down her cheeks. He tightened his grip around her neck, pulling her to a sitting position so he could stare into her frightened eyes.

"My name's not Taylor! It's not Taylor!"

He tightened his grip even more until his fingers were touching each other. Mya's face turned red. He dug his finger nails into his skin, making half-moon indents along her skin. She grabbed at his arms and hands making a feeble attempt to pry him off of her. She was too weak. Tears were falling from his eyes, running down his face.

"My name's not Taylor and you're not Sai."

Mya's eyes rolled to the back of her head. Her face went from red to purple. Her hand stopped grabbing at his, hers going limp. He leaned down so his lips were next to her ears.

"My name isn't Taylor. It's Sam."

He pushed her backwards. She fell over onto the ground, eyes closed, lips slightly parted. He fell backwards as well, sitting down about one foot away from her. He wiped his hands off on his jeans. He stared at the corpse, a change of heart quickly setting over him.

What have I done?

His hands covered his mouth. Tears started up again. He pulled his knife from his belt and looked at Mya.

"Look what you made me do! Look what you made me do!"

He cried. The tears were flowing down his cheeks. He clambered back over to her body and knelt over top of it. He plunged the hunting knife into her stomach. Blood spurted from the wound.

"I didn't want to do this! It could have been different!"

He brought the knife back down into her skin through the torn remnants of her clothing again and again. The tears wouldn't stop. Blood gushed everywhere, splashing onto his skin and clothes, drenching his face. The metallic, iron flavour of Mya's blood mixed together with the saltiness of his tears.

Several minutes later, he finally crawled away from the body. He shook his head and smacked himself, open handed.

"Sam, you idiot. It should have been different."

He whimpered. He smacked himself again. He sat in silence for what seemed like forever. It was the ringing of his cell phone that interrupted the silence. He slid the phone out of his pocket, careful not to get any blood on it, his hands shaking.

"Hello?"

He answered quietly, like he was afraid he'd wake up Mya. He looked at the corpse as if he expected it to zombify.

"Where are you?"

He instantly recognized Bella's shrill voice. And then it hit him. He'd forgotten about their dinner date with Saige.

"Sorry, I got held up."

He responded, pulling himself to his feet. He stepped over Mya's corpse and let himself out of the room.

"Held up where?"

Bella demanded. He could hear the anger in her voice. It was traced with jealousy. He knew the hint of jealousy whenever he heard it.

"At home. I'll be there soon. Goodbye Bella."

He hung up before she could interrogate him some more. He was standing in his hallway now, in front of the door with Mya's corpse behind it.

He slowly walked down the hallway, making his way to the bathroom. He stared at himself in the mirror. God. He looked like hell. He had dark circles under his eyes and his dirty face had jagged streaks that the tears had left behind. Blood spattered against his face, clothes and hands. His fingernails had chunks of Mya's skin and blood caked under them.

He figured he could just wash his face, but now, after seeing his appearance, he realized he'd definitely need a shower. He turned away from the mirror, his reflection haunting him. He reached into the bathtub and turned the tap into a gentle spray from the shower head. He peeled his clothes off, one by one until he was fully naked.

He held back the shower curtain and slowly climbed into the shower. He stood under the hot spray, letting it rinse his body of the blood and grime. He already felt rejuvenated. He looked down and saw black streaks running down his body.

What the fuck?

He thought. And then it hit him.

"Fuck!"

He cried. In a flash he shut off the shower and jumped out of the tub, almost tripping over the edge. He stared into the mirror. His hair was still black, but he knew now that the colour would start fading. Any day now. He'd need to stop and buy more.

He didn't look at himself for long. His phone started ringing again. He saw Bella's name pop up on his caller I.D. He rolled his eyes. He let it ring. He left the bathroom without looking in the mirror again. The phone continued to ring annoyingly in his hand. He moved across the hallway and entered the room directly across the hall from the bathroom.

It was used as a makeshift bedroom. He slept in there when he had to. When he felt like being closer to his girls. He always kept backup clothes in the armoire in that room. He always kept the bed tidy and made. He was obsessive about keeping that room in order.

He pulled open the doors to armoire and pulled out a pair of nice, blue jeans and a sport jacket. He pried a dress shirt off of a hanger. He wanted to impress Saige. His phone started ringing again. He looked down and once again saw Bella's name pop up, and once again, he decided he didn't want to deal with her. He ignored the call.

Instead, he finished dressing and looked at himself in the mirror behind the door. If he didn't know any better, he could easily pass off as a normal guy.

He left the bedroom and walked swiftly through the cabin and truly realized how quiet it was. Usually he'd hear the screaming and pathetic crying of the girls, his girls, the ones that just didn't work out.

The moment he was outside, his phone went off for the billionth time. He checked the caller I.D, expecting to see Bella's name flashing brightly across the screen. He thought his eyes were deceiving him. Instead of Bella, he saw Saige's name pop up.

So, she'd never actually given him her number, but he knew it. He'd made it the first number in his phone. He knew it.

He almost pressed answer, but re-thought it. He hadn't answered for Bella. How obsessive would it look if he answered for Saige? It killed him not to answer the phone. But he didn't. He let it continue until it finally died down. He bit one of his knuckles and held back the tears. Disappointing Saige was the hardest thing he would ever have to do. He continued on toward the front door of the log cabin. He squeezed his phone in his hands.

"Call back. Come on. Please call back."

He whispered. He wanted to hear her voice. He wanted to listen to the whimsical sound of her angelic voice. He couldn't think of anything better than sitting with her, listening to her talk day by day. He could dream.

He made it to the front door and looked around the kitchen to the cabin. Still kind of messy. He would need to clean up next time he was back there. He reached for the knob of the aged wooden door when his wish was granted. The phone had barely started to ring. He didn't look down at the caller I.D. He just pressed the green answer button before the end of the first jingle.

"Bella! I said I'll be there shortly. Just give me a minute!"

He said sharply.

"Hi Michael, it's Saige."

He was pulling open the door when she spoke. Her voice was as sweet as sugar tasted.

"Oh, hi Saige."

He said, trying to keep his voice steady. He shut the door behind him and began walking towards his car. It was a black Chevrolet Cobalt SS. He clicked the button on his key fob, unlocking the car from a distance.

"Bella was wondering when you'll be here. We haven't ordered yet."

He felt horrible. He was keeping his precious girl from eating.

"Oh, Saige, don't worry about me. Don't let me stop you from ordering."

He felt himself saying.

"Tell Bella I apologize for being so late. I got held up at home and then my mother called me. I'll be there in a flash. I'm just getting in my car."

He got into the car and slammed the door shut to make his point.

"Okay, see you soon."

Saige responded. She could practically taste the urgency to find an excuse in his voice, on her tongue. They clicked off the phone and he turned the key in the ignition, starting the engine. His car came rumbling to life. He was so frustrated with how disorganized Bella made him. She was completely ruining his routine. And she was one hundred percent fucking up his thoughts. He drove quickly, not paying too much attention to the road.

He had somewhere to be and people to see. People to see...He chuckled. Saige. He had his baby. His gorgeous Saige to see.

His car tore through the roads, passing people, children and pets alike, zipping in and out of side streets, trying to use low traffic areas to minimize his chances of being pulled over. Of course, Bella picked the restaurant located the farthest possible distance from anywhere convenient. He was so pissed.

He'd passed a Flying Squirrel, Ridge Tavern, Ridgeway's, and even a Castaways Grill and Bar. Any one of those would have sufficed, but of course not. Not nice enough for angel Bella. He scoffed. Angel. Please. In what world was Bella an angel? He hoped this restaurant would be nice enough for his real angel.

All of a sudden, every thought he was having dropped from his mind. He heard sirens. He looked into his rear-view mirrors and saw the flashing red and blue lights.

Fuck. Fuck.

He thought. Now he had two options. Pull over or car chase.

He quickly shook his head.

Don't be stupid. Don't give them a reason to arrest you. They won't.

He slowed down and signaled that he was pulling over. He came to a stop on the side of the road. The white and blue police cruiser pulled over behind him. He reached over and hit the glove compartment door. It popped open and he pulled out some papers. He sat up straight, calmly. He dealt with officers often enough in his life. He checked out his side mirrors. He watched the cop approach his already lowered window.

"License and registration."

He said sternly, without looking up from his notepad. He knew the cop was writing a speeding ticket. He handed the two pieces of legal work out the window.

"Do you know how fast you were go—Hey! You're..."

"Yes. I am. Hi Jack."

He smiled out the window towards the cop. The cop tucked the notepad back into his belt and reached a hand through the window. He shook Jack's hand forcefully.

"Why are you in such a hurry, bud?"

The cop's whole demeanor changed. He handed the paperwork back through the window and bent over, crossing his arms over the window ledge, leaning on them.

"Supposed to be meeting with a potential client. I'm about forty-five minutes late."

Jack, the cop, half laughed.

"That's the you I know. Hey, where's that gorgeous mustang o' yours?"

He shrugged, lifting a hand into the air.

"Shop. Thing's giving me a headache. Might sell it."

Jack's eyes lit up. A massive grin spread across his face.

"Come to me first, eh?"

He did his best to smile back warmly.

"You know I will, good sir."

"I don't want to keep you any longer, man. You've got my number. We should get together one night with our ladies. Have a barbecue or something."

"Sure thing, Jack. I'll get in contact with you lãter. See you."

He started to roll the window back up. Jack stood up fully.

"Just slow down a little bit okay?"

"Anything you say, Jack. Catch you later about getting together."

He finished rolling his window up, shoulder checked that no one was coming up behind the two of them parked on the road and signaled his way off the shoulder and back onto the pavement.

He grumbled to himself as he looked out the rear-view mirror and watched Jack climb back into the cruiser before it was lost from his sight.

After what seemed like too long, he reached the restaurant. It was called 'The Phoenix' and he was pleased to learn there was valet parking. Maybe this place would be satisfactory enough for his precious angel.

He was also curious as to how college students could afford this kind of luxurious fine dining. He pulled up to the nicely dressed valet and put the car in 'park' and then got out.

He looked at the man, a short, Mexican fellow who had a skinny black mustache lining his upper lip and a big, white smile. He read the name on the name tag, stating that the valet's name was Juarez.

He tried his best to give him a convincing smile. He placed the keys in Juarez' hand.

"Take care of it, my good man."

Juarez peered past him at the black car.

"Sure thing, senor."

He smiled at Juarez, who got in the car to park it a couple of yards away, after handing him a pink slip of paper with a number written on it.

He turned and walked steadily through the massive doorways and found himself in an exquisite looking dining area. He admired the red carpet, the huge archways he passed under to be fully inside. The walls had mirrors that extended almost to the ceiling. They were lined with gold and diamond trim. He had never felt so out of place before.

He scanned the restaurant. It wasn't overly busy. There were three couples sitting a couple of tables apart from each other. He immediately felt under dressed in his blue jeans and coat. The males of the couples were in full suits.

"Table for one?"

He turned from the dining area and came eye to eye with a hostess and smiled.

"There's a reservation. Donaldson."

He responded. The hostess gave him her best toothy grin.

"Oh! Donaldson! Sure thing, sir. Follow me."

She turned her back and walked out of the main dining hall. He looked around before following her.

"Where are we going?"

He felt inclined to ask. He wanted to be sure that nothing was going to surprise him. No one was going to ambush him. The hostess kept walking and pointed ahead of her.

"Miss Donaldson requested the four of you eat in private. In one of the ballrooms."

She paused as they reached another massive oak doorway, which had a sleek, shiny finish to it.

"Restaurant and ballrooms?"

He questioned. The hostess grabbed both door handles.

"The ballrooms are hardly used. Only for special occasions or on request."

She flashed him another dazzling smile.

"I present to you, the Sierra room."

With a flawless flourish, she pushed open the double doors and he found himself starting at what could be perhaps the most stunning room he had ever laid eyes on. He was in complete and total awe.

The floors were made of white marble, the incredibly expensive kind, and it glittered and sparkled up at him under the overhead lights. The ceiling arched high over his head. The walls were made of glass and dark ebony wooden trim. More mirrors that made it look even bigger. Soft, classical music was playing in the background. He recognized it as something by Tchaikovsky.

"Finally!"

He recognized the shrill squeal instantly. It echoed around the room. The beauty quickly shattered as Bella suddenly appeared in front of him, throwing her arms around his neck, hugging him tightly. He hugged her back and then twisted out of her arms. Looking at her was like a throwback to the nineteen fifties. Her blonde hair was done up, pin-up girl style, her lips had a red lip stick on them. Her overly make-upped eyes were done in a smoky eye style. His eyes travelled down her body. She had a tight-fitting red dress on and some sparkly, diamond encrusted jewelry hanging around her neck and wrists.

"So how do I look?"

She asked, smiling massively. He noticed a little bit of red lipstick on her teeth. He would let it slide without telling her.

"Beautiful."

He still felt very under dressed. Bella grabbed his hand.

"C'mon."

She said. She led him back to the table in the middle of the room. He didn't see Saige.

"Matt, this is Michael. Michael, Matt."

Finally, he could put a face to that name that kept popping up.

"Nice to meet you."

He said, reaching across the table to shake Matt's hand. Matt shook it firmly, trying to put across an alpha feel towards him.

"Watch out for this one, man."

Matt teased, nodding at Bella. Her jaw dropped.

"Hey!"

She exclaimed. Matt laughed loudly.

"I'm kidding. Jesus."

He pretended to laugh and tried to keep his mind off of where Saige could be. He pulled a chair out that was situated between Bella and the empty spot that he knew was Saige's.

"We've already ordered appies."

Matt said. He nodded and picked up a menu from the side of the table.

"Hi! I'm back! Oh! Hi Michael!"

He immediately perked up, and then hoped he wasn't too obvious in his joy that Saige had returned. He slowly lowered his menu and he swore, his heart stopped.

Saige's hair was half up, half down, curls framing her face. She had minimal makeup; liner and mascara, and a little bit of pink lip gloss shimmered on her lips. Her outfit of choice...a dark, plum coloured dress that reached the floor and flowed around her feet. It was strapless and fit her tightly until it expanded into a flowing A-line style at her waist. She looked stunning.

Breath-taking.

She shocked him again when she didn't sit down right away. Instead she stood next to him.

"Don't I get a hug?"

She asked, smiling. He pushed himself away from the table and stood up next to her. She slid her arms around his waist and he wrapped his around her neck, hugging her close to him.

It felt too soon that it ended.

"Allow me."

He said as he grabbed the back of her chair and pulled it away from the table for her.

"Why thank you."

She smiled at him and sat down, brushing her long skirt under the table cloth. He sat down between her and Bella who automatically grabbed his hand. He saw Saige lean over and press her lips gently into Matt's.

He felt his blood start to boil. That was not okay with him. Not in the slightest. He had to ignore it. Couldn't allow himself to show anger. Not yet.

"We've already ordered appies."

Saige said to him as his eyes scanned the menu. He wasn't really seeing what was on it. Saige completely took over his thoughts. There was no light chatter amongst the four of them as they waited for their waitress to return. He was curious.

"So, how do you guys afford this place?"

He caught Bella's gleaming, proud smile.

"My dad owns the restaurant. None of us have to pay tonight."

She was bragging. He knew she was bragging. He wanted to strangle her.

"Anyway, you got that poem for me yet?"

Saige asked, changing the subject. He smiled at her, sitting next to him.

"I wrote it the other day."

He saw Saige's eyes light up.

"I don't suppose you brought it with you, hey?"

He shook his head, feeling sad and upset with himself for disappointing her.

"That sucks...Next time!"

She said, smiling. She touched his hand gently. He really didn't want to disappoint her. Not ever.

"I know it, though. I could recite it for you."

He piped up. Saige's smile returned. He looked around the table, meeting Bella's adoring stare and Matt's blank gaze.

"That is, if it is okay with both of you."

Matt slowly nodded and reached up, taking Saige's hand. Bella latched onto his, smiling widely at him.

"So romantic."

She gushed. He tried to give the best heartwarming smile that he could muster. Before he could start the poem, a redheaded waitress stepped up to their table.

"Miss Donaldson, I was just wondering if y'all were ready to order? Y'all's appies are on the way."

He noticed she had a slight southern drawl. Texas. He figured.

"Thanks, Hannah. I think so. You guys?"

Bella looked around the table. Saige and Matt nodded.

"Yea. We're ready if you are."

He nodded his head as well.

"All on one bill?"

Hannah asked. Bella shot her a menacing glare.

"Daddy said we don't have to pay tonight."

Oh great. I have to pretend to be into a chick that calls her father, 'Daddy'.

He desperately wanted to kill her then so that he could be out of that miserable hell hole.

"Oh, yes. That's right. I'm so sorry, Miss Donaldson."

Hannah apologized promptly. She had her notebook in hand, pen stuck between her thumb and index finger.

"What can I get for y'all?"

She twanged.

"I'll get the tossed salad, please."

Bella said, smiling at Hannah, but clinging to his hand. He could see the look of pure rage in her eyes.

"Lobster. Babe?"

Matt said next. He squeezed Saige's hand in his. Saige bit her lip.

"I'm kind of torn between the tossed salad and a big ol slab of ribs."

She paused momentarily.

"Screw it. I'll get the ribs. Please."

Hannah chuckled but wrote the order down on her notepad. Bella was staring at Saige in shock.

"Sai."

She said. Matt patted Saige's hand.

"That's my girl."

He muttered affectionately. Hannah looked between Saige and Bella, directly at him. She smiled at him and he smiled back. He admired her eyes. They were bright, emerald green. Beautiful.

"What about for you, sir?"

She twanged happily.

"Steak, rare. Baked potato. Thank you."

He said, even toned. Hannah flashed him a dazzling smile and wrote that down too.

"Let me know if I can get y'all anything else."

Right as she said those words, a male server entered the exquisite room, carrying a massive, heavy looking tray loaded with appetizer platters.

"Cactus cut potato chips. Bacon wrapped steak skewers. Calamari. Enjoy."

The server did a half bow and backed out of the room followed by Hannah. They left just as quickly as he'd entered.

"Oh, yum!"

Saige said, her reach extending towards a bacon wrapped steak skewer. Matt and Bella dug into the cactus cut potatoes.

"So. Michael. The poem."

Bella said through a stuffed mouth. He looked at her, a slight grimace on his face.

"Bella..."

Saige muttered, trailing off after swallowing her bite. Bella realized she had spoken with her mouth full. She brought a hand to her mouth and covered it.

"Sorry."

She mumbled through the food stuffed in there. He turned his face towards Saige who took a delicate bite of the skewer.

"You want to hear it?"

He asked, genuine sincerity in his voice. Saige nodded, staring deep into his eyes. He took a deep breath and dug into his memory, grabbing the poem he'd written the day she first spoke to him, out of his mind.

"My mind, my soul, my entire body feels weak. My spirit feels shattered. Until I see her. She sits there. Like an angel sent from the heavens. She deserves the best. Pain shoots through me. I am not the best. I sit still, motionless. Watching her. Loving her from afar. If only she knew. If only she knew. I get cold. I get cold waiting for her. Until the day she remembers our love. I will wait. I will watch. I will always love. Her."

Saige's breath caught in her throat. Bella's jaw dropped. Matt sat still, blank faced.

"It's still a work in progress..."

"It was beautiful!"

Bella and Saige interrupted him in unison. He sat back in his chair; a small smile crept onto his face.

"It was okay. Like you said. Work in progress."

Matt said suddenly. Saige playfully shoved his arm.

"Matt."

She exclaimed. Bella shot a death glare at him.

"It was gorgeous."

She said, through gritted teeth. He stretched his arms over his head. He could practically taste Matt's jealousy on his tongue. He certainly felt it rippling over his skin. He felt goose bumps.

"Matt's right. It was okay."

He said, looking across the table at Matt. He smirked. He saw Matt flinch in his seat, anger and jealousy coursing through his veins. He had Saige's attention. Matt didn't. Right now, he was winning.

Saige touched his hand.

"It was beautiful, okay?"

Bella touched his other hand.

"Yea, baby. It was."

He paid Bella no mind. He stared at Saige.

"Well, thank you."

He and Saige seemed to be lost in their own world. That's what it felt like to him. He couldn't even see Bella or Matt, although he knew they were there, staring at Saige and himself. He had to break their moment. He didn't want to, but he knew he had to.

"So. How about this calamari?"

He said, grabbing a piece from the plate.

"Ugh, I still can't believe you ordered that appy, Sai. It still has its legs!"

Bella exclaimed. Saige chuckled and plucked a piece as well. She popped it into her mouth and chewed, satisfied.

"Tentacles, Bell. They're called tentacles."

Bella gagged. Saige looked at him, they both had mouthfuls of calamari. Saige covered her mouth with her hand right before a huge laugh could erupt from the deepest parts of her belly. He swallowed but not before almost choking on a tentacle.

"Is everything okay, Matt?"

Bella suddenly asked. He and Saige turned their attention to Matt, who was sitting silently, just staring into nothing. Saige touched his hand softly.

"Matt?"

She said quietly. Matt jerked away and seemed to re-focus on what was happening. Saige was taken aback by Matt's pulling away.

"Sorry, sorry babe."

He said quickly, re-taking her hand in his, intertwining their fingers together.

"Is everything okay?"

Saige said, repeating what Bella had previously asked. Matt nodded, smiling at Saige.

"Yea, I'm great. Just got my mind on my human kinetics papers."

Saige patted his hand.

"Don't think about school tonight. We're having fun."

Matt sighed.

"Well, I have to think about it a little bit. One more visit with Williams and that's it for me."

He could feel Saige tense up beside him.

"You're so smart, though!"

She forgot about him. She forgot about Bella sitting mere inches from her.

"Is that what he said in your meeting?"

Saige said, her voice shaking. Matt's eyes darted towards Bella and then him. Matt certainly hadn't forgotten about them. He glanced back to Saige; whose eyes had gone watery.

"Maybe we should talk about this later."

He said softly. Saige wiped at her eyes.

"Yes. Yes of course. This isn't the place."

She turned towards Bella.

"Sorry Bells. Sorry Michael."

She didn't face him. They sat in an uncomfortable silence for what seemed like hours. He picked at the last bits of calamari. Saige screwed around with a pile of wooden skewers. Matt fidgeted. Bella chewed her lip and studied her nails.

Another few silent minutes passed and the door to the room swung open, clanging against the wall with a loud bang. He sat up straight and looked towards the door. Hannah was back, a big silver tray hoisted over her shoulder.

"Alright."

She drawled as she approached the table.

"Tossed salad for Miss Donaldson."

Hannah said as she set a fair-sized bowl filled with green lettuce and spinach, tomatoes, cheese flakes, a couple of mushrooms and carrots garnishing it, in front of her.

"Slab of barbecue ribs for Miss D'Leo."

Hannah juggled the tray in one hand while barely managing to place a tray of ribs the size of Saige's head in front of her. The barbecue sauce was dribbling over the side of the platter.

"Lobster for Mister Grant."

Hannah placed a medium sized lobster in front of Matt. The butter was melting over it, bubbling slightly.

"And finally, steak and a baked potato for Mister..."

She paused and looked at him apologetically.

"Michael. Michael's fine. Thank you, Hannah."

He piped up, saving her from embarrassment. She put his dish on the empty spot in front of him. He looked down at it. A pool of red surrounded the steak. He picked up his dinner knife and fork, stabbing the two utensils into the meat so violently, the table shook. The steak started to bleed a little bit more. He cut off a small bite. The inside of the meat was a perfect pink. He smiled and popped the bite into his mouth. He looked up from the dish.

Matt, Saige and Bella were all staring at him. Bella's face was twisted into a sickened, distorted expression.

"What?"

He asked, after swallowing.

"How do you eat that? It's bleeding so much!"

Bella exclaimed, coughing. He shrugged.

"Gives it more flavour."

A loud, guttural laugh exploded from Saige's gut.

12

PJ held her head in her hands, her chin resting in her palms.

"Cheer up, P. You know what this means?"

Brock exclaimed, hand on her shoulder. He squeezed gently. PJ sighed heavily.

"It means Mya was alive. Was. Earlier. Who knows if she still is."

Brock squeezed her shoulder again.

"No. It means we may have a lead. If GPS is turned on, Ella can track its location."

PJ lifted her head and turned in her chair, Brock's hand falling from her shoulder. She looked at him.

"That's a big ol 'if' Brock. What if it's not?"

She felt frustrated and drained.

"Then we can see which cell tower it pinged off of. That's a start. Investigate the radius around it. Investigate the area a few kilometers around it. We will find something."

"I'm glad you have more confidence than I do."

PJ said gingerly. Brock grabbed both of her shoulders and pulled, effectively bringing her to her feet.

"P. You have got to think positively."

PJ brushed his hands off of her and swiveled around. She stared at the white board. Only one name was written on it. David Swanson.

"That's hard to do when you keep getting a big steaming pile of shit."

She replied, grumpily. Brock didn't know how to answer. PJ was one of his closest friends. He loved her dearly, but when she got into this negative state of mind, there was no trying to get her to see any other kind of light. He would just let her crawl out of the pit she'd put herself in.

PJ threw her hands in the air and let out an exasperated sigh. She slammed her hands down onto the table in front of her.

"I need someone to tell me what to do."

As if on cue, Brinker burst into the room.

"Chief. Richards. You'd both probably be interested in joining me."

He said breathily. Brock and PJ both looked at him.

"What's going on?"

Brock asked. Brinker gestured at them to hurry.

"Janet got back to me with a profile. The BAU's put together a good one."

PJ leapt into the air.

"Finally!"

She yelled. She grabbed Brock's elbow and pulled him out the door past Brinker. He followed her down the hallway. Upon reaching the conference room, PJ was slightly surprised to see it so full. She expected the feds that she'd been introduced to, Daniel and Phil and herself. Who she also saw where a few other detectives and a Sergeant, one above herself, Raymond Telley.

"If you'd both take a seat."

Brinker asked, sternly. PJ flopped down between Daniel and Raymond Telley. Brock sat opposite her. Brinker paced in front of the group of officers and Agents.

"I've invited Detectives Brady and Sheen, as well as Sergeant Telley to join us. I've also invited another Agent of mine, Agent Dilworth. You all know PJ Richards. She is lead on this case with myself. I want all of you to listen to her. If she has any concerns, you are to help. Now, Janet Ellings at the BAU has gotten me a profile of a likely unsub. Listen carefully."

Brinker paused, looking around the room. He nodded at every person, who all nodded back, showing the SAC their utmost respect and attention. Brinker tapped the envelope in his hands right before ripping open the seal and sliding the important piece of documentation out and tossing the envelope to the side.

"Our unsub is likely a man, judging by the brutal beatings. The bruising is differentiated, unlikely caused by a blunt object. The way the bodies are found is unfeeling. If a woman had done it, now I don't mean to be sexist, but had a woman done this, she would have clothed them, maybe washed them and cleaned them up. The way our guy murders these girls is way over kill.

"He's getting angry with them. Goes into some kind of rage. One of the connecting factors is each girl had a younger boyfriend. He could have been fucked over by an older girl before. However, a second connector is the University. He's been snagging girls attending or visiting the school.

"He seems to know their routine, he knew each was going to be where they were, when they were at the times they were. He's been watching. Observing. He probably doesn't go to the school. He probably has a decent job, perhaps a blossoming career. He is probably attractive. He probably looks easy to approach. He's probably late twenties, early thirties. He'll be quiet, reserved but friendly.

"He'll become infatuated with people quickly. He'll be tidy. Organized. He won't be someone you could pick out from a crowd. He'll be as ordinary as he can be, to be hidden in plain sight."

Brinker paused, letting the new information sink into the observers. PJ's jaw dropped. Her eyes widened. The room was silent.

"Mom. Melissa's...she's right."

PJ said through tears.

"She was right. That's why she's gone now. Mom, listen to me. Please."

PJ was holding onto her mom's arm. Lauri Richards was staring blankly at the wall.

"Mom!"

PJ screamed, shaking her mother's arm. Lauri snapped back to reality.

"Penny Jane Richards, control yourself. Do you realize how idiotic you sound?"

PJ dropped her arm.

"You...Melissa's been kidnapped! We didn't listen to her before. She was afraid and we didn't listen! Mom!"

Lauri brought an open palm across PJ's face. PJ stumbled backwards, putting her own hand over her stinging cheek.

"You're a bitch. You're an unfeeling, heartless bitch."

PJ spat. Lauri stood up.

"Go to your room!"

She yelled. PJ didn't move.

"You didn't believe her.'

Her voice wavered slightly.

"Neither did you."

Lauri retorted, snorting. PJ's eyes were watery.

"No. I didn't. And I should have. We both should have."

Lauri and PJ stood face to face, not speaking. PJ finally dropped her eyes to the floor and shook her head.

"I can't even believe you."

She muttered. Lauri didn't answer. She turned away from PJ.

"I saw him."

PJ said. Lauri didn't turn to look at her.

"He talked to me and Melissa."

She kept talking.

"A few days ago. Mellie and I were walking home. She was telling me about him. I didn't believe her. But we both had a feeling we were being followed. I turned to see and there he was. But he was nice and really cute. Blonde hair. Blue eyes. Very good looking, surfer dude complex. He had that going on. I asked him if he was following us. He said, no. That's silly. He lived the same way. I felt Melissa tensing up beside me. He introduced himself to me as Sam Thomas. He didn't even pay attention to Mellie...When we got home, she said, that's him.

"He's the one. PJ please. Please believe me.' I still didn't. He was too cute and too into me to be her stalker. So, I ended up continuing to talk to him. I actually ended up going out with him.

Like on a date. Remember when I said I was going to the library? Well I went out with him. He was so sweet..."

"How do you know it was him? He's too nice and cute."

PJ knew Lauri was mocking her.

"Because...Because he left me a note the day Mellie disappeared. He said, 'I'm going to date your sister instead."

"PJ? PJ are you okay?"

PJ blinked a couple times and realized she was still in the meeting. She sucked in a deep breath and choked on it. She coughed a couple of times.

"She looks like she's seen a ghost."

Someone in the room commented. PJ felt her stomach turn. She stood up and walked to the garbage bin, dipped her head inside and heaved, promptly puking up her guts.

"Someone, get her a glass of water. Now!"

Brinker shouted over the sudden commotion. Someone else was rubbing her back. She straightened, slowly, just as Phil was extending a small paper cup of water towards her. She took it, tossed it back and gargled before spitting it back into the cup. Daniel took the cup from her and disposed of it. Brinker grabbed both of her shoulders.

"What's going on, PJ?"

His voice was filled with genuine concern. He was looking right into her eyes. PJ turned her head and coughed again. She avoided coughing in his face. The stench of her vomit still heavy on her breath.

"His name is Samuel Thomas."

The entire room went from chaos to utter silence in point two seconds. Brinker stared at her.

"What are you talking about, Richards?"

PJ brushed Brinker's hand off of her shoulders.

"Everyone, please sit back down. I am about to tell you all something that I should have mentioned a long time ago."

PJ requested, not really caring if they did or not.

They did.

Brinker sat in the chair PJ had been in. They all gaped at her, not saying a word.

"His name, our unsub's name, is Samuel Thomas. I know this because I've met him. It was a few years ago, about thirteen, to be precise. He kidnapped and killed my sister. Her body was found the same as these girls. I thought it was purely coincidence until Agent

Brinker mentioned hiding in plain sight. That was his specialty. Samuel would probably be around thirty-two, thirty-three years old by now. When I met him, he was six feet, around one hundred and seventy pounds. He's got blonde hair and blue eyes. Thirteen years ago, he had no identifying marks visible. No scars. No tattoos. He'd kidnapped an eight-year-old girl about a year after my sister's death."

PJ paused, feeling tears sting her eyes.

"What happened to the girl?"

FBI Agent Hamm asked. PJ turned to him.

"I do not know. My family moved from that town about a week later. Too painful for us to stay there."

"How do you know this is his work?"

Brinker asked.

"This is Samuel. This has Samuel written all over it. If it isn't him, then it's a copycat."

PJ bit her lip and looked down.

"That's it."

She felt her knees go weak. She crumpled to the floor. Daniel and Brinker rushed to help her back up. Daniel had his arm around her waist. She felt too drained to stand. Brinker started barking orders.

"Hamm, Darbyshire, you two dig and see if you can find out what happened to that little girl. Is she still alive? Where is she now? Find out. You two, Dilworth. Walters. Find out what happened to Samuel Thomas. Was he incarcerated? Taken down? What happened? Go!"

The room jumped to life with activity as people responded to Brinker's barks. He turned to Daniel.

"You. I want you to take Brady and Maynard. Stake out the university. Watch for anyone suspicious that fits our description. You are to arrest anyone meeting our profile. Get anyone that looks like they shouldn't be there. We will figure out who is innocent later. We have one, maybe two days before he picks his next vic."

Daniel didn't hesitate. He wasn't about to argue with a federal officer. Brinker hooked his arm around PJ's waist.

"Okay, and you."

He said, looking at her. She shot him a look.

"Are you okay to give the description to your sketch artist?"

PJ nodded.

"I'm having a press conference in the morning. It would be nice if I had a picture to go along with the information."

Brinker smiled at her.

"I don't think you should drive like this. I'll take you home after."

PJ wasn't about to argue. She thought was going to pass out. That wouldn't help her operate a motor vehicle. Brinker escorted her out of the chaotic room. PJ told him where Hank Tyler's office was. Hank Tyler was the best sketch artist for miles around. His steady hand and attention to detail made him the best.

Brinker knocked gently. It was almost eight pm. PJ was sure Hank would have left by then.

"Brinker, I don't think Hank is going to be in there."

PJ said, suddenly aware of how quietly she was speaking.

"If he isn't, we will call him."

Brinker was determined. PJ also became aware of how tense she was. Brinker's arm was still around her waist. She was exhausted, but she didn't want to lean against him. She couldn't let herself fall into his charm.

She had Nick. He was all she wanted. All she needed. Brinker knocked once more, a little louder.

"One minute!"

PJ and Brinker looked at each other. He was in there. The door swung open.

"PJ! Always nice to see your lovely face!"

Hank said excitedly as he pulled open the door.

"Hank, this is special Agent Brinker. James Brinker."

PJ said, the two men shook hands firmly.

"Who can I draw for the two of you?"

Hank asked and chuckled like he made a joke. He stepped to the side and held the door open wider for them to get inside. The office was messy. There was no question that it was an artists' studio. Half drawn sketches, ripped papers and notepads littered the floor. Pens, pencils and erasers were everywhere.

"Sorry about the mess."

Hank apologized. He took a seat at his desk. PJ and Brinker stood in front.

"His name is Samuel Thomas."

PJ began. Brinker's arm still snaked around her waist, holding her up. Hank pulled out a big sketch pad, flipping it open to a fresh page.

"Start with the face shape. Meaty? Baby faced? Pubescent?"

Hank said, pencil positioned over the paper.

"Squared. Chin went into a little rounded point. Strong jaw. Slim nose that also ends in a nice point. Almond shaped eyes. Lips are not too plump, not too thin. His eyes are blue."

PJ paused and watched intently as Hank's steady hand flew across the paper.

"What kind of blue?"

He asked without looking up. He picked up a box of pencil crayons.

"Ice. Cold. Very cold, icy blue eyes. And blonde hair. Like honey. Wavy."

PJ paused again.

"What kind of hairline?"

Hank asked, not taking his eyes off the forming masterpiece.

"A good one. It wasn't receding. It was very much there. I should mention that this description is from nearly thirteen years ago. He was around twenty when I met him. He's probably early thirties now."

Hank paused in the sketch but did not move his eyes.

"Any identifying marks? Tattoos? Scars? Birthmarks?"

PJ shook her head.

"None visible."

Hank bit his lip and furrowed his brow. Pencil returned to paper, moving rhythmically in quick, wild swipes.

"He was clean shaven back then."

PJ added. She swayed on her feet a little bit and felt Brinker's arm tighten, keeping her steady.

"Okay."

Hank said. He put the pencil down on the desk.

"I give you, Samuel Thomas."

He said, lifting the sketch book and turning it towards PJ and Brinker. PJ gasped and immediately her knees went weak, giving out on her. She fell towards the ground, but felt herself flop over Brinker's arms. Had he not been holding onto her; she would have toppled over right onto the ground. Her eyes welled up at the sight of the sketch.

Upon seeing it, she rapidly went back thirteen years.

She was cuddled against Samuel's side. Their first date. She hadn't thought his eyes were cold back then. They were sitting on the beach, it was evening, right before sunset. They were side by side, his arm around her waist, his free hand clutching hers. Her head was resting on his shoulder. The slight breeze lifted their hair playfully.

"This is so romantic, Sam."

She whispered. Samuel gave her hand a light squeeze.

"I'm glad I could share this with you, Penny. You're something."

He whispered back as the sun dipped below the horizon. The sky turned all sorts of pinks, oranges and yellows. It reminded her of Halloween candy.

The wind became brisker. PJ shivered against his side. He grabbed the edges of the blanket that was draped around their shoulders and pulled it tighter around them.

"You're right. This is romantic."

He whispered again, rubbing his face against her hair. She turned her face up to him. They stared into each other's eyes.

"You're so beautiful."

He murmured, not taking his eyes from hers. She blushed and looked away. His hand came up to her cheek, cupping it gently. He turned her face back to his.

"Can I kiss you?"

He whispered, stroking his thumb along the edge of her cheekbone. She gulped and nodded. His hand moved from her cheek, down to her chin and tilted her face up where her trembling lips met his. The kiss was an instant explosion. They were caught in a moment of such intensity.

A moment of a fiery passion for each other.

"I love you, Penny."

"PJ?"

Brinker's voice broke through the taunting image. She didn't hear Brinker. She heard Samuel. She opened her eyes and saw Sam's face on Brinker's body. She realized his arm was still around her.

"Don't touch me!"

She screamed. She clawed at Brinker's arm, prying it off of her waist. She tumbled to the ground and crawled away from him. Hank had put the sketch back down on the table.

"PJ, relax. PJ, it's me, it's Agent Brinker. James Brinker."

He exclaimed, taking a step towards her. He held up his hands in front of him to show her that he meant her no harm. He was safe. Tears had overflowed from her eyes. She pulled her knees up to her chest and breathed deeply.

"It's me. It's James."

He said again, in a calming tone. PJ looked up and focused on him. Samuel was gone. Brinker's face had returned. He reached her and slowly reached out. She grabbed his hand and pulled her to her feet. She wrapped her arms around his waist, hugging him firmly. He didn't know what to do. He settled for hugging her back, rubbing her back in small circles.

"That's him alright."

PJ murmured too quietly for Hank to hear. Brinker grabbed her shoulders and detached himself from her.

"Are you going to be able to do the press conference tomorrow?"

Brinker asked, staring into her eyes. She could see the overwhelming look of concern lingering in his. PJ brushed the tears from her eyes. She looked towards Hank. His hands were on his head, fingers twisted in his graying hair.

"Yes. I have too. That—you hit the nail on the head with that picture, Hank. At least, that's him. Thirteen years ago, that's him."

Hank relaxed his hands and let out a sigh.

"Are you going to be okay, P?"

He asked, leaning over his desk. PJ stepped away from Brinker and reached for the sketch book.

"I need to take this with me. For tomorrow."

Brinker grabbed PJ's wrist. He turned her to look at him again.

"Let me take it. It affects you so negatively. I'll deal with it."

PJ gave him a small smile. He returned it and averted his attention back to Hank. He picked up the book and tore the sketch from its place. He slowly folded it up and slid it into his pocket.

"Thank you for your help, Mister Tyler."

Brinker said, addressing Hank formally. Hank acknowledged him with a nod.

"Yes. Thank you, Hank. Sometimes I wish you weren't so good at your job."

PJ added, which resulted in a chuckle from Hank.

"Agent Brinker, I assume you're taking PJ home, yes?"

Hank asked, eyes on Brinker.

"You bet. Have a goodnight Mister Tyler."

Brinker turned towards the door, his arm hooked around PJ's waist again, keeping her steady.

"Goodnight Hank."

PJ shouted her goodbye just as Brinker shut the door behind them.

"I can probably just drive myself."

PJ began to say when they reached the outdoors. The sky was black, but sparkled with millions of glimmering stars.

"No. I won't allow it."

"But my car..."

PJ protested. She started to pull away from him, but he held his grip firm.

"I'll pick you up in the morning."

Brinker assured her. She realized then that she was not going to win that argument. She gave in and let Brinker walk her to his car. She let him open the passenger door and she let him help her inside the car. He climbed into the driver's seat, beside her and slid his key into the ignition. The newer model silently came to life, PJ was floored by how quiet it was.

The short drive to PJ's was also quiet. It was a comfortable silence. PJ was okay with not talking with him as he drove. Besides, it was a nice night. Why ruin it with pointless small talk?

"Great."

PJ finally did say as they pulled into her driveway. Nick's car was no longer in her driveway. She knew she'd upset him that morning, but she had a job to do.

"Everything okay?"

Brinker asked, the car idling in the driveway.

"Everything's fine..."

She paused and looked towards her darkened house. It seemed slightly disturbing with how silent it was.

"Thanks for the ride."

She said, un-buckling her safety belt with a click. She pushed the door open, but didn't get out right away.

"Uh, did, did you want to come in for a drink?"

She heard herself saying. She knew she'd caught the Agent off guard. She caught *herself* off guard.

"You don't have to."

PJ said quickly. She slid out of the car.

"Thanks again."

She shut the door firmly and turned for her front entrance. She heard the car shut off behind her, and then the door open and slam shut.

"I'd love to have a drink."

She heard him say from behind her. She paused in her walking and turned back towards him.

"I think I only have Budweiser."

She said in an apologetic voice. He smiled at her, making her feel less silly.

"That's perfectly fine. I'm a Budweiser kind of man."

She shot him a quick smile back and they walked up to the short stoop to the front door. She pulled her set of keys from her bag and slid one of the gold ones into the key hole. She was surprised to find the door unlocked. She resisted the urge to grab her twenty-two from her holster. Nick must have forgotten to lock it. No need to fret.

She pushed the door open, remaining calm. She was so glad that there were light switches right beside the door. She flipped all three to the up position. The room illuminated immediately. They entered her house through the kitchen.

"I'll grab us a couple of cold ones if you'd like to make yourself comfy. Living room is right through that door."

PJ gestured towards the door on the left of the kitchen. Brinker took off his glossy black shoes and placed them neatly beside the door. PJ crossed the kitchen to refrigerator. She caught sight of a small piece of paper in the middle of the fridge door.

"P—I have some things to do tonight for a client at work. I don't know when you'll be back, so I'll just stay at my place tonight. Hopefully see you tomorrow. Love you, Nick."

PJ rolled her eyes at the note.

"You're just mad with me because I couldn't spend the day with you."

She crumpled the note and tossed it like a basketball into the waste bin. She turned back around and pulled the fridge open. It looked pretty barren. She'd need to grocery shop soon. She found the case of Budweiser on the shelf at the bottom and pulled out two bottles. She opened a drawer right beside the fridge and pulled out a bottle opener. She cracked both of the beers open easily, shut the drawer with her hip and walked back across the kitchen to the living room.

Brinker was sitting on the couch closest to the door, his back to her. She felt herself sigh quietly. She walked up behind him.

"Here's your cold one."

She said, bringing them around in front of him.

"Oh, thank you."

He said politely, taking the beer from her. She didn't sit down right away.

"Are you hungry? I think I've got chicken wings in the freezer."

Brinker gave her a reassuring smile. He could tell she was tense and apparently nervous to have him in her home.

"That would be awesome. Thank you."

PJ set her beer on the coffee table and hustled back to the kitchen. She dug out the box of honey garlic flavoured chicken wings. She scanned the instructions on the back and broke open the box. She dumped the entire box onto a cookie baking sheet and popped it into the oven.

"Shouldn't be too long."

She said, entering the living room again, and taking a seat beside him. She noticed his beer was still full.

"I was waiting for you."

He told her, answering her silent question. She lifted her bottle from the table and held it out to him. He clinked his against hers and they both took a gulp.

"So, miss Richards."

He said, looking at her. She swallowed hard.

"Mister Brinker."

She responded, mocking his formality.

"Now that we're off the clock, tell me about you. I'm intrigued."

He leaned back, crossing one leg over the other.

"You're intrigued?"

She questioned, staring at him.

"You seem strong. Put together. Headstrong, I should say. Like you've got no fear, and beautiful to boot."

PJ giggled like a little girl, took another swig of bear and regained her steady face.

"Short version. My dad passed away early. My mom kind of checked out. She loved him so much. She didn't care anymore is what it felt like. I'm the eldest of my brother and... deceased sister. When my dad passed, I had to step up and take care of my siblings, mom wouldn't do it."

"How old were you?"

"I was twelve. My brother Joseph was ten and my sister, Melissa, was four. So, I guess that's what made me this way. At twelve years old, I had to take care of my siblings and my mother. She didn't start caring again until after Melissa left us. That was nearly eight years later."

PJ hadn't realized she was subconsciously drinking her beer as she spoke. Her bottle was almost empty. Brinker's was still half full.

"Your sister...she was killed by this Samuel Thomas guy."

He noted. PJ immediately stood up.

"I need another if I'm going to talk about that."

She walked around the couch to the entrance to the kitchen.

"Would you like another?"

Brinker shook his head.

"Good for now, thanks."

She dipped into the kitchen and yanked another bottle from the box. She checked on the chicken wings. Not quite ready.

"Yes, Melissa was kidnapped and killed by that monster."

She said, returning to her seat.

"You don't need to tell me if you'd rather not talk about it."

Brinker assured her. She gulped back a big swig of her second beer. She could feel the buzz starting to hit her.

"She got murdered by him. He's ignorant, cheeky and stubborn. But he was so good looking, friendly, helpful and romantic. So romantic. It wasn't hard to fall for his charm."

PJ said, slurring slightly.

"How do you know so much about him? You said you only met him once."

Brinker said, curiosity filling him.

"I didn't say that. Want another?"

PJ asked. She stood up, wobbling slightly. She was a lightweight and she knew it. Brinker nodded and PJ stumbled her way back to the kitchen. She pulled open the fridge and grabbed out four bottles so she wouldn't have to make another trip anytime soon. She cracked all four open and help them by their skinny necks and made her way back to the living room, again. She handed Brinker a bottle and set the other two on the coffee table.

"I met him. Talked to him. Began to date him."

PJ blurted. Brinker almost choked on his booze. PJ tipped her bottle fully back and began to chug the alcohol. She gulped down every last drop of the bitter tasting drink. Brinker did the same.

"He was sweet. His eyes weren't so cold back then."

PJ rambled on. Her eyes filled with tears. Brinker sat next to her, unsure of what his next actions should be.

"It's my fault Melissa's gone. I didn't listen to her when she accused him of stalking her. I thought she was jealous because I had such a handsome boyfriend."

Brinker's eyes widened. He put his hand on PJ's knee. He'd never seen her so vulnerable.

"PJ. It is not your fault. Don't you dare say that."

PJ looked at him, her face flushed.

Wine blush.

"Let's talk about something else. Want to hear a funny story?"

Brinker said quickly, trying to change the painful subject. PJ wiped the tears with the back of her hand.

"It happened a couple of years ago. Probably about five or six. I was taking this lady out on a date. I had this whole romantic idea where she'd get picked up by horse-drawn carriage. It would take her to

Woodland park where I'd be waiting with a bouquet of flowers. Turns out, I'm allergic to bee stings. When she got there, as I was handing her the flowers, a bee was zipping around and stung me on the cheek.

"At first, I thought it was no big deal, right? So, we started walking along the path along the creek. I had set up a picnic of us in the clearing just past the creek. Well the sting was really starting to itch. It was becoming very irritated. Before I knew it, the entire side of my face swelled up like a balloon. I was trying to keep it hidden from her by walking on the opposite side of her, but I ended up tripping over a branch and shoving her into the creek. Needless to say, she never called me back."

PJ looked up at Brinker. She tried to keep a straight face.

"That's...that's truly unfortunate."

She slurred. Brinker smirked, a tiny dimple forming in his left cheek. She'd never noticed that before. She burst out laughing. A loud, obnoxious, guttural laugh that no doubt stemmed from her intoxication. She put her hands on her gut and tried her damndest to stop laughing. Brinker watched her gasp for air and wipe away the single tears from her eyes as she managed to finally calm herself.

She looked up and met Brinker's eyes. She'd never actually seen him. All day, she'd look at him, but now, since the first time she'd met him, she was seeing him. His eyes were like the deepest parts of the ocean. Blue. So blue. She lifted a hand and ran it through his hair. She was seeing how thick and wavy it was. The dark blonde that could only be achieved by someone who lived in the sun. It was such a dark blonde. She was seeing the dimple in his left cheek. She was seeing his crooked smile and the way his nose crinkled oh so slightly when he did. Her eyes travelled down his body.

He'd taken his jacket off so she was seeing the way his muscles rippled under the silk of his dress shirt. She was becoming intoxicated by him. She looked back up, meeting his eyes again. His bore deeply into hers. His hand grabbed hers, holding it tightly. Her breath caught in her throat.

"You're so beautiful, PJ."

He muttered. She could feel herself beginning to blush.

"Brinker..."

She started to say. He kissed her hand.

"We're not at the office anymore, P. James. Please."

He whispered. PJ didn't respond. She breathed heavily as he pulled her into him. He pushed her hair away from her neck and collarbone where he started planting quick, soft kisses.

"James."

PJ whispered. His hand cupped her cheek, brushing her brown hair behind her ear. His lips were an inch from hers.

"Just say no if you want me to stop."

PJ continued to breathe heavily; her eyes closed. She didn't utter a sound. Brinker closed the gap between their lips. PJ was suddenly filled with such an intense amount of bubbling nerves. She brought her arms up and around his neck. His hands, one was still cupping her face, the other had found its way to her back, holding her against him.

His lips were soft, touching hers with such a gentle intimacy that PJ had never known. She tightened her arms, pulling herself into him. His hand left her face, travelled down her body to the bottom of her sweater. Both hands tugged at the bottom, sliding it up her slim torso. They broke their kiss momentarily as Brinker slid the sweater over her raised arms.

As soon as it was off, his hands returned to her body, feeling, sensing everything. He didn't want to miss one single minute. Her fingers went to work on the buttons of his dress shirt. She got it open, he pulled his tie over his head. Her hands traced the finely toned abs, running over the rigid definition.

She looked back up, into his eyes. Both pressed their lips into each other again, hungry for more. He grabbed her ass in his hands and pulled her into his lap. She was straddling him now, their most private parts grinding against each other. His hands moved up her spine, stopping at her bra clasp. His fingers worked frantically to undo the clasp. PJ held his face in her hands, kissing him passionately. He managed to get the bra undone, it slid down her arms stopping at the bend in her elbows. She let her hands fall from his face so she could grab the bra and yank it off of her.

They stared at each other. Want and need completely enveloping one another. PJ pushed at the dress shirt that was still on James Brinker's back. He pulled it off as quickly as he could. One of his hands found the small of PJ's back, bracing her as he gently urged her to lie on her back. Their lips met again, tongues dancing together. Brinker lay on top of her, his hands running up and down her body. He moved his lips from hers and started kissing her neck, collarbone and along her jaw-line. She had her arms around his back, holding him against her. She leaned her head back and let out a soft moan.

The shrill sound of the timer on the oven interrupted the two. Brinker stopped kissing her. She looked at him and giggled.

"Chicken wings are ready."

She whispered. They both started laughing. Brinker pushed himself off of PJ so that she could slide off the couch.

"I'll be right back."

She said, standing up, wobbling slightly. She was only wearing her leggings. She left the living room, knowing very well that Brinker's eyes were trained on her ass.

In the kitchen, PJ turned the oven off and pulled open the door. She grabbed a dish towel and gently pulled the piping hot stoneware baking sheet that she'd placed the chicken wings on, out of the heat. She put them on top of the stove, resting on the elements.

She bit her lip. She knew neither of them wanted chicken wings, especially not now that things were getting good between them. Then, with a sly smile, she turned from the cooling wings and hooked her thumbs into the waistband of her leggings. She pulled them down, over her slim hips, letting them drop to her ankles. She was now wearing just her thong. She stepped out of that too, leaving herself completely clothing free. She walked slowly back into the living room where a shirtless Brinker was waiting patiently, back to her.

"James."

She whispered, voice sultry and seductive. She strode around the couch and stood in front of Brinker, hand on hip, staring deeply at him. His eyes widened when he saw her.

"Oh, PJ."

He whispered. His eyes travelled her whole body, taking in her athletic build, the tightness of her tummy, the perkiness of her breasts and the tautness of her butt. His eyes landed on the scar on her leg. He stood up and put on hand on her waist, the other traced the scar.

"Hit by a truck."

PJ whispered; long story short. Brinker brought his other hand, the one on the scar, up her body, tracing her cheek. A single tear fell from the corner of her left eye. Brinker kissed her softly. He kissed her with so much passion. He grabbed her waist and hoisted her into the air. She wrapped her arms around his neck.

"Upstairs."

She whispered against his lips; he needn't respond. He walked towards the hallway, carrying her, kissing her. She held herself tightly against him, her bare breasts pressing into his bare chest.

Getting up the stairs was a little more difficult, but he refused to put her down. At the top of the stairs was the entrance to the master bedroom, PJ's room.

He crossed the room to the bed, tossing her onto it. She leaned back against the pillows, watching him as he un did his belt and dress pants. He slid them down his muscular legs, letting her look at how truly astounding he was. Both in and out of clothing.

PJ held out her arms, Brinker climbed onto the bed and crawled on top of her, once more pressing his lips against hers. She parted her lips slightly, allowing his tongue entry to her mouth. She ran her nails along his back, his hands running along her body. Neither of them seemed to get enough of the feel of the other.

He pressed himself down onto her, breaking the kiss and looking into her eyes.

"Is this okay?"

He whispered. PJ didn't respond. Instead, she grabbed onto him and pulled him into her. He moved slowly, adjusting to her body. Her eyes were closed, mouth open slightly, soft moans barely escaping her lips.

He thrust hard, shocking PJ, sobering her up. She arched her back, accepting him, wanting it. Needing it. She dug her nails into the skin on his back, raking them down his spine.

13

The bright sunlight shone through the master bedroom balcony window. The rays sliced across PJ's face. She yawned and slowly opened her eyes. She blinked a couple of times, adjusting to the brightly lit room. And then she realized she was naked. She slowly turned over, noticing a nicely toned, muscular arm draped just below her bare breasts. She saw him, still sleeping soundly next to her. The blanket they'd been under was lowered to their hips.

It sat just under his v-line, just covering his most private part. The night before came rushing back to her. The beers. The kissing. The love-making. The intense, best love-making she'd ever experienced. She gasped and shook her head furiously. She tossed his arm off of her. She shoved the blankets away from her hips and scrambled out of bed. She ran across the room and grabbed her robe off of the door. She tied it closed around her waist, the soft fabric hanging around her skin like a warm, motherly hug.

"Brinker."

She said, loudly. He grunted and rolled over, face down. The muscles in his back tensed and flexed. PJ became fixated on them. She watched as he breathed. Why did he have to be so perfect? She shook her head and came to.

"Hey. James. Get up."

PJ said, taking a step towards the bed. She lifted her leg and rested her foot on the edge. She jostled the bed. Brinker rolled over again, back onto his back. His eyes were still closed as he lifted his arms over his head and stretched. The muscles in his arms and abs flexed as well, defining themselves. He yawned widely. Slowly, he opened his eyes, squinting through slitted eyelids, he too, adjusting to the lit bedroom.

"Oh, good morning sunshine. What time is it? Why don't you come back to bed?"

He managed to say through another yawn. PJ shook her head and pointed at the clock on her nightstand.

"Get out of bed. We have to get back to the office."

Brinker shot up in bed and looked around the room. He let it sink in that PJ was in her robe and he was in nothing but a bed sheet.

"Did we..."

He trailed off as his eyes scanned the room, catching sight of some of his clothing items tossed into a pile on the floor. PJ nodded her head.

"So that wasn't just a dream. That was amazing."

He said, a smile cracking onto his face. It was. PJ knew it was. It was also the best she'd ever had.

"That can never happen again."

"What? But why not?"

PJ held up a finger to shush him.

"Absolutely never. We're never going to speak about it. I have Nick. I'm happy with Nick. Last night happened because of a drunken stupor. Never again. Now get up, get dressed and let's go. We have a press conference to attend."

Brinker lazily slid out of the bed, standing naked in front of PJ. She caught herself staring at his perfectly tanned body. How did he look so great? He must vacation a lot. She shook her head and averted her eyes so she wasn't obvious about the staring.

"I'll get your clothes. Your shirt and tie. Here."

She slid her foot under his pants and kicked them up into the air. Brinker caught them in his hands and started pulling them on, never taking his eyes off of her.

She hastily turned around, breaking the eye contact. She rushed down the stairs. She was tingling all over. Her mind kept flashing back to the night before. She could still feel Brinker's hands running up her body, his soft lips planting kisses everywhere. She liked it. She didn't want to. But she did.

She found his white dress shirt and tie scattered on the ground. She gathered them and tried to push the night from her mind.

"You can have your bedroom back."

PJ jumped at the sound of his voice. She pivoted and saw Brinker standing behind her. He was wearing his black dress pants, but was still shirtless. PJ's eyes skimmed over his bare chest. She longed to have his weight on top of her again. There was no better feeling.

She shoved his button-down shirt and tie into his hands and clutched her robe tighter together. She moved past him and had to remain calm so she wouldn't run full speed down the hall and up the stairs.

Brinker turned to watch her make her exit. He leisurely slid his shirt over his muscular arms and did the buttons up, one at a time. PJ lingered on his mind. He couldn't shake the memory of last night no matter how hard he tried. It was the best night of his life, easily trumping the night he spent with Rachel or Randee or Rebecca or whatever the fuck her name was. She was some chick that he'd met at a bar. Kinky and freaky as hell. But fun. PJ easily made that night seem insignificant. She knew what she was doing.

He gradually did up his tie, thinking all the while about the curves of PJ's body, the way her brown hair fell around her naked shoulders, the way her lips felt against his shivering skin.

He started picking up the empty beer bottles from the coffee table. It was the least he could do since he made the mess as well.

"You don't have to do that."

He heard her voice from the hallway behind him. He turned at the sound and saw her leaning against the hallway wall. As soon as his eyes landed on her, he felt his breath catch in his throat.

She was wearing black dress pants, a white, short sleeved blouse and a black blazer was slung over her arm. She looked ridiculously professional. She looked utterly, overwhelmingly, drop dead gorgeous.

"It's no problem."

He said, stuttering slightly, trying not to stumble over his words.

"We don't have time..."

She trailed off as her cell phone began to jingle. It was still situated on the coffee table, right where she left it the night before. She locked eyes with Brinker and strode across the room, brushing past him and picked up her phone. Brinker noted that she didn't check her caller I.D.

"Detective Richards."

She answered smoothly. She could hear commotion in the background.

"PJ, where the hell are you? Press is here. Everyone's going crazy. Is Brinker with you?"

Brock Carter's frantic voice came loudly through the phone.

"Yea, we're almost there."

PJ replied. She met Brinker's eyes and gestured towards the door. He didn't hesitate to leave the room, PJ following him.

"Hurry up."

Brock hung up before PJ could say goodbye. She slid the phone into her dress pants' pocket and locked eyes with Brinker again. He was pulling his shoes over his socked feet. She spotted a pair of black, slightly heeled shoes. She decided that's what she should wear for a professional press conference. She slid them onto her feet and swiveled towards the counter behind her. She grabbed her purse off of the counter and stepped over her leggings and thong on the floor. Her holster and twenty-two were still down there.

She bent and swooped them into her hands, lifting her blouse momentarily to buckle the belt around her waist. The Glock fit nicely against her leg, comforting her. Brinker's hand was on the door knob. PJ nodded at him.

"We really got to go. Brock's losing is mind."

Brinker thought it seemed easier for PJ to push the night from her mind. He opened the door, grabbing his jacket off of the coat hook to the right. PJ closed the door behind them.

She shut the door to the house making sure that she turned the lock and tested it to be sure it was firmly locked tight. She turned back towards the car to see Brinker holding the door for her. She felt her heart flutter. She walked to him and resisted the urge to jump into his arms right then and there and kiss him again, bringing back the passion from last night. She nodded a thank you to him and climbed into the passenger seat.

Brinker gently shut the door and moved swiftly towards the driver's seat, getting in behind the wheel. PJ was holding a note book in her lap. She'd written down most of the things she wanted to mention in the press conference. She was skimming over her notes and written questions when Brinker started the vehicle and put it into reverse. He backed out of PJ's short driveway, the two not exchanging any words.

They drove in an uncomfortable silence for several minutes before Brinker decided to break the quiet.

"PJ."

She didn't dare respond, or look up.

"We do need to talk about it."

He said, continuing on when he realized that she wasn't going to reply. PJ didn't look at him.

"Last night was...spectacular. I've never experienced anything as exhilarating as that. It was..."

"Stop."

PJ said, looking up, cutting him off. She slammed the notebook closed with a loud clap.

"I already said that last night should not have happened. We are not going to talk about it. We are going to forget about it."

"I don't want to forget it."

"Stop. I swear if you do not shut the fuck up, I will have you sent back to base. I don't care if you're a federal Agent. Harassment suits apply to you and I have the best lawyer around for a boyfriend. I will slap you with a harassment charge so hard your grandchildren will feel it. Do we have an understanding?"

She felt hot with anger. She didn't want to be angry. She hated it. She didn't want to forget but it was completely unfair to Nick.

Brinker pulled into the parking lot of the precinct. News crews, many, many white news vans and reporters littered the parking lot.

"I'm sorry, P."

"And from here on, it's Detective Richards. Or just Richards."

She unbuckled her seatbelt and opened the door. She calmly got out, regaining her composure and slammed the door shut which very quickly attracted the attention of the news crews.

"There she is!"

"Detective Richards!"

"What do you have to say about the slayings?"

Like ants, they all scurried over, circling her, shouting their questions. PJ knew how to handle them. She held up her hands.

"If everyone could just meet me at the stairs of the building, I will answer any and all questions you may have."

Brinker got out of the car when the reporters turned to follow PJ back to the front of the building.

God, he liked her.

Fuck.

Brock Carter was standing on the stairs, leading up to the glass front doors of the RPD building.

"PJ. There you are. Ah, Agent Brinker."

Brock welcomed them to the gathering. The reporters were still shouting questions, which PJ successfully managed to tune out. They were nothing more than some annoying, buzzing flies.

PJ shook Brock's hand.

"Sorry I'm late. My alarm didn't go off and Brinker didn't pick me up in time."

She shot Brinker a look, throwing him under the bus, but all she really wanted to do was jump into his arms and kiss his perfect lips. She turned to the forming crowd.

"Good morning everyone. My name is Detective PJ Richards. This is Special Agent in Charge, James Brinker. He's joining us today from the FBI headquarters. Before I answer your questions, I'd like to make a few points. We've been dealing with several murders of teenage girls to very early adulthood girls. Our top unsub is named Samuel Thomas. We have a sketch of him from several years ago..."

She trailed off and looked towards Brinker, who pulled the drawing from his pocket. He held it out to PJ who took it and unfolded it, holding it up to the crowd so they could all see.

"Who is Samuel Thomas?"

"Why don't you have an updated sketch?"

"Is it true that you're next?"

The questions were being fired at her as if someone had put a rapid-fire attachment onto a gun and aimed it right at her.

"If everyone could just, here. Ask one question at a time, please."

PJ said, feeling flushed.

"Detective Richards."

Someone called out. PJ glanced down to the front of the crowd. A smartly dressed woman with jet black hair done up in a neat bun on top of her head was waving her hand. PJ nodded at her.

"Hi! I'm Bianca Simmons, Ridgeway Daily. Is it true that you are this guys' next victim?"

PJ narrowed her eyes and leaned forward. Bianca Simmons held out her microphone towards PJ.

"No. That is not true."

PJ responded, monotone, although there was no way to be sure.

"How involved are you now that the main suspect is the same guy that killed your sister several years ago?"

PJ froze. A small, sly smile spread across Bianca's lips. The only thought that ran through PJ's mind was *How the fuck did they find out about that?*

Brinker stepped up beside her.

"No comment."

He said, answering for her.

"Detective Richards! Rachel Barker, Ridgeway Channel nine news. Do you have any idea who is next?"

PJ locked eyes with the woman. She couldn't have been more than thirty. She had golden blonde hair that curled around her shoulders in a cascade of ringlets.

"No. As of this moment, we aren't sure. We're looking into many possibilities."

PJ was trying to keep her answers short and to the point. It was always better that way.

"Detective Richards! Naomi Wilkins. Global news. Is it true that a professor from the university is also a suspect?"

PJ frowned.

"Yes."

She said, bluntly. Naomi brought her microphone back to her mouth.

"Are you allowing him to continue work?"

PJ narrowed her eyes.

What kind of idiotic question was that?

"No, as of this moment he's in custody."

PJ glanced around the crowd.

"Unfortunately, that's all the time we've got..."

PJ began to say.

"Detective Richards."

Someone else in the crowd cut her off. She looked around, trying to spot the bodiless voice.

"One last question."

PJ raised her eyebrows.

"Yes?"

She still couldn't see who was speaking.

"Could you identify yourself, please?"

She asked, gently.

"Ross Jennings. GTV. What do you guys plan on doing next? You seem to be moving slowly. You don't seem to have any real leads. How do we know our daughters are safe? What are your guys' next plan of action?"

PJ felt her face going red.

"No comment."

She said, turning her back and walking up the remainder of the stairs. Brinker and Brock followed her up them.

The mass of reporters broke into a chaotic frenzy, shouting more questions up the stairs at PJ's back. They went unanswered.

"That was fucking brutal."

PJ shouted the moment the doors closed behind her. She felt herself start to slump over. She grabbed the reception desk to balance herself.

"I think that went just fine."

Brinker said, meeting PJ's eyes. She glared at him. She could taste his bitter sarcasm.

"Brock, have any of the teams come up with anything?"

"Last time I checked, no. But we've still got Martin, Brady and Maynard at the university. I'll radio them and see what they've got."

"What about Hamm and Darbyshire? Or Dilworth and Walters? Neither of them have anything?"

PJ exclaimed. She was becoming frustrated again. Brock slowly shook his head.

"Not yet."

PJ let her head drop into her hands.

"That guy, Ross Jennings, was right. We are moving too slowly. We need to step it up."

She felt depressed. She felt completely unbearably useless. Brinker grabbed her shoulders and squeezed.

"Don't be too hard on yourself. There's only so much you, or any of us can do."

PJ brushed his hands from her shoulders.

"We should be doing more."

She said, resentment filling her voice. She pushed herself away from the reception desk and glanced quickly at Brock.

"I'm going to the tech lab. Maybe they could use an extra set of eyes on the computer."

Brock gave her his best smile. He knew how she was feeling. It couldn't be easy on her knowing this guy was getting away with what he was.

"Sure. I'll go with Brinker, talk to Swanson again."

Brinker tried to catch PJ's eyes. She wouldn't look at him. She couldn't. She knew if she looked at him, she just might fall under his charm. He was almost too irresistible. The guilt was eating her up from the inside-out.

She turned on her heels and strode down the hallway opposite of Brock and Agent Brinker. She shoved her hands into her pockets and bit her lip. All kinds of torturous thoughts invaded her mind. They ranged from her guilty conscious, reminding her of the way Brinker felt against her body, to the way she absolutely, undeniably loved every waking minute of it. The thoughts shifted from Brinker, to Samuel Thomas.

She couldn't shake her feelings towards him from the brief time they were together. She did not want to think about it. No way did she ever want him in her thoughts. She shook her head furiously.

"You can't be in my head. You can't be. Leave me alone."

She muttered. She squeezed her hands into tight fists, clenching until her knuckles turned white.

"Oh shit!"

PJ exclaimed as she slammed right into another body. Neither of them had been paying attention as they walked down the hall. PJ fell backwards, catching herself on a door handle.

"Oh. Oh wow. I'm so sorry PJ. I wasn't watching where I was going."

PJ met his eyes and gave him a soft smile.

"Don't worry about it Phil. No harm done. I was just coming to find you."

She gave him another quick smile as she rubbed her elbow. She'd caught it on the door handle, sending shooting pain through her arm.

Funny bone.

Yeah right.

"I was coming to find you. We found some stuff."

PJ couldn't help but grin at his choice of words. Phil was still rather new to the RPD. He'd only been on the team for just over a year.

"Would it be too much to ask for good news?"

She said. She wasn't feeling overly hopeful. Phil let her get herself together before answering. She brushed herself off, gave her elbow one more rub. The pain had mostly subsided. Now it was an annoying tingling sensation. Like when someone's foot falls asleep.

Not pleasant.

She got in step with Phil as they both headed down the corridor.

"No. Not a whole lot of good news, I'm afraid."

He replied, bluntly. PJ let out a breathy sigh.

"I figured as much."

Phil fiddled with his hands as they walked back to the tech lab. PJ chewed on her lip.

"He's not in jail."

Phil piped up. PJ looked at him. The door to the tech lab was coming up on their right.

"Not in jail."

PJ repeated. She put her hand on the cold metal of the door handle and gave it a smooth twist. The tech lab was a completely foreign place to her. She'd been in that particular room twice in her whole career. She found herself anything but tech savvy. She spotted FBI Agent Jason Dilworth sitting at a computer a couple of rows down on her left.

His eyes were half closed. He was slumped forward in his chair, yawning. PJ didn't blame him. She knew he had to be exhausted. While he, Phil, Agent Hamm and Agent Darbyshire were up all-night doing recon, she'd been at home, getting drunk and getting laid. She was kicking herself.

"Agent Dilworth."

She said, approaching him. She lay her hand on his shoulder softly.

"Detective."

He responded through another lion sized yawn.

"Phil tells me you don't have very good news for me."

"Depends on how you look at it."

Dilworth replied, sitting up straight in his chair. PJ remained standing.

"Talk to me."

She stated, eyes travelling towards the screen. The page on the screen then was an article from the Springfield newspaper. A big photograph of a grisly plane crash was positioned at the top of the article. Flames engulfed the air craft.

"Turns out, right after Samuel Thomas murdered your sister, he kidnapped an eight-year-old girl. Just like you said. Well, she got away. So, Sam ran. He eluded the police for a couple of years. I don't know if he got any kids but he was gone. Like he dropped off the face of the Earth for those years that the police couldn't find him. The stories were buried pretty well, I guess the families of the victims didn't want to be reminded of the horror. This article in front of me is from May sixth, two thousand twelve. That's almost three years ago.

"Anyway, the article basically says how the plane went down, every person on board perished. According to the records, Sam was on board. Sorry Richards. Sam's not our guy."

PJ's mouth hung open.

"Dental records?"

She said slowly.

"Excuse me?"

Dilworth replied, looking up at her from his chair.

"Dental records! Do you know for sure Samuel was on that plane?"

She exclaimed. Her hands grabbed her head. Her heart started to race. She felt panicky.

"No. The fire was too bad. Anything to do with records was gone. The tower had an extra copy of who was on the flight, but the remains of everyone on board were too charred to tell anything from medical or dental records. There was a man's body in Samuel's seat."

Dilworth explained. PJ started pacing.

"It doesn't feel right. It just doesn't feel right."

She whispered. Jason Dilworth pushed himself to his feet. He grabbed PJ's shoulder and stopped her monotonous movement.

"Sorry, Richards. I think we're dealing with a copycat. Someone researched him. Probably found the stories that I did. They became attached to the thought of what he was doing. He must've looked up to Sam. Sam's death must've been what broke him."

PJ glanced from Phil to Dilworth.

"Three years. Three years. Our guy hasn't done anything until a month ago!"

She couldn't wrap her head around the information.

"Generally, if a copycat's mentor or idol kicks the bucket, they start their shit right away. It doesn't take three years."

She stated, turning to Phil.

"Can you guys look, just to give me peace of mind, to see if there was anywhere else, he could have been? Did he miss the flight or give away his ticket?"

"PJ"

"Please. Just look for me. Please."

She cut Phil off, pleading with him. Phil smiled at her and pulled himself up to the monitor next to Dilworth's. Dilworth sent the article to an email address and closed the browser.

"I'm not wasting my time with this. He's dead. Okay? Detective? Get it through your head. Dead. Stop chasing ghosts and start searching for something your team could actually use."

He shut off the monitor.

"Excuse me?"

PJ said. She stared at him, appalled.

"You. You are a community police officer. I am a federal Agent. I am more important than you. If you want to chase ghosts, be my guest. I am not wasting my time with this. My boss, SAC James Brinker, gets to assign assignments to me. Not you."

PJ felt like she'd just been slapped in the face.

"I want to speak with you in the hall. Please."

She said, lowering her voice. She became uncomfortably aware of the other officers and Agents working in the lab. Dilworth yawned again, but didn't reply. Instead, he followed her out of the lab. She shut the door behind them.

"Agent Dilworth,"

She paused and stared at him. He was leaning casually against the wall, yawning.

"I understand you're tired. Everyone is. But that's no excuse to speak to me the way you did in there."

She stated slowly. Dilworth was paying her absolutely zero mind.

"Agent. You may think I'm 'chasing ghosts' but I *knew* Samuel. He was smart, conniving and cunning. It just doesn't seem right to think he died on that pl..."

"Will you just shut up? You sound like a complete fucking idiot. People die. Sam died in that plane crash. You knew him. You were fucking him. Boo fucking hoo. I'm not doing this miniscule job, especially not under your direction. How you became a Detective, I have no idea."

He said, loudly. He turned to walk away from her. She grabbed his arm.

"Okay, whoa. Hold on a minute!"

She yelled, pulling him back to her. He spun around so fast and shoved her away from him, hard. He pushed her against the wall. She knocked her head off of the hardness. Pain automatically rippled through her skull. He punched the wall next to her ear.

"Get your hands off of me."

She said, trying to push him away from her.

"You do not put your hands on me!"

He screamed. He grabbed both of her wrists in one of his hands and kept her pinned against the wall.

"You do not have the authority to touch me!"

He shouted, inches from her face.

"You're a pathetic excuse for a police officer."

He spat. He tightened his grip on her wrists. She let out a little squeak of pain.

"Dilworth! What the fuck do you think you're doing!"

PJ recognized the deep, manly voice as Brinker's. Dilworth dropped her wrists and backed away from her. She narrowed her eyes at him, rubbing her wrists, making the circulation start up again. Brinker stormed down the hallway.

"Sam died in a plane crash, Brinker. She's still trying to..."

He didn't finish his sentence. Brinker's fist connected with Dilworth's cheek bone, knocking him sideways. PJ gasped. Dilworth looked stunned. He tasted the salty coppery taste of blood in his mouth.

"You do not, *ever*, put your hands on this woman again. You hear me? Never!"

Brinker screamed.

"Get your shit together. You're going back to HQ. You get your shit from there and you're done."

Dilworth stared at him.

"You aren't serious?"

"You bet your ass I'm serious. Go."

He said sternly. Dilworth shot PJ a look and started making his way down the hallway to the main lobby.

"I'm so glad I'm not a pussy-whipped bitch."

He muttered to himself out of ear shot of Brinker and PJ.

"Are you okay?"

Brinker asked, genuine concern lingering obviously in his voice. PJ didn't look at him.

"I'm fine."

She replied.

"What did he do to you?"

Brinker wondered. He wanted to touch her. Hug her and hold her.

"He just pushed me. No big deal."

She stated softly.

"He didn't hurt you?"

"No. Well, my head hurts from smacking it off the wall but I'm fine."

She edged herself down the hallway, moving away from him. She wanted him to embrace her. Love her.

"Thanks for your concern."

She turned her back and reached for the tech lab door handle so she could re-enter. She wanted to know what Agent Hamm and Darbyshire were coming up with.

"PJ"

Brinker whispered. PJ paused, hand on the handle.

"What?"

She said after a moment or two had passed. Brinker stayed unresponsive.

"Okay. I need to get back to my team."

She spoke quietly, as if there was some big secret no one else was allowed to know.

"I don't know what to say."

Brinker said. PJ turned back to him, locking her glimmer brown eyes with his blue ones. The tears from Dilworth's attack finally hit her. She gulped hard, trying to swallow the hard lump that had formed in her throat.

"I really, really..."

"Stop."

PJ interrupted. Brinker took a step toward her, closing the slight distance between them.

"You can't do this right now. I can't do this right now. I can't. You need to drop it."

"I can't just drop it."

He felt himself whisper.

"Why not?"

"You awakened a fire deep within me. I didn't know I could feel that way about someone."

He grabbed one of her hands in his, interlocking their fingers.

"You're delusional. It was only one night."

She said, even though she knew what he was saying was true. She felt that fire too.

"One amazing night. I can't forget it. I can't do it."

PJ held her breath as he leaned his face closer to hers.

"I can't do this."

She whispered, hushed. He squeezed her hand, leaning his face closer to hers again, their lips mere inches apart. She didn't move. Not until his lips brushed against hers. She pushed him away from her and quickly turned the handle and ducked inside the tech lab, leaving a distraught Brinker in the hallway.

"Good morning to you both."

Saige sang out that morning. She was wearing extremely small shorts and a baggy tee shirt that hung loosely around her shoulders. Her silky hair was piled in a thick, messy bun a top her head.

He didn't think he'd ever seen her look so beautiful. He sat up and realized he had passed out on the couch in an unknown apartment. His mind travelled back to the night before. They'd, meaning Bella, Matt, Saige and himself, had eaten a fancy dinner at a glamorous restaurant owned by Bella's father. Then they'd came back to Matt's apartment, had a few drinks, watched a few movies and apparently gotten too drunk to get back to their own respective homes.

He glanced next to him and laid eyes on a half sleeping Bella. By half sleeping, he wasn't sure if she was fully gone or not. Her eyes were open a crack, but she was snoring ever so slightly. He quickly slid out of the make shift bed and realized his next issue. He was in his boxers. Saige's eyes fell on his body. She grinned as she checked him out.

"Nice."

She giggled. He didn't want to put his clothes back on. No, he wanted to take hers off.

"Would you like some tea?"

Saige asked, turning away from him. She studied the kettle on the counter, watching for the water to boil. She reached up and pulled a plastic Tupperware container down from the top shelf. It was over flowing with hordes of mini tea bags and what looked to be the remnants of spilled bags of Insta-Coffee.

"Unfortunately, Matt drank all of the coffee."

Saige said absent-mindedly as she dug through the Tupperware box.

"And apparently all of my honey lemon."

He couldn't stop the smile that crawled across his face. She was just so perfect.

"Hmm? Tea?"

She turned back to him. He quickly re-focused on reality.

"No. Thank you."

He couldn't seem to muster more than those three little words. Saige shot him a smile and turned her attention back to the kettle which had finally started boiling. She unplugged it and slowly filled up her blue mug.

He found an incredibly high amount of pleasure watching her putter around the kitchen, doing such mundane tasks.

"What...what's going on?"

A quiet mumble came from the couch-bed. Bella sat up, rubbing her eyes. She was in her bra and g-string thong, her red lipstick had been smeared all across her face, her dark eye makeup was rubbed half off, making her resemble a raccoon.

He had to do his very best not to flinch and grimace at her scary appearance.

"Oh, good morning sleeping beauty."

Saige joked, holding her piping hot mug of English Breakfast tea between her hands. He turned away from Bella.

"Sai, where are my clothes?"

"Awe, no. Come on back in here, boo."

Bella pleaded.

"Oh gee, I'd love too but it's Monday. I've got classes today.'

Saige's eyes widened.

"Oh shit. Oh shit.'

She gently placed the mug on the counter and dashed out of the kitchen. He could hear her saying Matt's name. He started looking around the tiny living room. He found his jeans on the other side, under a chair. His dress shirt and sport coat folded nicely on the seat of the chair. He felt a pair of hands wrap around his firm chest, a pair of lips placing gentle kisses all over his back.

"Bella. You've got to stop."

He said, turning in her grasp. For a split second, Saige's face was looking at him. He blinked hard, erasing her image and allowing the gnarly morning version of a hung-over Bella re-configure. He pried her hands off of his body.

"Why don't you let me show you affection?"

She whispered. He wasn't looking at her.

"You're my boyfriend. Why don't you let me..."?

"Hold on. No. I'm not your boyfriend. I don't know where you got that idea from. I've known you for two days. No."

He snapped. He met her eyes. She teared up.

"You don't like me?"

He rolled his eyes. She moved back over to him and grabbed his arm.

"Michael, Michael please."

She cried.

She's acting like such a child.

He was filled completely with frustration. He didn't think he could last another day. He needed to get rid of the whiny, annoying, parasitic thing called Bella.

"You know what?"

He looked at the pathetic girl hanging off his arm.

"How about..."

He paused. Was he really about to do it? Yes.

"How about, after classes, you come to my house. I'll make dinner. We'll eat, drink wine, get to know each other."

He watched her entire face light up. She shook his arm excitedly.

"Yes! Okay, yes. Just us?"

He struggled to make himself nod.

"Yes. Just us."

"What's just us?"

Saige asked as she re-entered the kitchen.

"Wining and dining Bella tonight."

He stated matter-of-factly, like it was no big deal. He wished she'd react in a jealous manner. Instead, a big toothy smile stretched across her lips.

"Oh my god! Yes! Cute!"

She exclaimed, very teenage girl like. He noticed at that moment she was now wearing tight fitting, faded jeans and a plain black tee shirt. Even in the simplest outfit possible, she looked like a glamour model.

He worked up his best smile.

"So where is Matt?"

Saige rolled her eyes as she picked up her mug.

"Being a moron. Hey, do you guys want to drive to school together?"

Bella looked down at her attire.

"Sai, lend me an outfit?"

Saige bit her lip to hold back a giggle.

"You mean you don't want to go looking like that?"

Bella shot her a stern look.

"I joke. I joke. One second."

Saige threw a saddened glance at her mug of tea, still full, before disappearing back into the bedroom. Bella still clung to his arm. He gently pulled away from her. She threw him an upset, heartbroken look and that was really when he knew her character. This Bella had some serious separation anxiety issues. Once again, it took his entire soul not to knock her out right there.

Instead, he bent over and picked up his jeans. He almost fell over trying to put them on. Damn, his head hurt. Did he really drink that much last night? He didn't think so. He could remember almost everything. At least he thought he could. Dinner. Matt's apartment. Drinks. Movies. Sleep. He wasn't sure if he had gotten out of his clothes voluntarily or not. Had he slept with Bella? No. He couldn't have. She would have said something vulgar if they had.

"Here Bell."

He immediately perked up at the sound of Saige's voice. He wished she didn't have such a massive effect on him. He looked up and saw Saige re-enter the room with an armload of clothes.

"Oh my god. Saige. Are you serious?"

Bella exclaimed. He could practically hear the agony and devastation in her voice. Drama queen.

"What?"

Innocence.

Innocence lingered heavily on Saige's voice. Bella threw her hands in the air and let out an exasperated sigh.

"Are you trying to make me look like a fucking nun? Do you want me to join a convent? You got jeans, a tank top, a tee shirt, a sweater and a hoodie. *And* a hoodie. Really? Were both necessary? Are you trying to cover me up? You can't nun-ify this!"

Bella twirled around, still wearing her delicates, showing off, tight stomach, toned butt and perky breasts.

"Yea. There's no way you'd ever be mistaken for a nun."

Bella, Saige and himself turned to see Matt coming into the kitchen. He was wearing low riding jeans, revealing his v-line and no shirt. Red scratches marked his shoulders and pectorals. That really pissed him off.

Matt, this young, foolish kid did not deserve to have those marks. He did not deserve Saige. He didn't deserve to have those marks defining him as hers.

"You never fail to be a complete dick, Matt."

Bella said, partly angry, partly humored. He shrugged, yawned and turned towards the sink. More red scratches ran jagged down his back.

"I never fail to be a dick and you never fail to get dicked."

"Hey!"

"Okay, okay."

"What the fuck is your problem this morning? Hmm? Matt, what the fuck is your problem?"

Bella screamed. Matt whirled back around, hatred filling his eyes, anger creasing the lines on his face.

"You! You are my problem! I'm sorry babe, you told me to be nice. I tried. I can't. I'm going to have to throw out that couch...hey man, you might want to get yourself checked. Bella's a dirty, dirty girl."

"Matt, calm down."

Saige said, before Bella or he could say anything else. Or rip each other apart.

"Matt..."

Bella started, but Saige held up a hand. She was acting as mediator. Bella grabbed his hand and gave a gentle squeeze. He reciprocated, mainly to keep up appearances.

"I'm sorry, Sai."

Matt said. He was so pissed off that he was physically quivering.

"What's with you?"

Saige whispered, touching Matt's arm gingerly. He flinched at the gently motion, shocking Saige. Matt didn't reply.

"Maybe you guys should leave..."

Saige said slowly. Bella pulled the pair of jeans over her hips, doing up the button and slid the tank top over her torso. She left the other clothing items on the ground and urged him to get his shirt on. He did, remaining silent.

"I'll see you guys later."

Saige said as he and Bella went to the door. Matt stopped him by grabbing his arm.

"Hey. Nice to meet you, man."

He didn't reply. How could he? Matt slowly pushed the door closed behind them, hearing it click into place.

Outside of the apartment, he couldn't help but think about Matt's goodbye. Nice to meet you, man? What? When Matt had spoken those words, he could feel the unspoken threat coursing through his veins. He wasn't sure what that threat was, exactly, but it was there. It was definitely there.

Matt's eyes were cold, his words filled with some kind of fear. Or maybe it was an abundance of such acrimony and cynicism that he couldn't help but over think to an irrational amount.

"Can you fucking believe him?"

He bounced back to the moment, leaving his thoughts exactly where they should be left. Bella was still clutching his arm. He'd grown accustomed to the constant cling, he barely felt it. He just shrugged.

"I haven't known you guys long enough to believe him."

He said bluntly. Bella gasped.

"Saige's on his fucking side. You're supposed to be on mine."

He raised his eyebrows. He didn't know how to reply without sounding like a sadistic bastard. Even though he was.

"Let's just go alright? Relax. Sai will straighten him out."

Bella let out a long groan.

"Mother fucker."

She muttered.

"You curse a lot, don't you?"

He retorted as they exited the building.

"Fuck yea, I do."

Bella replied with a big smile, like she was proud of herself for her limited vocabulary. He didn't smile back.

"Is it really necessary?"

Bella frowned, biting her lip. She didn't reply. They walked in silence to the car in the lot.

"Do you do it to express yourself?"

He was genuinely curious. He'd never heard a female, or met one, for that matter, that used the amount of obscenities as she did.

"Why the fuck does it matter?"

Bella finally said, becoming angry. He stopped walking; they'd reached his vehicle. Bella dropped his arm and made her own way to the passenger side door. He unlocked the car and climbed in, Bella hopping in next to him. As he started up the engine, he looked out the corner of his eye.

Bella was sitting with her arms crossed over her chest. She stared straight out the window.

"I just don't think it's very ladylike. It's a very ugly thing."

"Okay, I fucking get it."

Bella snapped. He smirked. He was getting to her and he knew it. He loved the feeling that pissing her off gave him. The rest of the drive to the university campus was quiet. He didn't turn on the radio, he let it remain silent.

Serene.

Blissful silence seething with anger from Bella who was not getting her way. The university appeared in the distance. It loomed massive through the trees and the thin layer or morning fog.

"When is your first class?"

He asked as he pulled into the parking lot. He glanced around the lot. A few, cheap looking vehicles were the only other ones in it. They clearly belonged to students who couldn't afford school and a car.

"Did you hear me?"

Bella asked.

"Hey. Michael."

She snapped her fingers in front of his face. He once again, re-focused. Bella was snapping her fingers in front of his face over and over. He grabbed her wrist.

"Must you?"

Bella pulled her hand free.

"You asked me a question and then zoned out. Pay attention."

She paused, opened the car door and stepped out. She shivered slightly. It was still early; the sun was still trying to make its way out from its hiding place behind the clouds.

He climbed out of his car and locked the door. He couldn't help but feel like something was off. The atmosphere of the school was shifted somehow. Bella's grumpy phase had obviously passed. She latched herself back onto him protectively.

"I don't have classes for another hour. I'll leave you at the door, but I'll see you after. My house."

He did his best to give her a convincing smile. She grinned back, tightening her grip on his arm as if he'd vanish if she let him go. They passed the Raven fountain in the courtyard. That Raven fountain would be the death of him. The massive, gaudy raven in the middle of the fountain was very old. Old and rickety. As beautiful as the rest of the marble and granite fountain was, he was terrified, truly terrified that the raven would collapse one day when Saige was sitting there, studying, crushing her.

That fucking fountain.

The main doors were on the other side of the fountain.

"I'll be back later. See you. Have fun in your class."

He smiled down at Bella. She hugged him tightly.

"Bye, Michael."

She swooned. As annoying as she was, he had to admit, she had some great cleavage.

The moment the doors shut behind Bella, he immediately turned and headed back to his car. He had to prepare his home for his newest guest. He also needed to prepare Mya's corpse. That wasn't right. No, it shouldn't be corpse. She should still be living. He'd bring a new girl home. Give them hope. But he'd gotten too enraged.

Mya was dead. He fisted his fingers through his hair. Everything was going wrong.

"Excuse me?"

He looked up. Someone was coming towards him.

"May I help you?"

He said to the stranger. He sized the important looking man up. He noticed the man was wearing an expensive looking black suit. Probably Armani. He had sandy brown hair, styled into a nice, quaffed flip. His eyes were framed by a couple of fine wrinkles. He couldn't be more than forty.

"My name is Sean Maynard. I am an Agent working with the FBI."

He froze.

FBI Agent.

What the fuck.

"Hi sir. What can I do for you?"

Sean Maynard looked him up and down.

"Nice coat."

He noted.

"Thank you. Limited edition."

Sean Maynard smirked.

"Looks like a Brioni Vanquish."

"Desmond Merrion. Good job though. You know your suits. Now, what can I do for you?"

Maynard grinned.

"Actually, you can come with me, down to the station."

He felt himself start to panic.

Don't show it.

"What for?"

He asked, keeping his cool.

"Nothing major. Questioning."

Maynard responded, just as coolly.

"Questioning?"

He said.

"Yes, sir. Please, come with me."

"You can't take me with you if you don't tell me what this is about."

He stood his ground. He knew his rights.

"What's your name?"

Maynard stated.

"It's none of your business. You haven't answered me, so I don't need to answer you."

"Listen, if you don't start being cooperative, I can arrest you for being disorderly."

Maynard put his hand on his belt, towards his gun.

"We don't want to start a scene."

He held up his hands.

"Okay, fine. Take me down. I did nothing wrong. I'm coming from a meeting."

Maynard scoffed, he walked slowly towards him. He wasn't about to fight an FBI Agent.

"Matt, please. Talk to me."

Saige pleaded. Matt was wandering the apartment, cleaning the various, small messed and gathering the empty liquor bottles.

"Matt!"

Saige screamed. Matt turned to stare at her momentarily.

"I don't want that girl in here again, okay?"

He returned to his chores.

"Why?"

Saige asked, her voice wavering between inside voice and yelling. Matt didn't reply. He didn't even acknowledge Saige had said anything. She stormed over to him, grabbed his arm and forced him to face her.

"What the fuck?"

He growled.

"That's enough, Matthew."

Matt burst out laughing.

"Matthew? Really Saige. You sound like my mother. 'That's enough, Matthew.' Funny."

He mocked her. She frowned at him.

"What the fuck is your deal?"

Matt grabbed her shoulders.

"I do not want that girl in my house."

Saige pushed him away from her.

"You said that. But why? You can't seriously hate her that much."

Matt tried to grab her again.

"Sai."

"No. Don't touch me. You acted like a complete asshole the entire morning. Why?"

Matt swiveled away from her. She swore she could hear him sniffle. Was he crying?

"Matt."

She said, lowering her voice. She couldn't yell at him if he was crying. No, she'd feel just awful. She touched his shoulder softly. He jerked but didn't move away. He'd become jumpy. He didn't use to be.

"You want to know why? Because of him."

Saige circled Matt, stood in front of him, her hands on his waist.

"Michael? I don't understand."

Matt grabbed her face in his hands. He stared into her eyes. She didn't think she'd ever seen so much concern, worry, maybe even fear, in one person's eyes, let alone, Matt's. Matt was always so brave and strong. The amount of emotion in his eyes seemed to age him.

"Babe?"

Saige whispered. One of her hands ran up his body, cupping his cheek. The moment her palm touched his face, he closed his eyes. A couple of tears squeezed their way out of his closed eyelids and streaked their way down his cheeks, colliding with her palm. He pulled her into him and hugged her. He buried his face in her hair.

She felt compelled to hug him back even harder. Confusion enveloped her. She had no idea why he was acting this way. She felt his body shake. She realized he was crying. Not just a couple of tears. He was actually crying. She felt awful. She felt like her heart was breaking. She squeezed him into her as tightly as she could.

"I don't trust him."

She heard Matt whisper.

"Why not?"

She whispered back. She wasn't as concerned about what he had to say. She was more worried about how he felt right then. Matt lifted his face from her hair and slowly slumped to the floor. Saige kept her hold on him, but sunk down with him.

"Please don't hang out with him."

Matt said. He was clutching her hands now. She stared at him; a look of total perplexity sewn onto her features.

"Matt..."

"Please, Saige. I don't trust him. I can't put my finger on it, but there's something...not right. Not right about him. He just pops up out of nowhere and suddenly you guys are best friends. And what about that poem at dinner. What the fuck was that all about? I just don't like the way he looks at you."

Saige didn't mean to, but a soft chuckle escaped her lips.

"You make it sound like I'm a piece of meat."

She had to stifle another laugh. She closed her eyes and took a deep breath. When she re-opened them, she saw Matt's eyes filled with so much...pain.

He looked genuinely hurt over her reaction. He was still clutching her hands, though not as tightly. Saige could feel him shudder, his entire body quivered and he dropped her hands. She thought he was acting ridiculous.

She reached for his hands again. He pulled away and turned his head from hers.

"Matt. Stop."

Saige said. She touched his knee. He shocked her by pushing her hand off his leg. Her eyes widened.

"Here's the thing, Sai."

He paused, voice trembling. Saige could tell it took everything in him not to continue crying.

"Look at me."

She said softly, scooting across the linoleum floor, trying to get him to face her. He avoided her gaze.

"Here's the thing,"

He repeated, pausing to gulp hard. He was trying to push the lump in his throat back down.

"I love you and I care about you, so much. More than I ever thought I could."

He paused again, coughing.

"I love you, too."

Saige said. She tried to move closer to him. He disregarded her.

"You think it's funny, that I don't trust him. You think it's funny and..."

"I think it's silly because it is."

Saige interceded. She slapped the floor, open palm.

"He's just a guy! Like you. Like Troy. Like Jared. Like Michael. He's just a guy. Another university guy."

Saige felt her face flush, her cheeks growing hot.

"I think your behavior is silly. I don't know why you don't like him. You haven't given me a logical reason to dislike him. Because something doesn't *feel* right. Because he *looks* at me weird?"

She paused in her tirade to push herself off of the kitchen floor. She stood over Matt, hands on her hips.

"So, come on. Hit me then. Hit me with a good enough reason why I should be wary of him and I will. Come on."

She waited, glaring down at the poor guy hunched over on the floor. He didn't respond. She rolled her eyes and huffed out heavily.

"Fine. Whatever. I'll see you later when you're not acting like such a child."

She turned on her heels, snatched her purse off of the counter top and made a beeline for the door.

"So, it's him then."

Matt's voice came from behind her. She stopped walking and turned around. Her hand was frozen on the door knob.

"What?"

"You walking away right now means you are picking him over me."

Saige's jaw dropped.

"Seriously? No. Me walking away right now means I'm going to be late to my Criminal Justice class."

She turned the knob and pulled open the apartment door.

"Can you pick? I... I need you to pick. You can stay friends with him or stay with me."

Saige felt herself tear up.

"You're giving me an ultimatum? Really?"

He didn't reply. He just lifted his head and looked at her with big, sad, puppy dog eyes.

"What if I pick staying his friend?"

Matt let out a heavy breath.

"Then that's it."

A single tear rolled over the rim of her left eye and went barreling down her cheek.

"Bye, Matt."

She slammed the door behind her and slid to the floor. She hit her head against the wall and pulled her knees up to her chest, wrapped her arms around them and began to sob.

15

PJ's chin rested in her hand. She was sitting at her desk, twirling a pencil between her fingers. Phil was working in the lab, trying to find out if Samuel Thomas was somehow magically still alive.

Federal Agents, Charlie Hamm and Ansyn Darbyshire were still working feverishly to find out about the little girl. She hadn't heard back from Daniel, Detective Derek Brady or Agent Sean Maynard, who Brinker stationed at the university on surveillance.

She felt hopeless. She had no idea where to go from there. None. She twirled the pencil too fast, it slipped from her fingers and it tumbled to the floor. She stared after it, watching it roll under the edge of her desk. She sighed and let her chin drop from her hand. She crossed her arms on the desk and buried her face in the crevice.

She didn't know how long she stayed that way. Had to be a good five minutes at least, before a soft knock resounded through her door.

"What?"

She called out, her word, muffled in her arms. The knock came again.

"What?"

She screamed, lifting her head, glaring at the door. It slowly squeaked open. Brock poked his head into the room.

"You okay in here?"

PJ let her head drop back down to her arms, banging off the desk. She didn't bother to answer Brock. She knew that he knew very well she was not okay in there.

"I have something. You may want to come with me."

Brock said softly. PJ's shoulders lifted and fell.

"Why?"

She said, loud enough for the words to make it past her arms.

"Martin, Brady, and Maynard are back from their shift."

He paused while his words hit PJ. She shifted in her seat and slowly lifted her head.

"And they've got a few creeps with 'em."

Brock had never seen PJ move so fast in all of the years he'd known her. She was out of the chair and standing at the door in seconds.

"Let's go."

She said bluntly. Brock couldn't help but smile.

"Not wasting any time."

He stated. PJ glanced sideways at him, but continued her long strides down the hall.

"We literally have zero time to waste."

She said, refocusing on the task at hand.

"Tell me. What have they found out? Anything?"

Brock chewed on his lip for a moment.

"They brought back three men. They all say they have reasons to be there, at the university. They very well might. Our men took into consideration other aspects other than the description you gave them. Hair dye, coloured contacts. That sort of thing."

They turned down a different hallway. The door they were looking for was fast approaching.

"Do any of them look like Sam?"

PJ was hesitant to ask.

"You're really the only one that can actually answer that."

PJ knew he was going to say that. They reached the door. Brock grabbed the handle and twisted it open. PJ held her breath. They both stepped into the observation room. PJ peered through the window. Three men sat at the steel table in the interrogation room. They all looked sweaty and nervous. PJ looked at each of them.

Blonde hair, slightly chubby face. She couldn't tell what colour his eyes were. His head was tucked and he was clasping and unclasping his hands.

"Andrew Hopkins."

Someone in the room said as if they were reading her mind.

"Says he goes to the university."

She studied the next man. His eyes darted around the room like he was trying to find a way to escape. He had thick, black hair and a square, meaty face. PJ squinted, bit her cheek and shook her head.

"Kellan Nix. Apparently, a janitor at the school."

PJ pursed her lips and moved her eyes to the third and final man. He had black hair as well, a strong jaw line, and sturdy shoulders.

"What the fuck!"

PJ exclaimed. She whirled away from the window and glared at the officers in the room.

"Nick Red..."

"I know who the fuck he is. Why the fuck is he in there?"

PJ pointed at the window.

"He was prowling around the school."

Detective Derek Brady said. PJ turned back to the window. Nick was sitting calmly at the table, hands clasped together. He was staring down at his interlocked fingers.

"You do know who he is right?"

PJ yelled. She was furious.

Livid.

Brady nodded.

"Of course, but our orders were to pick up any one who looked suspicious."

PJ shot him a nasty look and stormed over to the door. She pulled it open as if it were weightless and slammed it shut with so much force, she was surprised when the room didn't quake.

She turned a quick corner and entered the interrogation room. Andrew, Kellan and Nick looked up in unison.

"Oh, thank god."

Nick muttered.

"Nick, come with me."

PJ gestured. He slowly stood up. She looked at Andrew and Kellan for a moment. Andrew had blue eyes. Kellan had blue eyes. Neither seemed overly cold. But she couldn't be sure. It had been thirteen years. She had grown accustomed to his icy gaze. PJ turned towards the heavy metal door, Nick right behind her.

The minute she pulled it open, Brinker's sturdy build filled out the frame.

"Richards, what are you doing?"

He tried to sound heated, but PJ did not miss the sadness tracing her name when spoken from his mouth.

"You can't release the suspects like this."

He said smoothly. PJ's eyes widened.

"Nick's not a suspect."

She replied. She hoped she sounded strong.

"He was prowling the school. He was defiant with one of my Agents..."

"Nick."

PJ interrupted. She turned her back to Brinker and looked at Nick.

"What were you doing at the school?"

Nick looked from PJ to Brinker then back to PJ.

"I was meeting with a client."

He said, directly to PJ.

"Who? What for?"

Brinker cut in, glaring at Nick.

"Lawyer-client confidentiality."

Nick responded. Brinker narrowed his eyes. PJ could feel the testosterone. She started to push her way past Brinker.

"I'm sorry, Richards. You don't have juris..."

"Jurisdiction? Are you kidding me? Get out of my way, Agent Brinker."

PJ shoved him sideways and let Nick out of the room, leaving a ruffled James Brinker blocking the door of the interrogation room.

Once back in the office, PJ sat down beside Nick and grabbed his hand.

"Thank you, P."

He said. PJ smiled at him, leaned in and kissed his cheek.

"I'm sorry you had to deal with that."

She said softly, giving his hand a gentle squeeze. He reciprocated and smiled at her. Then he looked around for a clock.

"Shit, P. What time is it?"

He asked, upon not seeing any form of telling time on the walls. PJ pulled up her sleeve and looked at the little silver women's Rolex on her wrist.

"Ten fifty-six."

She told him. He stood up so fast it made PJ's head spin.

"Fuck!"

He yelled. He started moving towards the door.

"Nick? What's wrong?"

She questioned.

"Before those assholes picked me up, I was supposed to be meeting my client. I don't have my phone. It's in my car. Which is at the university. She's probably so pissed. This is not good lawyer etiquette."

His words were spewing out of his mouth. PJ grabbed his shoulders.

"Are you forgetting I do have a vehicle?"

He stopped fidgeting and stared at her.

"Do you need to get back to the university? Come on babe. I'll take you."

She slid his hand back into his. He smiled quickly at her and cupped her cheek, kissing her gently. They exited her office and walked swiftly towards the lobby.

No one was in the entrance. Not on the inside anyway. Just past the glass doors, PJ could see the hordes of the reporters milling around outside. It seemed as though even more had accumulated within the past hour. She turned back towards Nick who was staring out at everyone outside.

"You already know this, but the minute we open those doors, they will be on us like white on rice."

Nick chuckled at her comparison.

"Oh, I know."

"They'll be shouting questions at us, just, for your own image, do not respond."

Nick turned PJ to look at him.

"Relax, P. I know. I'm a professional."

PJ let out a breath and nodded at the door.

"So, let's go then."

Using her free hand, she shoved the glass doors open. They squeaked loudly on their hinges, alerting the reporters of their existence.

"Detective Richards!"

"Look, Nick Redford!"

"Detective Richards! Did Nick kill those girls?"

"Nick! Say something to the camera!"

"Admit you murdered those girls!"

Someone shoved a big, black TV camera in Nick's face. He ducked out of the way of the swinging lens, ignoring them. They were almost at PJ's vehicle.

"Detective Richards! Where's Agent Brinker?"

PJ felt herself tense up at the mention of Brinker's name. She pulled her keys out of her purse and unlocked the car with the automatic button. She and Nick ducked into the car, turning the screams of the reporters into muted yelps.

"That wasn't so bad."

Nick noted. He looked out the window. The reporters were still shouting questions at them. PJ started her car and peeled out of the parking lot.

"Parasites. Vultures. They're fucking parasitic vultures. That's what they are."

PJ spat. She had a serious distaste for the likes of those reporters. Nick's hand fell on her knee. He gave a gentle squeeze.

"Thanks for getting me out of there, P."

She shot him a sideways glance, but returned her eyes to the road.

"You've already thanked me."

Confusion sat on her voice like a weight on her chest.

"Besides, I know you. And I know Sam. You are not Sam."

She realized right then that she had never told Nick about that time in her life. She clamped her mouth shut.

"Sam?"

Nick wondered. PJ cursed herself.

"PJ? Sam who?"

Nick was asking, pressing her for an answer. PJ could see the university coming up ahead.

"Short version. Sam is Samuel Thomas. He murdered a bunch of girls a few years back, including my sister. Before I knew who he really was, I spent a little while as his girlfriend."

She coughed and choked back tears just as she pulled into the parking lot. Nick could see how hard it was for her to talk about. About that part of her life.

"It's okay, P."

He said, languidly. He wasn't sure what else to say. This was all a huge shock. She swiped at her eyes, wiping away the moisture.

"It's okay. Yea. Now, where is your car?"

She shot him a smile.

"Don't worry. I have to go inside."

Nick waited until PJ shifted her car into park before unbuckling his seat belt.

"Are you coming over tonight?"

PJ asked as he pushed open the door.

"I doubt it. This little set back will probably result in me working late. I'll see you tomorrow though."

He gave her a quick peck on the cheek and slid out the door. PJ watched him jog towards the doors of the school. She admired the massive Raven fountain.

Tacky, but beautiful.

As soon as he disappeared into the school, PJ pulled out of the lot and started making her way back to the department. She couldn't help but notice his beautiful Mustang was not in the parking lot.

16

He let out a heavy sigh. Thank god PJ was in love with him. He didn't think he'd have gotten off half as easy if someone else was working the case. He didn't realize it, but he had been chuckling to himself just inside the doors of the university.

"I know you and I know Sam. You are not Sam."

He repeated her words, a gut bursting laugh erupted from deep within him. He regained control of his laughter and looked around the empty hallways. Classes would be letting out soon. He'd need to hurry home and get ready for his guest. He figured he couldn't be touched.

PJ was a very highly respected unit of the force. She'd get back to the office and yell at everyone for detaining him. She'd make sure they left him alone from then on. He exited the school and peered around the brick wall. PJ's car was gone.

He kept smiling to himself. He was a lot smarter this time. He sauntered towards the lot, eyeing his car. Nick was no fool. He couldn't drive around in his sixty-nine Mustang and act like a university student. He needed a vehicle that could mask his identity. Keep him hidden in plain sight.

He took big strides across the school grounds, reaching his car quickly. He didn't hesitate to clamber in and start the car. On the drive back to his beloved cabin home, he cursed himself. He thought he was smart. Involving himself with PJ again.

In the long view of the plan, it was a good idea. At least the beginnings of one. Date the enemy. She won't suspect a thing. If anything, she will want to defend him. Which is exactly how it was working out for him so far. He thought it was a brilliant idea. PJ had been so in love with him all those years ago.

PJ had fallen hard for him again, without knowing it. He didn't expect her to be the top cop on this case. He knew it would reach the cops; he knew she would be involved. He just didn't think she'd be the top shit. He didn't expect her to push so hard. Especially since her sister was involved.

PJ was full of surprises. He slammed his hands down on the wheel, blaring the horn loudly.

"Fucking PJ. Fucking bitch."

He muttered. He yanked the wheel sideways, taking a sharp turn to the left.

"Goddamn it, PJ. Why'd you have to become a cop?"

He yelled, even though he knew why. It was actually his fault she changed her school major. She had originally been studying veterinarian courses. He knew she changed her major the day Melissa had turned up as a doornail.

He knew PJ didn't suspect anything. If she had, she wouldn't have let him out of that room. For fuck sakes, she thought he was some hoity toity lawyer named *Nick Redford.*

Still.

She'd become a liability. She was digging too deep. He slammed his foot down on the brake pedal, skidding to a stop. Gravel flew everywhere. He shoved open the door to the car, leaving it running. He'd be right back. He sauntered up the gravel driveway, bypassing and ignoring the beautiful nature surrounding his woodland cabin.

He shoved the door open so hard it crashed into the wall, resulting in a round dent in the wood. He stormed through the cabin, tidying things on the counter in the kitchen and straightening the pictures on the walls in the hallway on his way to the one room. That one room.

He could smell it from where he stood. The awful stench of a rotting, decaying corpse. He wondered how the smell could be so rancid after only one day. Did the others smell this bad?

He wouldn't know for sure. He disposed of them the same day they died at his hand. He wouldn't know for sure, but he could assume the others were just as bad, if not worse. He resisted the urge to plug his nose as he reached from the door knob. It wasn't locked. Why would it be? He took a deep breath of air before pushing open the door and stepping inside.

Now he could understand half of the reason it smelled so bad. The dead girl had soiled herself. A lot. She'd released all of the contents of her bowels, it spilled out of her pants and onto the carpet.

He clasped his hands, digging his finger nails into the palms of his hands, making half-moon imprints in his skin. He could get as pissed off at her as he wanted, but it would do nothing. She was already dead. Instead, he marched over to the body and knelt down beside it. Holding his breath, he ripped at the remainder of her clothing, pulling it away from her body.

She looked bloated; her skin pulled tight like she'd had some bad plastic surgery. She was purple. She was not beautiful. He felt disgusted with himself. How could he have visualized his perfect angel's face on this body?

He reached down to her and started stripping the remainder of her clothing off of her. After he'd pulled it all off, he grabbed one of her arms and dragged her to the doorway. At the door, he picked her up, gasping slightly. She was all dead weight. He chuckled slightly at the pun as he struggled to carry her out of the room. He was so thankful his cabin was in such a remote, isolated area. He didn't have to worry about any nosy neighbours peeping into his business like in Springfield.

He lugged the limp body out the front door, dropping her with a thud to the ground beside the car. He popped the trunk by hitting the button on his key fob and stared down at his two boxes inside. The ones that held his identities. He very carefully removed his precious boxes of cargo. He wouldn't need them right now, so he wanted to be sure he put them away safely and securely.

After gently placing his items down at the front door, he returned to where Mya's body lay. With a heavy sigh, he reached down, hooking his arms under her arm pits and hauling her to her feet. He dragged her the rest of the way around the car and carelessly shoved her into the trunk, pushing her as far back as she could go, then he slammed the lid closed with a loud bang.

With a second heavy, strained sigh, he moved back around to the front of the car and climbed into the driver's seat behind the steering wheel. The car still rumbled away, the radio playing quietly in the background. He threw the car into reverse and backed out of the gravel and dirt driveway as fast as he could without spinning out.

The road back into town wasn't long, but at that moment, it felt like the longest possible route. He felt stressed and pressed for time. He was. He reached for the radio and slowly turned up the volume. The song "*All About That Bass*" was playing. He grimaced and immediately turned it back down.

"Turn that shit off."

He mumbled to himself. His foot felt heavy on the gas. It wasn't much past noon and he was panicking. He'd have to be careful when he rid himself of the burden currently occupying the space in his trunk. He pulled into town and slowed his speed, lifting his foot off of the accelerator. He did not need to get pulled over. That was the last thing he needed.

He knew where he would go. It would be the same place where he rid himself of all his burdens. He would go to Woodland Park. He could see the massive mahogany sign to his right. There weren't any vehicles in the lot, but that certainly didn't mean that someone couldn't pull in while he was doing the dirty deed.

He held his breath as he shut off the car. He slid out of the door and slinked his way to the trunk, popping it open by the fob again. He had no idea how to act in broad daylight. He had always gone out at night. He glanced around at the park and took in his surroundings. It was the middle of the day at the beginning of a work week. No one was around, everyone was at work. Or should be. He breathed a sigh of relief.

He bent at the waist and reached in, grabbing Mya's body by a handful of hair and pulled her to the opening of the trunk. He quickly double checked the area to make sure he was still in the clear and hooked his arms under her armpits. He pulled the naked girl from his trunk and dropped her on the ground beside the rear wheels.

He closed the trunk with a hard slam and slouched over to pick up the corpse again. He pulled her into his arms and rearranged her so he was carrying her like she was a baby. He looked towards the forest in the park and began walking as casually as possible, although, he wasn't sure how one could walk casually while carrying a dead girl.

He shrugged the thought from his mind and checked out the fields as he strolled. He was almost at the edge of the small patch of woods when he heard the laughter. He figured it was a kid. A very little kid, maybe five or six by the sound of the giggles. He picked up his pace as he past the first layer of trees.

His heart quickened as he heard a grown woman shouting.

"Faye? Where'd you go? Faye, this isn't funny. Where'd you go?"

He was about six layers of trees in by now. He could still hear the giggling and a couple of hysterical shouts. He could feel the pestering beads of sweat dripping down his face. He couldn't go any further. He dropped the corpse on the ground and stared at it.

She was twisted and mangled, gross looking. He squinted and knelt down. Very carefully, he moved her legs so they were straight, instead of the pretzel form they had taken. He straightened her face and that's when he realized he didn't close her eyes. They say eyes are the windows to the soul. He felt his own eyes well up. She was definitely dead. When she was breathing, she'd had one of the most beautiful sets of blue eyes he had ever seen. Now, they were cold, staring up at him. Dull. Like fish eyes.

He gasped and sucked in a breath. He gently slid his fingers over her eyelids, closing over the soulless, scary eyes.

"Hey!"

He heard the little voice shout. He scrambled away from the body on his hands and knees. He clambered to his feet.

"What are you doing?"

He spun around and found himself staring at a little girl. He was frozen in place.

"Is she okay?"

She asked him, trying to peer around him to the body. He panicked. He turned around and ran. He ran as fast as he could, cutting through the winds, dodging trees, smacking away the skinny branches that swiped at his face and jumping over fallen logs. He could hear the childish screaming.

He could only assume now that she had marched over to the body to investigate, only to see the deep gashes, the bruising...a whole bloody mess. He needed to get back to his car. Any minute now, the woman with the child would find her, staring and screaming at a purple corpse. She'd call nine one, one and within minutes, the whole area would be taped off, swarming with police and the feds.

He figured he probably had about ten minutes to loop around back to his vehicle and get the hell out of dodge. He realized his breathing was coming in quick, short gasps. He could see the edge of the small patch of forest by then. He could no longer hear the screams. Instead he could hear the sirens wailing. Had it been ten minutes already?

He burst through the trees and made a beeline for his car. The sirens got louder. His heart was pounding. He yanked open the door of his car and started the engine and peeled out of the lot, sending pebbles flying. The minute he was back on the main road, headed into town, he let out a sigh of relief. He'd made it out. He drove carefully and watched with wide eyes as four different police cruisers sped past him. Blue and red lights flashing. He glanced into his rear-view mirror and watched them turn into Woodland Park.

The little girl entered his mind. What would she say? Would she be too terrified and surprised to say anything? Or would she describe everything in perfect detail? Explicit detail...

His foot pressed down harder onto the gas pedal. He sped down the road, heart beating utterly fast, sweating profusely.

"She was just a little kid. No way she'd speak after seeing a mutilated body. No. She'll sit there and stare off blankly. I'm okay. It'll be okay."

He said out loud, as if he was trying to reassure himself that his fate did not lie in a little girl's hands. He pulled into a parking lot and turned the key in the ignition, turning the vehicle off. He dropped his head onto the steering wheel and stayed like that for several minutes. He needed to recuperate.

His heart slowed. He didn't re open his eyes right away. He kept his head bowed, breathing deeply. A couple of light raps on his window startled him, making him jump. He slowly lifted his head and looked out the window.

A stout Mexican looking man with a skinny black moustache wiggled his nose and knocked again. Nick sighed and pressed the automatic button. The window gradually made its descent. Nick noted that the Mexican man was wearing a cement grey jumpsuit. The name "Juan" was stitched into the upper left breast pocket.

"What can I do for you, Juan?"

Juan shifted on his feet and glanced over his shoulder at the building the parking lot belonged to. Nick followed his gaze. Costco.

"Senor, I noticed you pull in about ten minute ago. Is you okay?"

It took everything in him not to drop his jaw.

"Ten-ten minutes?"

He stuttered. He didn't think he had been regrouping that long.

"I'm fine. Thank you."

Nick said. Juan didn't leave. He kept staring at Nick. He narrowed his eyes.

"Is there something else?"

He asked, snidely. Juan wiggled his nose again.

"No, senor. I go now."

Juan turned on his heels and started walking back up to the front entrance of Costco. Nick shook his head and pressed the button for the window. He noted that Juan's accent was pretty thick. He must have just gotten to the Canadian country not long ago.

"Dirty. Dirty fucking foreigners."

Nick spat with a grimace on his face. He slowly re-started the car and backed out of the parking lot. He figured he'd calmed down enough to drive safely. He wanted to drive back to the park and grab that little girl.

He figured he'd be safe; she wouldn't say anything. But he had to be sure. He'd cruise by. Hopefully she'd be away from the officers. He knew what he was planning was extremely risky.

He drove the speed limit as to not draw attention to himself. He slowed down as he approached the beautiful park. Just as he expected, yellow "Do Not Cross" caution tape roped off the entrance to the lot.

Uniformed officers swarmed the lot and the perimeter of the small thatch of woods.

He didn't see the girl at first. He scanned the area as he was slowing down. That's when he noticed her and who she was with.

"PJ. Fuck."

He whispered. He saw PJ helping the woman and child into one of the police cruisers.

"Fuck!"

He slammed his hands down on the wheel. He continued on past the park. He'd missed his shot. He should have just grabbed her when she spoke to him. He could only hope and pray that she kept her fucking mouth shut.

He made the sharp left turn down the old, dusty, dirt road, eyes straight ahead, glued to the road. He grumbled to himself. When had he become so disorganized? His mind flashed back to when Saige had first introduced herself a few days ago. That's when.

Now that she was an active piece of his life...she was closer to him now than she ever was. The excitement was almost too much for him. Knowing she was so close to being his again...that's when he became messy. He pulled into the drive way of his cabin, this time turning the car off. He jumped out of the driver's seat, slamming the door shut behind him. He took massive strides towards the door, reaching it quickly. He pushed it open hard, the door slamming against the wall with a loud bang.

He pulled the boxes just inside the door and closed it gently, as if he was apologizing to it for being so rough. It didn't last long. He stormed down the hallway and kicked open the door to the room Mya had occupied for her short stay with him. Her bodily fluids left a small stain on the rug. He squinted at it. He knew a little bit of vinegar and water could clean the majority of it, but it would absolutely leave a mark.

He examined the old rug and truly noticed how abhorrent it was. He grimaced and bit his cheek. It would do for Bella's stay, but he would get a new one in for when Saige returned to him. He'd purchase a new bed, new sheets, maybe even paint the walls a cheerier colour than the depressing blue. He'd make it perfect for his girl. He rushed back to the kitchen, stopping at the first cupboard on the outside.

He flung it open and spotted the large, clear bottle. It was a little under half full and had the words "Pure White Vinegar" printed neatly in block letters on the label. He pulled it from the cupboard and tucked it under his arm.

He didn't bother closing the cupboard, he'd be right back. He yanked a dish towel off of the stove handle and made his way back to his guest room. He dropped to his hands and knees beside the fresh stain. He gingerly twisted the vinegar cap off of the jug and tipped gradually. He splashed some vinegar over the spot, being extra sure it was on the whole thing. He breathed deeply. The foul smell of coppery blood, urine and fecal matter was quickly over taken by the strong scent of the vinegar.

He loved the smell of vinegar. He sneezed. He wiped his nose with the back of his hand and got to work scrubbing with the dish towel. Momentarily, he pulled away from the spot. It was faded, but not gone. He didn't expect it to be. He sighed at his efforts. It was a very short couple of seconds of silence before his phone started ringing. The sound was muffled in his pocket. He almost didn't hear it. He rolled his eyes as he pulled the phone from his pocket.

He assumed it was Bella, wondering his whereabouts. He, unlike PJ, did not have a habit of not checking his caller ID. Mainly because he always wanted to be sure he used the right alias when addressing himself. The caller was not Bella. It was PJ.

He swallowed hard and pressed the flashing green answer button.

"Hello? Nick Redford."

He said, using his best lawyer voice.

"Hey hon."

He really liked the sound of PJ's voice. Not more than Saige's but PJ had a very wonderful voice as well. Musical.

"Oh, hey P. What's up babe? I'm just with my client right now, can I call you back in an hour or so?"

He heard PJ shuffling around the background and a couple of muffled voices.

She must have returned to the precinct.

"Well yea, I guess."

She said slowly, trailing off. Nick bit his lip.

"Everything alright?"

He questioned, although he was positive, he knew what was upsetting her.

"I'll be fine. I'll let you get back to your meeting. Talk to you later."

She replied quickly.

"Wait, you're upset. Something's bothering you. I don't like when you're upset. When I'm done here, how about I pick you up and we go to my cabin for the night? Let me take care of you."

He heard himself saying. PJ was too deep. He needed her gone. Maybe he was going out of his comfort zone, bringing both girls that night, but Bella was annoying and PJ was too smart.

"Cabin? Since when do you have a cabin?"

Nick chuckled.

"It was supposed to be a surprise. I just bought one."

He heard PJ gush happily.

"Okay babe. That sounds nice."

"It might be a little late, though."

Nick said into the phone.

"That's okay. Let me know when you're coming. I'll be sure I'm ready. Bye babe. I love you."

"I love you too, Peanut."

He replied, using the incredibly stupid pet name for her. For some reason, she loved it. They both clicked off, effectively ending the call. He shoved himself away from the floor. He let the bottle of vinegar fall from his grasp. It splashed onto the floor immediately scenting the room with the sour smell of the liquid.

"Fuck!"

He screamed. He swiveled and slammed his fist into the wall. This was it. He'd have Bella and PJ in the cabin tonight. He needed to move fast and do his job. Everything was coming apart quicker than how it came together. He shouldn't have gotten involved with PJ again. He shouldn't have. But if it wasn't Saige, it would have to be PJ. She was the closest thing to his second favourite girl, Melissa that he had in his godforsaken life.

17

Nick finished cleaning up the mess as best as he could and then he looked down at his watch to check the time. It was just after one pm. He was running out of time. He only had about fifteen minutes to get to the university in order to meet with Bella. He exited the room and walked swiftly down the corridor towards his kitchen where he gave the boxes of his items a little kick. He reached for the door knob and twisted, effectively opened the cabin's door.

He was suddenly paranoid and he wasn't sure why. He was outside and headed towards his car. He noticed that his vehicle was the same as the one that Saige's boyfriend drove. He made that mental note as he climbed inside the car with ease and turned the key in the ignition and backed out of the driveway. He looked at his stereo as he turned the volume up. The words, "Boyfriend" by "Justin Bieber" flashed across the small screen. Now, he'd never heard any of the kid's music for himself, and he never wanted to. He seemed like such a douchebag. However, he had heard Saige pouring out her love for him one day with her blonde friends as they reached the fountain. She had been obsessing over how "utterly perfect" he was and how he had the "voice of an angel." Nick slowly turned up the volume. He'd give this Justin Bieber a shot. Especially if he was Saige's favourite. Part of him still didn't care to listen to it.

He drummed his fingers on the steering wheel as he drove. He tried to keep a clear mind as he passed Woodland Park. There were no more cruisers in the lot. Actually, there were no vehicles at all. The park seemed abandoned. Sad. Yellow police tape was still surrounding the entrance to the part of the forest that Mya's body had been found in. He was still reeling on his escape. How close he'd come to getting caught. It was not time for that yet. Not time at all.

He figured the cops would be back if that tape was still up. The park quickly left his view as he drove. He rounded a corner into town. The university was located almost directly in the middle of their quaint little city. He felt his fingers tighten on the grip of the wheel. How was he going to pull it off? He didn't want to change his game more than he already had. He knew he would have to kill one of them right away. He didn't want to. He wanted to be able to have some fun with them first. Perhaps there was another way. Perhaps he'd be able to overpower the two if they got to be too aggressive. He sure as shit knew that PJ would be a challenge. She was the best on the force for a reason.

He pulled up to the school and drove smoothly into the parking lot. He turned the automobile off and slid out of the seat and stood to his full height next to the car. He sucked in a deep breath as he began his stride across the lot towards the quad. As he rounded a corner, his eyes landed on the Raven statue. His blood began to boil. Even just looking at the thing pissed him off. One way or another, one day or another, he'd bring that fucking Raven down and smash it to smithereens. His eyes left the bird, travelling down the height and length of the statue, landing at the bottom of the fountain. He saw her.

He saw Saige sitting there like her norm, but this time, Bella was with her. He walked across the lawn towards them. It still felt off to him that he was able to approach his Saige so easily. He thought there was supposed to be more build up to their budding relationship.

"Hey gorgeous ladies."

He called out, catching their attention as he accosted them. Bella smiled widely and waved at him. He noticed Saige waved too, though her's was feeble. Something was wrong. Seeing her look so disheartened broke him. Bella rubbed Saige's shoulder.

"What's wrong, Sai?"

He said softly, his voice filled completely with genuine concern. Saige looked up at him, tearfully.

"I'm pretty sure Matt and I broke up."

He felt his heart jump for joy but he did not show it. He had to act like the concerned best friend.

"I'm so sorry."

He said apologetically, taking a seat next to her.

"You guys have a date to get to. You should go."

She stifled the urge to cry some more and forced a smile.

"Are you going to be okay, boo?"

Bella asked, giving Saige's shoulder a gentle squeeze. Saige nodded solemnly.

"Yeah, I'm just going to sit here and study. Midterms."

Bella kissed Saige's cheek. He felt compelled to do the same but fought it.

"Let us know if you need anything. Anything at all."

He said instead. Bella stood up and found her favourite spot on his arm to grab and latch onto. Nick put a hand on Saige's shoulder and gently squeezed. She looked up at him and smiled softly. He could see the pain and hurt and betrayal filling her eyes. It hurt him to see her so broken. Matt entered his mind.

That fucking asshole.

Anger filled him. Rage bubbled up from deep inside him. He did his best to keep it down. Hidden.

"Like I said, call either of us if you need anything."

He let his hand drop from her shoulder. He felt awful leaving her this way. Bella subtly tugged his arm, trying to pull him away from Saige. His Saige. He gave her one last mournful look before slowly starting to back away from her. She jumped up from her fountain perch.

"Wait."

She said. He slowed in his tracks and felt Bella tense beside him. She obviously wanted to get back to his place for their "date." Little did she know... Nick turned slightly as Saige hurled herself at him. She wrapped her arms tightly around his waist. The sudden embrace startled both Bella and himself. Bella let go of his arm. He gently wrapped his arms around Saige's shoulders, hugging her back in a bear like vice. His mind immediately flashed backwards, returning him to the day Saige first hugged him on her front lawn. Her tiny arms around his waist, his around her shoulders. Exactly this way. Exactly how it should be.

He shook himself back to the present day and looked down at the top of Saige's head, lovingly. After what seemed like several long minutes, Saige detached herself from his waist. He forced himself to let her go as well. She smiled up at him again, this time it wasn't so feeble. Bella grabbed his arm again and smiled at Saige.

"We really should be going."

She said wryly, tugging on Nick's arm.

"See you later, Sai."

Nick said to her before letting Bella drag him towards the parking lot. She knew what his car looked like, at least this car. She had no idea he owned a gorgeous Mustang. She spotted it in the lot and squealed. Nick felt the need to plug his ears from the piercing sound. They reached the car; Nick stuck a hand out for the handle. He pulled the door open and held it for Bella to get in.

"Gentleman."

She gushed before ducking her head into the vehicle. He shut the door after her and turned to walk to his side while rolling his eyes. He couldn't wait to rid himself of the persisting annoyance. He pulled open his driver's door with a huff of air. He sat next to Bella who immediately reached for his hand. He disregarded her and turned the key in the ignition and moved his hand down to his gear shift.

"We just have to stop at my house really quick. We're going to my cabin tonight."

He paused to make a left turn.

"Romantic getaway, am I right?"

His voice was deep and seductive. Bella started blushing heavily.

"I can't wait."

She smiled and grazed her fingers across his knee. Only a short, silent moment later, he pulled the car into the driveway of a cute, two story houses. It was strange. It looked like it had probably been white at one point, however the paint was now tinged gray. The trimming of the windows was a caramel coloured brown. The door was a much darker brown with a big window at the top. The small yard was kept incredibly neat the grass cut, the little chain link fence stood up straight. It looked odd, but was still cute. Bella smiled widely.

"This is adorable!"

She squealed. Nick winced at the sound but managed to keep himself composed.

"You can come inside if you'd like."

He said, smiling warmly at her. Underneath the warmth of something as easy as a smile, lay a deep abyss of cold, icy hatred and a fiery rage. She unbuckled her seatbelt. She wouldn't turn down his invitation. She'd be too stupid to. Stupid, but safe, for the time being. Nick slid out of the car, hustling towards the passenger side of the vehicle to let his companion out, acting like the complete and total gentleman package that he knew he was not. Bella had what seemed like a permanent grin plastered to her pink lips, revealing her perfect pearly whites.

She slipped her arm through his as he led her up the front steps to the little house. He held his big bunch of dangling keys in his palm. He chose a large silver one from the hoard and slid it smoothly into the lock. He gently pushed the door open, Bella quivering with excitement next to him. He rolled his eyes as he flicked the light switch next to the door, illuminating the entry way. Bella squealed again, clutching his arm in her grasp. She shook his arm ferociously.

"Look how cute it is!"

She exclaimed. The interior of the place was much more exquisite than the exterior. The walls were simple; they were painted a light cream colour, like an eggshell. A big mirror with a gorgeous Celtic looking black iron frame hung on the wall above a brown suede couch. The matching love seat was positioned right next to it. A multicolored tile coffee table sat between them on a very plushy dark brown carpet. A massive flat screen hung on the wall opposite the couches. It was simple but utterly beautiful at the same time.

Bella let his hand go. She kicked off her flats and ran across the room, launching herself onto the couch. Nick shook his head at her. She chuckled and gazed adoringly at him.

"Make yourself comfortable. I'll just go pack up a couple of things. Personal hygiene. You know."

He shot her a quick smile before disappearing around the corner. He held his breath and counted to sixty. He poked his head back into the room.

"Bells, I need to run back to town momentarily. Looks like I'm out of a couple of things. Stay here. I'll be back shortly."

For emphasis, he blew her a kiss and she giggled, relaxing backwards into the warm cushions of the expensive couch. Nick backed out of the house and shut the door. He quickly climbed back into his car and tore out of the driveway. He had to do his best to stay within the speed limit. He was in a very quiet suburban neighborhood, but he had to be very careful. The entire way back to town, he had only one thought about only one person. Matt. How could he hurt Saige like that? Anyone who hurt Saige like that deserved an even more horrible consequence and Nick was intent on giving it. He wanted Matt to suffer at his wrath.

He frowned at the road. He was angry, pissed off even, but more so sad that his baby girl was in pain. He'd deal with it. Oh, would he ever. He wasn't far now. He was sure he could make Matt's death look like a suicide. It wouldn't be too hard. He'd done it plenty of times before. He could see it. The apartment buildings that Matt resided in. He felt a sort of sick pleasure at the thought of slicing up Matt's arms. Sure, Matt's death certainly wouldn't be one of his more rewarding kills, but it had to be done. It would be thrilling, as thrilling as he could possibly make it. He pulled into the parking lot and came to a stop in the visitor space.

He got out and locked the door. He scanned the lot and his surroundings. There were many cars in their spaces but not a single soul lingered around outside. He smiled in spite of himself and made his way to the apartment building. He tried his best to seem inconspicuous. He hoped he was doing a good job, although it didn't matter. There wasn't any person inside the building. It was creepy, almost eerie, at how deserted the place was. He knew which apartment Matt lived in. It was, in his opinion, the mots conveniently located. Right next to a set of getaway stairs. He put his ear against the door and listened closely. There was a slight background noise, could be the TV.

He lifted his fist and knocked lightly, quickly scanning the hallway once more for any suspecting eyes. He heard rustling behind the door and a click. The door slowly opened, revealing a distraught looking Matt.

"Oh. It's you."

He said without smiling.

"What do you want?"

He asked. Nick could hear the anger in his voice. It took everything in him not to smile. He tried to peer around him. Matt glanced over his shoulder and the turned back to Nick.

"Can we have a word?"

Nick asked, stepping towards Matt and over the threshold to his apartment. Matt stepped back at the sudden advance.

"What about?"

He said, remaining as calm as he possibly could. Nick took another step fully entering the apartment. He shut the door behind him.

"Saige."

He replied bluntly. Matt reached passed Nick and grabbed the door knob.

"Look, man. I know you're friends with her, but I just can't. You need to leave."

Matt kept his voice low, like he was afraid the neighbours would hear them. Nick took a step towards Matt resulting in Matt taking a step back, letting his hand fall from the door knob.

"Michael. You're not welcome here. You need to leave before I call the police."

Nick chuckled.

"I just want to have a word."

Matt yanked his phone out of his pocket.

"I don't want to. You're really over stepping your boundaries. Get out of my apartment."

Matt said firmly. He held up his phone threateningly. Nick let out a laugh. Matt narrowed his eyes.

"What's so funny?"

Nick shrugged.

"Look, I'll go. Just humor me first. Have a word."

Matt sighed and lowered his shaking hand.

"Fine. One word."

That's when Matt made his first mistake. He turned his back to walk into the little living room. Nick lunged and grabbed Matt from behind. He wrapped him in a headlock and started squeezing. Matt gasped and dropped his cell phone. He thrashed about and started clawing at Nick's muscular forearms. Nick stepped kicked Matt's phone off to the side, out of reach. Matt slowly stopped struggling and went limp in Nick's grip. Nick could still feel Matt's heart beating. The veins in his neck were still pulsating. However, Nick had knocked him out. He hadn't intended to kill him that way, and he didn't. He let Matt's unconscious body drop to the floor with a thud. He slid a pair of stinky plastic surgeon's gloves from his pocket and pulled them over his hands. He wiggles his fingers and knelt down to the blacked-out university student.

He lifted his hands and studied his fingers. He didn't think Matt had scratched him in his scramble. He didn't see any marks on his own arms but he wanted to be sure. He studied Matt's fingernails closely. They were surprisingly clean. Not even one speck of dirt was caked under them. Nick dropped Matt's hands back down to the floor. He stood up and unzipped his jacket pocket. He pulled out a small roll of duct tape and yanked a strip off. It made a loud ripping sound as it unraveled. Nick knelt back down and wrapped the tape tightly around Matt's bare ankles. He did the same thing to his wrists.

Nick sighed. Now he just had to wait for Matt to wake up. He hoped it wouldn't be too long. He still had to get Bella to the cabin, put her out, and pick up PJ. He began to wander the apartment. He wanted to see what Matt possessed. To his disappointment, the university student barely owned anything. Nothing that interested Nick by any means. He made his way into one of the rooms in the hall by the kitchen. The apartment was bigger than he'd expected. He found himself in a bedroom.

The bed was unmade, blankets strewn across it. Clothes littered the floor in two piles. Nick noticed that one of the piles was made up of women's clothes. He held his breath as his eyes landed on the top of the pile. He took the two steps towards it and with a trembling hand, he reached towards, lifting it gently from the pile. RU was etched into the front in a gold fabric. This was Saige's sweater. He hugged it to his chest tightly and bent his head so he could smell it. It smelled faintly of vanilla and cinnamon. He knew that smell. and held it close to him.

He had spent far too much time in the bedroom when he suddenly heard groans coming from the kitchen. Matt was coming to. He hadn't realized his wrists and ankles were bound together. He was blinking and shaking his head. Nick leaned against the wall and watched Matt pull himself together. The minute Matt tried to push himself up and failed, is also the moment he saw his hands and feet trussed up like a deer.

"What the fuck?"

He exclaimed. He looked up and met Nick's eyes. Nick smirked.

"Okay, ha-ha. Very funny."

Matt joked. Nick could taste the fear that clung to his sarcasm.

"Where do you keep your paper and pencils?"

Nick asked. Matt stared at him, wide eyed.

"You're crazy."

He croaked. He lifted his hands to Nick.

"Cut this shit off. We can talk."

He pleaded. Nick clicked his tongue and shook his head. He turned and started pulling open drawers. Matt brought his wrists to his face and tried to gnaw on the thick and tough tape.

"Ah. Here it is."

Nick was digging through a drawer next to the sink and dishwasher. He pulled a stack of scrap papers and a blue ink pen from the drawer. His motions were rhythmic and quick. He had the papers and pen in one hand. He reached across the counter towards the knife block. A sick smile spread across his face as he pulled a stainless-steel steak knife from its spot. It was sharp, making a shing noise as it slid from the slot. It was music to his ears. He turned back to Matt, who was still furiously trying to chew his way through the binding tape.

"Knock it off."

Nick spat. He brought his foot back and swung it forward with so much force that when it connected with Matt's gut, it knocked him backwards. Matt sputtered and coughed. He wheezed hard, trying to suck in a breath. He lay on his side, gasping for air. Nick dropped to the linoleum beside him.

"Why are you doing this?"

Matt gasped. Nick set the knife down on the floor. He looked directly into Matt's pain filled eyes.

"You're going to write your suicide note now."

Nick replied, hatred piercing his voice, slicing through the air and stabbing Matt.

"This isn't funny, Michael."

Matt whispered.

"It's not a joke. Although, I find it deeply pleasuring."

Nick said, picking one slip of paper and putting it down on the floor in front of Matt.

"Michael..."

Matt started to protest. Nick's fist collided with Matt's face. Blood immediately started gushing from his nose.

"Fuck!"

Nick shouted.

"Look what you made me fucking do."

Matt coughed and spat blood out of his mouth.

"Fuck, Matt, just keep your fucking mouth shut and do what I fucking ask."

Nick said through gritted teeth. Matt was resistant.

"What did I ever do to you? Michael, stop, man, please."

Matt sputtered, blood spattering from his lips in all directions.

"Not me. Saige. You hurt Saige."

Nick growled. He grabbed Matt's collarbone and pulled him in close.

"You do not hurt my girl."

Matt coughed again and struggled against Nick's grip.

"Your girl? She's my girlfriend. I would never hurt her."

Nick tightened his grip, hitting a pressure point, causing Matt to cry out in pain. Nick ignored what Matt had just said.

"My name isn't Michael. It's Nick Redford. Though, you might know me better as Samuel. Samuel Thomas."

Matt didn't reply. Nick's eyes widened in surprise.

"Wait. Our girl never told you about me, did she?"

He chuckled as Matt stayed silent.

"I should be offended that she never mentioned our love."

He slowly slid the stationary closer to Matt.

"What are you talking about?"

Matt whispered, stuttering. His nose had stopped gushing. It was just a trickle now. Most of the scarlet was caked under his nose like the cocaine he used to snort.

"Sai and I have quite the story."

Matt shook his head.

"She would have said something,"

He started to say. Nick pinched the pressure point again. Matt winced and closed his eyes.

"It was around twelve years ago. We spent a year together before her family moved and she left me. She always said we'd find each other again. And now we have. Her family never approved of us because I was so much older. But we cared about each other. We still do. You can't fake our kind of love. You just can't. Anyway, her family forced her to see this shrink, Cara Martin. That bitch. She erased me, most of me, from Sai's mind. She'll be mine again soon. You'll see..."

Nick paused. He burst into laughter. He dropped his hand from Matt's shoulder and put it to his gut. He held it tight as he laughed. Moments later, he lifted his hand and wiped a tear away from his face.

"Actually, you won't."

He grabbed Matt's bound wrists and shoved the pen into his hands.

"Now, I want you to write, 'Dear Saige, I'm sorry I hurt you. You don't deserve that. I wish I could give you what you deserve. I wish you all the happiness you deserve. This is goodbye. Love, Matt.' Write it. Now."

Nick said sternly. Matt's hands were shaking, tears overflowing his eyes, threatening their descent down his cheeks at any moment. Nick grabbed the knife and held it to Matt's face. Matt began to sob quietly. He shakily wrote the words that Nick had spoken. He wrote in all capitals, darkening a couple of letters slightly, not enough that Nick noticed as he held the knife to Matt's throat. He knew this was it for him. He knew there'd be no bargaining for his life. Matt could just hope that Saige would see the clue he left in his note. He looked up at the ceiling just as the tears fell from his eyes. He closed them slowly.

"I love you, Saige. I never stopped and never will."

He whispered. Nick rolled his eyes and with one quick slashing movement, brought the knife across Matt's throat. Blood immediately squirted out, spraying across the kitchen and onto the floor in front of him. he started gagging as blood flowed steadily. Nick had to duck out of the way to avoid the warm spray.

The scarlet liquid poured out of the gash and down his shirtless chest. Nick watched with pure ecstasy as Matt choked on his own blood. He slumped to the ground in a puddle of his own life. Nick watched him as he twitched a couple of times and then came to a complete and still standing. A smirk made an appearance on Nick's face. That was a joyous scene to witness, although he preferred doing his deeds more intimately. He edged closer to Matt's motionless, lifeless body and cut the duct tape away from his wrists and ankles. He rolled both pieces into a ball and shoved it into his pocket. He took one of Matt's hands and started putting the knife oh so carefully into his hand but paused in doing so. He chuckled to himself and grabbed Matt's wrists and slid the knife over them swiftly. Deep red gashes appeared simultaneously under the large steak knife.

He needed to be sure the coroner would deem it as a suicide. After he decided Matt's wrists were sliced up enough, he put the knife back in his cold hands and curled his fingers around the handle. His eyes landed on the note. Blood spattered on it, making it look like some piece of sadistic artwork. He smirked once more. He really admired his handiwork. He slowly stood up and backed away from the mess, double checking his shoes as he stepped away. No bloody foot prints. He was safe. He turned and made his way back to the front exit. That's the thing about apartments. They only have one exit. He reached for the doorknob when still wearing the latex gloves, when his heart stopped. He heard movement on the other side of the door. His hand flew back to his body, but he didn't move. He was frozen in spot. He hoped whoever was on the other side of the door would just be passing by to get to the staircase. He took a small timid step back. And then he heard the door knob being jiggled.

"Matt?"

A female voice so angelic and innocent it could only belong to one person, echoed through the door. Saige.

"Fuck..."

He whispered. He knew Saige had keys. He heard the clicking sound signaling the lock being manipulated. Nick didn't think he'd ever moved so fast in his life. So fast or so silently. He ducked into the hallway leading to the bedroom. He held his breath.

"Matt? I really want to talk. I don't want us to be over."

He heard Saige say. And then a blood curdling scream. He knew he wouldn't be getting out of there any time soon. Not if she intended on staying and waiting for the police. He knew he had two options. Try and sneak out or knock Saige out. He moved into the bedroom while he tried to decide what to do.

He threw himself into a pile of the clothes on the floor digging as quietly as he could. He had to find something to conceal his face. Anything. With no luck of a mask, he saw a pair of nylon tights laying on top of Saige's pile. He had never tried this tactic before, he never had to. He slid them slowly over his face, squishing his features. He had no idea if he was recognizable or not but he sure as shit felt stupid. He gradually left the bedroom and pressed his back against the hallway wall. He could hear Saige's loud crying and her loud sobbing. It broke his heart.

He didn't feel anything for the boy's death, he had deserved to die. Nick knew that Saige was close with him so she'd grieve, but she'd get over it. He peered around the corner of the wall. Saige was sitting on the ground; she'd pulled Matt into her lap and was stroking his face. His head bobbed, unsteady, thanks to the thick gash. Saige's head was bowed, she didn't see him carefully enter the kitchen. He watched silently for another moment, wondering when she was going to call the police. His thoughts were quickly answered as Saige came to the realization that Matt was truly, one hundred percent dead. She suddenly screamed again and while hugging Matt's bloody body, pulled her phone out of her pocket with a trembling hand.

"Hi, my name is Saige D'Leo. I'm at the Rubytop Apartments, number four dee. I need the police and the ambulance. Please. My boyfriend is dead."

She screamed into the phone, tears exploding from her body. She bent her head again and dropped her phone onto the floor, and pressed her face into Matt's hair. Now was the time for him to move. He jolted out of the hallway and made a run for the door jostling Saige as he passed her.

"Hey!"

She cried out. He didn't dare look back. He flung open the door and dashed out. He took the stairs to the main floor doors three at a time. It wasn't until he was outside that he'd realized the nylons were still on his head. He grabbed them by the top and yanked them off of his face without hesitation and threw them on the ground as he ran towards his car. They landed in a small puddle. He reached his car and in one movement, unlocked it and jumped inside, started the engine, and floored it out of the parking lot, sending a spray of gravel and dirt into the air.

He was breathing heavily, beads of sweat dripping rampant down his face. He then noticed that the latex gloves were still on his hands, concealing his prints. He was going to set them on fire. His breathing was labored as he drove like a madman to the Wal-Mart. He still needed to pick up hygiene items to make his story believe able to Bella. He could hear sirens now and realized he was going forty kilometers over the speed limit. He lifted his heavy foot off of the accelerator and gradually slowed down.

Cruisers and ambulances sped past him the moment he reached the ideal speed limit. Their lights spun wildly, their sirens piercing the air at their shrill squeal. He let out a slow relaxed breath. There was no way Saige could call him out. She hadn't seen his face. He'd be safe.

18

The first thing PJ saw when she entered the apartment was one of the most disturbing sights she'd ever laid eyes on. She was the last to enter the crime scene, Dan, Phil, Brock, Agent Hamm, and SAC Brinker along with Marta Camson and Robert Hampshire who were the EMTs with the ambulance and Gregory Deschaneau, the coroner and Heather Hendricks, the Crime Scene Specialist had all set up shop in the small apartment. But what PJ saw was a girl clutching the corpse of a man, sobbing and tears flooding her face. Marta was trying to get her to release the body, but she refused.

The girl was covered in blood. PJ felt like her heart had shattered. She knew the pain this little girl was in. This exact scene brought PJ back to when they'd first found Melissa, the only difference was this scene had a lot more blood. However, the girl clutching the boy, not being able to let go, sobbing so hard her chest felt like it was going to explode was all too familiar to PJ.

She strode towards the girl, taking in what was going on around her. Dan and Phil were poking through drawers with gloves on, using pencils to move around the items inside. Brock stood off to the side of the door with Agent Hamm, their heads close together, murmuring to each other, observing the horror that was taking place around them. Heather Hendricks was photographing the blood and the steak knife. She couldn't get a photo of the body with the girl in the way. Brinker was discussing something with Gregory Deschaneau who had a solemn look plastered across his face, creasing it, making him look ten years older than his forty-two. Brinker was jotting down some notes as he spoke. PJ made it to the girl and knelt down next to her.

"Honey."

She said softly. She gently put a hand on her shoulder.

"You need to let him go now, hon."

She whispered. PJ didn't know how to be nurturing. She just tried her best. She'd grown up as a hard ass especially when Melissa had died. She'd just stopped caring.

"I can't. He's dead because of me."

She stuttered through her blubbering.

"That's not why. Don't say that. C'mon sweetie, let him go so Marta and Robert can help him."

She whispered, trying to sound as calm as she could. The girl shivered and looked up, meeting PJ's eyes. A pang of heartache blasted through her. The look in the girl's eyes was the worst thing that PJ had ever seen. Her deep brown eyes were filled with the heaviest anvil of sharp stabbing pain that just ripped PJ apart.

The girl slowly let go with one hand and reached towards PJ. She dropped a crumpled piece of paper into PJ's palm. PJ immediately dropped it, straight out of habit. She slid a hand into her pocket and pulled out her own set of gloves. She snapped them onto her hands and picked up the paper. Her eyes scanned the note. It was written in all capitals; some letters were slightly darker than the others. She narrowed her eyes. Strange.

"Brinker."

She called as she stood up. Brinker glanced up from jotting notes. He hustled over to her. She held up the blood-stained paper.

"Dear Saige, I'm sorry I hurt you. You don't deserve that. I wish I could give you what you deserve. I wish you all the happiness you deserve. This is goodbye. Love, Matt."

He read out loud and then he too, squinted. PJ let her hand fall to the side.

"Why was it written like that?"

Brinker asked. PJ bit her lip.

"Look, some letters are darker."

Brinker nodded.

"That's just weird..."

PJ turned back to the girl.

"Hon, is your name Saige?"

She slowly nodded.

"Saige D-D'Leo."

She stuttered. PJ knelt down again.

"Let's get you cleaned up, okay? Let's let Marta and Robert take care of Matt."

Saige shook her head violently.

"This is because of me. I can't forgive myself. I'm never going to see him again."

She let out a heart wrenching wail and bowed her head back down as tears began to pour down her cheeks again.

"You'll see him again. But let's get you cleaned up. Let's let Marta and Rob clean Matt up, okay?"

Saige didn't reply. She tried swallowing a lump in her throat. She slowly nodded. With what seemed like a great effort, she let Matt go. She sat there; PJ had to help her to her feet. Marta and Robert rushed over. Robert handed PJ a thick blanket, which she wrapped around Saige's shivering shoulders. PJ motioned for Brinker to follow her. She led the distraught girl down the stairs and out to the parking lot. An ambulance waited with the back doors open. PJ helped Saige sit down.

"What can you tell me?"

She asked, slowly, letting the words float to Saige. She looked up at her with watery eyes.

"Matt and I got in a fight earlier this morning. He gave me an ultimatum. Him or our new friend. I told him he was acting stupid and I just...I just walked out. He was crying, but I didn't care. I got out of class and didn't want to fight with him. So, I came here and I walked in and saw.... saw that."

She burst into another fit of sobs. PJ bit her cheek.

"Did-did you guys catch him?"

PJ stared blankly at her.

"I'm sorry. Who?"

Saige coughed.

"The guy that did that. Did you catch him?"

"Saige, I'm sorry, Matt committed suicide."

PJ said slowly. Saige became hysterical.

"There was a guy! He was in Matt's place. I SAW him. He was hiding in the bedroom."

She said through tears. PJ could see Brinker furiously taking notes. PJ looked back down at the suicide note in her hand.

"Brinker."

She said. Brinker didn't hesitate to step up towards the ladies.

"Look. The darkened letters,"

She paused and pointed at the note with her other hand. She couldn't believe what she was seeing.

"Take those letters, minus a few of them. It says Sam."

Her heart began to race.

"Do you know a Sam, Saige?"

"Why does it matter? You should be sending out a search party for that man. Not playing word games."

PJ drew in a calming breath.

"Please, humor me. Do you know a Sam?"

"Yeah, I mean, I think so. I just...I don't know."

She closed her eyes, trying to draw in a memory.

"Richards, Richards! Phone!"

She turned and saw Agent Hamm running across the parking lot holding his cell phone out to her as he approached. His eyes were wide and wild.

"Agent,"

"Darbyshire. On the phone. You're definitely going to want to hear this."

He tossed his cell phone into her hands. PJ looked at him and held the phone up to her ear.

"This is Richards. What is it, Agent?"

Ansyn Darbyshire sounded rushed and breathless as he began to speak.

"I found something. I fucking found something! Figures the moment Rick's gone, I find what I'm looking for. What I think we're looking for."

He sucked in a breath. PJ clenched and unclenched her fist. He found something.

"Springfield, Ohio."

He said as he tried to suck in more air. PJ nodded and held up a finger, signaling Brinker to give her just a moment. Saige remained silent as PJ walked a few feet away from the ambulance.

"What about it?"

She said, lowering her voice like they were sharing some big secret. Perhaps they were.

"That's where the little girl went missing."

"I know, I told you guys that."

PJ sighed.

"But I found more! She escaped! Somehow, she got away. She was missing for a year."

PJ's jaw dropped.

"Did you get a name? Age? I guess she'd be twentyish by now. Is she still in Springfield? Is she safe?"

PJ was asking feverishly.

"No, that's just it. She's here."

PJ thought she was going to drop the phone.

"Like, here, like Ontario? Or here, like Ridgeway."

"The latter."

PJ flailed around for something to grab onto. She looked like she was a drunk lunatic.

"PJ are you okay?"

Brinker shouted from a few feet away. PJ gave him the thumbs up.

"Tell me everything. Short version."

"She lived in Springfield, born and raised. Samuel Thomas kidnapped her in two thousand three, she was eight years old. She got away a year to date after her abduction. For the record, that was July twelfth two thousand four. Shortly after her return, the family moved from Springfield to Ridgeway. Fresh start. They, the parents, put their daughter in a program for PTSD in youngsters. When she turned thirteen, she asked to go to a hypnotist. Night terrors. I guess the hypnotist, her name is Cara Martin, was partially successful. She managed to block what Sam looked like from her mind, but not everything that happened to her. Now, she is a student at Ridgeway University studying Criminal Law. Her name is Saige Laeyke D'Leo. I have the contact info for Miss Martin as well."

PJ dropped the phone and stumbled backwards. She could hear Ansyn Darbyshire's voice through the phone.

"Richards? Richards are you okay? Hey!"

PJ bent down and picked the phone up off the ground. She could see Brinker staring at her. His hand was on Saige's shoulder. They both had a look of utter concern twisted into both of their features. She held up a hand.

"I'm fine!"

She shouted towards them. She put the phone back up to her ear.

"No fucking way. That call we responded to? The caller was a Miss Saige D'Leo."

"The same chick?"

"It's got to be. Thank you for the intel, Darbyshire. Good work."

She clicked off the phone and began walking back to the waiting ambulance, uniformed officers, and Saige D'Leo.

"Thanks Agent Hamm. Here's your phone back."

Agent Joe Hamm took the phone and slid it back into his pocket.

"Crazy shit, hey?"

PJ nodded and caught Brinker's eye. She could tell he had no idea what they were talking about and why would he? PJ turned back to Saige.

"Sweetie, I have some important questions to ask you. Okay?"

Saige started blankly at her.

"More?"

"These are different. First, what is your full name?"

Saige let out a heavy sigh. Her shoulders slumped forward. She put her elbows on her knees.

"Saige Laeyke D'Leo. Need me to spell it for you?"

Saige knew she was being sassy. She hadn't meant to be.

"That's okay. When is your birthday?"

PJ made sure that Brinker was writing everything down in his little note pad. She wanted to compare those notes with Agent Darbyshire's when they returned to the precinct. Brinker was writing everything down verbatim.

"Did you hear me?"

Saige said softly. She was still shivering. She pulled the blanket tighter around her shoulders.

PJ gave her a soft smile.

"April seventeenth nineteen ninety-five."

Saige wanted to smile back but she just couldn't yet.

"Have you lived in Ridgeway all your life?"

Saige pursed her lips and slowly shook her head.

"No, I was born and raised in Springfield, Ohio."

PJ bit her lip. She knew what was happening. They'd found her.

"Does the name, Samuel Thomas, ring a bell?"

PJ crossed her fingers behind her back. She hoped beyond hope that this girl would have the memory.

"I know that name. I just know it."

PJ gave her a small smile and then heard a door slam. She looked over her shoulder and saw Marta and Robert wheeling a gurney towards the ambulance. Gregory and Heather followed closely behind. A white sheet covered the body shape that lay still. Red stains soaked through the sheet. Saige gasped and covered her face with her hands. PJ laid a hand on her shoulder and rubbed it gently.

"I'm sorry, we gave you guys as much time as we could but we've really got to get to the morgue."

Marta said gingerly. Saige hiccupped into her hands. PJ gently guided her to her feet.

"Here hon, I'll drive you home."

PJ said softly. Saige's whole body shuddered; her knees shook. PJ used her strength to keep Saige from collapsing to the ground.

"I was in the middle of moving in here."

She exploded into another fit of sobs. More tears managed to squeeze their way out of her eyes. PJ bit her lip and exchanged a look with Robert who stayed silent.

"Do you have a friend you can stay with until we figure something out?"

PJ felt so useless. This poor kid.

"I'll-I'll call Bella."

She stuttered. She wiped her eyes with the back of her hand. PJ stood next to her, watching as Saige pulled her cell phone from her pocket. She slowly dialed a phone number from memory and held the phone up to her ear.

"Her phones off. That's weird."

She trailed off and started scrolling through her phone.

"She left me some texts."

PJ stayed quiet as Saige's eyes narrowed, her brow furrowed and knitting together.

"Mind if I make one more phone call?"

Saige asked, turning to PJ.

"Please. Do."

Saige clicked on a contact and pressed the call button on her phone. She glanced sideways as Marta and Robert finished loading the gurney into the back of the ambulance. Saige looked away quickly.

"Hi, Michael. It's Saige. Is Bella around? Oh, yeah. That's what she texted me. You don't know where she is? Okay well if she goes back to your house please let me know. Thanks, bye."

Saige hung up and looked at PJ. Her eyes were big and glossed over with tears. PJ felt awful for this poor girl.

"You don't have anywhere to go?"

Saige let out a heavy sigh that came from deep within her. She typed in another number and brought the phone up to her ear for the final time.

"Jenn? It's Saige. Matt's dead. Can you come stay with me at my dorm tonight?"

Moments later Saige hung up the phone and turned back towards PJ. She shrugged the blanket off of her shoulders. She gradually handed it to PJ who draped it over her arm.

"My friend, Jenn, is going to stay with me. I have my dorm until the end of the month..."

PJ had no idea if Saige would be strong enough to continue living in the apartment after this ordeal. The memory of Matt's death would haunt her for the rest of her days.

"I still have a few questions for you if you don't mind."

Saige let PJ guide her towards her car. Saige felt numb and empty. Dead to the world. PJ pulled open the door and helped Saige get inside before strolling towards the driver's side. It was so quiet inside the vehicle as PJ turned the key. The car rumbled to life. It was a strange sound in the ill quiet.

"Can you tell me what you remember about Samuel Thomas?"

Saige scrunched her features.

"I think he used to live up the road from me...I don't know if it was a dream but I think he killed my old babysitter...The details are jumbled. Cara, my therapist, she was...she was excellent at helping me...That is until recently. I think I'm starting to remember."

Saige paused and put her hands on the dash in front of her. She counted to ten and closed her eyes, breathing deeply and evenly. PJ glanced at her out of the corner of her eye.

"Saige? Whoa, Saige, are you okay?"

She slowed down and came to a jerky stop on the shoulder of the road.

"Saige?"

PJ asked again, panic tracing her voice. Saige held up a hand.

"I'm okay. I'm okay. Whatever Cara did...oh god...it's all true. Cara told me I'd remember for my own safety. Oh god...oh god..."

Saige took a pause as PJ stared at her, trying to portray sanity even though her insides were telling her that indeed, Samuel was back.

"I remember he had blonde or reddish hair. Blue eyes...oh Detective, they were awful. They were so icy and filled with such anger...until he looked at me."

Saige's face dropped back down to her hands. She stifled another heavy sob.

"What happened?"

PJ inquired. She knew this was hard for Saige. Saige dug her fingernails into her scalp. PJ let her hand fall gracefully onto Saige's shoulder. She felt Saige instantly relax under PJ's touch.

"He would look at me with such affection. His eyes were still cold but the hate and anger were replaced with...well me...I guess. He would look at me like I was the only person in the whole world."

Saige shuddered.

"How messed up is that? I was eight years old! I remember I had just turned eight. I remember I had this My Little Pony party. I was dressed as Applejack...I had just turned eight before he..."

Saige trailed off and choked on a cough. PJ leaned away from her and put the car back into drive. She looked out her window and shoulder checked to make sure there were no other cars coming before pulling back onto the road.

"Would you remember his face if you saw a photograph?"

PJ wondered. She flicked her indicator and made a right turn. Saige drummed her fingertips on the dashboard. Her knee shook as she tapped her foot.

"I really don't know."

She tilted her head backwards until it came to a stop on the head rest.

"What's going on? Why is this happening? Isn't he supposed to be dead? Why is this happening?"

PJ pulled into a small lot of a couple of buildings close to the university. She turned off the vehicle and unbuckled her seatbelt.

"What did you just say?"

She asked, starting wide eyed at Saige.

"He's...he's supposed to be dead."

She said in a lower voice. Her eyes darted around, like she was looking outside for something, or someone.

"How do you know that? If you barely remember, how do you know that?"

PJ demanded. She hadn't meant to sound so intimidating. Saige shrunk back in her seat, her back pressed hard against the seat.

"A few years ago, I saw my mom on the computer. She exited out of the window when she saw me coming. Later on, when she left, I checked the history. She was looking at an article from Springfield. A plane went down. She had written a note on a sticky pad that she forgot to take with her. It said that Sam was on the plane. That he was dead. I didn't think much of it then...I didn't remember...but...he's dead. He's supposed to be dead."

PJ knew very well what article she'd read. It was the same one that former Agent Dilworth had come across.

"I have officers digging online to see if he really perished on board."

PJ pushed open the door and climbed out. Saige mimicked her actions. The air had gone chilly, a slight breeze blew around the two, ruffling their hair. Saige shivered and rubbed her hands along her arms.

"So, do you guys think there's a copycat or do you think Sam really killed Denae, Carly, Kelly...and even Josh... and....and Matt?"

Saige didn't wait for PJ to ask the next question. She could see the astonishment in her eyes.

"Denae was my cousin, Carly and Kelly were my sister's friends and Josh was my therapist's brother."

PJ looked around and took Saige's arm.

"Let's talk inside."

She ushered Saige towards one of the dormitories. She flung open the door and let Saige go in before herself. She looked over her shoulder and scanned the lots. Her eyes landed on a group of bushes towards the back of the lot. She could swear she saw the glint of a camera lens in those bushes.

19

Once inside, PJ took a seat on a wooden chair. It was one of the only pieces of furniture in the small dorm room. Besides that, there were two beds, one made, one unmade with a purple flower comforter strewn across it. A blue eggshell chair was off to the side. A four-drawer dresser sat between the beds.

"It can't actually be Sam, right? Not possible, right? Tell me it's not possible."

PJ could hear just how frightened that poor girl was.

"We won't know for sure until one of my officers dig up whether or not he actually died on that plane, but Saige, I don't want to alarm you, but you seem to be a major part of this. Everything is starting to revolve around you. I'm going to order round the clock supervision on you okay? It's imperative."

Saige started to tear up again. This was all so much. She began to shake her head.

"I don't want this. I don't want any part of this. I just want to live my life normally. I just want to be able to go home to Matt and be loved and bitch about everything with Bella and Jenn and worry about practicum. I don't want to be trapped."

PJ was feeling a connection to Saige. She reminded her so much of Melissa. Saige's shoulders heaved with every heart wrenching sob.

"I know you don't want to. I know. But we want to keep you safe. We need to."

"Okay."

Saige replied, wiping tears from her face. PJ noticed the frightened tone had dissipated. A certain calmness settled over whatever nerves had been there. PJ glanced down at her wrist and looked at the Rolex that sat there.

"I need to go back to the precinct and finish up my report. Here."

PJ paused as she slipped her notepad out and mini pen out of her pocket. She let her hand fly across the page. Saige tilted her head, trying to see what PJ was writing down but to no avail. She let out a sigh that made her chest quake and sunk to the floor beside the spot that PJ was standing in. PJ tapped her shoulder and held the piece of paper out to Saige.

"That's my cell phone number. You, please call me as soon as Jenn gets here. Call me if you need anything at all, okay?"

Saige swallowed hard. She nodded and looked up at PJ.

"Thank you so much, Detective."

"Please, call me PJ."

PJ gave her a warm smile. Saige did her best to return it. PJ was not going to force her to act like she was happy when she knew damn well, she wasn't. PJ had no idea when she'd be okay again.

"I'll make sure that whoever I send to watch over you has a code word so that you know you're in the right hands. They're going to want to speak with you. Find out where all the entrances and exits are. Do you have a word you'd like to use?"

"I don't know. Uh...Philadelphia."

"Where it's always sunny."

PJ half chuckled at her joke. Confusion was plastered across Saige's face. PJ shook her head with a smirk.

"Nothing. Philadelphia works. Do not, and I cannot stress this enough, do not let anyone in unless it's Jenn or my men. Capiche?"

Saige nodded. She walked PJ to the door. She clutched the paper with PJ's number on it in her hand.

"Thank you, PJ"

PJ smiled once more and closed the dorm door behind her as she left. She felt horrible leaving Saige behind. PJ shook her head to herself as she started down the hallway to the doors from which they entered in.

"Wait, wait, PJ!"

She stopped in her tracks as the shout hit her ears. She pivoted and watched as Saige ran down the hall after her.

"What are you going to do with Matt's note?"

"Bring it back to the precinct. Get the boys to do a fingerprint scan on it."

Saige inhaled deeply and on the exhale she nodded understandingly.

"Thank you, again."

She whispered. PJ patted her arm. She turned on her heel and finished walking the length of the hallway to the exit. With a heavy sigh, she pushed open the glass door and stepped into the day. The sun was low in the sky signaling the end of the afternoon and the beginning of the evening. PJ pressed the button on her key fob, unlocking her car.

When her hand reached the handle of her door, she paused and glanced over her shoulder at the dorm building. The name of the dorm was Becker Hall. In the windows of Becker Hall were a few girls scattered throughout, peering down at her, the look of intrigue was the look they all shared. She turned back to the car and yanked the door open. It made a loud squeaking sound. She winced. She climbed in behind the wheel and turned her key in the ignition. She felt her phone begin to vibrate in her pocket.

"Detective Richards."

She said as she held the phone to her ear. She turned the car back off, the rumbling as it idled was loud and distracting.

"Hey, PJ, it's me."

PJ frowned.

"Hi, Brinker. It's Detective Richards to you, remember?"

She felt crushed. She hated to be a hard ass cop to the handsome FBI Agent. She really just wanted to cuddle up to him and perhaps make love again and again.

"We found something you might be interested in seeing."

PJ sat up in her seat, straightening her back.

"Like what?"

She could hear people moving around in the background. She assumed they were back at the department.

"We found a pair of nylons in the parking lot."

PJ waited for him to continue but when he didn't, she shook her head.

"So?"

She listened to Brinker yell at someone in the background.

"So that man Saige mentioned may have used them to conceal his identity."

PJ groaned and bowed her head until it hit the steering wheel.

"Or they could belong to someone in the building. You do know that putting it over your head doesn't really work, right?"

Brinker chuckled. PJ was trying so hard to fight with him and he knew it. She just didn't want to admit her feelings towards him.

"We brought them with us anyway. We're going to examine it for DNA."

PJ smacked her head against the wheel.

"Don't you think that's kind of a long shot? Who knows how long they were there for? I saw that lot. There were tons of puddles. Muddy water can fuck up the examination. Who's to say the DNA would still be there?"

"Thanks for the vote of confidence, Detective. We're going to go ahead with it."

PJ sighed and straightened up again.

"Alright. Good luck. Can you get the boys to set up a printing? I want to get a finger print done on Matt's note."

Brinker coughed and PJ could hear him moving things around in the background.

"Don't you think that's kind of a long shot?"

PJ knew he was mocking her. Professional. She turned the key in the ignition again and pulled away from the dormitory building.

"Just do it, please."

"Already done."

PJ was thankful that the office wasn't far from where she currently was. She was sick of driving. She couldn't wait to be pampered that night at Nick's cabin. She could use it. When the Ridgeway PD came into view, she felt a sharp pang of dread hit her forcefully in the gut.

"Fucking vultures."

She spat as she saw all of the news crews that were there bright and early, still sitting there. By the looks of it, even more crews caught wind of the press conference and had made their way to the department in hopes of receiving a quote. Now they were all camped out next to their vans. PJ laid her eyes on a food truck that was just packing up.

"They ordered a fucking Taco Time food truck!"

She exclaimed. She pulled into a parking space near the back of the lot and shut the car off. Without a doubt, they'd see her. Especially if they hadn't already. PJ sucked in a gulp of air.

"Here we go."

She said to herself. She got out of the vehicle and felt the cold chill of the wind. It stung all of her joints and right down to the bone. She pulled her blazer tighter around her waist and ducked her head as she started the trek to the front door. Like flies on shit, the reporters bombarded her. It was chaos. Anarchy.

"Detective Richards! Sam's back?"

"Detective! Who is your prime suspect?"

"Miss Richards! Is Nick guilty?"

"Hey, Detective Richards! How many girls are you going to let Nick kill before you throw him in jail?"

PJ shielded her face from the camera lenses. She ignored the hoard as she made her way up the stairs. The flashes of the camera and the buzzing of microphones rang in her ears. She gave them one thing. They were excellent at keeping out in the cold. She made it to the door when one of the reporters grabbed her arm. She froze in her spot and stared him down with a deadly gaze.

"Detective Richards, how does it feel being in denial about dating a serial killer?"

PJ ripped her arm out of the reporter's grasp and turned so her body was facing the malicious crowd. It looked like there were more than there actually was. They were all pushing at each other, thrusting their microphones towards PJ. They were snapping photos of her and getting some video footage for the nightly TV news. It resembled a scene from the Walking Dead. They couldn't get enough of her. Now they were waiting for her to answer their questions. She started laughing and shook her head.

She turned her back and pushed open the glass doors and walked inside without another look at the crowd. Brock was the only one standing in the lobby. PJ got to look forward to her relaxing night with Nick. When the doors shut behind PJ, Brock leaned forward, pushing himself off of the reception counter.

"Animals."

He said, staring out at the groups. PJ had to agree. She and Brock both began walking down the hall towards the labs.

"Special Agent Brinker is testing the pair of nylons we found in the lot."

Brock stated. PJ sighed.

"He said you were going to do a finger print scan on the suicide note."

PJ chewed her lip as they strode down the silent hallway.

"That's just it. I don't think it's a suicide note. Saige said she saw someone run out of the apartment while she was there. I think someone forced Matt to write that note and then that same person killed him."

"There weren't any prints in the apartment. What makes you think they'll be on the note?"

PJ shrugged as they approached a door. Brock reached for the knob.

"Kind of a long shot, isn't it?"

He mimicked Brinker's words from the phone call. PJ shot him a look.

"Just let me do my job, Chief."

She retorted and pushed open the door when Brock turned the knob. Right inside the door was a box filled with plastic gloves. They both pulled a pair from the box and slid them over their hands. Right beside the glove box was a second one filled with blue plastic shoe covers. Again, they both grabbed a pair and slid the ugly items over their shoes. Everything in the room was stainless steel and incredibly high tech. Everything had to be sterile. PJ and Brock made their way across the room to where Brinker stood, leaning against one of the counters, watching a shorter man with a bald head and white lab coat testing the nylons.

"How's it coming, Andy?"

PJ greeted as they reached the counter. Andy leaned away from the nylons. He was wearing a pair of glasses with extra thick lenses. He chuckled.

"Hard. You'll need to wait awhile for the DNA testing, that is, if there is anything for me to test."

PJ shot Brinker a look that said, 'I told you so'. She carefully pulled the crumpled note from her pocket.

"Could you do me a solid and run a finger print scan on this for me."

She laid the note in the plastic Ziploc bag carefully on the counter. Andy stared at it like it was some foreign object but he picked it up momentarily. He held it up in the air under the fluorescent lighting. He studied it intently.

"Sure, yeah. I can do that for you."

He brought the note back down and put it back on the counter. He immediately began digging through drawers, pulling out a container of powder and thin brushes. PJ smacked her lips and clapped her hands together.

"Alright, I'll leave that with you."

She paused and turned to Brinker.

"Can you send one of your Agents and some of my officers to Saige's dorm? I want her under supervision."

Brinker chuckled.

"What for?"

PJ shot him a look.

"You should know damn well that our only witness should be under supervision."

Brinker started laughing.

"I'm just yanking your chain, PJ... Richards. Lighten up."

Brinker crossed his arms over his thick chest, guarding himself.

"I'll send Darbyshire."

PJ nodded and looked at Brock.

"By the way, Saige is the girl that was kidnapped after my sister's death."

Brock's eyes widened. His jaw fell to the floor. PJ nodded and glanced back over her shoulder and flashed Brinker a massive smile. Brinker's look matched Brock's.

"Brock, I'm sending Brady and Sheen with Darbyshire."

Brock nodded and unclipped a small, two-way radio from his belt. He pressed a button the side.

"Brady, Sheen, come back from patrol. You're on surveillance now."

He let the button go and seconds later the radio crackled. Through a static, they could hear Sheen replying.

"Ten four. Over."

PJ turned back to Brinker. One more time. He grinned at her.

"Where can I find Darbyshire?"

Brinker raised a hand.

"Don't worry, I'll retrieve him. Just give me the address."

"It's easy. Building C - Becker Hall - of the dorms at the university. Saige is in room one a. First floor, first room. I know my men are going to want to speak with her. If Darbyshire does too, the password to let her know he's in the clear is Philadelphia."

"Where it's always sunny."

Brinker muttered. PJ stared at him. He'd made the same reference she had. She shook her head quickly.

"Yeah, right. Anyway. Please get him out there asap."

She turned her back and quickly got the hell out of the lab. The minute she was in the hallway, she peeled the gloves off her hands and the booties off her shoes. She rubbed her arms and shivered. She walked swiftly down the hall, back to the main entry way. She knew she wouldn't have to tell Brady or Sheen anything. Brock would take care of it. She reached the lobby and pulled out her cell phone. Dialing a number from memory, she held the phone up to her ear. He answered on the second ring.

"Hey, P."

He said, his voice seductive in her ear. She bit her lip.

"Hey babe, I'm leaving work now. Pick me up at home?"

She strode to the door and that's when she heard the first deafening clap of thunder. She stared out the door. The evening skies had turned dark and gray. Thick clouds loomed overhead. Rain drops the size of buckets fell from the sky.

"Raining buckets."

PJ whispered.

"What's that?"

Nick responded. PJ pressed a hand against the glass.

"It's storming. Better meet me at my place. Be there in ten. Be careful. Love you."

PJ hung up and slid the phone back into her pocket. A jolt of lightning lit up the dreary sky. It was creepy and ominous. PJ breathed in deeply and clutched her blazer closed with both hands. She shoved the doors open with her hip and ducked her head.

The winds were furious. They were so strong they made PJ sway on her feet as she ran for her car. She noticed that the news vans were gone. They must have heard the forecast from others on their teams back at their own respective offices and packed up their gear and got the hell out of there. PJ wasn't sorry to see them gone. By the time she reached her car, she was drenched.

Her hair was plastered to her forehead. She yanked open the vehicle door and ducked inside. Thunder clapped through the sky just as she shut her door. The rain pellets were cold, they sunk into her skin, stabbing like knives into her bones. She'd never felt rain so frigid. She was glad to be out of it. She started her car with a shaky hand and blasted the heat. Her skin felt like ice. She flipped on the wipers to full blast but that didn't seem to help the down pour.

The minute the wipers shot the rain off her window, another couple of buckets took over. She couldn't sit in the parking lot and wait for it to subside. Who knew how long that was going to take? She slowly put her car into drive. Leaning forward, she lay her foot gently down on the gas. She inched forward. She found that she could see less than a foot in front of her before it looked like everything was drowning in despair and sadness. She let out a frustrated sigh and held her breath. If she was lucky, she wouldn't hydroplane.

There were zero cars on the road. She thought about how smart those people were. She should have stayed at the office and waited out the storm with her fellow officers and feds. She should have rescheduled with Nick. For one, she hadn't spent the night with him in a while, and second, she wanted to question him about where his Mustang was when he was supposed to be with a client at the school. She tried not to think of the possibilities. She didn't really believe that it was possible for Nick to be the killer. She didn't want to believe it. She had to be sure.

She noticed another flash of lightning as it lit up the sky. The lights in the houses around her flickered. More thunder shook the sky. She held her breath as her house appeared. She could just make it out through the ripples of the windshield. She saw the candy apple red nineteen sixty-nine Ford Mustang sitting in her double car driveway. He was there already? She pulled into the driveway next to the gorgeous old car. The Mustang was in the best shape of its life. Nick took excellent care of it. When she turned the car off, she listened to the pounding of the rain drumming off the roof and hood of the car. She stared at the Mustang.

"How the fuck long did I take?"

She questioned herself out loud. She pulled her blazer sleeve up her arm and looked at her Rolex.

"Seventeen minutes. Oh, dear Lord."

She stared gloomily out the window and saw a shadow flash through her living room window. She normally would have drawn her gun had she not known Nick was there. Another flash of lightning and a booming clap of thunder. PJ stopped wasting time and jumped out of the car, locking it, and made a mad dash for her front entrance. She shouldered it open and stumbled inside, slamming the door shut behind her. She was surprised to see the lights still on. With all the rain and wind, she thought it would have knocked out the power lines.

"Hey babe, you okay? You took a while to get back here."

PJ lifted her head and smiled at Nick.

"It's crazy out there."

She kicked off her shoes and strode into Nick's arms.

"Do you mind if I have a quick shower and change before we go?"

She planted a kiss on Nick's lips.

"Change, but don't shower. I have some special plans to pamper you when we get to the cabin."

PJ giggled and hugged him tight

"Can't wait."

She de-tangled herself from him and ran up the stairs in the hallway leading to her bedroom. She stopped dead in her tracks. Something felt off. She put a hand on her gun and slowly entered the room. She scanned the room, making sure to check behind the door and ensuite bathroom for any unwanted guests. She could hear the rain louder in her room and it was colder than usual. She zeroed in on her curtains to her mini bedroom balcony blowing around. She ran across the room and pulled the curtains apart and was almost knocked over by a cold gust of wind. Rain blew into the room thanks to the wind.

Immediately, she coughed and sputtered. She reached for the door and struggled to pull it closed. The minute it latched shut, she twisted the lock to make sure it was secure. Then she whirled around towards the bedroom door.

"Nick!"

She yelled. She jogged to the door.

"Nick!"

She yelled again. She was about to run down the stairs when Nick appeared in the hallway below the stairs.

"What? What's going on!?"

He exclaimed. He scrambled up the stairs and grabbed PJ by the shoulders.

"Are you okay? What happened?"

The worry in his voice was convincing. PJ was shaking when she glanced over her shoulder and stared at the balcony door.

"Did you - were you up here earlier? Did you open the balcony door?"

She stuttered, pulling out of his arms to stare at him. He narrowed his eyes at her,

"No. Why? What happened?"

He was still holding onto PJ's shoulders. He squeezed them gently.

"The door. It was open."

Nick looked over her head to stare at the door himself.

"Maybe the wind opened it."

He suggested. PJ immediately shook her head.

"It was locked. It's always locked."

Nick squinted. He squeezed her shoulders again.

"Hon, you've been pretty stressed the last few days. Maybe you unlocked it and went out there and just forgot to lock it again."

PJ stared at the door again.

"Maybe."

She responded, unsure of that excuse. She brushed Nick's hands off of her shoulders.

"I'll change and be down in a minute."

She said, giving him a gentle shove towards the door. He gave her a concerned smile before exiting the room. The minute he was out of sight, PJ made her way back to the balcony doors. She could hear the whistle of the howling wind outside. With a great feeling of unease, she pulled the curtains closed so she could no longer see the doom and gloom outside. The lights in her bedroom flickered. She decided she better hustle and get back downstairs before the power went out.

She ran across the room to her dresser. She peeled the damp blazer off of her torso along with the now transparent blouse and shimmied her hips out of her dress pants. She was now standing in her black lacy underwear and matching bra. She pulled open the drawers to her dresser and saw a flash out of the corner of her eye. She instantly straightened and stared towards the darkened window to her bedroom. She didn't believe the flash was lightning. It didn't make any crackling sounds. It was just a flash. She yanked a chunky dark brown knit sweater out of a drawer and slid it over her head. It fell down to just above her knees.

She took a few quick steps to the window and peered out. She didn't see anything suspicious but the downpour could have easily masked anything ominous outside. She shut the curtains in front of the window and turned back to her dresser. The lights flickered again the same moment that she heard another loud clap of thunder that seemed to shake the whole house. She quickly dug a pair of black leggings out of her drawers and pulled them up her long legs and hips. She slammed the drawers closed and knelt to the ground where she picked up her belt and holster with care.

She lifted her sweater so she could strap the belt around her waist. She let it settle and then adjusted it so the twenty-two sat comfortably around her hips. She let the sweater fall back down around her waist and checked herself out in the mirror behind her door. She looked a mess. Oversized sweater and leggings were her lazy day outfit. Not only that, but her hair was finally starting to dry, becoming slightly frizzy.

Her makeup was running down her face, mascara leaving jagged black streaks down her cheeks. She let out an exasperated sigh. She turned towards her makeup table and grabbed one of her make up remover tins. She popped it open and pulled out one of the wet disposable cloths. She wiped it hard across her face, the black smudges disappearing from sight. She tossed the dirtied wet nap into the trash bin next to her table and stared at herself in the mirror again. Her blue eyes seemed even brighter without the makeup surrounding them. She sighed again. She looked tired. Heavy purple bags were visible under her bright blues. She threw her hands up in frustration. She didn't care that night. Nick would pamper her. She'd feel and look rejuvenated in the morning. She turned away from the table and mirror before she could change her mind and exited the room. The lights started to flicker again. She entered the kitchen, the lights going off incessantly, casting creepy shadows to bounce around the walls. Nick was sitting at the kitchen table.

"Nick, let's go."

She said softly. Nick jolted in his chair like she scared him

"Yeah, okay, c'mon."

PJ approached him and he stood up. He smiled down at her and kissed her nose. The minute his lips touched the tip of her nose, the lights flickered one last time before shutting off, leaving them in total darkness.

"Do you mind if I follow you in my car? I need to get up early and come back here and change for work."

Nick gave her hand a reassuring squeeze.

"Leave your car, hon. I'll bring you back as early as you need."

PJ smiled up at his silhouette.

"Thank you."

She whispered. She turned towards the door, Nick's hand sweeping across her side, feeling the lump of her gun under the sweater.

"Hon, leave your gun here. I want this to be romantic."

PJ narrowed her eyes, turning back to face him.

"I can't do that. I need it."

She replied, her voice shaky. Nick touched her hand.

"Please?"

PJ thought about it for a moment. She could survive one night without it.

"Alright, just for you."

She replied. She slowly lifted her sweater, feeling for the belt. At that moment, lightning lit up the sky, coming through the window, lighting up the kitchen, throwing not two but three shadows along the walls. PJ's eyes widened in fear and immediately as the lightning subsided, dimming the room again, she pulled her gun from the holster within seconds and took the safety off. Nick backed up and held up his hands. PJ was swiveling towards the living room doorway and hall doorway.

"Someone's here."

She said in a hushed tone. She had the gun trained on the hall door. Nick took a step towards her.

"No one's here, P. You must be seeing things. Put the safety back on and put the gun away."

PJ didn't take her eyes off the hall door.

"I saw three shadows when that happened. Call nine one one. Nick, now."

PJ heard a creak come from the hall.

"Nick."

She said again as she took another step towards the hall. She reached for her phone which to her horror, she'd realized she had left in her pocket in her pants upstairs. She didn't turn to Nick. She couldn't take her eyes off of the hall entrance.

"Nick, seriously, call Brock at the office or nine one one, now."

Nick sighed.

"I wish you didn't have to make this so hard."

He said softly. PJ furrowed her brow and started to glance over her shoulder. She didn't have enough time to protect herself when Nick's fist came bashing down on her head. Her gun fell out of her hand as she slumped to the floor. Nick's fist connected with her cheek and eye two more times before she stopped moving. Nick looked towards the hall.

"You stupid fuck."

He called out. He bent to pick up the gun, put the safety back on and slid it into his belt.

"I brought you here under the condition you remain unnoticed. I'll give it to you, that escape on the balcony was brilliant but you should have shut the fucking door."

He shook his head and looked down at PJ on the floor.

"You want to touch her? Come help me get her in the car."

Nick watched as a skunky looking man stepped timidly out of the hallway. His eyes were big and wild, his hair jet black with a white streak in his bangs. His eyes, although big, resembled nothing but a dark pit of blackness. Nick couldn't tell where his pupils ended and irises began. Think Charles Manson.

The small man came fully into the kitchen. He was wearing a completely black sweatshirt and matching sweatpants. He had a big professional Nikon camera slung over his shoulder. His thin lips were pressed together tightly. Nick rolled his eyes at him as he stood over PJ's still body.

"Shithead, get your fucking shit together and help me the fuck out."

The small man came to and swung his camera over his head. He flipped up the flash.

"What are you doing?"

Nick grumbled.

"I need a picture."

His voice was pitchy and had a hint of a squeak to it.

"Hurry the fuck up before she wakes up."

Nick growled. The man held the camera up to his face and pressed on the capture button. The flash went off, lighting up PJ's sullen face. He then put the cap back on the lens and slid the carrying strap back over his head. He giggled with excitement as he reached for PJ's arms. Nick grabbed her legs and they hoisted her into the air. Nick peered outside. It looked like the rain was getting heavier. They'd have to be fast but he was certain no one would be able to notice them through the thick shower.

They started moving towards the door which luckily was only a few feet away from them. Nick struggled to pull the door open without dropping PJ. When he got it open, it was just as expected. The rain was coming down bucket after bucket, making the quiet street look even darker. He surveyed the surroundings. No lights were on, that he also expected. He pulled PJ out the door. His accomplice wasn't much help. Although he was holding up PJ's upper body, he was also leaning down, smelling her hair.

As soon as they were no longer covered by the roof, they both hustled towards the car. Nick let one of PJ's legs go so he could get the door to the passenger side of the Mustang open. That startled his helper who shrieked and dropped PJ's upper half.

"You idiot!"

Nick said through gritted teeth. The man stared down at PJ in the mud and grime, the rain pelting down on her. Nick got to where he was standing and pushed him backwards. He rushed to pick PJ up before the icy rain could awaken her. He grunted as he dragged her to the door. He bent the seat forward and pushed her into the backseat next to a black briefcase.

"Squinty, get over there and open that case."

Nick whispered, growing frustrated with his partner. Squinty, ironically nicknamed, hustled over to the driver's side. He pulled open the door and pushed the seat forward so he could reach the case. Then he remembered his camera. He shrieked again and resembled a fish out of water as he scrambled to pull his precious Nikon off of his person. He placed it gently on the front seat of the Mustang.

"Squinty, stop fucking around. Get me the chloroform from the case, now!"

Nick said again, his teeth still shut, lips pursed. Squinty reached to unclasp the snaps on the case. He was highly uncoordinated. He stumbled and fell to his knees, smacking his face against the seat. Nick watching from the other side, frowned. Squinty pulled the small glass jar out of its cozy spot in the briefcase along with a white handkerchief. Nick reached across the backseat. Squinty almost dropped them as he handed the items over. Nick glared at him.

"This is why I never bring you."

He muttered. Nick twisted the child proof lid off of the bottle and covered the top with the handkerchief. He tilted the bottle and let a small amount soak into the cloth. He glanced around again to be sure no one was looking or spying on them. Nothing. He slowly and carefully put the lid back onto the bottle, tightening it, ensuring it wouldn't spill. Squinty reached for it, cupping his hands. Nick shot him a look but handed the bottle back to Squinty. He was more careful this time, gently cradling the bottle like a fragile baby.

He slid it carefully into its pouch inside the briefcase. Nick brought the cloth over PJ's mouth and nose. He held it there briefly until he could feel PJ's breathing slow even more.

"Squinty, Squinty."

He said quietly. Squinty was staring down at PJ in awe. Nick knew Squinty didn't love her like he claimed he did. He knew Squinty was infatuated by who PJ was. Squinty was in love with her power. He lusted after that power. Not her being. Nick tossed the cloth to Squinty who tucked it next to the bottle. He snapped the clasps shut tight.

He clambered away from the back seat and stood up straight in the drenching and freezing rain. He and Nick switched sides. Nick jumped into the driver's seat while Squinty stumbled into the car beside him. The minute the doors closed; Nick grimaced as he started the engine. The sports car rumbled to life loudly. Nick hoped the sounds of the rain, wind, and thunder would drown out the sound of the raucous muffler. He drove the speed limit through the suburban neighbourhood. Why draw more attention to himself as he was already driving in a horrific storm, that was already strange enough.

As soon as they left that street, hitting the outskirts of town, he stepped a little harder on the gas. The road was slick, the rain pelting against the windshield. Truth be told, he couldn't see much more than a foot in front of him. Squinty was turned around, mouth slightly opened so he could stare at PJ. His eyes were bigger than before making the blackness of them look substantial which in turn, made him seem crazier. Something about the way he held himself and his mannerisms reminded Nick of some kind of fucked up mix of Charles Manson and Ted Bundy.

"She's beautiful, isn't she?"

Squinty whispered in his high pitched, squeaking voice.

"Yeah, top Detective on the force. Pretty beautiful."

Nick replied. He glanced out the side of his eye and saw Squinty's tongue loll out of his mouth. He smirked and yanked the Mustang around the corner that brought him onto the long dirt driveway that lead to his secluded cabin. The Mustang wheels spun on the dirt turned mud, rotating slower each time.

"Fuck."

Nick said as he realized they were becoming stuck. He shifted the car into a higher gear and realized they were moving forward, inch by painfully slow inch. He slammed his hands down on the wheel and grumbled angrily. He shoved his foot down on the clutch and changed gears into the highest one. The engine revved meanly but haltingly moved forward. He knew the minute they were out of the sludge because the vehicle suddenly lurched forward. He almost didn't gear down in time. He pulled to a stop inches from the cabin.

"Okay, Squinty, help me out here. Can you grab the briefcase for me?"

Squinty nodded furiously and then peered out to the sky. It was truly amazing how the weather was acting. Nick breathed deeply. He and Squinty both shoved the doors open hard. The rain was heavier still, battering them hard. It felt like they were getting baseballs thrown at them. Squinty shrieked and ran around the car to where Nick was standing. He'd left his Nikon in the car. Nick moved swiftly to the passenger side of the car. He bent the seat forward and stepped in place a few times. The mud was beginning to stick to his feet, sucking them back to the Earth. He grabbed the still unconscious PJ under her arms and pulled her out of the car. Her feet hit the muddy ground and he promptly began dragging her towards the cabin entrance.

"Squinty, eh Squints, shut the door for me."

He faintly said to Squinty. He had the briefcase in hand and was standing under the roof of the cabin. His wild eyes looked even crazier through the rain. His hair looked blacker when it was fastened to his pale face. He gently set the briefcase down and bolted out from under the roof. In a flash he was next to the car, pulling his precious camera out and slamming the door.

He tried shielding his camera from the rain to no avail. He shrieked again and ran back to the shelter. Nick shook his head with a smirk on his face. For how little and clumsy that meager man was, he was also fast. Incredibly fast. Nick dragged PJ up the two steps. He nodded towards the door. Squinty jiggled the knob.

"It's locked."

Nick rolled his eyes.

"I know it's locked, moron. Here are the keys."

Squinty nodded expeditiously.

"Oh, yes. Yes, yes, yes."

He reached his hands out and caught the keys as Nick tossed them to him. The wind picked up, swirling around them wildly, making the rain feel even colder.

"The gold one. With the twists on the end. Hurry the fuck up."

He said, trying to hold PJ up. Squinty's hand shook as he slid the key into the hole and turned. Nick was overly glad that his cabin was so nicely isolated. His nearest neighbours were several kilometers in the opposite direction. He pulled PJ with a huff into the door and Squinty pushed it shut. The wind resistance on the door was a workout. Nick continued to drag her through the cabin, spotting the mud from her legs leaving a grimy trail through the kitchen and hallways. He flinched at it. In the hallway he stopped at the door, the one Mya, Kelly, Carly, and Denae had once resided. Now it was going to be home to not one, but two of his girls. He pressed his ear to the door and listened intently. He heard no sound. She must still be out.

"Squinty."

He said in a hushed tone. Squinty was standing at the edge of the hallway, camera in hand.

"Come here."

He said again, voice still hushed. Squinty walked slowly up the hallway to where Nick stood. He still had the keys in his hand, tucked under the camera. He slid them out.

"Silver key. Squared."

Nick directed. Squinty languidly unlocked the door. He pushed it open just a little bit, just wide enough for Nick to squeeze through with PJ. The shrill, ear piercing scream he heard next caused him to drop PJ onto the floor. Squinty stood in the doorway staring at the anarchy that was unfolding in front of him. A skinny, blonde girl had jumped onto Nick's back, wrapping her arms around his neck and legs around his waist. She was screaming bloody murder and clawing at Nick's face. He spun around, trying to swing the girl off of his back.

She was little but she had a grasp on him. Squinty stared in awe. Nick grabbed the girl's arms and pried them away from his face and neck. A one hundred ten pound twenty-one-year-old was absolutely no match for a two hundred pound thirty-five-year-old man. Her only advantage were the claws she had glued to the ends of her finger tips.

She screamed again and tried to dig those claws back into his face. He yanked her off of him but not before she managed to drag her nails over his face, leaving behind thin red gouges. He tossed her over his shoulder like she weighed no more than a feather. She hit the ground with a thud. He grabbed PJ's gun from his belt and aimed it at the bruised blonde. He saw a flash out of the corner of his eyes and knew Squinty was taking more pictures of the helpless PJ.

"Oh, little Bella, why don't you just listen?"

He swooned. Bella cowered on the floor.

"Michael, I'm so sorry for whatever I did to you. I'm so sorry."

She said, whimpering, pleading. Tears sparkled in her eyes. He took the safety off of the gun.

"Tell me...Why don't you deserve to die?"

Nick said. He was squinting. She'd cut him over his eyelids. It was painful. Bella didn't have an answer. Nick kept the gun trained on her.

"You're nothing. You're just one less person between my girl and I."

Bella's eyes widened in fear.

"Saige?"

She choked out. Nick laughed. Another flash.

"First, the cousin, who was glued to her side. Next the two friends of her sister who idolized her followed by the girl who was secretly crushing on her and finally the boyfriend who was always guarding her."

"Matt... what did you do to Matt?"

Bella cried, choking back tears. Nick laughed again, disregarding her.

"Then you. And your other blonde friend. What's her name? Oh right, Jenn. Poor little Jennifer. Alexis. Kassidy. And lastly, that woman behind me. Detective PJ Richards. They have no idea what's coming to them. But neither did you. Isn't that right, Isabella?"

He sneered.

"Don't you dare hurt Jenn or Saige. I swear to God, I'll,"

"You'll what? Kill me?"

Bella didn't reply. She glared at him.

"You can't kill me, honey. Not if you're already dead."

Without a second thought, he pulled the trigger of the gun. Bella screamed. Nick's arm flew to the side, the gun was knocked out of his grip. The bullet had missed its mark, but not the target. It seared into Bella's shoulder, lodging itself in the tissue and muscle. She lay flat on the floor screaming as blood seeped from the wound.

Nick whirled around to see PJ standing up, looking woozy but aware. Squinty was laying on the ground behind her, the strap to his camera twisted around his neck.

"Oh, PJ, so glad you could join us. A little sooner than expected, but glad all the same."

He said, smiling. He eyed the gun on the ground to his right. PJ swayed on her feet.

"Don't kill that little girl."

She said, her words tripped out of her mouth. Nick chuckled.

"You don't look well, PJ. Maybe you should sit down."

He took a step towards PJ. She narrowed her eyes.

"I can't believe it's you. I was so wrong. You're the copycat. You were right under my nose."

Nick stepped closer to her; she balled her hands into fists. Nick had the advantage.

"Not a copycat. Think about it, Penny."

She froze. No one called her just Penny. No one except...

"Why do you think you've never seen any baby pictures of me? Where do you think I came from? Why do you think I was so taken with you? Come on, Penny. I'm actually a little hurt that you didn't realize sooner. We were so good together. Although I was pretty good with Melissa too."

PJ dropped her fists.

"Sam."

She whispered. He laughed menacingly. PJ's eyes fell to the floor

"But why? Why now? Why here? Why *her*?"

She whispered. Sam shrugged and made his move. He bent and picked up the gun from the floor with PJ's eyes still down.

"I think you know why."

"Why her, Sam? She was just a kid. She's still just a kid."

PJ raised her eyes and saw Sam pointing the gun at her. She caught her breath, but remained calm.

"She's more than that. She's my angel. My only reason for existing. I love her."

PJ took a gradual step towards Sam.

"No, you don't. You're lusting after her. She's still just a kid."

Sam kept the gun pointed at PJ.

"I love her. I love her and she loves me. She's said so. Before her family forced her to move away. Away from us. Away from me."

PJ swore she could hear him choke back tears.

"Sam, just put the gun down. Look at me."

She said slowly, putting her hands up. She took another step forward.

"Remember us? You said you loved me, remember?"

Sam started shaking his head. He still had the gun on PJ.

"You're a fool. I didn't love you. You were entertaining for the time being. Melissa. I did love Melissa. But she had to go. She was just training. I didn't want to make any mistakes when it came time to express my feelings to Sai. I didn't need to. She told me she loved me first."

PJ took one more step, bringing herself within arm's reach of Sam.

"But Sam..."

She started to say. That's when he realized she was slowly advancing.

"Back up, PJ."

He said quietly. PJ didn't reply, she kept her eyes locked on Sam's.

"I mean it, Penny. I don't want to kill you, yet."

"Why do you want to kill me at all?"

Sam still had the gun on her, his eyes turning into dangerous slits.

"You're helping them. You're helping them."

"It's my job, Sam."

Sam didn't move the gun. PJ could almost reach him.

"I will not hesitate to shoot you if you come any closer. Sit down."

He warned. PJ didn't sit. Sam waved the gun wildly.

"I swear, I will fucking shoot you. Sit the fuck down."

He threatened. PJ kept her eyes locked on his and took one more step. Sam pulled the trigger. The shot blasted through PJ's gut, it echoed through the cabin. Bella screamed. PJ didn't utter a sound as she dropped to the ground. She put a hand over her gut, the blood gushed from the wound. She bit her lip and held back tears. The pain seared through her.

"Is this the only way to get you to listen? Huh? Is it?"

He yelled. He stood over PJ and bent down. He grabbed her hair in his free hand. She yelped in pain. He held the gun to the side of her head.

"I could kill you right now. Right fucking now."

PJ could feel the barrel of the gun trembling against her temple. Sam was shaking. The pain burned in her gut, but she tried to ignore it. Both hands were pressed to her wound.

"I could do it, y'know."

He said, his voice lowering.

"You won't."

PJ replied, challenging him.

"Why not? Why the fuck not? Because you're still useful?"

He responded, his voice wavering.

"Exactly. I'm still useful to you."

She said softly. Sam narrowed his eyes and slowly removed the gun from her head. He gradually stood up.

"You're right. But she's not."

He swiveled around, took aim, and fired.

"No!"

PJ screamed. The blast was loud and reverberated through her ears. The tears streamed from her eyes. Blood soaked through the front of Bella's shirt, making it darker and grimmer. The gun was fired at close range, ripping a hole in Bella's chest. Her eyes were wide. She gurgled on the blood bubbling up in her mouth. PJ scooted across the dirty carpet, pulling herself up next to Bella. She held her, cradling her in her lap.

"Guns. They're loud but they get the job done a whole lot quicker than choking bitches out."

Sam laughed. He tucked the gun back into his belt.

"Not sure I like it though. That wasn't very exhilarating."

PJ didn't reply. She glared at him.

"You're so different from the Sam I knew."

She whispered.

"No, I'm so different from the Sam you thought you knew."

He paused to walk to the door. He looked down at Squinty.

"Shame."

He said. He bent down and grabbed one of his feet.

"He wasn't much, but he was company."

He dragged the unmoving body out of the room.

"I'll be back later."

He said, looking straight at PJ. He slammed the door shut, leaving her clutching a dying Bella. PJ looked down. She couldn't feel the stinging pain anymore.

"Bella. It's Bella, right? Don't die on me hon. You can get through this. You will be okay."

She put her hand over the hole in Bella's chest and pressed down, trying to prevent any more blood from pouring out. Bella coughed, blood splattering into the air.

"You have to save Saige."

She whispered, barely audible.

"And Jenn. He said he's going after her next. And then Saige."

She coughed again. PJ pressed down harder. Bella talking was a good thing. It meant Sam had missed her heart.

"Shh, it's going to be okay. She's under surveillance. It's going to be okay. I'll get us out of here."

She whispered, tears stinging her eyes. Bella coughed for the third time. Her eyes lolled backwards. PJ held her tighter.

"Don't close your eyes, hon. Stay awake, look at me. Come on."

All of a sudden, Melissa's face took over Bella's body. PJ was clutching Melissa.

"Keep your eyes open. Stay awake. Stay awake."

She cried, the tears rolling over her bottom rims. Was this how it had ended for Melissa? Bleeding to death from her stab wounds? Bella was laying there, the hole in her chest not giving up the gushing of blood. PJ hugged her.

"Don't go."

She whispered, still seeing Melissa's body and face. That's when she felt Bella go limp. Her head fell to the side, her arms dangled next to her. PJ gasped, bowed her head, and let the tears fall.

21

The next morning. Eight nineteen am. Saige shot up in her bed, screaming. She was sweating profusely. Jenn shot up next to her. Officer Derek Brady was opening the door and next to her bed in seconds.

"Everything okay? What's going on?"

He asked. He'd been standing just outside the dorm room, armed and watching the hallway. Jenn was staring at her from the twin bed she had pushed next to Saige's.

"Yes, I'm sorry, I'm okay."

She said apologetically. Derek Brady slowly slid his gun back into its holster. He touched a button on the radio attached to his lapel.

"The mouse is fine. False alarm, I repeat the mouse is safe, over."

"Ten four, over and out."

Came the staticky response.

"The mouse?"

Saige asked, regaining her composure.

"It feels like this guy is playing a game of cat and mouse with you. He's the cat. You're the mouse."

He answered simply. Saige clutched the comforter in her hands.

"Do you need anything?"

Brady asked. Saige shrugged.

"No, I think I'm okay."

Brady nodded at her and began to exit the room. The minute the door closed behind him, Jenn was out of her bed and sitting on Saige's.

"Are you okay?"

She whispered, well aware that the walls and the door were thin. Saige frowned.

I think so. Do you know any Michael's at our school? Tall, broad, dark hair, blue eyes?"

"Well, uh, I know Michael Morley and Michael Anderson but neither have dark hair."

Saige closed her eyes.

"No, not Morley. Not Anderson. This one is majoring in arts. Poetry."

Jenn laughed.

"How does he make a career out of arts? Do you know how tough that is? All of the competition?"

She paused to chuckle some more.

"Jenn, seriously."

Saige said languidly. Jenn wiped a tear from laughing so hard.

"No, I don't know. I don't think so. I'll ask Kendra. She knows everyone."

"She's majoring in arts too, right?"

"Yeah, that's also why I'll ask her. Wait, Michael? The one Bella's been talking about?"

Saige nodded.

"Yeah. That one."

Jenn could now see the disdain on Saige's face. The tormenting look of despair.

"What is it, Saige?"

Suddenly she sat up straight.

"Bella. I couldn't get a hold of her last night. I just got this gut feeling that something is wrong. Very wrong. Fuck."

She shoved the blankets off of herself, sending Jenn to scramble out of the way.

"Okay, you just cursed. This is serious."

Saige looked at her.

"You bet your ass this is serious."

Saige began running around the room collecting the clothing items she'd snagged from Matt's apartment. Jenn watched her turn into a whirlwind of "Oh God's" before she finally stepped in front of her and grabbed her shoulders.

"Relax. Saige, what's the deal?"

Saige's eyes were wide with terror.

"Michael."

She managed to say. Jenn's look of confusion told Saige she'd need to explain. She let out an exasperated sigh.

"Michael. Matt was always so wary of him. He said it felt off. He said Michael didn't feel right and that he didn't like the way Michael looked at me. Even I noticed that Michael would look at me like...like I was his. I have only seen that look once before and that was when Sam would look at me when I was younger. I remember now. This is going to sound crazy but Sam is Michael. Michael is Sam. Oh God."

Saige pushed past Jenn and finished gathering her things.

"Michael. Like Bella's Michael."

Saige could tell that Jenn definitely thought she was crazy.

"Bella, oh God, Bella."

"I'm sure Bella's okay, Sai."

Saige spun around and grabbed Jenn by the shoulders.

"No, no you don't get it."

She said through gritted teeth.

"You don't know Sam. You don't know what he's capable of."

Jenn stared at Saige who was now donning black leggings and her maroon coloured RU pullover sweater. Jenn was in a baggy tee shirt, feeling insignificant next to Saige.

"I have to go. I have to go talk to Detective Richards. Oh God."

She turned and swiped her purse off of the dresser. She hesitated before heading to the door and turned back to face Jenn.

"Coming?"

Jenn glanced down at her attire. She turned and leapt across the room, grabbing her pair of jeans off of the floor beside the second bed. She wiggled them over her hips and did up the snap. She was still wearing her bra from the day before.

"Good enough."

She said, not caring about her baggy Rolling Stones tee shirt. Saige wasted no time in pivoting on her heels and taking the couple of steps to the door. She grabbed the knob, twisted, and flung open the door startling the officer stationed in the hallway.

"Is everything okay?"

Brady asked the second they stepped into the hallway.

"I need to go to the station, right now."

Saige said urgently.

"Why? What's wrong?"

Brady's eyes bore deep in Saige's.

"I need to speak with Detective Richards. Immediately."

She moved past officer Brady who grabbed the radio on his shoulder.

"The mouse is on the move. Coming down to the field."

Saige assumed that meant parking lot. She thought it was both amusing and frightening. Amusing because they were like spies using the code names. Frightening because it meant there was real danger out there. It meant Sam was definitely back. Saige and Jenn exited the building and right away they were flanked by two officers and agents surveying the outside, watching the exits.

"Agent Darbyshire, officer Sheen."

Saige greeted.

"I need to get to Detective Richards immediately. Like, immediately. It's an emergency."

The urgency in Saige's voice was apparent. Sheen and Darbyshire exchanged a look.

"I'll take them. You stay here and watch the outside for Brady."

Agent Ansyn Darbyshire said, the urgency in his voice matched Saige's. Officer Sheen nodded and mumbled into his radio. Darbyshire put a hand on Saige's lower back and guided her to the car. It took everything in her not to burst into a sprint to get to the vehicle. Darbyshire opened the door for her and she and Jenn both climbed in, careful to avoid hitting their heads.

Both stayed silent on the drive to the station. Saige stared out the window, gloom, anxiety and a mess of nerves washed over her face. Ridgeway University flashed past the window. Tuesday and Wednesday were the only two days that Saige had free. The next thing Saige knew, the Ridgeway Police Department came into view through the windshield. She held her breath as they pulled into the parking lot. She could hardly contain herself, waiting for Darbyshire to open the doors to the backseat. Stupid child lock.

Darbyshire turned the car off and got out. Saige clutched her purse tightly. The minute the door cracked open, she pushed on it, shoving Darbyshire out of the way. She took off towards the building running through the parking lot, splashing through puddles. She almost didn't notice the news vans who had parked themselves in the lot, the reporters camping out in front of the vans, mikes in hand, ready to get the scoop.

When they saw a young woman running full speed towards the station's front doors, they took their shot. They were on her in an instant, surrounding her, blocking her entry to the large doors. She was ambushed.

"Is that an RU, Ridgeway University sweater?"

"Are you a student there?"

"What's your name?"

"Are you Sam's next victim?"

"Are you running for safety?"

"Is Samuel Thomas after you right now?"

It was overwhelming. Saige spun in a circle looking for an escape. She started breathing heavily, hyperventilating. Then her rescuer appeared. Darbyshire shoved his way through the circle of reporters.

"Get out of the way! Move it! Back off!"

He yelled. The reporters took him in and their attention didn't last. It dissolved off of him. They continued shouting at Saige. Darbyshire grabbed her by the elbow and shoved through the two people deep line of reporters, microphones, and cameras. He dragged her up the short flight of stairs and shoved open the doors.

"Where's Jenn?"

Saige asked the minute the doors shut. Darbyshire looked towards the car in the lot.

"I told her to wait there."

Saige craned her neck to stare out past the frenzy of reporters. The gorgeous and tall blonde had gotten out of the vehicle and was making her way towards the group that were blocking the staircase.

"Figures she wouldn't listen. She's kind of theatric."

Saige said as they watched Jenn approach the news crews.

"If they talk to her, she won't say anything will she?"

Saige's gaze went from Jenn to Darbyshire.

"Well I don't know. She might if it'll get her on TV."

They both gawked as Jenn walked with ease and a certain calmness.

"No, no, she better not. If she leaks anything...Anything at all and our guy is watching..."

He paused and flung open the glass doors just as the reporters noticed Jenn.

"What's your name?"

"Who are you?"

"Are you connected to the murders?"

"Are you next?"

"Are you associated with Samuel Thomas?"

Jenn's bright smile beamed proudly.

"My name is Jennifer Kassidy, aka Jenn. I'm best friends with Saige D'Leo..."

"Stop talking!"

Darbyshire exclaimed as he burst through the crowd. He grabbed her arm and dragged her through the flock. She wouldn't stop smiling at them.

"Agent! C'mon Agent! Let her go!"

They were shouting. Darbyshire ignored them. Jenn started waving which sent the congregation into an even bigger chaotic mess. The minute the doors shut that second time, Darbyshire released Jenn's arm.

"You are now involved in the case. You are not allowed to speak to anyone regarding what's going on. You get that?"

Jenn looked over her shoulder, sullen and dismayed.

"I'm meant to be on TV."

Darbyshire shook his head.

"Not like this. You're meant to protect your friend and keep your mouth shut. Got it?"

Jenn sighed.

"Jenn, please."

Saige whispered. Jenn looked towards her. She could see her pleading eyes.

"Yeah, you're right. I'm sorry. Lips zipped."

Saige reached for her hand, squeezing gently.

"Now that we have an understanding, let's go hunt down Detective Richards."

Darbyshire said. Jenn and Saige exchanged a look.

"Darbyshire."

All three looked to their right and saw a man wearing a black suit walking towards them.

"Chief."

Darbyshire responded. He closed the distance between the three of them. Saige recognized him from Matt's apartment.

"Did I hear you say you were looking for Richards?"

"Yes, sir. Our girl here has something important to share with her."

"She hasn't come in yet."

Darbyshire narrowed his eyes. Brock Carter shrugged.

"I don't think we need to worry just yet. It's only nine."

He glanced at his watch.

"The last couple of days she's been here before eight."

Darbyshire trailed off. He stared at Brock. Brock didn't seem to think anything was wrong.

"Sir, it's urgent."

Saige piped up. Brock looked at her. He smiled at her.

"If you'd like, you can wait in her office."

Saige still had a grip on Jenn's hand. Jenn gave it a reassuring squeeze.

"Thank you."

Saige whispered. She hadn't meant to speak so quietly. She held onto the strap of her bag tightly as Brock escorted the girls to PJ's office. He unlocked the door for them and flicked the light switch. PJ's office had minimal furniture. Her desk and chair and only two other chairs that were situated on the opposite side of the desk were what was in the office. She did, however, have tons of large manila envelopes, pictures, mug shots, and photos of random items from each crime scene splayed all across her desk. Saige and Jenn looked around the room.

"PJ should be in soon. Make yourselves comfortable."

Brock said. They exchanged looks and slowly sunk into the two chairs by the desk.

"The receptionist will be in at nine thirty. Her name is Hilary. If either of you need anything, please don't hesitate to ask her."

Both girls nodded and Brock made his escape, leaving the office door open.

"Something isn't right."

Saige said, voice low. Jenn leaned forward, trying to peek at the confidential information on PJ's desk.

"You're just paranoid. Relax."

She said. She grabbed the arm rests of the plastic chair and scooted the seat closer to the big mahogany desk.

"No, Jenn. Something really isn't right."

Jenn turned to look at her.

"Do you know your cop?"

Saige narrowed her eyes, her brows knit together.

"I've met her once. Last night. You know that."

"You've met her, but you don't know her. She's probably just running late."

Saige's eyes dropped to the bag hanging off her arm. She pulled it into her lap and began rifling through it.

What are you looking for?"

Jenn questioned, this time without turning to face her. She'd picked up some of the files on the desk and was scanning them.

"My cell phone. I'm going to call her."

That made Jenn twist around. Her eyes were wide.

"Don't do that, Sai. You're being silly. Just let her get here when she gets here."

Saige had already dialed the number that was scribbled hastily on a piece of yellow notepad paper. She pressed dial and held the phone up to her ear.

"She told me to call her if I needed anything."

She paused and Jenn let out a frustrated sigh. She turned back to rummaging through the documents on PJ's desk.

"Her phone's off."

Saige said only a short moment later.

"It went straight to voicemail. That's not right. She wouldn't tell me to call if she'd have her phone off."

Jenn didn't reply. She was staring, mouth hanging open at the pages she was holding.

"I'll be right back."

Saige said, taking in the fact that Jenn was not paying an ounce of attention to her at all. Still clutching her phone and the piece of notepad paper, Saige brought herself to her feet and made her way to the office door. She looked down the long hallway to her right, seeing the abrupt curve in the hall, cutting off her view of people. She saw no one in the walk way at the moment. She twisted to her left and saw the short hall leading back to the main lobby. She stepped cautiously out of the room becoming all too aware of how scarily quiet the precinct was. Shouldn't there be uniformed officers up and down the halls? Shouldn't there be chatter echoing through the halls? On TV, police stations were always alive and buzzing with all sorts of activity.

She made her way down the short hallway, stepping into the reception area. The lobby. It wasn't nine thirty yet. She knew that. She surveyed the lobby, still seeing nobody. Not one person entered her sight.

"Chief Carter? Agent Darbyshire?"

She called out. She took a few steps towards the hallway opposite the one she had come from. That one extended far down the length of the building. She took a curve identical to the one in the hall she'd come from. She knew she shouldn't go looking for anyone but she was worried. About nothing, probably. She just couldn't shake the inkling feeling that something bad, something purely evil, was in their midst.

She took a single cautious step towards the hallway. Then another. And another. Before she knew it, she was in full stride down the hall, inside it in seconds. She stared blankly at each door she passed. Conference Room A. Conference Room B. Conference Room C. Chief of Police; Brock Carter. She read each plate on the doors explaining which rooms they were. She approached the bend in the hall. She could hear voices now. A door slammed; the voices got louder.

"She isn't here yet."

"What do you mean? She's always the first to get here."

"Well she's not here yet. Don't worry."

"Brock, do you realize what Andy just told us in there?"

Brock coughed. Saige could hear their footsteps becoming louder as well. She swiveled and ran back down the hall towards the lobby.

"; He found black hair follicles in those nylons. He tested em and you know what came up? A photo of what we can assume Samuel Thomas looks like now. Blonde hair, blue eyes. For fuck sakes, his fucking name came up."

"We already know, or at least assumed Sam was our guy."

"Think about it! The DNA proves it's Sam but he has blonde hair. The follicles Andy extracted from the nylons were black."

Brock and another FBI Agent that Saige recognized as SAC Brinker entered the lobby. She couldn't waste any time.

"Excuse me! It's Michael!"

She exclaimed, the words erupting from her body. Both men turned their attention from each other, focusing on her. They seemed surprised to see her in the lobby.

"What?"

Brock asked, finally breaking thc uncomfortable silence.

"It's Michael! Michael is Sam. Matt told me. PJ... I mean, Detective Richards isn't here yet. I'm afraid something's wrong. She knew about the letters. Maybe she figured it out. But it's Michael. It's Michael. He has Bella!"

Saige cried. She knew she wasn't making much sense. Brinker accosted her, putting his hands on her shoulders and bending slightly to look her in the eye.

"How did Matt tell you?"

Saige's brown eyes filled with tears.

"I never told him about Sam. He told me that he didn't trust Michael and that something was off with him. I never believed him until Matt died. But he was right. Michael was...Michael was off. Bella...oh God, Bella was with him. And now she's missing. Cara took away my interpretation of what Sam looked like but it came back. It's him. Michael is Sam. I don't know how, Sam was supposed to die in Springfield, plane crash. But Michael is Sam. It's him. I know it."

She was becoming hysterical, inhaling short and rapid breaths.

"Could you identify Michael in a photograph?"

Saige nodded furiously.

But...but Detective Richards..."

She muttered. Brinker met Brock's eye.

"Brock, take her to the lab. I'll go to PJ's house. I'll let you know."

He stepped away from Saige. He didn't have to nudge her towards Brock. He reached for her arm. Brinker pulled a radio from his belt.

"Agent Hamm, this is Brinker. Ten seventy-six. Richards' house. Repeat, ten seventy-six, Richards' house. Meet me at address forty-nine oh two, Maryland Crescent. Over."

Saige couldn't make out the staticky response. Brinker slid the radio back onto his belt and didn't waste another second. He shoved the lobby doors open instantly bombarded by the news. Saige didn't see what happened after that. Brock had his hand on her back, guiding her down the hall from which he and Brinker had emerged.

She didn't talk the whole way down. She fidgeted, nerves and worry biting at her insides. They reached the door marked "No Unauthorized Personnel Permitted". Brock pulled open the door and gestured to the blue bins that held the gloves and boots. She observed Brock slide a pair of the ugly surgical gloves onto his hands snapping them over his fingers. Saige immediately followed suit.

After she had everything on, she followed Brock further into the large, stainless steel room. Expensive. The one and only word to sum up Saige's perception of the room. They approached one station that Brock seemed to make a beeline for. The technician wasn't what Saige was expecting. Short. Bald. Big, black, square framed glasses took up most of his face. If it wasn't for the lab coat, Saige would have thought he was in the wrong place.

"Andy, can you pull up the photo of Sam."

Andy nodded obediently. He turned the computer screen so Brock and Saige could see it better. They watched him press on a file at the bottom of the screen. A photograph of a normal looking guy with a headful of thick shaggy blonde hair and light blue eyes popped up on the screen. Saige remained unphased. She stared at the picture, wishing something would come alive within her, wishing something would make her recognize the smiling man staring back at her from the monitor. Even in her dreams and flashbacks, his face had been fuzzy.

"I'm sorry. I don't recognize him."

She said, feeling disappointed. She was so sure that Michael was Sam. She had been so sure.

"That's not Michael."

Brock met Andy's eyes.

"Black. Change his hair colour to black."

Andy did as he was told, opening the Photoshop application on his computer. He quickly filtered the hair colour from the honey red blonde to jet black. Saige's heart jumped momentarily.

"Can you make his eyes darker? Like dark blue but fade them into a light blue green near the pupils?"

Saige hoped she was making sense. Andy did just that. He made it look so effortless. Saige squeaked and stumbled. With a gloved hand, she grabbed the counter top. Before she could say anything, someone walked up behind them.

"Sorry to interrupt. Hey, Andy, I - hey! That's Nick. What's he doing on your screen?"

Saige turned feebly. She looked the officer standing there up and down. Brock's voice rang in her ear.

"Hey, that is Nick. Saige is that..."

"Michael. That's definitely Michael. I'd know him anywhere."

Her voice came out shaky.

"Jack, could you give us a minute? Andy will be available shortly."

The officer, Jack, gave a smile to Brock, respecting his boss. He looked at the screen again and shook his head as he walked away.

"Who is Nick?"

Saige asked. Andy and Brock's eyes connected.

"Detective Richards' significant other."

They were silent. There was a crackling sound coming from Brock's pocket.

"Chief, come in. This is SAC Brinker. Come in, over."

Brock scrambled to pull the radio off his belt.

"Brinker, what is it? Over."

It didn't take long for a reply.

"PJ's car is still here. Her house is unlocked. Looks like there was a struggle. There are tracks in her driveway. Looks like someone dragged her from her house. Over."

Brinker didn't bother to hide the worry lacing his voice.

"I'm sending officers your way. Look around, see what you can find. I'm putting out an APB, over and out."

Brock slid the radio back to its spot. He met Saige's eyes.

"Do you know where Michael slash Nick lives?"

Saige shook her.

"No, no, I'm sorry. Oh God, Bella. Bella though."

"Who is Bella?"

Brock asked. Saige had said that name a few times.

"Michael...Sam... Michael was going to take her on a romantic overnight date. I don't know where...She's in trouble. She's in trouble. I just know it."

Saige started hyperventilating. Brock grabbed her by the arm. He nodded at Andy, who was observing quietly before dragging Saige from the room. The minute they were back in the hall, Saige pulled her arm from Brock's grasp.

"He's found me. He's back for me, right? He's back for me and disposing everyone closest to me, right?"

Saige cried out. Brock gave her a puzzling look.

"Everyone close to you?"

"Denae, Carly, Kelly, and now he's got Bella. What if Jenn's next?"

"Back it up. Denae, Carly, Kelly? What is your connection to them?"

Saige's big tear-filled eyes stared up at him.

"Denae was my cousin. Carly and Kelly were my sister's friends but they really idolized me. He's trying to isolate me. Trying to get me to come to him, isn't he?"

Saige sniffled and gulped hard. Brock didn't respond. He didn't know how to. Instead, he grabbed Saige's arm again and pulled the radio from his belt.

"Darbyshire, come in, Darbyshire. This is Chief Carter. Over."

Darbyshire responded instantly. His voice crackled over the radio.

"Darbyshire. What's up? Over."

"I want the mouse back in the hole. I want eagles on her at all times. Do not let her out of your site. Repeat, supervision at all times. I think the cat is getting ready to pounce. Over."

Saige felt frozen to her spot. Her feet felt like cement, immovable.

"Copy that. Over and out."

The radio clicked and Brock put it back down. He had Saige by her elbow and began escorting her towards the door to meet Darbyshire. She wasn't sure how her legs managed to move. She couldn't talk. The door clicked open.

"Animals!"

The girl screamed at the reporters. She slammed the door and let out a huffy breath and straightened the bag on her shoulder. She dusted off her blue jeans and turned around. She gasped when she saw Brock and Saige standing in the entrance.

"Oh, hi Chief. Hi, I'm sorry."

She chattered, glancing over her shoulder at the mob. Brock waved with his free hand.

"Don't worry, Hilary. Saige, Hilary."

He introduced her to the peppy blonde. She had a lot of similarities to Cara. Saige couldn't wave off her curvy body, long blonde hair, or emerald green eyes. She couldn't ignore the small beauty mark on her upper lip, positioned nearly the same as Marilyn Monroe's. If Saige didn't know better, she would swear she was looking directly at Cara Martin. Hilary waved at her and made her way to the reception desk. Saige moved her stare off of the blonde and out the doors. The multitude of reporters had sat down on the front steps. Some were tinkering with the video cameras and some were fiddling with their microphones. A couple of them were writing notes in their pocket-sized journals. Saige let out a heavy sigh.

"Let's go get your friend. Darbyshire will bring you both back to your dorm. Officers will be stationed inside near the exits, near your door, as well as outside in the parking lot. Round the clock, round the perimeter surveillance."

Saige didn't reply. She swallowed hard and followed Brock back down to PJ's office. They stopped at the doorway. It was closed now even though Saige remembered specifically leaving it open. She bit her lip and reached for the door knob.

"I'm going to grab some more officers to comb through PJ's house. You both meet myself and Darbyshire in the lobby in five minutes. Clear?"

Saige nodded.

"Crystal."

She understood perfectly and wasn't about to argue. Jenn's life and her's were at stake. She watched Brock exit the hallway and let her hand drop from the knob. She pressed her ear against the yellowed wood and could hear muttering.

"He's not dead anymore. You hear me? He's not. It's solidified now. No, you listen to me. Stop. Shut the fuck up. Listen, whoa. Okay whoa. Keep talking like that and I'm going to hang up. Marky isn't dead anymore. Okay? You asked me to tell you when I saw. Marky is alive, okay? I got to go. I'll see you later. Yeah, okay, yes. Bye, Collin."

Saige pushed open the door. She saw Jenn sitting back in a chair putting her cell phone back in her pocket.

"Collin?"

Saige asked, meeting Jenn's eye as she turned to see who opened the door.

"Yeah, Collin James. From school."

Saige stayed standing by the entrance.

"Can't say the name rings a bell."

Jenn shrugged.

"So, who is Marky then?"

"What?"

"You said, 'Marky isn't dead anymore.' Who is Marky?"

Jenn burst out laughing.

"You sound so nervous. Relax, Sai. Marky's a character on this show Collin and I watch. It's called, 'The Ruins'. Last week's episode, Marky supposedly died in an explosion. I didn't get to watch this week's episode but I saw a tweet that Marky's back. He got out alive. Collin's away right now and was positively dying for me to tell him."

Saige didn't answer. Jenn gave her a reassuring smile. It helped ease Saige's nerves. She couldn't help being on edge.

"What's going on, Saigers?"

Jenn's voice was low. Saige gestured to the door behind her.

"We got to go. I was right. PJ, Detective Richards is in trouble."

Jenn lurched out of her seat.

"Oh no!"

That was all she said. Saige turned and left the room, Jenn on her heels. Saige rubbed her hands together nervously. When they re-entered the lobby, she saw Brock and Darbyshire waiting for them. They both looked alert and on their toes. The minute their eyes landed on Saige and Jenn, they both reached towards them.

"We're going to get you guys out of her without a disturbance. Get you back to your dorm undetected."

Brock explained. He and Darbyshire escorted the two girls down the longer hallway where the labs and interrogation rooms were located. They approached a wide steel door at the back of the station. It resembled a loading dock door but was the entrance for the cell block of the station. Saige felt Jenn grab her hand and squeeze. Saige returned it but didn't look at her. Brock broke away from the group and veered off to the edge of the door. Darbyshire signaled for the girls to stop walking. They did and watched in awe. Brock put his face up against the side of the door. There was a peephole there.

"Yeah."

He said finally after what seemed like ages. Darbyshire pushed a red button on the opposite wall. The steel door groaned as it gradually ascended. Saige grimaced at the sound. She coughed a couple of times. She put her hand over her mouth to try and suffocate the sound. No one even looked at her. The door finished opening, slamming into its spot in the roof with a bang.

"Undetected, huh?"

Jenn said, the sarcasm heavy in her voice. Saige stifled a laugh and coughed again. Brock and Darbyshire looked at her and the smile immediately left her face.

"Come on."

They both said, reaching towards the girls again.

"Darbyshire's car is just out here."

Brock said smoothly. Darbyshire walked out onto the concrete outside. Jenn and Saige followed suit. Brock stayed back.

"Get them back quickly and quietly. Radio upon arrival."

Darbyshire nodded and watched Brock hit the red button a second time. The door made a sound like it was about to detach from the roof and plummet to the ground. Saige winced again as it made its descent and reached the ground without incident. She felt Darbyshire's hand on her back, ushering her towards the vehicle. She knew just how urgent the situation was. She just couldn't believe it. She and Jenn stayed quiet as the three of them marched across the back-parking lot. Darbyshire got the door for Saige but she didn't duck in right away.

She grabbed Jenn's hand and pulled gently. Jenn was staring off into the distance, just past the edge of the building. Beyond that wall were the news crews, unsuspecting as they lay in wait, hopeful that someone they could pester with questions would emerge from the front doors.

"Jenn, no, Jenn."

Saige whispered, trying to pull Jenn and get her into the car. She knew how badly Jenn wanted to be on camera, regardless of the apparent circumstances. Darbyshire stepped in front of Jenn's longing gaze breaking her focus.

"I need to get both of you to protection. Please, get in the vehicle."

Darbyshire's voice was soothing and low. Saige pulled at Jenn's hand again. Finally, Jenn turned and met Saige's eyes. She gave her a soft smile before ducking her head and sliding in behind the driver's seat. She scooched her way over so Saige could slide in beside her. Darbyshire shut the door as quietly as he could. They didn't need the reporters hearing and come running over. He climbed in behind the wheel and started the car. All three of them held their breaths as the car rumbled to life. It seemed louder than it really was. Maybe that was just Saige's heart pounding in her ears. Her only thought on the drive back to the dorms was, 'Fuck. I hope PJ is okay.'

22

Brinker didn't know what to do. He paced back and forth in PJ's kitchen, clasping and unclasping his hands, clenching them into fists. How did he not see this coming? The very person that murdered her sister had come back for her. No, that couldn't be it. He didn't believe that PJ was the initial target. The team had already determined he had found that little girl, D'Leo. Saige D'Leo again. She was the initial target. She was who he was after. She was the one that got away. PJ just knew too much. She was a loose end. That's what he was doing. Brinker rammed his fist into the wall next to the open door. A half circle shaped indent broke the plaster. He was tying up loose ends.

"Brinker?"

The voice came from the hallway. Brinker looked up and met Charlie Hamm's eyes. Agent Hamm was re-entering the kitchen. He could see the pain in Brinker's eyes.

"I found some interesting stuff upstairs."

"What interesting stuff?"

Brinker responded quickly. He strode across the kitchen and met Hamm in the middle.

"The lock on the deck door in PJ's bedroom has been fucked with. It's loose. Slides right open from the outside. There's prints all over it."

Brinker narrowed his eyes.

"Broken? PJ's prints?"

Hamm shook his head.

"I don't think so. It was tampered with. And then there's this." Hamm extended a hand. Brinker noticed it was gloved. A small black chip was in Hamm's palm.

"Found this sucker in the light above her bed."

Brinker stared at it.

"A bug?"

"Camera. Mini "Spy Kids" video camera. Someone was watching her."

Brinker's jaw dropped.

"I don't think it was Sam. Doesn't feel like his style."

Brinker was astounded. He had no words, nothing to say. Hamm pulled a small Ziploc bag from his pocket and slid the camera inside before tucking it into his jacket for safe keeping. Brinker's eyes fell to the floor. He stared down at the yellow markers he'd placed around the crime scene. Hamm put a hand on his shoulder.

"Don't beat yourself up, Brinker. How were you, or I, or anyone supposed to know this was going to happen? There was no way for us to know."

Hamm tried to comfort Brinker. He shrugged him off his shoulder and knelt down. He stared intently at the blood stain on the linoleum.

"Hamm, do you have an extra set of gloves?"

Agent Hamm always had an extra set. He pulled the latex gloves from his pocket effortlessly. Brinker grabbed them out of Hamm's outstretched hand and snapped them over his own hands.

"Swab?"

He asked without looking up. Hamm patted his pockets.

"Yes, here."

He slid a thin Ziploc from a different pocket. It contained several long q-tips. In his other hand he held a vial for the swab to go in. Brinker accepted the items and very carefully slid the cotton end of the q-tip across the blood, scraping it slightly. There was a high chance it was PJ's but he wasn't about to take the chance of missing out on a possible clue or evidence.

He dropped the bloodied q-tip into the vial and handed it back to Hamm. Before he could say anything, he heard the sirens. He knew Brock and a couple of other officers would be there shortly. He was hoping he wouldn't have to call back to HQ and have more agents fly out but that wish was looking less and less bright. He made himself stand back up. The squealing of tires coming to a stop, spraying gravel from the driveway resounded through the kitchen.

Not a second was wasted. Brock, followed by four other officers swarmed into the kitchen like bees. Brinker recognized Daniel Martin and Philip Walters. He also recognized Sergeant Raymond Telley from the meeting a short few days ago. There was one officer he had never met before.

"Brinker? Agent Brinker, we're going to need you to tell us exactly what you've found."

Brock said, his voiced wavered slightly. Brinker knew that he and PJ were incredibly close friends. He almost wondered if he and PJ had ever been intimate. He shook the thought from his mind as he shook the officer's hands that Brock had recruited.

"If you don't know me already, my name is James Brinker. I am the Special Agent in Charge. PJ Richards was abducted sometime late last night or very early this morning. If you noticed in your entry, the disturbed driveway. With all of the rain last night, it left the driveway a bit of a mess. If you saw, it looked like someone had been dragged. Come inside and instantly you know something malicious happened. Her purse,"

He paused to point out PJ's feminine handbag on its side on the kitchen floor. A few of the items had rolled out, spreading across the ground by the fridge.

"Her gun cannot be found. Agent Hamm and myself searched when we got here. The gun is definitely missing. Cell phone. Her phone was upstairs in her pocket. It was dead. Probably remained on since she had returned home from yesterday. Here, blood on the floor. Most likely from Peej but I'm not about to rule out the chance that she got a piece of her attacker. Now if you'll follow me upstairs, Agent Hamm found some interesting contributions on his second scan of PJ's bedroom."

He turned on his heel, leading the small group through the kitchen into the hallway. Agent Hamm was right behind him. They moved swiftly through the corridor and soundly up the staircase. That was what they were trained for. Stealth. Entering the bedroom, everyone turned back towards Brinker. He stepped back and gestured to Agent Hamm.

"On first run through, all I found was her cell phone, dead. Second run through I paid closer attention to detail. Exhibit A, balcony door."

Hamm paused to lead the officers to the door.

"Look at the lock. Locked, yes?"

The officers agreed mumbling their yeses and mhms. Hamm gestured for Brinker to step forward. With his gloved hand, Hamm unlocked the door and stepped onto the deck. Brinker closed the door and locked it. He could tell the officers were puzzled. Hamm, on the other side of the door, pulled his wallet out of his pants pockets and removed a bank card. He slid it into the crack of the door and jiggled the knob once. The door cracked open with ease.

"That lock has been tampered with."

Hamm stepped back into the room. He shut the door again and looked at the group of uniforms.

"There's really no telling how long its been screwed with. I don't think PJ even knew it was broken. I also found this."

Hamm paused again as he reached into his pocket, pulling out the camera in the baggie.

"I've really only seen these on TV. It's a very small, very hi-tech video camera. This had been strategically placed up there."

He pointed towards the light overhead.

"I've seen one of those before."

Piped up one of the officers. The only one Brinker didn't recognize.

"My wife has one. We use it as a nanny cam for our daughter. You're right. It is extremely hi-tech. And expensive. Thing costs a small fortune. You can't buy them from any stores here. You'd have to go across the border."

Brinker trained his gaze on the officer.

"What's your name?"

He asked quickly.

"Clayton. Ryan Clayton."

"Well Ryan Clayton. Where did you buy yours? What was the store called?"

Ryan Clayton nodded enthusiastically. He pulled a yellow notepad from his pants pocket and a pen followed. He immediately began jotting down the information as he spoke.

"They're fairly new. Not available anywhere except this place in Akron, Ohio. It's a tech shop that advertises spy gear. The real deal. Night vision goggles, bugs, and you guessed it, mini cameras. Guy who owns it is named...uh...Schmidt. Keith Schmidt. Place is called KSSG. I think the guy develops and makes all of the products himself. Far as I know, he keeps records of everyone that purchases from him. Names, addresses, phone numbers."

Officer Clayton tore the yellow note paper from the pad and handed it off to Brinker. He wildly scanned the information. He looked up and met eyes with everyone in the room.

"Okay, I think this goes without saying. Split up. I want this whole place finger printed. I want photographs and swabs. You,"

He paused and pointed at Ryan Clayton.

"You're coming with me."

Clayton didn't hesitate. Every person in the room broke into a frenzy. Jogging down the stairs to their vehicles to grab their finger printing tool boxes, latex gloves, and Ziploc bags to gather evidence. Brinker pulled his cell phone from his pocket. He dialed the phone number that Clayton had supplied to him. The two hustled down the staircase, bypassing an officer headed back up to finger print PJ's bedroom.

"Thanks for calling KSSG. Satisfying all your hi-tech needs. This is Keith."

"Keith Schmidt?"

"Speaking."

"My name is James Brinker. I'm a Special Agent in Charge with the FBI. I'm working on a case across the border in Ridgeway, Ontario. It's come across my attention that we have a piece of evidence that may have come from your store. A mini video camera. I need you to fax your records of everyone who purchased one within the last few months."

Keith Schmidt didn't respond right away. He seemed a little shocked.

"Sir?"

Brinker repeated.

"I'm sorry, Mr. Brinker. I cannot provide that information over the phone. I can arrange a meeting with you here at the store in a few days..."

"That's not going to work for me. I'll be there in twelve hours. Goodbye."

Brinker hung up the phone without a second thought and turned to Clayton.

"Feel like going to Ohio?"

Clayton nodded quickly. They had made their way to PJ's living room, facing each other.

"We'll swing by your house and grab your passport."

He pivoted on his heel and exited the living room into the kitchen where Daniel Martin was on his hands and knees dusting the radius around the blood stain. Heather Hendricks, the CSS, had shown up while Brinker and Clayton were in the living room. She was busy taking photographs of the scene. Everything that Brock had put markers around needed to have its picture taken.

"Chief, I'm taking Clayton. We're going to Ohio. We'll keep you updated and I'd appreciate if you'd do the same."

Brock turned away from watching Heather and turned to Brinker.

"Will do. Good luck."

Brinker nodded at him and swiveled again, hustling quickly out the door followed closely by officer Ryan Clayton. They moved fast out of the house and towards one of the cars. Brinker jumped in behind the wheel, Clayton right next to him.

"I need directions to your house."

Brinker stated. Clayton didn't hesitate. He gave the address and pointed Brinker in the right direction. It was only ten short moments later that they arrived at Clayton's house. A car was in the driveway, a little silver Dodge Caliber.

"I'll be right back."

Clayton clambered out of the car and ran to his front door. He disappeared inside, leaving Brinker waiting in the idling vehicle. Brinker tapped the steering wheel. He was impatient. He needed to get on a helicopter and get the hell to Akron. The more time that passed was more time wasted.

Finally, Clayton reappeared in the doorway followed by a petite redhead who was holding a small child. Clayton's daughter. Clayton gave his wife a kiss and then placed a delicate peck on the child's head. He jogged back to the car; his wife waved at them. He threw himself into the vehicle and slammed the door shut. Brinker backed out of the driveway as quick as he could. They sped off towards the airport. Brinker looked from the road to Clayton.

"That was Amelia, my lovely wife and Haydn, my daughter."

Brinker smiled and nodded.

"They were both beautiful."

The next thing he did was tap the screen in the car and typed in the number one and then hit dial. It was speed dialing Head Quarters.

"FBI."

"I need to speak with Director Traynor. It's Brinker."

The person who had answered the phone patched him through to the Director.

"Director Traynor, It's James Brinker, SAC on the Ridgeway murder case."

"Brinker, what can I do for you?"

Brinker didn't waste any time.

"I need a helicopter at the Ridgeway Airport as soon as possible. I'm headed to Akron."

"You got it."

Director Traynor replied.

"It'll be there as soon as it can be. Be waiting."

Director Traynor hung up the phone and Brinker did the same.

23

Sam tucked Squinty's body into the trunk of his Chevy Cobalt SS. Penny was better than he had anticipated. She'd managed to grab Squinty and strangle him all without making a sound. He'd give her that. She was well trained. Smart. He couldn't get rid of her yet. She made him think of Melissa. He had loved Melissa almost as much as he loved Saige. He would have kept both if he could. He slammed the trunk shut with a thud. Images of Saige floated through his mind.

So close. She was so close to being his again. The thought made his body tremble all over. He wanted to call her. Hear her voice. He wanted to be with her. He had to play his cards exactly right if everything was going to work out in his favour. He couldn't afford any fuck ups. Not when he was so close.

With a shaking hand, he slowly reached towards his pocket for his cell phone. His palm brushed against the Glock that was stuck in his belt. A rush of adrenaline jolted through him. He pulled the phone from his pocket, allowing his hand to bump against the handgun a second time. The gun was not his preferred method of disposal but it was fun to use.

He stared down at his phone and pressed the message icon. The only conversation he kept was his one with Saige. He opened the text messages. Very slowly his fingers tapped on the letters. Soon, he had a short message typed out. He re-read it back to himself.

"Hi Saige, Bella's okay. She called me this morning and said she'd see you later."

He scrunched up his nose and pressed send before he could change his mind. The minute he pressed send, the phone rang in his hand. The name on the caller ID put a smile on his face.

"Yes?"

He said smoothly.

"Have you fixed my issue yet? Impossible, I don't like hearing that. You know better. I'd gladly swing by but I have some stuff to do first. Yes, that stuff. Okay? Okay, bye."

Sam chuckled as he hung up the phone. Foolish. Foolish girl. He looked over his shoulder at the cabin and sighed heavily. Almost. It was almost the right time to house him and his angel. Almost.

He pulled his keys from his pocket and jingled them in his hand. He shoved the key that unlocked the car into the lock and twisted. Poor car. He didn't want to do what he knew was inevitable. He slid in behind the wheel and started the vehicle. It came to life, purring like it was brand spanking new. He started feeling emotional over his plans. This car wasn't his antique but it was still a nice car. One silly mistake and this is what it boiled down to. He sniffed hard as he hit the road driving smoothly over the terrain.

The storm the night before had done some damage to the road. Potholes had begun to form. He grumbled to himself angrily as he drove. He had to find the perfect spot and he was pretty sure he knew where that was. He wanted to be positive that his location was far enough away from his cabin, letting him remain undetected. He drummed his fingers on the steering wheel and thought about the jerry can filled with gasoline that was tucked in the trunk next to Squinty's body.

In a way, Squinty's untimely death had been beneficial for Sam's planning. No one knew Squinty. Just a guy that worked for his own newspaper. Never married. No kids. Not even a friend. Except Sam though Sam was more of an acquaintance than friend. He just helped Squinty get close to the one he claimed to love. He smiled at that fact. The one Squinty 'loved' had ended up being the thing that caused his death.

Sam couldn't help but laugh at the irony. Suddenly, he gasped. He checked his mirrors to make sure no one was tailing him. Upon not seeing anyone, he pulled over without signaling. With a sigh, he unbuckled his seatbelt. He left the car running as he got out of the vehicle and made his way to the trunk. He thought it was strange that not another automobile had passed him. Thought it was odd the highway was so unpopulated.

He shook his head as he fiddled with his trunk managing to pop it open. He swiveled his head, searching for any spectators. Still not a soul. Not a vehicle. He struggled for a moment to pull Squinty's body from the trunk. Even though the other man was significantly smaller than himself, getting him out of the trunk proved to be a difficult task. Hell, he'd learned getting anybody out of a trunk was hard work. After he managed to pull the man out, he dragged him to the car and with a great effort, pulled him up into the driver's seat.

Sam checked his surroundings again making sure he was still alone. He was. He reached across Squinty's body with the seatbelt and clicked it into place. He went back to the trunk and dragged the jerry can out, un twisting the cap. The overwhelming scent of gas filled his nostrils. It put him into a high. The smell of gasoline was near the top of the list of his favourite smells.

Holding the jerry can close as if it were a child, he made his way back to the open driver's door. There still wasn't another soul to be seen. He tilted the can and splashed the clear liquid over Squinty's body, soaking it. The heavy aroma over took the car. Sam could feel tears welling up in his eyes. His car. After he emptied the can, he went back to the trunk and tossed the can inside. He turned a three sixty and surveyed his surroundings one more time.

How weird that not one car had passed by. Lucky. Weird, but lucky. He slammed the trunk closed and walked back up to the idling car. He didn't think he had much time. Sam shut the driver's side door with a loud bang that echoed against the cliff next to him. He was happy with himself for parking so close to the edge of the cliff. Hopefully it would make the next step of his plan easier.

He rubbed his hands together and placed them shoulder width apart on the shiny black door of his Cobalt. With a big intake of the fresh nature filled air, he pushed. Hard. The Cobalt rocked back and forth but did not topple. He huffed out and turned, pushing his back up against the vehicle. Digging his heels into the ground, he shoved again, grunting. The Cobalt slid across the ground by an inch, more than enough to knock the front and back wheels on the passenger side over the edge. It sent the un balanced car tumbling down the cliffside.

Sam stumbled as the car left his back. He dropped to the ground to prevent himself from falling too far backwards. He was on his hands and knees, gasping for air. The car was a lot heavier than expected. Sucking in gulps of air, he crawled to the edge of the cliff and watched the beautiful car bounce over the jutting rocks and come to a crashing halt against a massive pine tree.

"Come on. Come on."

He mumbled; eyes trained on the car.

"Light up, light up."

He narrowed his eyes, straining, concentrated. He didn't want to have to climb down there and light it himself, risking death in an inevitable explosion. He was beginning to think that might be what had to happen. He leaned further over the edge and glared at the car.

Right when he pulled himself to his feet to lower himself down, he heard the crackling. He glanced back at the car. The gas had found its way to the broken engine. Sam backed away from the cliffside just as the car exploded. It was a massive explosion, sending rocks and chunks of metal flying in all directions. Flames licked the air below, catching the pine needles, racing their fingers up the trunk and engulfing the tree. He started smiling to himself, tears lingered in his eyes. He grinned down at the crispy, red, half blackened arm that lay on the ground in front of him. The flesh was still bubbling, the awful, wonderful smell of it burning, wafted through his nostrils. He did it. He managed to kill himself. Now he had to be reborn.

He turned on his heels, leaving the arm, Squinty's arm, in its resting place on the ground behind him. He still did not see anyone. Unfortunately for Sam, someone did see him. They saw the entire event play out from their perch on the hill opposite the road. Dressed from head to toe in camouflage clothing, face painted to match the trees, he sat, tucked in the brush, rifle in hand, witnessing the scene through the scope. With a shaking hand he scrambled to pull his cell phone from his pocket. It was on silent to avoid frightening the animals away. His fingers worked to press the buttons quickly, dialing nine one one.

"Hi, my name's Chet. I'm up at Riddlin Point. I think I just witnessed somethin' crazy."

24

PJ looked around the room. The smell of the dead woman and the itching pain from her wound came into play as she studied her captivity. The room was dirty but not overly small. The carpet was so filthy, she couldn't even tell what the original colour could have been. The walls were blue, or they used to be blue. They were dirty and had ripped mangy looking posters pinned to the walls. PJ had her knees pulled up to her chest.

She was doing the best she could to stay calm and think rationally. She didn't know how long she'd been held captive for. Couldn't be more than a couple of days. Sam still hadn't removed Bella's body out of the room. PJ struggled to stand on her feet. Once she did manage to stand, she pressed a hand over her wounded stomach. She winced at the pain. She bit her lip as she pressed.

The bleeding had subsided, thankfully but she knew she'd need a hospital to remove the bullet and stitch her up. She wasn't sure how much longer she could go with a hole in her gut. Every movement made her well up with tears.

"Sam?"

She called out. Her voice was a lot stronger than she imagined it would be. No response. She slowly edged closer to the door.

"Sam?"

She called again. Still no answer. She reached out to the door knob. She jiggled it hard but came to the realization that it was exactly as she had expected. Locked. Who knew how many locks were on the outside of the door, keeping her trapped in the smelly room with a decomposing body.

With an exasperated sigh, she slumped back to the ground. There were no windows in the room. If at one point there had been, they were long gone now. PJ screamed. She hadn't meant to; it just escaped her lips. A tear finally fell from one of her eyes. Followed by another and another. Eventually the tears continuously flowed from her eyes, soaking her cheeks.

She slammed a fist into the ground, sending a shiver of aching pain through her arm. Her wound pulsed.

"How did I let you fool me? How did I fall for you, again!"

PJ yelled, slamming her open palm into the floor, ignoring the pain. The tears flowed harder.

"You were supposed to be dead you fucking bastard! You died!"

She yelled again. Her heart was full of pain. She glanced over her shoulder at the bloated purple corpse of the very young Bella. Images of Melissa coursed through her mind.

Melissa never got to grow up. Never got to go on her first date, have her first kiss, get married or have children. This young woman had met a fate all too similar. PJ imagined Sam strangling and stabbing her sister. The way Bella died, choking on her own blood, gasping for air and needing a savior...PJ couldn't help but realize that was how Melissa had gone. She couldn't stop thinking about how she failed Melissa and how she failed this girl, Bella. She couldn't stop thinking about how many girls and women died at the hands of Samuel Thomas and how many she failed to save.

She looked up, catching her breath in her throat. She could hear the faint slamming of a car door in the distance. She couldn't tell what was happening. Sam must have returned. She scrambled backwards towards the bed. A blood curdling scream escaped her mouth as her hand grazed the squishy flesh of the corpse. No screams were intended. She heard the door open.

"Thanks so much, sir. Crazy girlfriends, man. I tell ya. Have a good one."

The door shut. PJ knew then that he was talking to someone. But who? She could hear his footsteps in the hallway, getting louder with every step. She managed to pull herself to her feet. She stepped over the corpse and onto the bed pushing herself as far back onto the bed as she could go, which wasn't very far since it was a twin.

The door knob to the room jiggled. She could hear clicking and knew instantly that he was undoing the locks. She prepared herself to see a monster emerge. Sam entered and laid his eyes upon her. She almost shocked herself by sighing. She knew Sam and when he wasn't around, she could swear he was the Devil himself.

"Ah, Penny."

Sam said, her name rolling off his tongue. She felt herself frown and she glared at him.

"Hi, Sam."

She said, his name tasted vile on her tongue. She was so disappointed in herself for not seeing the similarities between Sam and "Nick." Even though he looked nothing like the Sam she knew, he was still the same. His body movements, the annotations in his voice. He was totally the same, but she'd managed to miss all of the signs completely. Sam was smiling at her.

"What do you want, Sam?"

PJ asked, keeping her voice steady even though the pain in her gut shot through her whole body. Sam's eyes fell off her to the body on the floor.

"Just came to get rid of our friend here. Can't have Princess Penny in a room with a rotting girl."

He slid his hand in his belt to retrieve PJ's gun. She was shocked, letting the nickname sink in. He'd always called her his princess. Now he was mocking her. She looked up and he was slowly approaching, gun raised, barrel trained on PJ. He knelt down and grabbed one of Bella's swollen wrists and pulled. He was always surprised at how heavy dead people could be.

"Let me guess. Woodland Park? About six or seven rows in?"

PJ said. He looked at her as he drug the body towards the door.

"Have I really become that predictable?"

PJ swore he almost sounded disappointed.

"After not one, but five bodies show up, yes. Yes, we can assume."

Sam dropped the fleshy purple wrist. He stood up straight and held the gun tighter, his finger tense on the trigger.

"Smart ass."

He murmured.

"I'm not going to Woodland Park."

PJ sat up on the bed. She kept her breathing steady.

"You're not?"

He shook his head.

"Nope. You all think you know me so well. Let's make an example then."

He backed out of the doorway, pulling Bella's body the rest of the way out. He paused before he shut the door.

"Hell."

He said. He turned back to PJ, raised the gun, and fired.

PJ fell back on the bed, blood spurted from the wound on her shoulder. He hadn't shot to kill, just to maim. He just couldn't bring himself to kill her. Yet. Sam left the room, shutting the door firmly behind him, closing all of the locks.

PJ lay there, pressing a hand over her shoulder. Two g.s.w's. She needed a hospital. She wasn't sure how much longer she was going to last. The gut wound she had was aching. She leaned her head over her body and slowly lifted her sweater so she could get a look at her gut. The skin around the wound was bruised, purple and blue. Closer to the injury site was also extremely red and irritated. There was a greenish hue surrounding the small hole and pus was visible just inside.

Tears stung PJ's eyes. She squeezed them shut as she reached a hand down and pressed on the wound again. Pain rocketed through her. She needed a damn hospital. First, she needed to get out of the room. She had to if she was going to survive. It was only a matter of time before he really did kill her. She opened her eyes and held back the tears. She was tough. She could do this. She could escape. She just needed a plan.

She looked around the room, looking for anything she could use to make an escape. Her eyes landed on the posters hanging around the room. The tacks. She wasn't sure how she could use them; they weren't very long, but maybe she could try and stick one into his eye. It was better than nothing.

She slowly rolled off of the bed, wincing in pain as she did. She crawled across the filthy floor towards a wall with a motivational cat poster hanging off it. Once she reached the wall, she braced a hand against it and stood up gradually. Pain pulsated through both her gut and her shoulder.

She pulled a tack out of the bottom corner of the wall and held it in her hand tightly. She didn't want him knowing she had it. She sunk back to the floor and sat against the wall; her head leaned back on it. Once again, tears were welling up in her eyes. She couldn't contain them this time, they fell over and barreled their way down her cheeks.

She lay on the ground, breathing hard. He would be back soon. He had to be. He was constantly checking on her. She was going to make her move the second he came back into the room. She sucked in a breath and held it in as she started crawling across the floor towards the door. She had to be ready. She had to be waiting.

She made it to the door and braced herself on the wall as she slid up it to her feet. She decided she didn't want to wait. She exhaled hard, pushing the air out of her lungs.

"Sam!"

She yelled, hoping he hadn't let the house yet. If he had, she would have missed her shot.

"Sam!"

She called again; her voice strained.

"Please!"

She cried out.

"Please! Sam!"

Then she heard the footsteps. They sounded loud and angry as they stormed down the hallway towards the door. She could hear him unlocking the many locks. Now was her chance. The minute the door opened and he stepped inside the room, she flung herself onto his back, ignoring the shooting pain. She was screaming. She pulled the tack back and slammed it forward into his eye. He shrieked out and grabbed PJ by the arm. He ripped her off of his back and tossed her over his shoulder. He threw her to the ground.

"Fucking bitch!"

He yelled out as he retracted the tack from his eye. He pressed his palm to it while staring down at her with the other eye.

"Fucking bitch!"

He screamed again and brought his booted foot back. He kicked her hard right in the stomach over her wound. She screamed in pain. Tears rapidly fell down her cheeks. He kicked her again. She shielded her head with her arms and curled up into a ball. He kicked her a third time and then a fourth for good measure.

"You're fucking lucky I don't blow your fucking head off right now."

He turned grabbed the door knob, palm still pressed to his eye. Blood seeped through his fingers. He slammed the door shut behind him and did up the locks. PJ lay on the ground, battered and beaten.

25

"My name is Brock Carter, Chief of Police. Could you please tell me exactly what you just told Sergeant Telley? Thank you."

Brock stood firm in front of a large and hulky man sitting at a wooden desk. More specifically, the wooden desk in Brock's office. The man was wearing camo print pants and a grey V-neck tee shirt that clung tight to his tree trunk sized arms and beer gut. A camo print jacket hung off the back of the chair he was sitting in. He had his hands folded on the table in front of him.

"My name's Chet Riley. I think I witnessed a murder. I was up in tha' mountains at Riddlin Point doin' a little huntin'. I'm lookin' through the scope on Georgie, my rifle, and I done seen the craziest shit I ever seen. This guy pulled anotha' guy from his damn trunk and put him in the front seat of his car. Then he's, get this, then he's pourin' gas on the feller. Then he's pushin' the car over the edge of the damn cliff. Boom! Explosion."

Chet leaned back in his seat. He spoke wildly, using his hands a lot, twanging with a southern accent. Brock put a hand on the desk and leaned in.

"Can you describe the man?"

Chet tapped his chin and thought for what seemed like too long. Brock started to pace.

"The one was pretty little. Looked like it anyway. Black hair, couldn't see his face. The otha' one was much taller. He too had black hair and was wearin' jeans and a black shirt. He was tall and built, I could see his big arms from where I was. He had a chiseled face and a strong jawline. Feller kept lookin' around though I would too if I was doin' what he done did."

Chet leaned back in the chair again, tapping his foot on the ground.

"How about the car? Make? Model? Estimate a year? Colour?"

The questions were coming rapid fire out of Brock's mouth. Chet sat forward again.

"One at a time!"

He coughed and a smile crawled onto his face.

"The car was black. I think it was a Chevy, not sure what model. If I had to guess a year, I'd be thinkin' maybe a twenty ten? I'm not sure."

Brock looked over his shoulder to Raymond Telley.

"Told you."

Telley said. Brock sighed.

"You're sure it was another man that was pulled from the trunk?"

Chet was nodding wildly.

"Sure as sugar."

He placed both hands flat on the table and began to push himself to his feet.

"Are we done 'ere? I feel like there's a buck callin' my name up at the Point."

Brock shot Chet a warm smile.

"Almost. If you could just sit tight for a few more minutes."

Chet sighed heavily but sunk back down into the chair. He tapped his foot repeatedly. Brock turned to Raymond Telley.

"Has anyone gotten a hold of SAC Brinker? He's oughta found Schmidt by now."

Telley shook his head.

"Last time I tried, he and Clayton hadn't found him."

Brock chewed his lip. He glanced past Telley to Chet. He was studying his hands now, picking at the dirt and grime that was under his finger nails. His foot was still tapping. Brock noted that Chet's face was creased with worry. He looked anxious and even a little scared. Brock couldn't shake the feeling that the hick knew something else.

"Try him again. I'm sure he'd like to know what we were just told."

Telley pulled his cell phone from his pocket and dialed a number. Brock kept an eye on Chet who continued to fidget.

"Agent Brinker? It's Telley. Sam killed again but this time, we have a witness. Guy says he was hunting and a man matching Sam's current description pulled a body from his trunk and put it in the front seat and then push the car over the cliff's edge at Riddlin Point. Chief wants to know if you've spoken to Schmidt yet? He wants you to keep him updated!"

Telley hung up the phone and turned back to Brock and Chet Riley. Telley must have noticed Chet's behavior too. Before he said anything about the phone call, he exchanged a look with Brock. Telley knew Brock was thinking the same thing he was. Telley didn't have to say anything. Brock spoke first.

"Hang tight for another few minutes, Mr. Riley."

Brock gestured towards Telley and they both exited the room, shutting the door to the office firmly behind them.

"What are you thinking?"

Brock asked the minute the door was shut. Telley stared through the cracked blinds into the office. Chet's foot was still tapping nearly uncontrollably under the desk.

"There's something else."

Telley finally said.

"He definitely knows more."

Brock said next as he too stared through the blinds.

"My thoughts exactly but what is it?"

Telley replied, momentarily forgetting about the phone call with Brinker.

"I doubt it'll be hard getting it out of him. He's been cooperative."

"But why hide part of the story in the first place? I just don't get it."

Telley had to agree with Brock. What was Chet hiding and why? Brock grabbed Telley's shoulder.

"Give it a shot, Ray."

He urged Telley towards the door. He grabbed the cold metal of the door knob and twisted. Chet's head snapped up at the sound.

"Hi."

He said through dry lips. He smacked them a couple of times trying to moisten them.

"Would you like something to drink, Mr. Riley? Water?"

Telley said smoothly. Brock hadn't heard any of his other officers offer water before, except for PJ. He couldn't help but look down, deep sadness heavy on his heart. Chet nodded slowly.

"Please."

Telley glanced at Brock who nodded slightly and left the hallway.

"Chief Carter will be right back with some for you."

Telley stayed quiet for a minute as he made his way around the desk and sat opposite Chet. He could tell he was nervous. The sweat beading on his forehead proved that to Telley.

"What's going on, Mr. Riley?"

Telley asked, leaning forward on his elbows, resting his chin in his hands. Chet didn't reply. His eyes darted around the room. He gulped hard.

"What happened after you called nine one one?"

Chet didn't reply. He cracked his knuckles loudly.

"May I please have that water?"

Chet asked politely. Telley stared at him, trying to catch his eye. Chet looked everywhere but at Telley.

"Please?"

He repeated.

"It's coming. It'll get here a lot faster if you would tell me what happened after you hung up with nine one one."

Telley wasn't giving up. Chet finally looked at him. He was licking his lips. Telley could see how chapped they were. He needed a chap stick, badly.

"I helped him get away."

Telley's hands dropped from under his chin. He wasn't expecting that.

"After I hung up with nine one one, I waited for them ta show up. It didn't take very long for them ta show up. After they asked me a coupla questions, they let me get the hell outta there. I had my truck parked on a dirt path up ta where I was sittin' while I was huntin'. I got ta my truck, threw Georgie in the seat next to me and drove. I didn't expect ta see 'im. He was hitchhiking. I don't know why, but I pulled over and asked if he needed a ride. He said he an' his wife had a fight on their way back from campin' and she kicked 'im out and told 'im to walk the rest of the way home. I took 'im home and then went to my place. I was headed back up ta the Point this mornin' when you folks called me in."

Telley pushed himself away from the table and began pacing.

"Why didn't you tell us this earlier?"

Chet stopped tapping.

"Because I coulda got arrested. I helped a criminal escape. That's a crime, ain't it?"

Telley nodded.

"It is, but withholding information from the police is also a crime."

"Ya'll ain't gonna put me away, are ya? I got a daughter at home. 'Er mama's been gone some time. Neigbour's are watchin' 'er. She needs me."

Telley worked up a soft smile.

"No, we won't arrest you...Because if you drove him, you know where he lives."

Chet nodded his head.

"Great, then you can tell us where and we can finally take this maniac down."

Cue, Brock. He walked back into the room with a coffee mug filled with water. Ice hit the edges, clinking merrily. Brock placed the cup in front of Chet.

"Drink up, you must be parched."

"I've been in this fucking town for two days and I still haven't reached Schmidt. I told him I'd be here in a few hours and he just drops off the face of the fucking Earth."

Brinker said angrily. He was filling his coffee mug with his third filling of java. He hated the taste. The motel that he and Ryan Clayton had holed up in had some of the worst coffee he'd ever tasted. It was watery and thin, tasting like cheap dollar store coffee rather than a hot delicious and expensive brew. Hell, it probably had come from a dollar store, now that he thought about it. Clayton was sitting on the edge of one of the beds, bent at the waist, pulling on one of his boots.

"Why tell us he'll meet with us and then drop off the radar?"

Clayton said as he finished with his boot. Brinker didn't respond. It had now been four days since PJ went missing. If Sam stuck to his routine, that meant they only had three more to find her before they'd come across her body in Woodland Park.

Brinker had to find out who else was watching her and why. He was positive that it was Sam who physically took her but the camera was new. Maybe it would give them a clue. According to Sergeant Telley, they had a certifiable witness. He'd given them the address and directions to where he'd brought Sam after the car incident. Brinker knew they were devising a way to get in, unnoticed. He wanted them to wait for his return. He wanted to be the one to nail Sam's hide to the wall. He also didn't expect to be in Ohio that long. One more day and he'd need them to go ahead without him.

"Okay, let's get a move on. If possible, I want back on the helicopter by tonight."

Brinker said, putting the drained mug onto the counter. Clayton didn't hesitate to follow. They left the motel in a rush and jumped into their rental car that was at their disposal. Brinker knew the way to KSSG by heart now. The past couple of days he'd been back and forth from the store, talking to every person he saw. Didn't seem as though anyone could say where Keith Schmidt had gone. He'd just disappeared.

Brinker pulled the car up to a small shop on the corner of a dead road. He barely had the car in park before he was out and running towards the door of the shop. He already knew. It was the same as the last couple of days. Dark. He slammed his fist on the door.

"Dammit!"

He cried. He withdrew his phone and called the number that Clayton had given him. It rang five times and the automated voicemail rang in his ears.

"Thanks for calling KSSG. I'm away from the counter or we're closed. If it's urgent, please leave a message and I'll call you back asap. Have a wicked day."

Brinker didn't wait for the beep. He hung up. He'd already left six urgent messages and Schmidt hadn't returned any of the calls. Clayton had a helpless look plastered to his face.

"Good news is, we have crossed the border. You're the FBI. This guy's ran away from us, now you can involve the police with jurisdiction here."

Clayton said. Brinker stared at him.

"Why couldn't you have offered up that information two days ago? Clearly I've been too distracted to think of it myself."

Clayton shrugged.

"I didn't think of it either. I'll call the department."

Clayton said, trying to be helpful. Brinker turned back to the door and pressed his face to the glass and stared inside the silent and dark store.

"Hey! What are you two doing?"

Brinker stepped back and swiveled around. He saw a small, gray haired woman rushing towards them. Brinker pulled his badge from his pocket and held it out to her.

"Special Agent James Brinker. I'm with the FBI. This is official matter."

The little woman studied the credentials and gradually handed it back to Brinker. She let out an ample sigh.

"What's Kevvie done now?"

Brinker caught Clayton's eye.

"I'm sorry. Kevvie?"

The little lady had tears glistening in her eyes.

"Kevin, my grandson. He owns this store. Kevin Sanders Spy Gear. KSSG."

"Forgive my ignorance. I thought the owner was a Keith Schmidt."

The lady sighed and shook her head.

"Is that what he said his name was? No, oh no no. Uh..."

She paused to look around. The street was quiet.

"Let's talk inside."

She said. She pulled a set of keys from her purse and shoved past Brinker who was staring at Clayton in awe. They both followed her into the store and she shut and locked the door behind them. She typed in the alarm code turning it off. Brinker hadn't even heard it so it must have been a silent alarm.

"My name is Meredith Sanders. Kevin Sanders, the owner of this store is my grandson. I thought he gave up his Keith Schmidt identity a while ago. My grandson used to be a heavy-duty drug user. He ended up going to detox and rehab. After he left, he began selling drugs very regularly. He used the name Keith for that and, well anything illegal really. I love my grandson. I just want what's best for him. I thought was done with crime..."

Meredith shook her head sadly. Brinker stared at Clayton, letting the information sink in.

"Well, ma'am. As far as we know, he's okay. As far as we're aware, he's innocent. However, we found a piece of equipment from this store at a crime scene. We need to see his records."

Meredith nodded. She stood up from her seat at the counter that she had taken and made her way behind it. She pulled out a massive black binder stuffed full with papers.

"He didn't believe in computers."

She said as if apologizing for his records.

"Funny how he owns and operates a hi-tech store but doesn't have a computer."

Brinker noted. Meredith didn't reply. She was too busy flipping through the black binder.

"What item?"

She mumbled. Brinker looked at Clayton.

"It was small black video camera. Almost like a bug."

Meredith clicked her tongue.

"Ah, here, here it is."

She turned the binder towards Brinker. He scanned the list. It wasn't a very large one. Among the seven names of people who'd purchased one, four were from Ridgeway. That was already more than he thought there'd be. Also, among the list of names was Ryan and Amelia Clayton.

"Thank you so much Missus Sanders. I really appreciate your help. Just one more question. Do you have any idea where Kevin may have gone?"

Meredith shook her head.

"I'm sorry. I don't. He hasn't spoken to me in weeks until today. He telephoned me and asked if I could open the store for him. I have the spare key."

Brinker dug in his coat for a pen and notepad.

"Do you remember the number?"

Meredith's eyes fell to the counter.

"I'm sorry. He called from a blocked number."

Brinker and Clayton thanked her for her cooperation and made their exit. Once outside, they made eye contact.

"What the fuck?"

Brinker asked. Clayton's eyes were wide.

"What the fuck is going on?"

Brinker yelled a little too loudly. Clayton didn't know how to answer. Brinker looked at the list in his hands.

"It says that you bought yours on February twelfth. Isn't that the same day that your first vic went missing? I read the files."

Clayton nodded.

"Yes, and yes. We haven't had the camera for very long."

"It says that two of the other three people bought theirs the same day. Think. Was there anyone making the same purchase as you?"

"That only one at the time was a woman. I purchased mine and as Amelia and I were leaving, this redheaded woman intercepted us at the door. She asked about the video camera. After we explained about it, she got excited and said she would buy one to catch her cheating husband. That's when we finally left."

Brinker pulled open the door to the car.

"Why wouldn't Kevin meet with us? Why is he running? Did you get that number? Let's involve the state police and get them to hunt down Sanders and get let's get the fuck back to Ridgeway."

Clayton didn't reply, just opened the passenger door and climbed in next to Brinker. He was scrolling on his phone, finding the address of the local police department. Brinker's cell phone began to buzz. He frowned and looked down as he pulled the phone from his pocket.

"Ah, here. It's on twenty-two..."

"Shut up."

Brinker interrupted. He'd received a picture message from an unknown number. Clayton watched him from the passenger seat. Brinker slowly opened the message and found himself staring at a horrific sight.

"Call Brock. Right now."

Brinker said bluntly. He couldn't peel his eyes off of the picture. It was of a girl, dressed in a nice pair of black dress pants, a white, or what used to be white but was now spattered with blood blouse, and black blazer. A crude brown wig was placed on her head with no effort to hide the blonde hairs underneath. A single word had been printed on a piece of paper and brutally nailed to her chest. The word on the note said, 'PJ'. Clayton handed the phone to Brinker,

"Brinker? Brinker, what's going on?"

"Get people to PJ's house, now. I've just received a text. It's a picture of a dead girl. She's wearing PJ's clothes and is propped up on her couch.

He's making a fucking statement. You have got to find her. Go. We'll be back asap."

Before Brock could respond, Brinker's own cell phone started ringing in his hand.

"Wait, wait."

He shoved Clayton's phone back to him and told him to stay quiet. He pressed the green answer button and lifted the phone to his ear.

"Hello James. Or should I call you Agent Brinker?"

The male voice came through the phone clear and threatening.

"The latter. How'd you get this number, Mr. Thomas?"

Laughter.

"Mr. Thomas is my father. Call me Sam."

Brinker didn't respond.

"Did you like my gift?"

"Your gift?"

"Yes. Returning our dear Penny to her own home after death."

"That wasn't PJ."

More laughter.

"Oh, you got me. It wasn't. But it could have been. Oh! I have an idea. Would you like to talk to her?"

Brinker felt caught on his words.

"Yeah. I'd like that."

"Well, I'll try and be accommodating. See, I like you, James."

He paused, letting it sink in that he ignored what Brinker liked to be called.

"I like you, even though you were fucking my girlfriend."

"Ex."

Brinker said.

"Ex-girlfriend. I'm pretty sure when you were revealed to be a serial killer. The same serial killer that got her sister, might I add, that you officially became an ex."

Sam chuckled softly.

"That's why I like you. We could be such good friends"

"I thought you were going to let me talk to PJ."

Brinker said, glancing at Clayton. He had a hand over his mouth, phone clutched between white knuckles.

"Of course. Yes. Got distracted. Here you go."

Brinker held his breath.

"Brinker?"

Her voice broke his heart. She sounded so weak and frail.

"Hi, PJ."

He said slowly. He figured he was on speaker, so he had to be careful with what he said.

"Are you okay?"

He asked.

"'Bout as good as you'd expect. I don't know how long I've got. Sam's not in the room but he's probably right outside the door."

Brinker didn't reply.

"I can't tell you where I am, because I don't even know. But I know it's been four days. He keeps reminding me. So, if you guys don't find me soon, I'm fucked."

Brinker could feel the tears stinging his eyes. He'd only known her for a short while and they'd only had one night together but he cared about her so deeply.

"We'll find you. Everyone's working all hours. We'll find you. I promise."

"Don't promise me anything."

She paused and started coughing. The sound was awful in his ears. She sounded like death.

"Look, Brinker, I,"

"Time's up!"

Sam's voice rang out.

"No, wait!"

Brinker called out, feeling panicked.

"Brinker!"

PJ yelled. A sick slapping sound echoed through the phone. PJ went silent.

"Nice chat, James. Have a good day."

"You son of a bitch."

Brinker said.

"We'll find you. I swear to God we'll find you and when we do, I'll,"

"You'll what? Kill me? I've heard that before but look who is still kicking. Oh. Me. Good luck with that, James."

The line went dead. Brinker scrambled for the phone Clayton was holding.

"Brock, go. You guys have to get her now."

"On it. See you guys soon."

Brinker hung up and met Clayton's eyes.

"I need you to stay and talk to the state police. On my authority. I'm going back alone. Give them my number and they can verify with me if needed."

Clayton nodded. He wasn't about to argue. Brinker pulled out of the parking lot and sped off in the direction of the airport.

27

Saige stared out her dorm window, wide eyed. She couldn't see the agents put on surveillance but she knew they were there. Just like she knew that Derek Brady was now posing undercover as a security guard so he could wander the halls and keep an eye everywhere. The situation terrified her beyond belief.

"Saige, you got to stop. Just relax. You've got like half of the police and a bunch of FBI guys watching your back. Chill."

Jenn said. She was sitting on one of the twin beds in the dorm room painting her toenails.

"I'm relaxed. I'm just looking at puddles."

Saige said, knowing all too well that was the lamest lie she'd ever come up with. Jenn scoffed from behind her.

"Yeah, puddles. Alright."

Neither said anything for the next few moments. Saige continued to stare. What was she supposed to do about school? She'd already missed the last couple of days, ruining her perfect record. University was a big deal. She hated missing those days, especially when she was trying to make a career of being a lawyer. Knocking on the door made her spin around defensively. She met Jenn's eyes.

"Who is it?"

Jenn called out for Saige who was frozen.

"It's Brady."

Saige could feel the weight lifted off her shoulders.

"Come in."

She called. The familiar face of the male officer who'd been watching them the last couple of days entered the room. He looked run and ragged. Dark purple bags weighed heavily under his eyes. He'd been switched out twice but Saige knew it was hard for him to sleep, knowing Saige wasn't comfortable with Officer Riggs as much as she was with him.

"Saige, I've got some good news."

He said through a yawn. Saige walked away from the window and towards him.

"Good news? Finally! Does that mean you found Detective Richards?"

Brady smiled at her meekly.

"No, but we know where she is. Which means we know where Sam is and..."

"And you got him, oh my God! That is such good news! Oh my God!"

Saige squealed with delight and jumped into Brady's arms, hugging him tightly. Neither noticed Jenn slide off the bed and dig through her bag that was next to it. Neither paid any attention to Jenn as she pulled a switchblade from her bag.

"I'm so relieved that things are finally over!"

She said.

"I'm so happy for you, Sai."

Jenn said as she walked up behind Brady and rammed the blade into the back of his neck and twisted. Saige stumbled backwards, eyes wide, jaw open. Brady gasped as blood bubbled from his mouth, spilling over his lips. His eyes rolled back in his head and he dropped to the floor.

"Jenn...Jenn..."

Saige sputtered. Jenn studied the blood coated switchblade.

"Saige, you're pretty but you're not the brightest. How do you think Sam found you again? How do you think he knew Denae, Carly, and Kelly? I mean, yeah. He was watching you but there was stuff he needed help with. Like his false death three years ago. He knew where you were. I helped him because, well because he caught me doing some bad shit and he wanted me. Oh, Sai. He's known for the last three years. He's been moving slowly. Bound to get it right this time."

Jenn glanced down at Brady's body.

"And thanks to someone,"

She paused and kicked him in the side.

"now I have a chance to warn him."

She knelt down next to Brady and lifted the back of his shirt and pulled the gun from its holster on his waist. She aimed it at Saige as she slowly stood up.

"If you scream, I swear, I'll shoot you."

"Sam wouldn't like that."

Saige whispered.

"If you keep your mouth shut, you'll be okay. But if you so much as squeak, he'll understand a grazed shoulder, or maybe a missing toe."

Saige didn't make a sound. Her eyes sparkled with glistening tears, but she didn't say a single word. Jenn bent and grabbed her phone off of the bed and pressed one number. Speed dial.

"It's me...Some shit went down. They know where you are. Shut up and listen to me for once. I just killed a fucking cop for you...Yes, I've got her right here...Yeah, okay. So, get out of there, now! Will meet you at Ace."

She hung up the phone and continued looking at Saige.

"Come on, we're leaving."

The tears trickled over her rims. She still didn't say anything. Jenn waved Brady's gun at her.

"Come on, move."

Saige took a step towards the door.

"How are we going to get out of here? There's an officer at each exit. An agent outside."

Jenn smiled at her.

"Oh, Sai,"

She clicked her tongue and chuckled. She grabbed her bag and slid it over her shoulder.

"Go."

She said to Saige. Saige didn't argue. She moved quickly to the door and slid a pair of flip flops on her feet. She reached for the door knob and pulled open the door. Even if the officers didn't hear her, someone inside the rooms was bound to. She felt the gun against her spine.

"Don't think about it."

Jenn muttered through gritted teeth. She removed the gun from Saige's spine and slid it into her bag. They looked like regular joes. No one would guess that one was a murderer. They began their descent down the hallway. They moved all the way down to the side door where they could see an unmarked vehicle sitting at the back of the lot. An agent had a newspaper open.

"How do you think we're getting past him?"

"Shut up."

Jenn said quietly. Saige clamped her mouth shut. She followed Jenn up to the cop car.

"What are you girls doing out here? Where's Brady?"

Jenn flashed him a steadfast smile.

"I have something for you."

Jenn propped her bag onto the window ledge of the cop car. She reached into her bag and flipped the blade out. In one motion, she brought it out and jammed it into the agent's eye socket. It made a horrible squishing sound as scarlet squirted out. The agent didn't utter a sound. Saige put both hands over her mouth and suffocated a scream. Jenn looked around. She reached in and unlocked the car and opened the door. She reached across the dead agent and unbuckled his seatbelt. She pulled him from the driver's seat with a grunt.

"Get in."

She said. Saige slowly lowered her hands and gulped hard. Jenn put a hand on her shoulder and shoved. Saige stumbled forward, slapping on hand against the car. She ducked her head and slid in behind the wheel.

Jenn shut the door softly, trying not to alert the other members of the surveillance team located around the other sides of Becker Hall. Saige could gun it. She knew she could floor it or start honking the horn. She should do something but she was paralyzed. She couldn't stop shaking. Jenn. She would have never guessed Jenn was the other half of a psycho. Jenn got into the seat next to her.

"Drive the long way out."

Saige squeezed her eyes shut, trying to prevent the tears from finding their way down her cheeks. Saige put her foot on the gas and maneuvered her way out of the spot that the agent had parked in.

"Roll up the windows."

Came Jenn's command. Out of the corner of her eye, Saige could see Jenn pull the black Glock from her bag. She kept it lowered and out of sight from the world but her thumb danced over the safety. Saige kept holding her breath, hoping and praying that another surveillance car would spot her. They got to the exit of the parking lot without the slightest chance of another car catching them. They hit the main road through town, Jenn had the gun in one hand, pointed at Saige's side and her cell phone in the other. She was humming as she typed.

"Where are we going?"

Saige managed to say without stuttering.

"Turn left at Woodland Park."

Jenn replied. Saige knew there was still a good fifteen minutes before they would arrive at the park. Every time she checked her mirrors or shoulder checked or even just glanced out the window, she hoped someone would drive by and they wouldn't be so oblivious to her looks. She wanted someone to drive past. She hoped she'd be able to communicate with another road user that she was in danger. So far, she'd had no such luck. Thoughts ran through her mind as she drove. What was going to happen? What would Jenn do? More importantly, what would Sam do? Would he be holding a grudge against her for what happened twelve years ago? Or would he be so grateful to have her back?

She didn't know. She was terrified. In her mind, she started saying goodbyes. '*I love you, Mom, Dad, Ben, Leesa...I love all of you so much. I'm sorry this is happening again. I'll see you real again real soon, Matt. I'm so sorry.*'

"Turn here, now."

Jenn's voice broke through the thoughts jumbled up in Saige's mind. She didn't need to reply. She made a left turn onto a dirt road across the street from Woodland Park. Saige waited for her next command with anxiety racing through her veins.

"Okay, stop."

Jenn said when the highway was no longer visible. Saige narrowed her eyes but braked and put the car in park.

"Get out."

Jenn said sharply. Saige did as she was told.

"No, leave the car running."

Jenn said when Saige reached to turn the key in the ignition. Saige stopped her hand and slowly reached for the door handle. She opened the door and got out, backing gingerly away from the car.

"Walk to the gas compartment. Take the cap off."

She said, voice gruff. Saige did, the fumes immediately burning her nostrils.

"Okay, come on."

Jenn said. Saige looked at her, the gum aimed.

"Coming."

She said frantically. She moved quickly towards Jenn who was standing much further back than Saige had originally thought. Saige glanced around taking in the densely wooded area. She could take off. She should. Jenn grabbed her wrist.

"This will be loud."

She said. Before Saige could question her, Jenn raised the gun again, took aim, and let her finger tap the trigger. It only took one bullet. It hit the open gas tank. The explosion was deafening. It sent Jenn and Saige flying backwards into the air. They landed a couple of feet apart. The ringing in Saige's ears was loud and irritating. She pressed her palms into her ears and closed her eyes tight.

She shook her head a couple times, hoping the ringing would die down but it persisted. She slowly opened her eyes and saw the stolen vehicle engulfed by flames. The orange tongues were licking the air, climbing the trees, eating the bark, leaves, everything. She turned her head to see Jenn. She was squirming on the ground, holding her head. The gun was next to her feet. Saige knew it was now or never. She pushed herself to her feet, stumbling. She focused on the woods in front of her. For a moment, she didn't think her feet were going to work. It was like she'd forgotten how to run. She took a wobbly step towards the trees. She just needed to get away from the dirt road. She grabbed her head again as if she could suddenly hear the fire crackling, branches snapping.

Just as suddenly, her body remembered how to move. She tripped but regained her balance and headed for the woods' edge. The pain that came next was almost unbearable. She dropped to her knees and screamed. The bullet pierced the back of her shoulder and exited the front, just under her collarbone.

Blood spurted on the ground in front of her. The pain was searing through her. The tears began to pour down her cheeks. Her hand pressed against the opening in the front. Blood seeped through her fingers. She felt the barrel press against the back of her head.

"Get up."

Jenn ordered.

"Get the fuck up."

She grabbed the back of Saige's hair and yanked. Saige screamed. Jenn brought the gun across her face. The pain pulsed through her shoulder, collarbone, and face. The smack made her nose and mouth bloody, the coppery taste sick on her tongue.

"Come on you stupid little bitch."

Jenn spat. Holding Saige by her hair and keeping the gun pressed against her temple, she dragged Saige back to the road where another vehicle had arrived and was waiting in the haze of the fire that was chomping its way through the woods, away from them. The door to the vehicle opened and he stepped out.

His face came rushing back to her in a flood, completely shredding the wall that Cara had put up. She recognized him as who he was. She remembered his face. Samuel Thomas. Jenn shoved Saige forward, letting go of the fistful of hair. Saige fell forward, falling onto her hands and knees. The pressure from the fall sent a jolt of pain surging through her wound. She could feel her eye swelling up from being hit by the gun. She felt Sam's hand grab her good shoulder. It wasn't rough. He had a gentle touch.

"What happened to her?"

Sam barked at Jenn. She shrugged.

"She tried to get away. Couldn't let that happen. Not after all the planning, all the meticulous planning. Not after all the shit we went through to get her back to you."

Sam's other hand came up to Saige's bruised, bloody, and battered face. With his index finger, he gently tilted her face up towards his. She tried not to look at him. She tried not to be captivated with the handsome man he had turned into. He turned her head, studying the bruising and the blood.

"You wrecked her. You...You hurt her."

He stuttered. His hand fell from her face. He stood to his full height. Saige couldn't continue. She dropped from her hands and knees and fell to the ground, lying flat on her stomach. Her breathing was shallow.

"You hurt her."

He said again, his voice deepening. Jenn raised her hands.

"To help you."

She said, voice slightly shaking. Sam moved closer to her. She dropped the gun in an attempt to make him see a little forgiveness. Sam looked down at the gun on the ground and then back up to Jenn. He smiled.

"Come here."

He opened his arms, inviting her in for a hug. She smiled back at him and stepped into his arms. Saige managed to slowly raise her head to observe what was taking place. With one hand, Sam stroked her hair and with the other, he rubbed her back.

"Forgive me?"

Jenn asked softly, leaning into him.

"Of course not."

Sam whispered, lips against her ear. Jenn's eyes widened. She tried to pull herself out of his grasp. Both hands went to her face, cupping her cheeks.

"Thanks for all your help the past few years, Sara. I just don't need you anymore."

Jenn couldn't utter a word. She didn't have the chance to. Sam twisted her head, cleaning snapping her neck like a twig.

Saige clapped her hands over her mouth to suffocate the blood curdling scream. She immediately regretted doing so. Sam dropped

Jenn's body to the ground. It fell in on itself in a heap. He turned back to Saige. She couldn't keep her head up. She dropped her face back to the dirt, completely drained of energy. Sam moved over her. He bent to his knees.

"Sai. Come on, Sai. Stay awake, sweet angel. We're going home now."

He let his eyes drift over the bullet wound. The back of her shirt was soaked with blood. Tears filled his eyes but he would absolutely not let himself cry. He reached down and slid a hand under one of Saige's armpits, the side without the injury. Her eyes were closed but she was awake. The tears streaking her face had dried but she was shaking.

As much as she didn't want to touch him, she needed to. She needed his support to stay on her feet. She really just wanted to run, scream, find help. Instead, she allowed Sam to direct her to the truck. She wavered slightly as he held her good arm to get the door of the old Chevy for her. He helped her in and slammed the door shut. She slumped over to the side, leaning against the window. Sam climbed in behind the seat just as sirens resounded in the distance.

"Okay, Saigey angel. We're going home, baby."

He leaned across and planted a soft kiss on her cheek. She didn't jerk away. She couldn't, there was no room the cramped cab of the truck. Sam put it in drive and spun the tires, flinging dirt. The haze from the fire was thickening, it was headed towards the main road, the highway. Sam was glad to be out of there alive and with his girl.

His angel. His Saige. He drove quickly through the woods, the truck bouncing over the rough terrain. He'd momentarily forgot about the woman knocked unconscious in the backseat. He forgot about his handy bottle of chloroform that lay in the glove compartment in front of the spot Saige was in. Sam smiled. The devilish grin stretched across his face, marking his handsome features.

He glanced at her sitting, slumped over next to him. He needed to tend to her wound soon before infection set in. He'd also need to re-administer chloroform to PJ when unloading the two. The drive to his secondary location felt like it was taking much longer that the hour it usually took. He hoped it was the same way it had been when we was last there. He wondered if Kevin had ever returned there after the two went their separate ways three years ago.

He let out a slow breath of air when he saw the broken sign. It was illegible by now but it lay in the dirt, pointing inside the woods. Sam pulled over. This was as far as his truck was going right then. He turned the key, effectively shutting the vehicle off. He peered over his shoulder and laid his eyes upon PJ curled up in the small backseat. She looked so peaceful. He chuckled quietly before climbing out of the old truck. He made his way to the passenger side and grabbed the handle. Saige was awake but was drifting in and out of consciousness.

He pulled the door open and caught Saige as she tumbled from the seat. He held her tightly, putting pressure on the bullet wound. It wasn't bleeding as much but it was still trickling. He looked back at PJ once more. The million-dollar question hanging in his mind. Would he be able to make it to the location and back without her waking up? He decided it wouldn't be worth the risk. He gently lowered Saige to the ground and leaned her against the side of the truck. He popped open the glove compartment. To his horror, he saw the worst possible outcome imaginable in a situation like his. The bottle was not in the compartment.

"No. No, no, no, no, no. What the fuck? Where is it?"

He mumbled to himself. He started to sweat. He remembered putting it in the glove compartment before leaving his homey cabin, over one hundred kilometers in the opposite direction. He remembered Sara, "Jenn", calling him, warning him of the cops' impending advance. He remembered panicking. He remembered being confused about how the fuck they figured out his location and then he remembered that fucking hillbilly who drove him home. No wonder he seemed so nervous and didn't offer up much conversation. He remembered everything so where the fuck had he put that bottle?

Moving quickly without much choice, he had to trust that he'd given PJ enough to keep her out for just a little while longer. He'd given her more than he thought he had considering she'd been out for nearly two hours now. He'd have to hurry, just to be safe. He jingled the keys to the truck in his hand, making certain he had them and shoved them into his pocket. He slumped down, grabbed Saige under her pits and hoisted her up to her feet.

She groaned; her head lolled on her shoulders. Sam hooked his arm around her waist and grabbed her good arm. He held tight to her arm and pulled her to the box of the truck. He had a sizable shovel tucked under a tarp. He grabbed the shovel and began dragging her into the thick of the forest. It was tougher than he'd expected. The branches snapped back, cutting into his open skin, slicing into hers. He tried to push back the wild branches but every time he did, it seemed like even more appeared. He was becoming frustrated. He never remembered the foliage being so untamed. He and Kevin always did their best to keep their cave well hidden, but easily accessible to them if they knew where they were going. He knew where he was going but it had been so long since he'd been there.

He and Kevin had agreed that, in order to keep the place discreet, neither would return unless absolutely dire. That's when they had their falling out. Sam coughed once, wheezing slightly and then finally, finally he saw it. He was a little bewildered that the ribbon had stayed on the branch those past years. Tied so tight someone would have to cut it off, it was so frayed and dirty, but it was definitely the same cherry red ribbon that he and Kevin had used to mark their special place.

A smile spread again. This time it was genuine. He was excited to finally be back. He gently leaned Saige against a tree. She could barely keep her head up and her eyes open.

"Sam"

She mumbled. Sam glanced at her. His heart ached for her. He focused on the task at hand and dropped to his knees, dropping the shovel beside him. It was still there. A small pile of rocks was next to the trunk of that tree. He removed the rocks and began clearing away some of the debris and nature on the ground. He grabbed the shovel he'd tossed onto the ground and used it to help himself stand up. He began digging, barreling the head of the shovel into the soft dirt, removing heaps at a time and dumping it into a neat pile next to him.

It didn't take long to uncover what he was in search of. The shovel had hit something under the ground, resulting in a thunking sound. The already big smile on his face stretched even further. He threw the shovel to the side and dropped back down to his knees and cleared the remainder of the dirt.

Only a short moment or two later, he'd fully uncovered what he was looking for. A large wooden door stared up at him. The wood looked ratty and scarred, the rusty handle looked stiff. No wonder. It had been hidden away for the last three years. He reached for the handle, the possibility of contracting tetanus through his open cuts crossed his mind but he'd already wrapped his fingers around the harsh texture of the rust. With a heavy gasp, he pulled up as he stood. The old wood creaked and lifted out of the ground. He let the trap door fall with a thud.

"Back."

He whispered as he peered down into the dark and deep hole in the ground. He slid his cell phone out of his pocket and activated the flashlight app. He aimed it towards the darkness, illuminating the depths. He almost expected to see a zombified person sitting at the bottom of the few steps into the pit as if it were something straight out of the original Evil Dead. Upon not seeing anything out of the ordinary he backed away and turned back to Saige. His poor girl was so drained. The blood had stopped leaking from the wound but the bruising on her face was stretching across the rest of it. Blood covered her sweatshirt. It almost blended in to the material. Sam didn't realize a wound like that could bleed so much. For fuck sakes, he wasn't a doctor. He wasn't even a lawyer. Hardly. Stealing the identity of a lawyer and charading didn't count.

He grabbed Saige by her uninjured shoulder and helped her scoot over to the hole. She didn't try and fight with him. She was too tired to bother. Sam held her next to him tightly as he took the steps into the dark hole in the ground, the flashlight app on his phone shining brightly in the darkness. Rats scuttled around the huge room. Spiders disappeared into hiding places along the damp walls. Cob webs decorated the wooden beams along the ceiling, hanging off of them like false snow on the mantle at Christmas.

Sam helped Saige stumble towards one side of the room. A few shelves stood against one wall. Dozens of cans sat upon the shelves, layers of dust, dirt, and grime coating them. Three years of dust. He wasn't sure if non-perishables were really safe after three years but then again, isn't that what they were meant for? His eye fell on a case of water bottles next to the shelves. It was too dirty. He lowered Saige to the floor and moved to the bottles. He remembered the day he and Kevin had found this place and they'd stocked it with their supplies. Sam and Kevin had met six years ago. Both families had relatives that lived in Ridgeway. They had found the place on one of their mutual visits.

He touched one of the bottles. They were cold from being underground those last few years. He turned away from the water and let his eyes fall back on Saige. She slumped to the side in the fetal position. Her eyes were closed and her breathing was labored. He moved over to her and planted a gentle kiss on her cheek. She barely flinched.

"I'll be right back, my beauty."

He flashed his cell phone back to the staircase. It creaked and groaned under his weight as he walked up the stairs, two at a time. When he got to the top, he turned and peered back in. With a sigh, he grabbed the top of the trap door and let it fall closed, encasing and swallowing up his angel into its black grip. He didn't bother covering the entrance. He'd be right back. He took off in the direction of which he came. He had to get back to the truck before the remainder of the chloroform wore off of PJ. He didn't expect her to get very far, if she did somehow manage to escape.

He'd been purposefully under feeding her, keeping her tired and worn. Factor in the two bullet wounds he'd given her. He couldn't let her have her normal energy. No way. The branches swiped at his face as he ran through the heavily wooded area. He ignored the itching pain the cuts made on his face and arms. He burst through the trees at last and onto the skinny dirt path. The truck was still parked there, waiting for his return. He ran up to the door and froze. The backseat was vacant. He opened the door and leaned in, like he expected PJ to still be there.

"Where the fuck are you?"

He called. He pulled himself out of the truck and slammed the door shut.

"Penny! Penny, where are you?"

He grabbed the gun from his belt. Rage filled him, burning through his body. It was like a fire. Hot and moving through him quickly, eating up his insides. He pulled the trigger while aiming the gun into the air. The loud blast echoed through the forest. Birds that were hidden in the trees took off into the sky, chirping crazy. He had hoped the blast would draw her out of hiding. He didn't think she would have gotten very far, certainly not to a populated area. She didn't know where they were. And where they were was surrounded by dense and thick wood.

He moved swiftly to the other side of the truck and noticed the dirt that was unsettled next to the door. She must've fallen out of the truck and landed in a heap. He followed the disturbed dirt trail to the other side of the skinny dirt path to the edge of the forest. He shook his head and stepped into the woods.

"Penny, you're tired, injured, and hungry. Let me bring you somewhere safe. It's dangerous out here for you. Come on, Pen."

He ventured further into the woods, looking from side to side and keeping an eye on the flattened grasses. He knew she was too drained to stand. Her crawling through the brush, looking for an escape, seeking safety, was giving away which direction she went in. The flattened trail that wove its way through the trees and fallen logs was very helpful. Suddenly, the trail stopped cold. It was abrupt and more than a little surprising.

"Penny."

Sam said again. He stayed very still, quieting his breathing enough that he could hear a few crickets making their music. He tilted his head and listened closely. Then he heard it. The snapping of a twig. That sly smile made its appearance on his lips again. He turned to his left and saw a log laying on the ground between two trees. He began walking towards it, not bothering to cover his tracks or be wary of how much noise he was making. He knew that she knew he was there. He approached the log and placed a hand on top. He pulled himself on top of the log and stared down at the woman lying on the ground. PJ looked frail and thinner than usual. She was in rough shape. Sam clicked his tongue at her, smiling.

"Penny. What were you thinking? You're injured and malnourished. Come join me and Saige at our place for a bit."

He jumped down from the log landing with a heavy thud next to PJ"s head. She winced once and coughed, the act making her tremble from the pain it brought on. Sam put the gun back into his belt and clicked his tongue again. He bent down and grabbed PJ by her shoulder and pulled her to her feet.

She cried out in pain as he pressed his thumb into the gunshot wound on her shoulder, using it to punish her. Sam held her shoulder in a firm grip as he pulled her back towards the dirt path and the other half of the heavily wooded area. PJ was weak. She had a hard time keeping up with Sam's pace. All of her police training felt like it was going straight down the toilet. She should have been able to escape. She was smart, quick, and agile. One of the top cops in the province. She should have been able to escape.

Sam shoved PJ through the last row of trees. She stumbled forward, the branches cutting in to her skin, leaving behind thin bloody lines. She fell to her knees on the path. The pressure from landing on her hands shot through her arms and pulsed through her wound. She cried out and let herself drop to her stomach, lying face down in the dirt. Sam was chuckling.

"Get your ass up, Pen. Don't play this game."

PJ groaned; the sound muffled by the dirt. Sam rolled his eyes and took the few steps to reach where she'd fallen. He reached down and grabbed her shoulder a second time, lifting her to her feet. She staggered and closed her eyes for a moment. Sam tugged on her feet, leading her past the truck and back through the dense forest. Back to his hide-away. Back to what was a certain horrible, terrible, gruesome death.

28

"They're dead! Officer Brady and Agent Jeffries. They're fucking dead!"

The scream came loud and clear over the radio.

"Saige is gone. Repeat Saige is gone!"

The voice was frantic. Brock had received the message while he was at PJ's home, staring down at the dead woman on the couch.

"He's got her. He's fucking got her."

Brock replied, his voice filled with panic.

"I just got off the phone with Brinker. We need to move. Now."

The other officers and agents that were at PJ's house were already moving quickly, gathering their things and setting up police tape.

"Chief, there was a nine one one call. There's a huge blaze up at Jeffery Mountain. A car explosion. There is a woman up there with a broken neck!"

Brock looked around at the agents and officers.

"You three! Go check it out. I have a bad feeling. The rest of us, we're headed to Sam's house. Let's get a move on. Go! Go! Go!"

Everyone that was in the house started running. They all exited the house and ran to their respective vehicles. Brock shot into the driver's seat of one with Agent Hamm next to him.

"Do you have those directions to Sam's cabin?"

He asked, his voice shaking. Agent Hamm didn't hesitate. He immediately started giving the directions to Brock who backed hastily out of the driveway. He flipped on the lights and siren and sped down the road. The lights were flashing and the siren was wailing like there would be no tomorrow. The road crunched under the tires as they spun wildly. Two other cruisers were flying along behind them.

They passed Woodland Park ripping down the road. They didn't seem to be going fast enough. Brock's heart was racing. He had to save his friend. He had to. He wouldn't forgive himself if they were too late. Sam certainly made a statement with the dead woman on PJ's couch. He was saying that PJ would end up just like her. No question.

Hamm was directing Brock in the way he needed to go. The words almost weren't processing in his mind. He barely heard them. He prayed Brinker would be there soon. They'd need all the man power they could get.

Twenty minutes of speeding down the roads later and Hamm was giving his final direction. Brock yanked the wheel to the side and went barreling down the dirt road. The cabin came into view. They spotted the sixty-nine Ford Mustang sitting in the driveway and right away Brock knew they were in the right place. He knew "Nick" owned that car.

He pulled up and stopped beside the beauty, the other cruisers not far behind. They sprayed dirt and gravel as they came to a skidding stop. Brock was out of the car in a flash. He lifted his gun and held it up, trained on the door. The other officers did the same. They moved quickly around the house, surrounding it.

"Someone get me a fucking megaphone."

Brock said. One was pulled from a trunk and tossed into his hands. He still had the gun trained on the door as he crouched behind the car.

"Samuel Thomas. We have the place surrounded! Come out with your hands up!"

Brock shouted into the megaphone; his voice instantly amplified. He waited. They waited. Nothing. There was no sound. No movements.

"Samuel Thomas!"

Brock shouted again. No response. Not even the fluttering of a blind. He glanced at his officers standing near the side of the house. He pointed at them and then pointed at the cabin. They nodded understandingly. He wanted them to sweep the house. He gestured for his other officers and the agents around the rest of the house and behind him to start moving forward.

They were crouched, walking swiftly towards the front door. Brock was at the head of the pack. When they reached the door, he brought his boot back and kicked, hard. The door splintered as it shot open. He kept his gun trained as he moved through the house. Everyone with him split up and searched each room.

"All clear!"

"Clear!"

The shouts resounded through the cabin. Brock had found one door that was still closed. It had several locks on the outside but none of them were done up. Keeping his gun up and at the ready, he slowly twisted the knob and pushed it open.

"Clear."

He said as he looked around the room. He knew just from the looks that it was the room that had housed their victims and most recently, their very own, Detective PJ Richards. He felt the tears well up in his eyes. He would not cry. He couldn't. He had to stay strong for his team.

"They're not fucking here!"

Someone called out. Agent Hamm. Brock swiveled around and stared at him.

"I can see they're not fucking here. Where the fuck are they!? Tape this place off. Get an APB out on Samuel Thomas. Now!"

Brock shouted at his men. They were all moving like ants. Structured. Brock stormed out of the house, cell phone to his ear. He was calling Brinker.

"I'm on the 'copter. Please tell me you nailed Sam."

Brock pursed his lips and brought a hand to his hair. He ran his fingers through it and fluffed it out.

"They're not here."

He said, frustration apparent in his voice. Brinker didn't reply right away. Brock could tell that he was fuming just as much as he was terrified. Brock could see how Brinker felt about PJ.

"Where the fuck are they?"

Came Brinker's pissed off response.

"We don't know. We're at his cabin right now. There's no sign of him."

Brock replied. He grabbed a handful of hair and held the phone away from his head and screamed. He paced in the front yard as the other officers were taping off the house.

"Riggs! Jacobs! Comb the house for any sign of where he could have possibly taken PJ and Saige!"

Brock shouted. He held the phone back up to his ear.

"How far out are you?"

"I'm just under an hour away."

Brock could hear Brinker say something to the pilot of the chopper. There was a muffled response and Brinker was back on the line.

"Be there soon. Find out where they took her. I'm going to call Director Traynor at the FBI and ask him to deploy more agents. We will catch this bastard if it's the last thing I fuckin' do."

The line went dead. Brock stared at the phone in his hand. Officers Riggs and Jacobs were inside the house while Agent Hamm was standing a few feet away from Brock. He was looking at a map.

"Where'd you find that?"

Brock asked, walking over to the agent. Hamm took his eyes off the map and looked up at Brock.

"It was inside on the counter. Look, this whole area is circled off."

Hamm tilted the map so Brock could get a look at it.

"That's two hundred kilometers in each direction!"

Brock exclaimed.

"You think he brought them somewhere in this radius?"

Hamm nodded enthusiastically.

"Why else would he have it in his kitchen, circled like this?

"Okay but we're looking at an over eight-hundred-kilometer perimeter. We're never going to find them with that."

Brock said. He threw his hands in the air. Tears threatened to fall over his rims.

"Not with that attitude."

Hamm retorted. He pointed at the map again.

"See here. This little mark. That looks like an arrow doesn't it?"

Brock leaned back over the map and eyed the spot that Hamm was pointing at. There was a tiny mark on the map, invisible to the untrained eye but Hamm, being an FBI agent with vast and extensive training had caught it. Now that he was pointing it out, Brock could see it too.

"It looks like it's pointing North."

Brock observed. Hamm nodded.

"What do you want to do, Chief?"

Hamm asked. Brock didn't have to think for another second.

"Let's get some officers and agents out that way. Get them looking for the next two hundred kilometers."

"That'll be out of your jurisdiction, sir."

Hamm realized.

"Then my men will go as far as they can. I'm sure Brinker will okay it if you and some of your men go further. Just go, whatever you do, just go."

Hamm didn't wait. He grabbed the map and got into the car. Brock ducked in after him.

"We'll go to the station and wait there. Brinker said that he's asking Director Traynor to detach more agents. When they get here, you go. Please."

He started the car and peeled out of the drive sending a shower of gravel across the vehicles. Hamm nodded. Of course, he would. He too, knew how Brinker felt about PJ. He could see it in his eyes the day he'd come to the office with her.

29

Brinker sat on the helicopter, tapping his foot incessantly. He couldn't stop thinking about PJ. Where the hell had Sam taken her? He knew that Saige was missing now too. An officer and an agent watching Becker Hall had been murdered. They needed to catch the son of a bitch. Brinker wanted nothing more but nail his hide to the wall and mount his head on the mantle. Figuratively speaking.

Brinker looked out the window of the copter. He'd left Officer Ryan Clayton back in Ohio to talk to the state police about Kevin "Keith Schmidt" Sanders' disappearance. Of course, it was on his authority. Clayton was way out of his jurisdiction so thankfully Brinker had been with him.

The helicopter flew over the land and it was quite the sight. If Brinker wasn't so agitated, it could have been beautiful. He lifted a hand to his mouth and began chewing on the skin around his thumb. It was a habit he had long dropped but the current situation drove him back to it.

He lifted his other hand and run his fingers through his thick hair. When he retracted his hand, there were several follicles between his fingers. He let out a hefty sigh and shook the hairs out of his hand. Right then his cell phone rang. He dropped his hand from his mouth and grabbed the phone that was tucked between his knees. He looked at the caller ID. It was an unknown number. Brinker held his breath.

"SAC Brinker..."

He said, his name tapered off at the end.

"Ah, James."

The slippery voice came from over the line.

"Sam."

Brinker replied. His heart pumped steadily in his throat.

"Have you returned to town yet?"

Brinker wondered how he knew that he wasn't in Ridgeway.

"Sure am."

He responded in any case.

"You're lying."

Came Sam's retort. Brinker didn't respond right away. He held his breath. The pilot of the helicopter took a look at him out of the corner of his eye.

"Okay, so I'm not."

Sam laughed. His laughter was sickening to Brinker's ears.

"You'll be happy to hear that I was given warning that your men were coming for me. So, I got out of there."

Brinker exhaled through his nose.

"Why would that make me happy to hear?"

Sam laughed again. If Brinker didn't know better, he'd have thought he was on the phone with Satan.

"Anyway,"

Sam said, ignoring Brinker's question.

"I had to leave our darling PJ with my sweet angel, Saige. They're okay. They're both alive. PJ might not be for much longer. She's in rough shape."

Sam began to laugh menacingly. It was loud and full of all kinds of evil. Brinker felt his heart stop.

"You're lying."

He said back. Sam's laughter was persistent.

"I promise, I'm telling you the truth. Now, there's something you can do for me."

"Why would I want to do anything for you?"

Sam paused, his laughter subsiding just momentarily. It lasted only seconds before his chuckling started up again.

"You'll want to do this for me."

Brinker waited for Sam to say more. When he didn't, Brinker sucked in a breath.

"What is it?"

Sam's laughing stopped. The static in the phone was deadly. The air in the copter was tense.

"Call off the dogs."

"Why would I do that? What's in it for me?"

Sam didn't reply for several minutes. Brinker thought he had hung up. He didn't stand a chance at calling him back if that happened. Sam was calling from an unknown blocked number.

"Hello? Sam?"

Brinker finally spoke, breaking the silence.

"Call off the dogs. Or PJ dies."

More silence. Brinker didn't know how to respond.

"Don't believe me?"

Sam's voice rang out.

"No, I believe you."

Brinker replied. He wasn't about to call Sam's bluff. He'd already proven several times that he was no nonsense.

"What are you going to do about it then?"

"Let's make a deal."

Brinker heard himself saying before he had even thought about it.

"Give me PJ and Saige and I won't kill you."

Sam burst out in a fit of laughter again. He was always laughing as if all of it was a sick game. To him, it was.

"Good try, James. That's not enticing."

Brinker shook his head. He looked out the window of the helicopter and saw a city coming up underneath them. He put the phone on mute and looked at the pilot.

"Are we back?"

The pilot nodded without a word. Brinker unmuted the phone and held it back up to his ear.

"Meet me, James."

Sam said, his voice was smooth like butter. Brinker would give him that, the man sure knew how to work the people he spoke with.

"Why?"

"Do you want to see PJ or Saige?"

Brinker nodded.

"Yes."

Not only was he desperate to save PJ, he also wanted to save that little girl from the torment he knew she was going through. She didn't deserve to go through this a second time a whole twelve years later.

"Then meet me."

"Where and when?"

"Ridgeway University. Ninety minutes. Come alone or PJ's dead."

Sam ended the call without letting Brinker have the last word. That's how it always went. Sam always got the last word. Brinker quickly looked down at the phone in his hand. He immediately dialed Brock's phone. He had to update him. Brock answered within seconds.

"Brock, listen,"

Brinker said the minute the phone clicked signaling that someone had answered.

"Sam just called. He wants me to meet him at RU. I have to go alone or he's going to kill PJ."

He could hear Brock's breath catch.

"Well you're not going alone that's for sure."

He said. He wasn't about to let Brinker walk into that on his own. It didn't matter how highly trained he was. He needed back up.

"Of course not. We need to be discreet."

"Yes, absolutely. By the way, your Agent Hamm found a map at Sam's cabin. There are too many places that the girls could be but there was a small arrow on the map. We have a general idea of the direction he took them but there's a lot of ground to cover."

"I called Director Traynor. He's sending more men out. We'll find them."

Brinker said. He had a sliver of doubt tracing his words. He didn't want to be wrong.

"I'm just getting ready to land at the airport. I'll grab the car that Clayton and I left there and I'll meet you at the precinct, and Brock?"

He paused. Brock waited for the next words.

"Be discreet. Somehow, Sam knows our every move. We need to be careful. He's got eyes everywhere. Trust no one."

Brinker hung up the phone and braced himself in the helicopter as it began to make its descent. Floating down from the sky was effortless and light. He barely felt the landing.

The second the copter touched the asphalt; Brinker was undoing his seat belt. He climbed out of the seat and rushed back to the door. He slid it open and jumped out while the blades were still spinning. He was running full speed towards the black car that sat in long term parking.

The minute he reached the car, he was flinging the door open and clambering into the driver's seat. He was shoving the key into the ignition and twisting like his life depended on it. It almost did.

The car was running and he was speeding out of the lot and towards the precinct. Ridgeway was small enough that he could get there in fifteen minutes. He prayed it would be a fast fifteen minutes. He didn't have long before he was supposed to meet with Sam and he didn't want to miss that appointment. He couldn't.

He was flying through red lights and going forty over the speed limit. He had the lights in the car going so he wouldn't get pulled over. He could see the precinct in the distance. His foot grew heavier on the gas.

It was only moments later that he came to a squealing stop in the parking lot of the department. The rubber on the tires rubbed off on the cement as he did. He didn't even turn the car off. He flung the door open and jumped out, his legs carrying him fast to the entrance. He could see Brock through the window. His arms were crossed and he had a stern look written across his face.

Luckily there were no news crews waiting outside of the department. They'd been there the last few days after catching wind of PJ's abduction. However, they'd dissipated and left the police office alone. Brinker crashed through the front doors. Brock jumped back, hands up.

"Whoa, Brinker!"

He exclaimed as Brinker flew across the lobby and landed on the floor from his fall. He hurriedly scrambled to his feet.

"I have to go! I have to go, now!!"

He yelled in Brock's face as he grabbed him by the shoulders. He shook him in his place.

"Who is my backup? You need to be one hundred percent sure that you are so goddamn subtle even I can't see you. Do you hear me?"

Brinker was frantic. Panic was filling his voice to no end.

"Yes, okay, Agent Brinker. I've got it under control. He posed as a student, right? We're going to send in your agents undercover as students too. They'll be milling around in sight to make sure that nothing will go wrong."

Brock paused letting the words sink into Brinker's skull.

"We will save her."

He said delicately. His words floated through the air to Brinker, landing on him gently like a butterfly. Brinker puffed out his chest and nodded.

"We better. Let's get a move on, I have less than twenty minutes to meet with him. And we don't want to keep him waiting."

Brock nodded aggressively.

"Are my agents out searching the area you found? Did you direct them to it?"

Brock continued nodding.

"I sent a couple of them, yes. I figured you'd be okay with that."

"You're damn right I am."

Brinker and Brock walked down the corridor towards the back of the department. They had to suit up in their Kevlar vests before anything could happen. It was going to be a challenge hiding the bulky bullet proof vests under civilian clothing but it had to be done. They would make it work.

In a room at the backside of the RPD, Brock, Brinker and two FBI agents were standing with their backs up to the walls. They were staring at the rack of Kevlar vests on the opposite side of the room. Brock was the first one to step up and grab one. It was like the rest of them were too scared to touch them. It just made it all the more real. Brock handed the vests to the agents and all four of them suited up, buttoning their shirts back around the Kevlar.

Once they were dressed, Brinker and Brock shared a look. Determination along with doubt and worry was written across their faces.

"Let's do this."

30

Saige's eyes opened slowly. She blinked a couple of times, trying to get her eyes adjusted to the blackness. What had happened? Where was she? God, her head hurt. She lifted a hand and gingerly touched her cheek. Pain stung through, slicing its way across her face like a steak knife carving its way through a tender cut of meat. She felt something scamper across her other hand on the ground and let out a scream.

"Saige? Is that you, Saige?"

Saige froze. Someone else was in that black pit of despair.

"Who's…who's there?"

"It's me. PJ."

Saige let out a sigh of relief but stayed on edge.

"Where are you? Follow my voice."

PJ said tenderly. Saige slowly felt along the ground and crawled forward. Her eyes were finally starting to adjust and she could make out dark shapes in the depth.

"Where are we?"

Saige squeaked out, her fingers still traveling over the course ground. She could tell that it was dirt. She could feel worms and maggots crawling between her fingers as she felt her way across the ground.

"We're in a pit. Sam brought us here."

PJ said. Saige suddenly felt something hard. It was PJ's shoe.

"That's right. I'm right here."

She said, her words hitting Saige in the face. Saige finished inching her way forward until she was sitting next to PJ against the damp wall of the pit.

"Where is he?"

Saige stuttered.

PJ lifted her arm and groaned. The ache in her shoulder pulsed through her arm as she wrapped it around Saige.

"He left. I don't know where he went. Are you hurt?"

PJ questioned. Saige sunk into her arm sending a burning discomfort through the wound she had.

"I uh, I got shot… in the back of the shoulder. And Jenn, she hit me with the gun…"

Saige whispered; dismay laced her words.

"Jenn…Jenn's a part of this?"

PJ was appalled.

"Was. He… he killed her."

Saige sunk down further.

"Are you okay?"

PJ nodded even though she knew Saige couldn't see her.

"I'm fine."

She lied. She didn't need this poor girl knowing the extent of her own injuries. She was fading fast and she knew it. She wasn't sure how much longer she'd last.

"If he's gone, let's get out of here…"

Saige whispered. PJ shook her head.

"I already tried. There's something blocking the door. I can't lift it."

Saige bit her lip.

"Maybe both of us can push it open."

PJ looked towards her but could only make out the shape of her face.

"Let's give it a try."

She agreed. Both of the women shifted, both groaning when they jostled their injuries.

"The staircase is this way. Grab my ankle and follow me."

PJ murmured. Saige reached out and wrapped her fingers around PJ's tarsus and followed her over the damp floor of the chasm.

PJ reached the bottom stair, feeling the rotting wood moist and spongy under her fingers. It was a wonder they hadn't collapsed when Sam came down them. Gradually she inched her way up, stair by stair. Saige followed closely behind. When they reached the top of the staircase, Saige could feel the wood shuddering underneath them. She hoped and prayed it wouldn't break down. They needed to get out.

Saige edged her way up beside PJ. Both braced their shoulders along the bottom of the door and started to push. The door tremored above them. It shook as Saige and PJ jostled it but it did not give way.

"Fuck!"

PJ cried out. She leaned away from the door and sat back on the top stair. Saige did the same.

"I'm sorry, Saige. I'm so sorry."

PJ whispered through tears. She was trying to stay strong for that girl but it was proving to be more difficult than she had originally thought.

"We're going to die in here aren't we? We're going to die in here. Oh my God, we're going to die in here."

Saige cried. Tears began streaming down her face rapidly.

"No, no, that's not going to happen. We're going to get out."

PJ replied. She took in a deep breath and sat up on the stair and put both hands on the underside of the door and started pushing again. She screamed as she jiggled the door, dirt raining down on them from the cracks.

It wasn't locked. She knew there wasn't a lock on the door at all. She remembered making that mental note when she saw the door when Sam tossed her in. He must've placed a heavy rock on top of the door. Shaking it could work. She knew it could.

She started shaking it again. Saige lifted her arms up and began battering down on it, using her fists to hammer at the bottom. Both women were screaming as they pounded at the underside of the door.

"This is pointless!"

Saige cried out, stopping her endless clobbering of the door. Both sank down onto the top step again.

"There's shelving down there. You were sitting by it. Maybe there's something we can use."

PJ offered up.

"Wait here."

She clutched her gut and scooched down the stairs one at a time. She had noted that the shelving she'd seen was made of metal.

She hit the bottom step and moved across the soft dirt, feeling the bugs squishing and squirming under her palms. She reached out and searched in front of her, waiting for her hand to connect with one of the shelving units. The further into the chasm she got, the danker it began to smell. It smelled like mold and decaying matter.

She felt the metal on her hand. It was cold and bit into the soft skin on her palm. She held the bar as she raised herself to her feet. She felt along the shelves, her hand running over can after can of nonperishable food items. Lord only knew what they contained. A bug with what felt like hundreds of legs scuttled across her hand. She didn't flinch. She felt along the length of the shelving and didn't come across anything that she felt could be useful. Working in the dark without her sight was difficult but she made do.

"Ow, fuck!"

PJ cried out. She brought her hand to her body and felt the warmth sliding down her arm. She'd cut herself on a part of the metal shelving that was broken and sticking out. She had an idea. She carefully reached out, feeling for the shiv like piece of metal that stuck out. She made sure she didn't stick her hand with it again and she wrapped her fingers around the pole of the shelving unit. She shoved with all her might. The unit came down with a crashing thud, cans tumbled to the ground, jars shattering.

"PJ! Oh my gosh, PJ are you okay?"

Saige cried out. PJ heard the squeak of the stairs.

"Stay there, Saige! I broke a bunch of glass, do not come down here."

She ordered. Saige stayed put on that dirty stair. PJ felt for the part of the metal that stuck out. If she could just break it off, she might be able use it as a make shift battering ram. At the very least it would give her a little bit of support in trying to bash in the door.

She found it near the ground. She could feel that the shelf was rickety as it lay on its side. Screws were loose and some were missing. PJ didn't think it would be too hard to break the already broken piece the rest of the way off. She put a foot up on the side of the shelf and grabbed the broken piece in both hands. She used all of her strength to yank it backwards. Fire burned through her gut and shoulder. Tears stung in her eyes. To her disbelief, the metal pole came off of the shelving unit without much more effort than what she was able to give. She thanked her lucky stars that it was already broken.

She stuck one foot out and felt the ground in front of her. She wasn't sure how far the glass from the jars had flown and Sam had taken her shoes. She didn't want to risk cutting her foot open down in that shaft.

"Are you okay?"

Saige called out. She was shivering on the stair, under the one crack of light that came through the split in the door.

"I'm fine. Stay there."

PJ said. She was slowly making her way back across the distance of the pit towards the staircase. She could just make out Saige's figure thanks to that slit of light that ran across her face. It wasn't much, but it helped PJ navigate her way back.

Once she hit the stairs, she reached up for Saige's hand. Saige took it and helped her climb up the steps. She showed her the metal pole that she had managed to pry off of the shelf. Saige felt it and let her hand run the entire length of it.

"Think we can use this?"

She asked PJ, her voice faltered slightly.

"I'm damn well going to try."

PJ replied.

"Watch out."

She said faintly. Saige ducked her head. PJ turned her face away and brought the pole up against the wood, hard. It made a heavy thunking noise as it hit. Dirt came through the crack, sprinkling over top of the two women. Saige started coughing. PJ closed her eyes. She battered the pole against the door again. A dent in the wood became visible. PJ took a short look at the wood and when her eyes landed on the small dent, her heart began to race.

"It's working, Saige, honey, it's working!"

She exclaimed. Saige peered up and noticed the small dent too.

"Oh my gosh, oh my gosh."

She said excitedly.

"We're going to get out of here."

Her words were filled with hope and light. PJ sure hoped so. She brought the pole back again and slammed it upwards, sending the sharp end into the wood. It got stuck briefly. PJ used all of her remaining strength to pull it back out of the wood. She almost fell backwards down the stairs. Suddenly, she cried out. She dropped the pole and both of her hands went to her gut. The strain she was putting on herself made her gut wound open and it started to bleed again.

"Oh my gosh, PJ. PJ are you okay?"

Saige cried out. She didn't know PJ was bleeding. PJ keeled over on the stairs, holding her gut, tears pouring down her cheeks leaving streaks in the dirt and grime that coated her face.

"I'm okay."

She managed to choke out. She needed to hold it together for Saige. She needed to. Saige lifted the pole that PJ had dropped and started ramming it into the door. She slammed it over and over, screaming the entire time. She swung it up one more time. To her utter surprise the door jerked open.

"PJ!"

She exclaimed. The sun rays through the trees shone over them, lighting up their prison. PJ lifted a hand to shield her eyes from the brightness. Saige tossed the metal pole behind her and scrambled out of the pit. She stood up in the forest, letting the fleeting rays soak into her skin. The sun was beginning to set and there was a slight chill in the air. She turned around and reached down to help PJ climb out. She noticed the blood that coated PJ's hands.

"PJ…"

She whispered.

"Don't worry about me. Good job for getting us out of there."

PJ's voice was weak.

"You go. You have to go."

PJ said, her words almost inaudible.

"Not without you!"

Saige cried out. She put an arm around PJ's waist. Together they spun around looking at their surroundings.

"How do we get out of here?"

Saige said quietly. PJ lifted a hand and with a shaky, blood-soaked finger, she pointed.

"There..."

Saige looked to where PJ was pointing and saw a tiny cherry red ribbon tied around a branch.

"We... we came from... there..."

PJ sputtered. Saige tightened her grip around PJ's waist.

"Okay, okay, I got you, PJ. I have you. It's okay."

They both ambled towards the red ribbon and started fighting their way through the trees.

"Just keep going straight."

PJ whispered, growing weaker. Saige pulled her through the woods, trying her best to push the branches out of the way without having them come slapping back against their faces. They stumbled over twigs and roots and dipped and dodged their way around fallen logs. That's when they saw a break in the trees.

"Almost there, P.J. Almost there."

Saige whispered. PJ was drifting in and out of reality.

"Oh my gosh, P.J, look."

Saige exclaimed as they burst through the tree line. A green car sat parked in the middle of the dirt pathway. The Chevy truck that Sam had brought them to the location in was long gone.

"Help! Someone help us!"

Saige screamed. She was clutching PJ's limp body to her own.

"Someone!"

She cried. She dragged PJ over to the car and slowly lowered her down against it. Saige swiveled around, head turning in every which direction.

"Someone, please!"

Tears began to stream down her face. Suddenly, they heard a twig snap. Saige turned once more and came face to face with a tall and husky man with dark brown hair and forest green eyes that matched the pine trees perfectly.

"Well, well, well. What do we have here?"

He said.

"Please, you've got to help us."

Saige cried. She pointed at PJ.

"She's a police detective and she's hurt. Badly. A manic brought us here. We need help. Please, can you please help us!?"

The man glanced past Saige to PJ and then back to Saige.

"Well, Saige. You and PJ certainly will need help. Sam's not going to be happy to see you two got out."

He pulled a gun out of his pocket and aimed it at Saige. A blood-curdling scream ran from her mouth.

31

Brinker looked around the quad at the university. He was sitting on a black iron bench next to the Ridgeway Ravens fountain. The Raven at the top of the fountain hovered over head almost like it was protecting the agent. Every which way he could see his fellow agents, dressed undercover, posing as students and faculty. He hoped they were discreet enough that Sam wouldn't be able to know they were there. People passed Brinker in every direction. He looked around some more but still didn't see the monster he was waiting for. He slid a hand into his pocket and pulled out his cell phone. He checked the time. It was thirty minutes past the time Sam had told him he wanted to see him. Brinker was about to put the phone back in his pocket when it rang in his hand.

"James."

Sam's voice came through the phone loud and clear.

"Where are you?"

Brinker asked right away with no hesitation.

"You're not alone."

Sam's response was clipped.

"Yes, I am."

"Then who is that yard worker that hasn't stopped raking the same pile of leaves for the last ten minutes?"

Sam said.

"Oh, James. I thought I told you what would happen to our dear PJ if you didn't come alone?"

Brinker's heartbeat picked up speed. He could feel himself grow sweaty, beads forming on his forehead. His hands started to shake.

"Just come out so we can talk."

Sam chuckled; the sound was nefarious in his ears.

"I told you what would happen if you didn't come alone. But, because I like you, James, I'm going to give you another chance. Meet me at PJ's home in fifteen minutes. Fifteen, James. Not ten, not twenty. Fifteen."

The phone clicked and the conversation ended, the line was dead. Not even one second later and the phone was ringing again. This time Brock's number scrolled across the top of the screen. Brinker pressed the green answer button.

"He's not coming. He just called and said change of plans. He's not fucking coming."

Brinker could hear Brock's heavy breathing in the background.

"Of course, … What's next?"

"Tell me the team searching has found something. Anything."

Brock coughed.

"Not yet."

Brinker shook his head and slammed his open palm down onto his leg.

"Son of a bitch!"

He shouted. He looked up and around the quad with the phone pressed to his ear. A couple passersby gave him looks but continued on their way.

"You still have that map?"

"I do."

Brinker rubbed his chin.

"I'm going to need to take a look at it. But first I have something to do. I'll see you at the precinct in an hour."

Brinker stood up, stretching to his full height and hung up the phone. He slipped it back into his pocket and strode quickly across the property towards the parking lot. He had ten minutes. PJ lived just over ten away from the university. He had to make it. Sam was very particular on what he wanted and if he didn't comply to his exact specifications, the consequence would be terrible.

He reached his car and pulled open the door fast. He jumped in behind the wheel and slammed the door shut next to him. He wasted no time twisting the key in the ignition and starting the engine. He peeled out of the parking lot and towards PJ's house. The drive wasn't going fast enough. His foot was heavy on the gas as he tore down the road and he didn't slow down until he entered the suburban neighbourhood that PJ lived in.

He saw the house. Yellow police tape was in front of the door. He didn't see Sam's car yet. He hoped he wasn't late. Brinker pulled into the driveway and shut the car off but not before stealing a glance at the clock. It had been eleven minutes. He reached for the door handle and pushed it open. He climbed out of the car and ran to the front door. He didn't have a plan to get inside.

As he approached the door, he swiped the yellow tape out of the way and reached for the knob. Holding his breath, he turned it and to his utter surprise, the door slowly creaked open. He took a cautious step inside and shut the door behind him. He looked around the kitchen. The house was silent and still.

"Sam?"

He called out quietly. He wasn't sure why he was trying to be hushed. He knew no one was there. There wasn't even a whisper of evidence of anyone having been there. He walked across the kitchen and poked his head into the living room. No one. He turned and walked down the hallway and up the stairs to the bedroom. Nothing. He sighed heavily and turned around to head back down the stairs. He didn't want to be in the house anymore. It was hard to be there, without PJ. It was her home and it had been decimated.

On the first step down the stairs, he felt his phone begin to vibrate in his pocket. He slid a hand into the pocket and pulled the small iPhone out. It was an unknown number. Right away he knew who it was. He stopped walking down the stairs and held the phone up to his ear.

"Sam."

Chuckling. Laughter. Sinister.

"James. You were late."

"By one minute. One minute, Sam."

More laughter.

"I said fifteen minutes. Not sixteen."

"Where are you, Sam?"

Brinker said, anger filling his voice. He was sick of getting dragged around.

"I left you a clue, James. I left you a clue somewhere in PJ's home. Have fun."

Sam ended the call. Brinker hated that he always had the last word.

"A clue?"

He said out loud. What the fuck kind of clue did he leave behind? And where? He looked over his shoulder and back up at the entrance to the bedroom. He turned and walked the couple of stairs back up to the room. He glanced around. Sam knew him. Somehow, some way, Sam knew Brinker like the back of his hand. The clue would be something only Brinker would be able to find. Something that only Brinker would know was a clue.

He looked around the room. It had to be in here. Sam knew that Brinker had slept with PJ so he figured that the clue had to be in the bedroom. It had to be. Brinker was sure of it. He slowly walked around the bedroom. While he did so, he brought a hand to his jacket pocket and reached inside. He pulled out a pair of latex gloves and slid them over his hands, snapping them onto his fingers.

He let his gloved hand glide across the top of the dresser when he noticed that one of the drawers was cracked slightly. Curious, he reached for the knob and pulled it open. It was her underwear drawer. All of the garments had been pushed to the back of the drawer and in the middle lay a small pile of dirt.

"What the fuck..."

Brinker whispered to himself. He patted his pockets, in search of a Ziploc baggie. When he didn't find one, he turned on his heel and ran out of the bedroom and down the stairs. He charged through the hallway and into the kitchen.

"Bags, bags..."

He muttered as he began opening different drawers in the kitchen. PJ had to have Ziploc baggies somewhere. After a few moments of searching, he found what he was looking for. The bags were in a drawer next to the sink. Bag in hand, he turned and ran back through the kitchen and back up the stairs. Brinker entered the room and made a beeline back to the drawer that contained the dirt.

Brinker lowered the bag inside the compact space and used two of his fingers to swipe as much of the dirt as possible into the pouch. He zipped the baggie up and gingerly placed it inside his pocket. He tenderly shut the drawer back into the dresser and strode out of the room. He wanted to get back to the precinct as soon as he possibly could. He wanted to send the dirt sample to the lab and get it tested. He had an inkling that the dirt was from near the location or was actually from *the* location that Sam had taken Saige and PJ.

32

Sam tapped his fingers on his steering wheel. He watched James Brinker leave PJ's home, shutting the door firmly behind him and putting the yellow police tape back up over the entrance. A sly smile spread across Sam's features. Brinker must have found his little present or he wouldn't have left so soon. Sam chuckled to himself. The dirt wasn't a good tip. It would be difficult to trace back to an exact location. Sam wanted to play the game with Brinker. He liked dangling PJ in front of him, knowing he would never figure out where he had her. Not until it was too late.

Sam watched Special Agent Brinker as he climbed into his car in the driveway. He observed him as he pulled from his parking spot. Sam reclined back in his chair a little as Brinker drove away from the suburban cul-de-sac. He knew he wouldn't see him. He wasn't in his Mustang. He was in a shitty white Toyota Camry that he'd had put away. He had his own little arsenal of vehicles that no one but him knew about.

After Brinker had disappeared from sight, Sam quietly got out of his car and glanced both ways across the street. He looked up the road and back down, his head on a swivel, looking in all directions. There was not a soul in sight. He moved swiftly across the street towards PJ's house. Once he reached the door, he scanned his surroundings again. He still didn't see any person staring back at him from anywhere.

He grabbed the knob and twisted it, ducked under the yellow caution tape and stepped inside the house. He slowly shut the door behind him. Standing in PJ's empty kitchen was somewhat thrilling for him. Just knowing all of the pain and heartache he was causing was the most incredible feeling he'd ever felt. Causing that was something he strived for every single day he breathed.

He looked around the room. The police had done a number on the place while they were combing for their evidence and removed Bella's body. He laughed out loud. Bella's body. That kill was pathetic but fitting for the stupid woman he'd done it on. She was pathetic and didn't deserve his energy. He was glad to be rid of her.

He sauntered into PJ's living room. He looked at the cones and placards that were placed on and around the couch where he'd positioned Bella's body. Blood still stained the fabric. He crossed the room and stood in front of one of the comfy looking chairs that was situated in the corner. He turned around and lowered himself into it.

He stayed sitting in the chair for several long minutes, not thinking of anything in particular. He just enjoyed sitting in the middle of one of his crime scenes. It was electrifying, sitting there among the chaos that he had created.

His mind went back to his and Kevin's special place in the woods. To his Saige and PJ sitting down in the dank and deep pit with no way of escape. It brought a smile to his lips. He had surprised himself by keeping PJ alive for as long as he had. All this time, he was looking forward to being reconnected with his one and only Saige, but his feelings for PJ had surprised him. He didn't think he had any. He thought the only reason he kept her alive was because she was still useful. That didn't seem to be the case anymore. Saige was still his number one and if it came down to choosing between one or the other, he would pick Saige without a second thought. But for now, he'd decided to keep both.

It was about time to be getting back to them. He'd travel out to the location and visit them momentarily. He still had a game to play with Brinker. That wasn't over yet. He snickered to himself. The game. That was going to be exhilarating. He knew Brinker would play along.

He had to make him think he'd have a chance at saving PJ but that wouldn't be hard.

Twenty minutes later, Sam finally stood up out of the chair. He'd had enough screwing around. He had to get the next part of his game set up for his friend, James Brinker, and then get the hell out of dodge. He just had to decide if he wanted to amp it up already or if he should just continue on the way he was. Teasing and slow but so deliberate.

This game was gong to be one of the highlights of his killing career. He knew it. He'd never played a game before but he knew how strong Brinker's feelings for PJ were and he knew damn well that Brinker would be an excellent adversary.

He walked to the door and peered out the little window beside it. He didn't see anyone lurking around outside but he had to be sure. He couldn't just exit the house while there was still light and have the possibility of being caught. That wouldn't do. Upon still not seeing anyone, Sam reached for the doorknob and made his exit. He ducked back under the yellow tape and scurried across the street towards his Camry.

Once inside his car, he started it and began driving casually back down the road. He had to be careful so as not to get pulled over. That too wouldn't do. He needed to be safe and sure fire without being obvious that he was being conscientious. It was all about the planning. He was good at that. Meticulous planning.

As he drove, he hummed to himself. He thought about his girls trapped in their prison. He hated that he had to keep them there. He hated that he'd screwed up his cabin home by having the hillbilly drive him back. He should have known something was up when the hick wouldn't talk to him during that trip.

He slammed his fist down on the wheel. Thinking back on that mistake pissed him off. He was furious with himself. The cabin was perfect and it was ruined. And he couldn't go back to his home either. By now the police had to know where that was. If they didn't yet, they would soon enough once they finished tearing apart the cabin. Luckily, he didn't have anything on his location at his home. And that's when he remembered what he'd left on the counter in the cabin. The map.

"Fuck!"

He screamed inside the vehicle.

"The map! The fucking map!"

He cried out. He hit his palms on the wheel over and over as he drove. He couldn't believe he'd forgotten the fucking thing on the counter. Sure, it didn't give an exact location, but it gave enough of a clue that they'd be searching. They had a lot of ground to cover but they'd be searching endlessly. He held his breath as he rounded a corner and got onto the highway.

He hoped that they weren't smart enough to decode the clues on the map. They were small but they were there. He couldn't believe he was so stupid as to leave the damn map. He didn't need it to find the spot. He didn't know why he'd even kept the dumb thing.

He tried not to think about it as he drove. It was stressing him out and he didn't need to have a full mind. He didn't need to get into an accident. No, as he drove, he didn't think about the map. Instead, he thought about his friend. He wondered if Kevin had arrived at their special place yet. He remembered Kevin calling him a week and a bit ago telling him that the police found the camera at PJ's house and that they needed to come speak with him. He remembered telling Squinty to not put the camera there. He remembered telling him it was a bad idea. Now thanks to him, he made Kevin go on the run, leaving his incredibly successful business behind.

When Kevin had called Sam, Sam was livid. They hadn't made up from their falling out years ago. Kevin had begged and pleaded with Sam to help him. He had told Sam that he was going to go to their place. Sam had panicked.

"You can't go there. I'm using it."

Sam said. Kevin's voice went flat.

"I need to. They're coming for me."

"You didn't do anything wrong, Kev."

Sam replied; his voice full of frustration.

"No, you don't understand. Sam, listen. I've been rerouting classified information from the FBI. I hacked their systems and have placed a bug to gather private information. What I've been doing is beyond illegal. They're bound to find out. I need to get the hell out of dodge. I have to use our place. I have to."

"Shit, Kev, you badass."

Sam joked. He laughed loudly. Kevin was breathing heavily.

"I don't have much time."

"I'm using the location."

Sam replied, staring down at the girls in the pit. They were both unconscious. The sunlight lit up the chasm.

"I've got Saige."

Sam heard himself say. He had told Kevin all about Saige when they first became friends. They shared a lot of their lives with each other those first few weeks. They were just instantly comfortable with one another and their friendship grew fast.

"You've, … you've got Saige?"

Kevin stuttered. He seemed surprised.

"Yes, we're together again. She's so beautiful, Kev-o. She's stunning."

Kevin smiled on his end of the phone.

"I'm so happy for you, Sam. I am. But please, let me come out. I can help you."

Sam sighed heavily.

"Fine. Come meet me there."

Sam could hear Kevin let out a gust of air.

"Thank you. Thank you, Sam. You won't regret this. I can be useful."

Sam nodded his head as he held the phone to his ear.

"I know you can. See you in a few hours. Bye."

Sam hung up the phone before Kevin could say another word. He stared down into the deep cavity and smiled.

"You can't do this!"

Saige cried; tears streaming down her face. PJ held her tightly. Kevin sat at the top of the stairs; gun aimed at the two as they stood at the bottom of the depression in the ground.

"Please, you can't do this to us!"

Saige screamed. Kevin smiled, the evil of it stretching across his face. He still had the gun trained on the girls. He was too deep in it to let them go now. They knew his face. They knew Sam. If he let them go now, they would for sure be running straight to the police. Especially PJ. She was a cop after all. No, letting them go was completely out of the question.

"Sam will be back shortly. Just you wait."

Kevin sneered. PJ slowly let go of Saige's shoulders.

"What's your name?"

She asked, a certain calmness flooding her voice.

"Why do you want to know?"

PJ shrugged.

"Kevin, sweetheart. My name is Kevin."

PJ shot him a smile.

"Kevin... What did Sam offer you? In exchange for holding us here?"

Kevin burst out laughing.

"Good try, honey. You're not getting out no matter what you offer me. I owe it to Sam."

PJ let out a sigh. Saige trembled next to her. PJ glanced down. Out of the corner of her eye she spotted the metal pole that they'd used to bust open the door. She had an idea. It was risky, but she had to try.

"Kevin?"

She said softly. Kevin stared her down.

"What?"

PJ wrapped an arm around Saige. She pulled her into her side, wincing while she did. The strain on her wounds was almost too much.

"It's getting cold. The sun is going down. Can you come down and shut the door?"

Kevin glanced over his shoulder at the forest. He could no longer see the sun in the sky and the trees blocked whatever sunset there might have been. It was true, it was getting chilly. He thought about his car. He thought about the warmth he could have in there. But then he thought about how the girls had escaped once. He couldn't let that happen again. He'd have to join them in the pit so he could keep his eye on them. It was the only thing left to do.

"Okay. You twisted my arm. I'll do that for you, honey."

PJ held in her disgust. She couldn't let him see it. She needed him to trust her for just a few more minutes. She also needed to grab that pole without him seeing. She needed Saige as a distraction. Kevin pulled his cell phone from his pocket and activated the flash light app. He turned his back momentarily to shut the trap door above them.

"Saige, I need you to distract him."

PJ whispered nearly inaudibly into Saige's ear. Saige gave her a confused look. PJ nodded her head towards the metal pole laying on the ground, partially hidden by dirt. Saige understood. She nodded. Kevin turned back around and began his descent down the stairs. Saige stood up and met his eye.

"Sit back down."

Kevin demanded as he shone his flashlight over her face. She moved away from PJ and towards the other side of the pit.

"I just wanted to show you something."

She said slowly. She had no idea what she was going to say or do. She was winging it. She just knew she needed to help PJ with her plan. It was imperative. Kevin's back was to PJ as he was paying his attention to Saige. PJ crawled across the ground, making no noise. She reached out and grabbed the pole. She quickly hid it behind her back as Kevin turned back around to look at her. He shot her a look and returned to Saige.

"What is it? On with it."

Kevin said; irritation filled his voice.

"Uh..."

Saige mumbled. She didn't know what to say next. That's when PJ made her move. She sprang to her feet and ran across the pit as fast as her tired legs could take her. She came up behind Kevin and rammed the metal pole through his back. The weapon came out through his stomach. He coughed and sputtered and looked down. Blood poured from the wound. He dropped the gun and turned to look at PJ.

"You... bitch..."

He muttered. He fell to his knees as his hands went to the pole. He wrapped both hands around it and pulled, sliding it from his body with a sick squishing sound. Saige reached down and grabbed the gun and aimed it at Kevin's head.

"Fuck you."

She said and pulled the trigger. The bullet entered Kevin's skull, exploding through the front of his forehead. Blood spurted everywhere and over PJ's shaking body. Kevin dropped to the ground in a heap. PJ stood there, mouth open, the scarlet liquid dripped down her face. Saige gave her a look.

"Grab the phone."

PJ whispered as she brought a hand up to wipe the body fluid off of herself. Saige bent down and pried the phone out of the dead man's hand. The flashlight still shone, illuminating the depth of the chasm they were in.

Saige quickly moved back over towards PJ and handed her the gun. She wasn't comfortable with it and she felt overwhelmed with the fact that she just murdered a man. No matter how awful he was or what he was doing to them. PJ on the other hand, didn't care. She tucked the gun into the waistband of her leggings and took Saige's hand. Together they walked in the light towards the stairs. They ascended and shoved open the door.

"Wait. The car keys."

Saige reminded PJ. PJ looked over her shoulder.

"Shit."

She said quietly.

"I'll go get them."

Saige offered. She was less injured than PJ and they both needed to be able to move. Saige ran down the stairs as PJ wrapped her arms around her torso and shivered. The sun was low in the sky now, the evening turning into night. They needed to get the hell out of there.

Saige was back up the stairs in moments. She dangled the car keys from her fingers with a big smile on her face.

"We're getting out of here, PJ."

Her smile widened. PJ shot her one back.

"You're going to have to drive."

She whispered. She was beginning to feel faint. Saige nodded furiously. She approached PJ and wrapped her arm through hers. They both began to walk towards the tree with the red ribbon. That's how they had to get out of there. They knew their way back to the path. They were thankful for that.

They made their way through the trees, ducking under the branches that swung back in their faces. PJ held onto Saige's hand as Saige led them through the forest. The sun had finally finished setting and it was dark out. They had to be careful not to trip over the roots that threatened to catch their feet.

They could see the edge of the forest, the iPhone's flashlight glinted off of the car. That's when the headlights shone over the car. Saige and PJ froze. They hadn't burst through the trees yet but the headlights were definitely there. PJ tugged at Saige's hand. They had to hide. They had to get away from the edge. PJ pulled Saige through the trees and away from the makeshift trail.

They heard the door slam shut. The footsteps padded towards the trail. They could make out his shape through the trees even though it was dark. He started swiping at branches. Saige leaned in and put her mouth next to PJ's ear.

"Shoot him."

She whispered, her lips brushing PJ's lobe. PJ brought a hand up and clapped it over Saige's mouth. They saw him turn. His head was on a swivel. PJ and Saige held their breath. They didn't dare move. Sam stayed standing in his spot for another minute. PJ felt sick to her stomach. Both of their heartbeats pounded heavily in their chests.

"I see you."

They heard Sam whisper.

"Now, what happened to Kevin?"

PJ and Saige held tight. There's no way he could see them. Not possible. They were hiding in the shadows behind trees. He took one step in their direction. And then another. Saige screamed. PJ turned and shoved Saige.

"Run!"

She cried. They ran blindly through the heavy woods. They could hear Sam's feet pounding along the ground after them.

"Go! Faster!"

PJ yelled at Saige. PJ was moving a lot slower. The wound in her gut made it nearly impossible to run at her normal speed. The wound pulsed and sent pain through her entire body. Saige was a good few feet ahead of her. PJ tripped over a root. Saige heard the fall and turned around.

"PJ!"

She cried. She started to come back to her.

"No! Go!"

PJ screamed.

"Get out of here! Go!"

Saige had the car keys. If she could get out of there, she could go for help. She could map her way back using the stolen cell phone and get an exact location. She turned again and ran.

Sam approached PJ who lay on the ground in the fetal position. The pain shooting through her was unbearable. Tears stung her eyes. Sam reached down and grabbed her arm and yanked her upwards.

He turned her to face him, rage filled his eyes. PJ could see them at the close proximity.

"What have you done?"

He was seething, anger dripped from his voice. PJ couldn't respond. He brought a hand back and slapped her across the face with his open palm.

"You fucking cow."

He sputtered through gritted teeth. PJ held back the tears that threatened to fall. She could feel the gun that was stuck in her waistband. He didn't know it was there. He had her wrist in his hand and he turned and began to pull her through the trees, back towards the little trail.

"What did you say to her? What did you say to Saige? Why would she run from me?"

He said, his words cutting into PJ like knives. She didn't respond. She let her other hand go to her backside and reach for the gun. She wrapped her fingers around the butt and slowly began to pull it from her waistband. This was her only chance. If she didn't do it now, he'd kill her for sure.

"Bye, Sam."

She said. Sam turned to look at her and saw her holding the gun, pointed at his heart. His eyes widened. PJ pulled the trigger. Nothing happened. She pulled it again. Nothing happened. The gun was out of ammo. She stared at Sam. His fear turned back into animosity and PJ knew this was it. She tugged at her arm, trying to pull away from Sam He smacked the gun out of her hand and it flew to the side. He pulled the firearm that he was carrying away from his belt and aimed it at PJ.

34

Brinker stood in front of the steel table in the lab at the precinct. He'd called Director Traynor from the car and demanded he send in the department's Forensic Soil Analyst to conduct the testing on the dirt sample he'd found in PJ's dresser drawer. Director Traynor didn't hesitate. Anything Brinker needed to solve the case; he was more than happy to give. Any resources he needed, anything at all. The FSA was named Rita Barter. She'd been working as the FBI's FSA for twenty years and was impeccable at her job. She was the best that the FBI had ever seen.

Now, Rita was working feverishly on the sample in the lab. The FBI headquarters had sent her with everything she'd need to test the dirt. She was staring hard at the sample through a microscope testing the mineral content. Brinker watched her as she studied. He couldn't leave. He had to know. He didn't care how long it was going to take.

The next thing Rita did was take two skinny glass tubes and fill them both with a liquid. Brinker watched with curiosity as she added some of the soil to the tubes.

"What are you doing?"

He questioned. He was genuinely interested in knowing exactly what she was accomplishing.

"Density testing."

She replied quietly.

"If there's something else you can be doing, Agent Brinker, you should be doing it. This is going to take me some time and it'll go a lot faster without you staring at me."

Rita spoke softly without looking up. She was peering over the tops of her thickly rimmed glasses at the tubes. Brinker was a surprised at first but then decided that she was right. It was like the old saying goes, 'a watched pot never boils.'

Brinker didn't want to leave but he obliged. Rita knew what she was doing. He didn't need to supervise. He decided he would go check out the map again. He left the lab and started walking down the hallway. He put his hands in his pockets and sauntered down the corridor.

He passed by the conference rooms and then stumbled upon Brock's office. He could see Brock sitting inside at his desk, staring at the map they'd taken from Sam's cabin. The look on his face was that of pure focus. Brinker tapped on the door with his knuckles. Brock looked up from the map and caught Brinker's eye through the door. Brock stood up and walked to the door where he opened it and stared at Brinker.

"Come in."

He said casually. Brinker looked at Brock as they entered the office. They stood next to each other in the work space. Brock picked up the map from his desk and turned it towards Brinker.

"There's an arrow there. I have your team focused on that direction."

"I see the arrow. But what about these? Didn't anybody look at these?"

Brinker pointed at a small group of tiny circles. They were extremely faded, barely noticeable.

"They might not be anything. But they're worth checking out. Get their coordinates and send them to the team."

Brinker said. Brock was already on it. He held the map up to the light and took a long look at the longitude and latitude numbers written on it. Brinker sat down in the office chair and took in a long and deep breath. He needed to focus. It was late and dark outside. The one thing he was grateful for was the fact that PJ's body still hadn't turned up. That was a good sign if there ever was one. It meant she was still alive.

Brinker didn't know what to think. He needed to find her. He was getting desperate. He was also waiting for another phone call from

Sam. He didn't think he had heard the last of him. Something just felt off. It felt wrong.

Why hadn't he killed PJ yet? Brinker didn't think she was part of what he wanted. They knew he wanted Saige and that he got her. So, what did he want with PJ? That was the million-dollar question that the force was having a hard time answering.

"What the hell?"

Brock suddenly said. Brinker looked up from his thoughts and towards Brock who was sitting on the other side of the desk. He was staring at his cell phone.

"Hello?"

He asked as he answered it. Brinker could hear screaming coming from the other end of the phone. He sat up straighter in his chair.

"PJ, oh my God, PJ."

Brock said. He too sat up straighter. He pulled the phone away from his ear and pressed the speakerphone button.

"Brock, are you with Brinker?"

Her voice was hysterical.

"Yes, he's right here."

Brock's response was fast and frantic.

"PJ, I'm right here. Where are you? Are you okay?"

She screamed again as flesh connected with flesh.

"Don't you hurt her you sick fuck!"

Brock screamed into the phone. Laughter. The music of it was foul and sinister.

"James, did you find my gift?"

Brock knew right away the gift meant the dirt that Brinker had brought back.

"Yes."

Brinker said, anger rising in his throat.

"Our dear PJ has another for you."

Brinker held his breath. Another clue? It had to be.

"Brinker..."

The words came out feeble and strained. She didn't say anything else for a quite a few minutes.

"Saige got away."

"You bitch!"

Sam exclaimed. There was another loud smack and PJ's crying grew silent. Brinker knew then that that was not the clue he was supposed to get. It was better. If Saige had escaped, that meant she would be contacting them as soon as she could. She'd know where to go."

"I'm sorry, James. Look's like PJ needs to suffer a little time out. Goodbye, to you and Brock."

Before either man could say another word, Sam hung up the phone. The air in the room was tense. Momentarily, Brock slammed a fist down on the table. Brinker could see the tears in his eyes. Brinker had to look at the bright side in the shitty situation.

"Saige got away."

He said gradually. Brock turned to look at him, their eyes connecting.

"Saige… got… away."

They both said in unison. The look on their faces matched. It was written across their features. As soon as Saige showed up, they would go get PJ. That was as long as Sam didn't move her again which was a huge possibility given that one of his captives knew where he was. They could only hope that their search and rescue team could find them first.

35

Saige stumbled through the trees, the branches slashing into her tender skin. She was cold and shivering. She was tired and worn out. Her feet hurt from the running. Her soles were cut and bleeding. He had taken her shoes when he had taken PJ's. PJ. Saige thought about the fact that PJ was back with that monster. She needed to get away. She needed to find freedom. It was up to her now.

She clutched the cell phone in her hand. She still didn't have any service. She needed to get out of the godforsaken woods in order to make a phone call. As soon as she reached the road, any road, she could flag down a vehicle and get a ride to town. Was town even close? She had no idea where she was. Suddenly her foot caught on a root. The next thing she knew she was falling forwards fast. She thrust out her arms in order to catch herself. She hit the ground with a thud, smoking her face off of the hard dirt turf. She lay there for a moment, catching her breath, wincing in pain.

The cracking of a branch made Saige shoot up. She scrambled to her feet and stood perfectly still, holding her breath. Another branch cracked. She began to panic. Sam was right behind her; she just knew it. She hadn't managed to get away after all. This was it. The end.

She heard the rustling of leaves and her head snapped to the right. She stared out hard, clutching the cell phone to her chest and shaking. A deer emerged from the coppice. It stared at her as it munched on some kind of sustenance. She languidly let out a small breath. It was just a deer. She and the deer stared at each other, daring the other to make the first movie. Saige didn't want to scare the poor thing. Finally, she took one small step forwards, keeping her eye on the animal. He munched lazily and turned his face away from her. With each step, her feet hurt even more. They were beginning to bleed profusely from the twigs and rocks that she had been running on.

The steady stream of the crimson flowed from her extremities. She fell back to the ground and grabbed her soles in her palms and squeezed hard. She bit her lip and slowly let go of her feet so she could reach for her clothing. Her hands were covered in blood. The tears in her eyes warned her that they were going to fall over her rims at any second. She slowly lifted the bottom of her RU sweater and raised it over her head. She was wearing a white tank top underneath it. That too, she pulled over her head.

Once the tank top was in her hands, she used all of her strength to tug at the shirt. She pulled with all her might, trying to rip the tank in two. She cried out as she made a tear. The pain from her shoulder wound racked her body. She managed to rip the skimpy shirt into two pieces. She brought one half to her mouth and bit down on it. She led the other one down to one of her feet and began to wrap it around the injuries there. She tightened the fabric around and around as tight as she could make it and tied it there, holding it in place. She did the same thing with the second piece.

Once that was all taken care of, she stood back up and lifted one foot and then the other. The fabric made a small cushion between her foot and the rough terrain. It wasn't much but it would help. She started moving back through the woods in the line that she was making. She figured if she kept going straight, she'd hit something. Anything. She was limping and going much slower than she'd hoped but she was going as fast as her body would allow. The ringing of the cell phone in her hand scared her. She didn't realize she'd finally wandered into reception. As soon as she made that realization, her heart started beating faster. Reception. She could call for help.

She looked down at the phone and saw Sam's name pop up on the screen. She started shaking her head. It couldn't be. But of course, it could. It was Kevin's phone. Of course he had the number. She hesitated in answering.

"What do you want?"

She cried out as she pressed the green button.

"Saige, baby, why did you run from me?"

He sounded genuinely hurt.

"Sam, you're hurting me. You're hurting me by doing these things."

She decided she could try to reason with him. Maybe she could get him to let PJ go. Just maybe.

"Aren't you happy with me? What can I do to make you happy?"

It sounded like he was pacing. He sounded cold and sad.

"No, Sam. I wasn't. I need you to let PJ go. Let PJ go and I'll meet you and we can be together."

She heard herself say before she realized the words were even coming out of her mouth.

"I can't do that."

Sam replied. She could hear how tense he sounded.

"Why not?"

She whispered into the phone. She was still walking forward, slowly, being as quiet as she possibly could be.

"Why not, Sam"

She asked again when he didn't reply.

"She knows too much. I can't let her go. I would have to kill her."

Saige could hear squirming and whimpering in the background.

"Don't kill her. Sam, you're better than that."

She knew that wasn't true. He'd proved that time and time again that killing wasn't above him. She didn't know what else to say. She didn't know what else to do.

"Come back, Saigey baby. Please."

Sam began to plead with her.

"Please. I love you. I just want you to come back."

She could hear the tears in his voice. She could tell he was crying.

"I love you so much."

He said again when she didn't reply. She didn't know how to. Just thinking about saying those words back to him made her sick to her stomach.

"I love you too, Sam. Please, let PJ go."

She gagged on the words.

"I can't do that."

He said again, this time enunciating the word 'do.' Saige didn't know what else to do. She didn't know what else to say.

"I'm disappointed in you, Sam."

"Saige, stop. I'm right behind you. You can just turn around and come back to me. We can be together like we're supposed to be."

Saige's heart beat sped up. She glanced over her shoulder but didn't see anybody.

"I can't unless you let PJ go."

She whispered. She peeled the phone away from her ear and ended the call. This time she had the final say. She started running again. The phone started ringing again. She didn't answer it. She had tears running down her cheeks as she ran, swiping at the branches that poked at her.

The rumbling of vehicles rang in her ears. Her heart sped up. Cars. There were cars. She'd found the road. She tried to run faster and then she saw a break in the trees. Her feet ached but she ignored it. She was huffing and puffing, gasping for air when she tore through that last row of trees. She fell onto the side of the road. There weren't many cars but they were there. She tried to sit up and began waving frantically, trying to signal one to pull over. Her attempts worked. The first car that came up on her side pulled over to the shoulder. The driver jumped out of the vehicle, an uneasy look in his eyes.

"Miss! Miss are you okay?"

He called to her. He rushed over and put a hand on her shoulder. She glanced backwards into the forest from which she'd tumbled out of. The fear that Sam was right on her tail was still very much alive. She grabbed onto his wrist and pulled herself to her feet.

"You've got to help me. You've got to."

She started dragging him to his SUV. The man eyed her bloody sweater and her bloodied feet.

"Where are we?"

She cried as she pulled open the passenger door to the vehicle.

"We're near Isolet Mountain."

He replied as he climbed in beside her.

"Can I take you to the hospital? You look like you need a hospital."

He said.

"How far are we from Ridgeway?"

She questioned, ignoring him.

"About forty-five minutes. Is that where you're from?"

She began nodding furiously.

"There's a madman out there. He's got a woman. I need to go to the Ridgeway police department. Please, please, you've got to bring me there. You've got to."

She was begging the man.

"I was just on my way to Ridgeway. I'll absolutely bring you there. Do you want to use my phone to call them?"

He grabbed his phone out of the cup holder beside him and handed it to her.

"I need to ping this location."

She muttered to herself.

"I need to ping it so they can find her. They need to find her."

The man stared out the front windshield as he inched his way off of the shoulder of the road.

"My name is Hudson, by the way. What's yours?"

"Saige."

She replied without looking up from the phone. She was working her fingers over Google Maps and putting pins down on the location. After she made the pin, she opened the Internet browser and typed in the Ridgeway Police Department. The phone number and website popped up and she pressed the phone number. It began to ring.

"Come on… come on… pick up, pick up."

She mumbled to herself. The phone continued to ring. It was late, she knew no one would be at reception, she just hoped someone would hear the ringing and answer anyway. No such luck. The next thing she did was dial nine one one.

"Hello? Hi, my name is Saige D'Leo and I need to be connected with Chief of Police, Brock Carter, right away."

36

Sam was furious. He wouldn't be releasing PJ. No, that wouldn't do. His game that he wanted to play with Brinker was ruined now that PJ told them that Saige was gone. His Saige… He had to figure out what to do next. He needed to move PJ but he also needed to get Saige back. He needed to disappear but he also wanted to dangle PJ in front of Brinker for a little while longer. Not with the game. He'd come back to that. He just wanted Brinker to think they could find PJ.

With Kevin dead, he needed to figure out where to go. He and Kevin were a team, no matter what falling out they may have had. Kevin was the one that found the locations. Sam had other things to worry about. He figured he had approximately five hours to get out of there. That was a generous guess. If Saige had stumbled across the road, she was probably almost back in town. He stormed through the woods, back to his location. He had been following his girl. She was just a measly ten feet ahead of him when she stumbled out onto the road. He couldn't risk behind seen out there. He went back to the hole and pulled the gun from his belt. He flipped open the lid and aimed at PJ.

"Come on."

He said bluntly. PJ stared up at him from the darkness. She could make out his silhouette and that was it. It was too dark to see his face or any defining features. She stood up from the depth and slowly moved towards the stairs.

"Careful. Quick, now."

Sam spoke, his tone was becoming thin. PJ scrambled up the creaky wooden stairs.

"Let's go."

He grabbed her wrist and pulled her along behind him. Making their way through the trees in the blackness was difficult. There were plenty of roots in the makeshift trail that they could trip on. Sam was careful with himself but he was dragging PJ. She was stumbling over the roots but luckily, she hadn't fallen.

Once they made it through the thatch of woods and back to the dirt path, PJ could see the vehicle. It was different than the truck they'd come in. She didn't know where that was now. This vehicle was a sleek silver SUV. It looked out of place in the woods like that. Sam tossed her aside when they got to the vehicle. He flung open the back door and pointed the gun at her.

"Get in."

He ordered. PJ obliged. She climbed into the back of the immaculate SUV and wondered where in the hell he got it from. He slammed the door shut and she realized then that the windows were tinted. No one could see in. No wonder this is the vehicle he brought.

"Where are we going?"

She asked, her voice shaking.

"You'll see."

Sam replied even though he honestly had no idea where. He was just going to drive. They were a little way up Isolet Mountain. He'd continue going up. He started the car and began the drive. He went up the twisted and windy road. It was a thin road, enough room for one vehicle. Anyone coming in the other direction would need to get as close to the edge as possible for the other car to pass. The drive was bumpy. PJ was being jostled around in the back seat.

Sam desperately wanted to call Brinker and give him some sort of torture but the further up the mountain they went, the less likely there was to be any reception. There wasn't any at the pit so why did he expect there to be any up there?

PJ stared out the window. There were snow flurries coming down around them now. The road was becoming icy. PJ's nerves were shot. She was terrified. The car ride was silent. Sam didn't say a word to her and she didn't say one back to him. She didn't know what to say. He wasn't going to give her any information anyway.

"Aha!"

Sam suddenly exclaimed. PJ sat forward and stared out the front window. He was making a small turn off of the road and onto a little path. There was a small log cabin situated off of the path and in a clearing. Sam parked the car on the path and turned it off. The snow flurries had turned into a full-on snow fall. It was light but it was there.

"Your new home."

Sam said as he stared at the cabin; joy filled his eyes. It was a sick joy. PJ could see it.

"How do you know that no one is living there?"

PJ whispered, the chill from the outside settling into the interior of the car now that it was off and the heat was no longer circulating through.

"I don't. But I'll take care of that problem if it arises."

PJ knew exactly what he meant when he said that and it terrified her. He climbed out of the car and opened the door for PJ. She tripped out of the car and landed in his outstretched arms. Immediately she pushed herself away from him. She wrapped her arms around herself and shivered again. Sam put his hand on PJ's lower back and urged her towards the cabin. The snow on the ground froze her bare feet. She kept sliding on the thin sheet of ice.

They reached the cabin and Sam stopped PJ from walking. He put up a hand and signalled for her to wait. She was approximately eight feet from the cabin. She glanced over her shoulder at the car. She knew how to hotwire. Would she have time? Sam turned back towards her as if he read her mind.

"Don't you even think about it."

He stated directly to her. She stepped in place, her feet sticking to the ice. Sam turned back to the cabin and knocked on the door. He waited for a couple of short minutes. When no one answered, he jiggled the knob. It was locked. He peeked back over his shoulder and took another look at PJ. She was still standing in the spot he left her in.

He wandered around the side of the cabin, the side that gave him the ability to still see her. There were three windows that lined the side of the small house. Sam turned his face away and used his elbow to break one of the windows.

"Come here."

He ordered. PJ walked unsteadily over to the window. He pulled the gun back out and aimed it her once more.

"Climb in. Unlock the door."

He slid the gun back into his jeans and cupped his hands and made a makeshift boost. She stepped one frigid foot into his hands and he hoisted her up. Not all of the glass was knocked out of the window and it sliced into her skin through her sweater, making large rips in the fabric.

She bit her lip as she slid in through the broken window. The interior of the cabin was small, just one large room. There was a wood stove in one corner and a ratty looking couch in the middle of the room. Draped over the couch was a thick wool blanket. PJ was grateful for that. Especially now with the window broken open.

Because it was an open room, PJ had no where to hide. She thought she might have been able to hide and keep the door locked from him but he had his arm sticking through the window with the gun trained on her.

"Unlock the fucking door."

Sam said through gritted teeth. PJ stepped carefully over to the door and undid the chain lock and the dead bolt.

"I need some heat in here."

She said as Sam entered the cabin.

"You've got that blanket. You'll be fine."

Sam replied as he looked around the small, abandoned cabin.

"Listen. I'll be back. And you better be here when I return."

PJ stared at him.

"Where do you think I'm going to go?"

Sam shook his head with a smile on his face.

"You just better be here when I get back."

He turned on his heel and walked back to the door.

"Lock this behind me."

PJ didn't argue. She followed him to the door and as he exited, she turned the locks back into place and hooked the chain link back in its spot.

37

It was the middle of the night and the men were still at the office. They hadn't gone home. Neither wanted to. They were working tirelessly trying to decode the clues on the map. The FBI team that was out looking for PJ and Saige was still going strong. They were being swapped out every few hours to make sure that they were on their toes. Search and Rescue had joined them. They had twenty team members out looking. Brock's cell phone began to ring.

"Hello?"

He said into the phone, his voice was heavy with fatigue.

"What!?"

He suddenly exclaimed and shot up in his chair.

"Come in. Come in right away. Oh, I'm so glad you're safe."

He hung up the phone and looked across the desk to Brinker.

"You'll never guess who that was."

Brinker stared at him, wide eyed.

"Saige. That was fuckin' Saige."

Brinker slapped the desk and stood up from his seat.

"Saige!"

"She's coming in right now. Let's go meet her at the front door."

Brock and Brinker raced out of the room and ran down the hall. They reached the lobby and stared out into the night. It was pitch black outside. Headlights approached the lot. It was only seconds later that they saw a tattered looking girl running towards the door. Brock grabbed out his keys and quickly unlocked it and opened it. She didn't stop running. She ran full speed into the lobby and launched herself into Brinker's arms. A tall and lanky man with red hair and brown eyes followed her in. He extended a hand to Brock.

"Hudson Finn. I found this young lady up near Isolet Mountain."

Brock shook Hudson's hand.

"Chief of Police, Brock Carter. Thank you for bringing her, sir."

Hudson nodded and took a step back towards the door.

"Now that she's safe, can I go? I have a husband at home waiting for me."

"Not yet. If you don't mind, I'd love to take a statement from you. Where you were, what you saw. That kind of thing."

Hudson gave a smile and nodded.

"Of course, sir. Whatever I can do to help."

Brinker had Saige in his arms. She was crying.

"I know where they are."

She cried through hiccups.

"We have to go. We have to go get PJ."

She was hysterical.

"Slow down, Saige. Tell us what you know. I'll radio to the men."

Saige was breathing heavily, like she couldn't quite catch a full breath.

"Hudson said we were at Isolet Mountain. I don't know how far up but there's a trap door hidden in the woods. There's a pit. We were in the pit. PJ… PJ's still there."

"This young lady came spilling out of the woods onto the highway, I'm glad no one was close enough to her when she did. She would have been hit for sure. Poor thing looked like she'd been shot…"

"I *was* shot!"

Saige exclaimed. She pulled her sweater over her head so she was standing there in her leggings and bra. The bullet wound could be seen on her collarbone. It had gone clear through. It was green and filled with pus. It was definitely infected. Blood was dried all around the wound and down her front. It looked like it had bled quite significantly.

"We need to get you to the hospital."

Brinker said as he eyed the pieces of fabric on her feet. He could tell they used to be white but were now stained red.

"We need to find PJ first!"

She cried. Tears were streaming down her cheeks.

"I'll radio to the men asap. Your information is extremely helpful."

Hudson lifted a hand.

"I can take her to the hospital if that helps."

Brock smiled at him.

"Thank you for your help, Mr. Finn. I'll have an officer take her. I still need to get your statement on record."

Hudson nodded and Brock gestured down the hall.

"I'll show you the way to the interview room."

Hudson followed Brock down the hallway, stopping only for a moment when Brock grabbed an officer who was walking the opposite direction and asked him to take Saige to the hospital and stay with her no matter what.

Brinker ran to Brock's office and grabbed his radio off the desk. They'd been keeping in contact with the team that way.

"Come in, S and R team. Come in, over."

"S and R team here, over."

The response came quick.

"Isolet Mountain. Search Isolet Mountain, over."

Brinker said fast. A response came through but it was too staticky to make out. Brinker repeated himself and then set the radio back down on the desk. He took a seat in Brock's chair and rested his hands in his palms. His cell phone immediately began to ring. He pulled it from his pocket and looked at it. Unknown number. He knew exactly who that was going to be.

"James."

Sam's chilling voice came through the phone.

"Sam."

Brinker responded evenly.

"I want you to do me a favour."

Brinker waited for the next words to come out of Sam's mouth. When they didn't come, Brinker inhaled deeply.

"What would that be?"

Sam started to chuckle. He was always laughing. It didn't matter what was going on. Sam was always laughing.

"I want you to meet me. Just you. No one else."

"What for? You don't have PJ with you, I assume."

"No, you would assume correct. But I do have something else for you that might be of interest."

Brinker sat up straighter in the chair.

"I'm listening."

"I'm not going to just give it away, James. I want you to meet me. Alone. And seriously, alone this time."

Brinker nodded his head.

"Done. Where?"

"The university."

Sam replied. Brinker looked at his watch. It was after one am.

"When?"

"Forty-five minutes. I'm not kidding, James. Come alone, or I will seriously kill PJ. She's of no use to me anymore, I will not hesitate."

Sam hung up the phone leaving Brinker there to dwell on the words. He would go alone. He didn't care anymore. He would go alone. He peeked out the door of Brock's office. He didn't see anyone in the hallway. He slipped out the door and moved swiftly to the lobby. The door was still unlocked. He snuck out the exit and ran across the parking lot to his vehicle.

Once he got to the car, he flung open the door and jumped in behind the wheel. He started the engine and put the car in drive and began his route. It would only take ten or so minutes to get to the university but he'd be waiting. He'd be waiting to come face to face with the man that kidnapped the one woman he'd ever fallen in love with. That was a scary thought for him. Love. He loved her. He didn't even realize it but he had fallen in love with the feisty and determined cop. He had to save her. If it was the last thing he did.

He drove quickly to the school, blowing through the red lights he came across. No one was on the streets so he didn't care. He arrived at the school and parked in the lot. Now it was time to wait. As he sat in his seat, the heat running and circulating through the vehicle, he tapped his fingers on the wheel. He was growing impatient.

What felt like hours later, another set of headlights joined his in the lot. He looked up and noticed the other vehicle. It was a large silver SUV. It pulled up next to Brinker's car. He slowly unrolled the window and the driver of the SUV did the same.

"James. We meet at last."

Brinker recognized that slick voice anywhere.

"Samuel Thomas."

He replied.

"Get out of the car, James."

Sam responded, ice in his voice.

"You get out of your car, Sam."

Sam chuckled.

"Fine."

Both men unbuckled their seatbelts and climbed out of their respective vehicles.

"Tell me, where is Saige and PJ?"

Brinker tried. He wanted to see what Sam would say if he thought that Saige hadn't returned.

"Oh, they're somewhere safe. Don't you worry about that."

Sam's voice was cold and angry.

"What do you have for me?"

Brinker questioned.

"Is it another "gift" like the one you left me at PJ's house?"

Sam laughed out loud.

"Oh no, James. This is unlike anything you've ever received. Come. Walk with me."

Brinker eyed him suspiciously.

"Come on, James. Don't be shy."

Sam beckoned for him with a finger. Brinker pursed his lips and took short strides to reach Sam's side. The two men walked side by side away from the parking lot.

"You know, PJ is a wonderful woman. She's a real spark plug."

Sam said as they walked. Brinker didn't respond.

"But she doesn't compare to my Saige. You know, Saige and I have been in love for a long time."

Brinker nodded.

"So I've heard."

"I'm going to marry that girl."

Brinker glanced at him out of the corner of his eye. He saw that he was fiddling with something along his side. He narrowed his eyes.

"Sam, what are you doing?"

Brinker questioned. He slowed his walking. Sam immediately stopped fiddling.

"The question here, James, isn't what I'm doing. But what are you doing?"

Brinker furrowed his brow.

"I don't know what you mean."

They rounded the corner and came across the large fountain with the tacky Raven that Sam hated so much.

"Walking with me. That was your mistake."

Before Brinker knew what was happening, Sam was whipping his gun from his belt. He took aim at Brinker and fired without a second thought. He fired again and again. Brinker stumbled backwards. He tripped over the edge of the fountain and landed with a splash in the water. Blood poured from his shoulder and his gut. It turned the water in the fountain a shade of pink. Sam turned and ran. He ran across the quad and back to the parking lot.

Brinker lay in the fountain, his wounds bleeding profusely. He tried to climb from the fountain but slipped back in, scarlet poured from his gut. He pressed a hand to the shot and fumbled to pull his cell phone from his pocket. He heard the rumbling of a vehicle. Sam's car came barreling around the corner. He was headed straight for the fountain. He was going to crush Brinker. Brinker's eyes widened with fear. Sam was coming in fast, his SUV revving loudly as it ran over the grass towards the fountain.

Brinker splashed and floundered out of the way just in the nick of time. Sam's vehicle crashed into the fountain. He glared at Brinker from inside the SUV. Brinker rolled onto the grass. Sam tried to back the car up but the tires were stuck over the edge of the fountain. Brinker looked up. The Raven rocked on its perch. Sam followed his gaze. His eyes grew fearful. Brinker pulled his gun and took aim. He shot two shots into the front window of the car, hitting Sam in both shoulders.

The Raven came crashing down. It landed on top of the SUV. Blood splattered out in all directions. The windshield broke and glass flew. Brinker flopped down onto the grass.

Lights flashed in the distance. Students were staring out their windows, all of which were on their phones. The ruckus had woken them from their slumber.

Only a few moments later, police cars, fire trucks, and ambulances were attacking the school yard. Brinker lay face down, unmoving.

"Brinker! Brinker, oh my God!"

Brock's voice came out as a scream. He ran across the lawn and dropped down next to Brinker. He flipped him onto his back and saw his face was pale. His gut was still bleeding, staining his white shirt. Brock ripped open Brinker's shirt and noticed the bullet buried deep in the Kevlar he was wearing. Brock put both hands on the wound, pressing down hard.

"Stay with me, Brinker. You stay with me, dammit."

Brinker's eyelids fluttered.

"PJ..."

He whispered.

"Where is she? Is she here?"

Brock asked, frantic, glancing back at the vehicle with the giant Raven on it. He caught sight of all the carnage.

"No..."

He whispered. He looked back down at Brinker. Brinker was weakly shaking his head.

"I don't know where she is."

He said languidly.

"We'll find her. Dammit, we'll find her. We've got to get you to the hospital."

Brock said. He was still pressing down on the wound.

"Get the paramedics over here now!"

Brock screamed over his shoulder. Two came running over at his command. They both carried first aid kits in one hand and were packing a stretcher in their other. They dropped the stretcher on the ground beside Brinker.

"Careful now."

They were saying to each other. Brock was still pressing on the gun shot site. The two paramedics gently moved Brinker from the grass to the stretcher. They strapped him in and then hoisted the stretcher up with both hands, leaving the first aid kits on the ground next to Brock. He sat there, hands in his lap, head down.

"PJ…"

Brinker whispered again. Brock looked up. Finally, he stood.

"We'll find her."

Brock insisted. One of the medics put an oxygen mask over Brinker's nose and mouth. Brock glanced back over his shoulder towards the vehicle. He turned back to Brinker and patted his hand as the paramedics started to cart him off towards the waiting ambulance. After they'd left, Brock sauntered over to the SUV. He rounded the driver's side and stared in.

There was hardly anything to see. Sam was obliterated; the Raven had landed half on the roof of the automobile, completely pulverizing Sam's upper half. Blood leaked down the side of his mangled arm that was visible. Some type of matter was visible on the slammed in ceiling. Brock grimaced at the scene and shook his head.

"He got off too easy."

A couple more paramedics rushed over to check out the damage. As soon as they saw the inside of the vehicle, they shook their heads. There was absolutely nothing to save. Not a chance.

Brock headed towards the police cruisers. Once he returned, he picked up the radio that was inside the car. He turned the channel to the one they were using to reach the search team.

"S and R team, come in."

He said softly. The response came quickly.

"S and R team, over."

"Sam's dead, over."

Brock sat there, radio in hand. The chill in the air bit at his hands.

"We found PJ and it's not good, over."

To be continued….

Biography

Myk Richelle was born in Prince George, British Columbia, Canada in November of 1994. She moved to Vernon, British Columbia, Canada, in April of 2008. She grew up writing all kinds of short stories and novellas and in January 2015, she began her very first novel. She is a fervent fan of all things horror and it is her dream to bring to life words that keep her readers on their toes and full of suspense.

CPSIA information can be obtained
at www.ICGtesting.com
Printed in the USA
LVHW110924210520
655603LV00001BA/3/J

9 781796 099959